MW00584329

3.25.22

TO:

Rachel ♡

# A

# SYMPHONY

## OF

# STARS

BARBARA KLOSS

A Symphony of Stars

Copyright © 2022 by Barbara Kloss

Edited by Laura Josephsen
Cover Design by Damonza

THE WILDS

the Five Provinces

Túl Bahn

Skanden ◇          ◇ Craven

◇ Riverwood

White
Rock

HIDDENSEE

◇
THE CROSSING

THE RIM

THE FINGERS

DAVROS

StovichsHold ◇

CORINTH

Sanvik ◇

Skyhold ◣

BREVERA

GRAY'S
TEETH

BLACKWOOD

◇ Rodinshold

N

ISTRAA

BARREN MOUNTAINS

Trier ◣

THE

SOLVELORE

OTHER LANDS

# PRONUNCIATION GUIDE

**Akavit:** A-kuh-vitt
**Akim:** uh-KEEM
**Alma:** ALL-muh
**Anja:** AHN-yuh
**Asorai:** A-zuhr-eye
**Avék:** uh-VECK
**Bahdra:** BAH-druh
**Chakran:** CHAH-krun
**E'Centro:** EE CHEN-tro
**Felheim:** FELL-hime
**Fyri:** FEER-ee
**Gamla Khan:** GAHM-luh KAHN
**Hersir:** HER-sir
**Hiatt:** H-EYE-uht
**Il Tonté:** ill tahn-TAY
**Imari:** ih-MAH-ree
**Istraa:** ih-STRAY-uh
**Jadarr:** yuh-DAHR
**Jarl:** yahrl
**Jenya:** JEN-yuh

**Kahar:** kuh-HAHR
**Kai:** k-eye
**Kazak:** kah-ZAHK
**Kjürda:** kyerda
**Kormand Vystane:** CORE-mund V-EYE-stain
**Kourana Vidéa:** koor-AH-nuh vee-DAY-uh
**Kunari:** koo-NAH-ree
**Leje:** leh-zheh
**Lestra:** LESS-truh
**Liagé:** lee-AH-zhay
**Maeva:** MY-vuh
**Majutén:** mah-zhoo-TIN
**Mo'Ruk:** muh-ROOK
**Nazzat:** nuh-ZAHT
**Niá:** NEE-uh
**Oza:** O-zuh
**Qazzat:** kuh-ZAHT
**Ricón:** ree-CON
**Roi/Roiess:** roy/roy-ESS
**Sar Branón:** sahr bruh-NON
**Saredd:** suh-RED
**Saza:** SAH-zuh
**Sebharan:** seb-uh-run
**Sieta:** see-ET-uh
**Sol Velor:** soul veh-LORE
**Stovich:** STOVE-itch
**Su'Vi:** soo-VEE
**Sulaziér:** soo-lah-zee-AIR
**Surina:** sur-EE-nuh
**Survak:** SHUR-vack
**Talla:** TAH-luh
**Tallyn:** TA-linn
**Taran:** TAIR-in
**Tarq:** tark

**Trier:** tree-AIR
**Tyrcorat:** TEER-core-at
**Vondar:** vahn-DAHR
**Ziyan:** z-eye-ANN
**Zussa:** ZOO-suh

# 1

*A*zir Mubarék stood at the window of Vondar's high tower, gazing over Trier's smoldering remains. The fires had dimmed to embers, though smoke cast a gauzy film over the city, like some ever-present haze of retribution. Below, Sol Velorian guards moved like wraiths in the mist.

Azir's attention snagged on a group of Istraan fugitives being escorted to their new encampment. His guards were still uncovering Istraans within the city and without. Fear had rallied many of those fugitives to his numbers, while insubordination had fed Trier's steady flames.

Azir inhaled long and deep. "Do you smell it?"

No answer.

"My lord asked you a question, dog," the *leje*—legion—snapped in that delicious voice of many, of one.

Chains rattled, and the human whimpered.

"...yes..." the human managed.

"*Louder*," demanded the *leje*.

The chains rattled again, and the human cried out.

"Patience, my dear Zerxes." Azir turned his gaze from the

2 | BARBARA KLOSS

window to the room. "I do believe this tragedy has struck our poor sur mute, has it not?"

Sur Kai looked pitiful, naked and chained and covered in filth —much of it his own. What was left of his black hair had matted and clung to his face, which was bruised and swollen and bleeding. Kai's gaze met his, filled with great loathing and despair.

Azir smiled. "Bring him closer, Zerxes, so that he might gaze upon his beautiful city."

The *leje* kicked Kai forward, and Kai fell upon his face.

"Get up," the *leje* spat, yanking Kai up by the chains.

Kai gasped and winced, struggling upon all fours as the *leje* dragged him toward Azir. Once there, the *leje* bent over and grabbed the battered sur by the chin, forcing him to look out the window.

"What do you think of it?" Azir mused. "Is it not beautiful?"

Only jagged breath escaped the young sur.

"Fire is a wondrous thing," Azir continued, thoughtful. "It gives us light and heat, but it also has the unique ability to cleanse. If you want to know what a thing is made of, put it in fire, let it burn, and see what is left standing in the ashes of impurity." He looked down at the younger sur, who trembled upon all fours, eyes haunted as he gazed upon his city. Specifically upon a trio of Sol Velorian guards who tossed an Istraan woman onto the ever-burning pyre. The woman's agonized screams ripped through the city as flame consumed her. "I should thank you, Sur Kai. All of the information you gave Niá helped us considerably—"

Kai snarled and lurched forward, but the *leje* jerked his chain, and Kai fell instead. The *leje* then kicked Kai in the ribs so hard they cracked, sending Kai sliding across the floor and tumbling into a chair. The *leje* started after him, but Azir held up a hand.

The *leje* stopped, while Kai gasped and wheezed and gently cried.

It never ceased to amaze Azir how some only found the courage to fight once the battle was already lost. As if they might redeem their previous cowardice by railing against present futility.

The door to the room suddenly opened, and Su'Vi, his enchantress, stepped through.

Like his other resurrected Mo'Ruk, Su'Vi's face was a patchwork of skin and glyphs. The enchantress had been beautiful once—a supernatural force to behold—but Tommad the First's war had cost them everything. He had stolen their dignity and might, but Azir would not rest until he took it back. With Zussa's power now flooding his veins, he could heal those scars. And through the *sulaziér*—the singer of souls—he could restore their power unlike ever before.

Su'Vi bowed her head and her gaze. "You called, my lord?"

Azir glanced at the *leje*, who swayed in place, back and forth. Back and forth. Its power was too much for its rotting host, and its breath gargled and wheezed. Azir waved dismissively, and the *leje* bowed in deference, though the gesture was rendered awkward by a body so broken that only sheer will held it together.

Perhaps Azir would let the *leje* have Kai as a new host, once Kai had fulfilled his usefulness.

The *leje* jerked on Kai's chains and dragged the broken and whimpering sur after him.

Azir waved again, and the door closed.

He looked at Su'Vi. "It is time." Then, "You hesitate."

A breath. Her gaze lifted. "What if I cannot?"

"You must," Azir said, though he understood her concern. This new mortality was their tender heel, their vulnerability. Bahdra had brought them back, but they were not whole, for Bahdra had drawn together what nature had torn apart, and nature kept trying to pull them apart again.

Shah power leaked out of their pores, stealing their strength and efficiency. Azir had suffered this too, until Zussa's power filled the gaps and sealed them tight. Her power was a geyser of molten fire he could hardly contain—did not want to contain, nor could he completely. He needed the *sulaziér* for that, but everything must come in its proper time and order, and for this next task, he needed Su'Vi. She was the last one who could undo what had been made, because she had been one of three who had made it.

The other two were dead.

Su'Vi slid her eyelids closed and breathed in deep. Words still painted the backs of her lids. Words that proclaimed her devotion to his cause.

Azir felt the shift. The familiar surge of Shah as she drew from that vast well of power. Even broken, Su'Vi's pull was one of the strongest he had ever felt. Azir closed his eyes in ecstasy, shuddering as raw power infused the air. Oh, how he relished it, needed it. Craved it with a hunger that would not quiet.

It never had.

Shah energy poured into Su'Vi, and Azir followed it like a tether, drawn like a fish on a hook. The power pulled him physically and steadily toward her until she stopped drawing from that well. Her chest heaved hard and fast, and her eyelids snapped open.

Azir stood so close, he could see his reflection in her black eyes.

"It is not holding," she said quietly.

He grabbed her face between his hands, and she turned stone-still, staring at him. She had loved him once, though she had never said a word, because he had been distracted by...*her*.

"Let me help," he said.

Su'Vi did not move, did not speak.

"Try again," he instructed.

Su'Vi shut her eyes, closing out his reflection.

One breath, and then...

*Power.*

It pulled from everywhere, from every inch of this room, from the rafters and through the window, all drawn to a point—her. It poured into her body, where it welled inside of her, and Azir tipped his head forward to brush his nose against Su'Vi's cheekbone. He breathed her in, the scent of burning. The ash and earth.

"Don't stop," he whispered over her scars.

Such exquisite scars, he thought, knit together by sheer insistence. A veritable masterpiece of willpower.

Su'Vi placed her hands over his, and their fingers wove together as she channeled Shah into her body. Azir wanted to touch it, taste it. Wrap himself up and drown in it. He squeezed her hands tight, dug his fingers into her skin, and kissed her hard.

She gasped, sagging beneath him as Azir pushed his tongue and his power into her mouth.

"Draw from me," he growled.

Su'Vi hesitated.

"*Take it.*" He bit her lip hard, drawing blood.

Su'Vi snarled and kissed him back, pressing her mouth against his until it hurt. Until it bled. He opened his well to her, and she drank and drank, shuddering against him as she gasped and choked on his power, but he did not let go. He held her firmly against him, his mouth locked on hers as he poured power into her body, and she gulped it down. Once she was full, once her seams bloated and strained from the pressure of his power, only then did he let go.

He took a step back, watching her ingest what he had given. Watching her body process the raw and wild energy.

And then she opened her eyes.

She looked at her hands first, then touched her face. The patchwork had faded to thin silvery scars that now only slightly distorted the glyphs Bahdra had carefully re-inked upon her skin. She was old and she was new, past and present—reborn.

And she smiled.

"Hello, Su'Viatra."

Fire burned in her eyes.

Azir touched her lip where he had bitten it, and she licked his finger, the blood.

"I eagerly await your return," he said with a different kind of hunger.

"I shall make haste, my lord." She smiled viciously, in the way he remembered her.

Su'Vi closed her eyes, breathing in fully for the first time since Bahdra had brought her back, he was sure, and then she pulled upon the Shah.

Power—so much power, the air distorted with it.

"Yes..." Azir moaned with pure, intoxicating rapture. He took a step toward Su'Vi, and he considered making her wait.

Her lips curled as though she'd heard his thought—his *need* —but then crows exploded from Su'Vi's core.

They burst from her chest, leaving nothing of her human form behind as they filled this small chamber. They circled Azir completely, twisting around his body like a lover, and then they soared through the window and out into the night.

Some split from the group and headed west, for Brevera, while the rest flew north, over the jagged Gray's Teeth Mountains, which were buried in cloud and snow, and farther still, past The Rim. There, just at the edge of the infamous gorge of water that separated the Provinces from The Wilds, the murder dove.

Down...

Down...

Twisting and spiraling down....

To where the murder landed in a person.

Su'Vi's boots sank into the deep snow, and she gazed into the white, at the massive structure before her.

The Crossing Bridge.

Even from where she stood, she could feel the energy pulsing from it, warding off all creatures of Shah. Keeping them separate, holding them captive.

Su'Vi remembered when this bridge had been an idea; she remembered when that idea had become reality. She remembered when the Provincials had turned against them, designating The Wilds their prison, The Crossing its bars.

And she remembered the one who had sustained it. Her own flesh and blood.

Su'Vi stepped forward, and her boots crunched in the snow. A frigid wind cut at her cloak, though she did not feel cold. She felt nothing.

Except hate.

Su'Vi stopped before the magnificent stone archway. Up close, its energy tingled over her skin. Below, the Rotte Straight churned and frothed, hungry for blood sacrifice.

She would give it a different sacrifice this night.

Su'Vi knelt before one pillar, closed her eyes and placed her palm against the icy stone. Her body tensed from contact, from the energy woven into the fabric of this bridge, and though Tolya, the one who had sustained it, was gone, those wards remained as strong as the day they'd been made.

"May your pathetic ideals become ash like you, sisters," Su'Vi hissed and then focused, redirecting her power into that rock pillar. Smoke sizzled from her hand; the surrounding snow began to melt. The burning and pain intensified, and a low growl escaped her lips. Suddenly, the glyphs around her hand sprang to life with a fiery glow, as if Tolya and Taran were here even now, fighting back.

Always fighting her.

Su'Vi gnashed her teeth.

More glyphs caught flame, until the entire bridge was aglow with wardlight. Each and every enchantment that had ever been carved into this stone ignited, as though a sun had been unleashed inside of the bridge.

Su'Vi's growl turned into a scream.

The bridge flashed—blinding—and the earth shook. Fissures crackled as wards seared through rock, breaking it apart. The archway collapsed first, then other pieces broke away, all of it raining into the ravenous gorge below until all that remained of the great Crossing Bridge was a fractured spine of stone stitched between continents.

But no wards.

No limitations.

Su'Vi breathed in deep and stood tall. And then she walked over the bridge and into The Wilds.

·⌀·

GAVET, the smuggler, sat at his chair, mending a leather vambrace some traveler had pawned earlier this evening. Wind howled, rattling his door, and snow framed the creases of his window.

Winter had come, and she had come in a fury.

The gust slipped into the room, and Gavet shuddered. He set the vambrace upon the counter and crossed to the woodstove, and he was just tossing a fresh log upon the embers when a keening howl filled the night.

A shade. And it was close.

It wasn't unusual to hear shades this close to Craven's warded walls at night, though he was surprised they were out in this storm. Gavet closed the stove's grate just as another howl answered.

And another, and another.

Suddenly, the howling stopped.

Gavet frowned, walked to the window, and gazed out into

night, but falling snow masked the world. He couldn't even see the glow of the lantern across the street.

And then a face appeared on the other side of his window. Skin white as snow, eyes black as ink.

Gavet gasped and staggered back in surprise, nearly tripping over his footstool. He caught himself on a chair, heart pounding, but when he looked back at the window, the face was gone.

Had he imagined it? It *was* late...

He turned around to find the figure standing before him, just a few paces away.

On reflex, Gavet grabbed the nearest object—the stool—only to watch it sail right out of his hands, crack against the wall, and crash to the floor.

Gavet lunged for the fire poker. That, too, went sailing right out of his hands, but this time, it whipped around in midair and pointed straight at his face.

"Who are you?" he demanded, though terror rattled his voice.

"You have something that belongs to my lord," said a woman's rasping voice. She spoke in Common, though her Sol Velorian accent was strong, and he noticed a faint patchwork of scars all over her face.

Gavet backed away, but the fire poker inched closer. "I don't know what you're talking about."

The woman stretched out her arm, opened her pale hand palm up, and lifted, as if raising some invisible weight. Suddenly, the leather cord at Gavet's neck tugged, and the nightglass key beneath his tunic began to rise.

"What are you—?" Gavet started, but the cord pulled tight across his windpipe, and he gagged instead.

The key rose up and out of his collar until it hovered before his eyes. Those little silvery flecks glimmered like stars in the low light.

The woman's fingers curled into a fist, and she tugged, as if cracking an invisible whip. The cord snapped, and the nightglass key shot straight into the woman's open palm.

"Give it back," Gavet growled, catching his breath. He'd inherited that necklace from his great grandfather, the first collector, and he had never shown a soul. He'd never taken it *off* —until now.

The woman slid the object into the depths of her heavy midnight robe, and then she looked at Gavet.

Gavet took an involuntary step back and watched in horror as a murder of crows burst from her chest. Air whipped and wings flapped, and the crows soared out of his open door into the black night.

All except for one.

The crow carved a circle in the air above his head. Gavet didn't have a moment to react before its beak tore right through his left eye and exploded out the back of his skull.

His body lurched, his scream cut short, and he collapsed to the wooden floor in a pool of brain matter and blood.

## 2

---

$\mathcal{J}$eric scanned the barren stretch of sand, wondering why in the rutting hells he'd ever agreed to leave that cave. He *hated* the desert. Nothing in this godsforsaken place wanted them there. Even the godsdamned plants had spikes.

Dark clouds brooded overhead, and a gust of wind kicked sand into his face. He blinked fast and used the edge of his scarf to wipe the sand from his brow, only to find that his scarf had sand in it too. Jeric dropped the scarf with a curse.

The camels huddled at the base of the rocky slope, unaffected. They'd been designed to weather this landscape, and Jeric couldn't be sure, but it almost seemed like they enjoyed watching the rest of them suffer. Especially Braddok, who stood beside him, trying to spit sand out of his mouth. His beard was full of it.

At last, Braddok grunted in resignation. "It's official. I hate sand."

Aksel grinned. "We'll just add that to the list, then."

"Right next to your rutting name."

Aksel rolled his eyes.

Tallyn walked up the rocky slope and joined them at the edge of the escarpment, which overlooked a wide and sweeping stretch of dunes. "Do you see anything, Wolf?"

Jeric saw that this was a rutting waste of a trip.

They had, however, managed to recover two of the camels they'd lost when Fyri's tyrcorat—skin eaters—had attacked them. Where the other five had gone, Jeric had no idea, but it bothered him.

"No," Jeric said tersely, then stopped and said, "Wait."

Tallyn, Braddok, and Aksel watched him as he held up a hand and cocked his head, listening. He took a step. "Do you hear it?" he whispered.

"Hear what?" Tallyn asked.

A man's laugh boomed from where the camels waited.

"*That.*" Jeric held up a finger. "Yes, it's definitely a horse's ass."

Tallyn eyed him, while Braddok and Aksel chuckled.

Jeric ignored the deriding look Tallyn was giving him just then and glanced over his shoulder, down the slope and past the camels, to where Zas, Habback, Absom, and Jesriel were slowly picking through large rocks and old bones—all that remained of Fyri and her skin eaters that had plagued this land for a hundred years.

"He knows you don't like him," Tallyn said. He was referring to Zas, whose laughter was fading.

"Good," Jeric replied.

A beat. "You should at least try, Your Grace."

"There are a lot of things I should probably do." Jeric turned his attention back to the dunes, and he thought he heard Tallyn sigh.

It had been three days since they'd found the underground city. Three days of torrential downpour, which had made travel rutting impossible, and so they'd all been confined to the underground city, Av'Assi. Or "Little Assi," so named after Sol Velor's old capital that lay *above* ground in ruin: Assi Andai.

But once the rain had stopped, Zas, a Liagé guardian and son of a particularly imperious elder, had been elected to begin investigations on what remained of their homeland. To see if Sol Velor was habitable. Habback, Absom, and Jesriel—also Liagé—had been chosen to go alongside him, and Imari had *suggested* Jeric join.

His first answer had been a resounding no. He needed to return to Corinth; he'd already been gone over a month, and desertion was not a wise strategy for a new king who intended to hold on to an unstable throne. But Jeric would not leave without Imari, and Imari would not leave without a talla, and Av'Assi's master enchanter, Mazz, was struggling to create one for her.

In summary, Jeric was rutting pissed.

"Jeric, *go*," Imari had insisted immediately after the meeting where she'd volunteered his services. "It's only for the day, and I'm tired of watching you pace like a caged wolf."

He had stopped in his tracks, mid-stride. "I'm not pacing."

Imari had given him a look, to which he'd smiled, all teeth.

"Also, you're the best tracker there is," she'd continued. "Put that talent to good use, and maybe they'll even *like* you by the end of it. We need their help, and you know it."

He did know it; he wasn't fool enough to think Corinth could fight Azir with skal alone. Whatever their numbers, they needed power beyond the physical. They needed *Liagé* power. So here he was, sifting through this godsdamned bucket of sand with that arrogant little prick.

"There's nothing here but death," Jeric ground through his teeth.

"Speaking of death, I'm kinda hoping for a rattler." Braddok gestured to the cluster of rocks where Zas stood pontificating to Habback about various tracking methods, of which he knew complete scat.

But Habback and the others ate it up. Zas had status, and Jeric knew well that status always won the attention of those who wanted a share. Power was blood, and it drew vultures.

He'd seen that enough with his father.

Zas lacked Tommad the Third's nefariousness, of course, but he was still a self-important piece of scat. He was near Jeric's age, with half the experience and twice the ego. Normally, Jeric righted such discrepancies with a good ass-kicking, but he was supposed to be *making friends.*

"Jeric."

Jeric looked to the old alta-Liagé, who gazed steadily back with his one pale eye.

"Staring at the young master like you're about to end his life is not the best way to form alliances."

"But I *am* about to end his life."

Aksel snorted. "Surprised it's taken you *this* long."

"Five crowns says Wolf here gets his ass handed to him," Braddok said to Aksel.

Jeric gave him a look.

"What?" Braddok shrugged. "Your sword against a guardian? Sorry, Wolf. I don't care how good you are with a blade. My bet's on the Liagé."

Jeric drew a wardstone from his pocket.

Braddok looked at the stone, at Jeric. "The hells you get that?"

Jeric tossed the stone, caught it, and slid it back into his pocket. "Hiatt's." He'd snatched it from the matriarch's shelf before they'd left. Just in case.

Braddok folded his arms. "Yeah, well, you don't know if it'll work."

"It'll work," Tallyn said.

"I accept your bet." Aksel smirked at Braddok. "And I raise you one hundred."

"Jeric!" Zas hollered from below.

Jeric inhaled a very tight and irritated breath and glanced back to see Zas waving him over.

"Saddle up," Zas shouted in Sol Velorian. "I want to get to that ridge before we head back." He pointed farther behind them, southwest.

Braddok leaned closer. "What did he say?"

"He wants to reach that ridge," Jeric murmured to his men, who both frowned at the ridge. To Zas, Jeric replied in Sol Velorian, "We don't have time." He nodded toward the brooding sky, which grew darker with the setting sun. "We finish up here and head back."

They were supposed to return by nightfall. This land had been built upon spells and Shah power, according to Tallyn and Av'Assi's elders, and without Liagé to properly sustain it these past one hundred years, those spells had degraded and evolved in unpredictable ways. Dangerous ways. The elders were adamant that such uncharted circumstances be approached slowly, and with great caution. Today was strictly for local inventory and inspection.

But Zas, who had been gesturing at his companions to saddle up, looked sharply back at Jeric. "It wasn't a question."

Jeric flashed his canines. "Neither was mine."

Jesriel and Absom stopped and glanced between the two. Habback looked over from where he already sat upon his camel, with his long black and silver hair whipping in the wind like some Sol Velorian banner.

"What's happening?" Aksel whispered to Braddok.

"A pissing contest," Braddok whispered back.

"Huh. Didn't know Zas even had a pisser..." Aksel said, and Braddok snorted so loudly, it drew the others' attention.

Zas's gaze narrowed on Jeric. "You don't give orders here, *Corazzi*. And if you want our help, you'll go to the ridge."

Jeric's hand flexed at his side.

His men didn't ask, but they seemed to sense the direction the conversation had taken. Braddok stood a little taller, glaring down the slope at Zas. Aksel too, but to little effect, while the wind pushed and tore at Jeric's hair and clothes. The clouds shifted, and a ribbon of waning sunlight broke through.

"Jeric," Tallyn's voice warned.

Jeric ground his teeth together. *Godsdamnit*, this insufferable man.

Jeric was just starting to turn away from the escarpment's edge and head back to the camels when a wink of light caught his eye. A reflection, now visible with the sun, shining from within the huddle of cacti at the base of the escarpment.

And then it was gone.

Jeric frowned, his curiosity piqued. He stepped to the side to see if he could catch the light again...

*There.*

Jeric started walking, following the escarpment's edge as he looked for a way down.

"Where are you going?" Zas called after him.

*None of your godsdamned business,* Jeric thought. He found a climbable section and started down, half climbing, half skidding down the escarpment's steep face. Rock and sand tumbled after him, and dust rose in a cloud. He finally reached the base, where rock met sand, and his steps sank and slid as he trudged toward the tangle of cacti—jumping cacti, Absom had called it earlier today—then stopped and crouched, searching for the source of that light.

"What are you doing?" the little prick called out from above.

Jeric sifted through the sand, careful not to touch the cactus's many fine needles. More rock skittered and tumbled as someone else started down the escarpment after him, and Jeric was about to abandon his search when his fingertips grazed something cold and metallic.

He grabbed hold and pulled out a fine strip of leather.

A wrist strap, to be exact, dyed a deep red, though sand had chapped the surface and dulled the hue. Liagé glyphs had been etched all over the leather, though they'd frayed with time.

Affixed to the surface, at equal intervals, were seven hollow golden spheres—each bearing one etched glyph, all of them unique. They looked like bells, though these made no sound.

"Let me see that." Zas stood over Jeric's shoulder and held out his hand expectantly.

Jeric glanced at Zas's hand and briefly considered breaking it.

Zas snatched the strip from Jeric, and Jeric let him. In fact, Jeric didn't move at all. He didn't trust himself to.

Zas shook the strip, as if to hear the bells ring (they didn't), then frowned.

"What is it?" Habback called from above. He'd dismounted and now stood at the escarpment's edge. Wind whipped his long black and silver hair into Absom's face, and Absom stepped aside.

"I'm not sure. Some kind of talla, I think." Zas turned it over. "Whatever it is, it's broken."

"Hand it over."

It was as if Zas had forgotten Jeric were there. His gaze flickered to Jeric, only briefly and very dismissively, before he slipped the talla into his robe. "This doesn't belong to you, *Corazzi*."

Jeric should have let it go. "It doesn't belong to you either, prick."

Zas stopped. Everything about him stopped, and he took a small step closer, bending over Jeric as if to make Jeric feel small. "What did you call me?"

Jeric stood, forcing Zas to look up at him. "I called you a prick. In Common, it means pisser...asshole...pecker..." Zas's expression darkened. "I see you get the general idea."

"Listen here, *Corazzi*." Zas glared up at Jeric, who stood a good head taller, and that fact seemed to deepen Zas's rage. "This artifact belongs to my people, and just because you're putting *your* pecker in that Istraan bastard doesn't mean—"

Jeric slammed his fist in Zas's face.

Braddok started laughing. "Oi, Aks! Bet's *on*!"

"Hey!" Absom yelled as Zas stumbled back with a cry.

Jeric took a step toward Zas, who cupped his nose and blinked back tears. Behind them, rock crashed as Absom and Jesriel stumbled down the embankment.

"Hand it over." Jeric held out his hand.

Zas pulled his hands away and touched his nose. It was definitely broken, and bright blood trickled out of his nostrils. Zas spit on the ground with a curse, his furious dark eyes locked on Jeric, and then he pushed an inked palm forward.

Energy surged from his open hand in a warped wall of air. That wall rushed at Jeric, but the stone in Jeric's pocket warmed, and when the wall hit, the energy diffused, running over Jeric like cool water.

Sonofabitch, it worked.

Zas's gaze narrowed on Jeric, on the silvery wardlight now glowing from Jeric's pocket. His expression turned indignant, and he ran at Jeric with a growl.

Jeric easily ducked out of the way, but, unfortunately, he'd underestimated Zas. At the last second, Zas twisted and knocked Jeric's feet out from under him. Jeric fell flat on his back, utterly surprised. Braddok was too, by the sound of his booming laughter, but Jeric gathered himself fast and rolled over just as Zas's fist landed in the sand where Jeric's head had been a second ago.

*So the little prick* does *have some training...*

Zas's fist came at him again, but Jeric caught it with his hand and held it there between them. Zas's brow furrowed, his features strained as he pushed against Jeric's hand.

Jeric smiled, whipped their joined fists aside, and slammed his forehead against Zas's broken nose.

"*Ohhhhh!*" Braddok guffawed. "That's gotta hurt..."

Zas fell back with a cry, and Jeric jumped to his feet. The wardstone pulsed with warmth again, and another spell rushed over him like cool water.

"Not much without your power, are you?" Jeric chided.

Zas snarled and lunged at Jeric, but Jeric stepped around him, barred his arm across Zas's chest, and flipped him down to the sand, on his back. Right up against the tangled rope of cactus.

Jeric pressed his knee to Zas's chest, braced his forearm against Zas's windpipe, and leaned right in Zas's bloodied face. A few cactus needles dug into Jeric's thigh, but he hardly felt them.

"Say what you want about me, but say *anything* about Imari again, and I will—kill—you."

Zas gasped, trying to breathe. His entire left leg was up against a rope of cactus. Absom grabbed at Jeric's shoulder, but Jeric shoved him off.

"That's enough, Your Grace," Tallyn said from somewhere behind him.

"Do you understand me, prick?" Jeric said through his teeth.

Zas might have answered. Jeric's arm didn't make it easy, and now Zas's bloodied lips were turning blue.

"*Wolf*," Tallyn snapped.

A beat. Jeric removed his arm and plucked the talla from Zas's robe, then stood and walked away from a gasping and heaving Zas. Jesriel and Absom rushed to Zas's aid, while Tallyn moved to intercept Jeric.

"Get out of my way, old man," Jeric said.

Tallyn pressed his lips together, and fury lit his eye, but he did not try to stop Jeric as Jeric strode on by.

"We leave now." Jeric started back up the escarpment.

"We have to get these needles out first," Tallyn called after him, not bothering to hide his irritation.

Jeric looked at the dark clouds above, smelled the rain on the air. "You've got ten minutes," he snapped, hoping they weren't already too late.

# 3

*I*mari walked the ruins of Assi Andai while a cold, damp wind bit her skin. The former Sol Velorian capital still awed her, though it was only a skeleton of what it had been. Tallyn's shared memories of this place had never dimmed from her mind, so when she gazed over it all, at the cracked pillars and crumbling archways and shattered sandstone walls, her mind filled in the gaps. It put the pieces back together and rebuilt this fractured empire.

An empire Imari wanted to see thrive again, in the way the Maker had intended. Where they lived at peace with one another and used their gifts to help those who had need, as the verses proclaimed:

*I have blessed you so that you would bless others. Be a light in this dark and forsaken world.*

It had been three days since they'd arrived in this place. Three days since she'd fought Azir at the tree, since she'd given her life to Jeric only to have hers brought right back. Three days, on top of the four it had taken to travel from Trier, and now she was impatient to leave. Kai was still captive to that demon in Vondar

—hopefully he was still alive—and Ricón was out there too. Somewhere.

But as anxious as Imari felt, she knew Jeric felt it more. He'd been gone from Corinth for over one month, and he needed to assemble his jarls for the inevitable war Azir would bring. But Jeric wouldn't leave without Imari, and Imari could not go —not yet.

Her bone flute had fatally cracked the day she'd unwittingly freed the Great Deceiver, so Mazz, Av'Assi's master enchanter, had been attempting to make something new. However, none of the objects Mazz had brought before her would connect to her power —*talla binding*, he called it—and Imari was beginning to worry. She needed a talla in order to fully access her power, and apparently her easy binding to the flute had been extremely rare and fortuitous.

Imari wondered if fortuitous was the right word.

"Go on to Corinth," Imari had said to Jeric yesterday morning. "I know you need to get back, and I'll catch up with you when I can."

Jeric had given her a condescending look, then laughed and said, arrogantly, "No."

However, in the hidden deep of Sol Velor's underground city —Av'Assi—Jeric paced like a caged wolf. He couldn't seem to help himself; confinement wasn't in his nature. Imari wasn't entirely sure how that would play out once he returned to Corinth and formally assumed his role as the sole occupant of a very large and uncomfortable chair, but she decided now wasn't the best time to point that out.

Instead, when the rain had ceased and the elders had elected a young man named Zas to go above ground to see what Fyri's tyrcorat had left behind, Imari had suggested Jeric go with them. Also, because she wanted to make sure Zas gave an accurate report of his findings. After only three days of getting to know Zas and his father—an elder named Esaum—Imari was convinced that Zas would say whatever he needed to say in order to keep the people from leaving this place.

The place where Zas and his father held power.

"Jeric is the best tracker there is," Imari had said before the elders, earning herself a sharp glare from Jeric. "If there's anything to find, he will find it."

At first, Imari thought the elders would say no. Most had made no secret of their dislike for the Provincial king, due to century-old prejudices, and Imari couldn't say that Jeric had made an effort to win them over. She wished he'd try, and she thought this was the perfect opportunity to earn their support: Jeric could put his restlessness to good use, and these Sol Velorians might learn to respect and trust a Provincial king.

To Imari's surprise, the elders had voted in unanimous agreement. Unsurprisingly, Esaum was the only elder who had not agreed; however, thus overruled, Jeric was permitted to go.

"Why do I feel like I'm being patronized?" Jeric had said to her later as he packed his things in their shared bedchamber. Well, technically it was Imari's bedchamber, but he shared it with her.

"Because you are...?" she'd replied, and Jeric had chuckled. "But honestly, they could use your nose. And it's just for the day. Put your talents to good use."

Jeric had looked wolfishly at her and taken a step closer, slipping his arms around her waist as he pulled her close, hip to hip. "I have other talents I'd be more than happy to put to good use. Right now, in fact."

Imari had laughed, and Jeric had dipped his head low and kissed her deeply. Truth be told, she'd almost said to hell with it and taken him up on the deployment of those other talents right then.

"*Go.*" She'd chuckled instead and playfully shoved him away from her. "They're leaving in the next half hour. And who knows.

Maybe Mazz will actually find something that works by the time you get back."

"One can only hope..." Jeric had sighed.

And so he had gone, taking Braddok, Aksel, and Tallyn with him. Chez and Stanis had stayed behind, per Jeric's orders, and though he hadn't said specifically, Imari suspected he'd appointed them as her additional security.

Which Stanis had not looked thrilled about. He'd been increasingly quiet and withdrawn ever since arriving at Av'Assi. Imari knew Jeric noticed it too, though he hadn't said a word, but Imari guessed it was also why he'd ordered Stanis to stay behind. To give him space.

And she'd hardly seen Stanis after Jeric had left.

However, Imari hadn't had the time to dwell upon it, because she'd spent the day with Niá, memorizing basic Liagé glyphs, studying what they meant and how to use them. When Imari's head ached and Jeric still hadn't returned, Niá had suggested they walk outside through the ruins. So here they were, meandering through history with Jenya and Chez.

Imari's gaze trailed the darkening horizon, feeling increasingly anxious. She should have spotted them by now.

*Where are you, Jeric?*

Imari sighed and kept walking, through this scattered skeleton of another time. From her current vantage, she could just see the massive hole in the ground—all that remained of the Divine Tree.

Imari had investigated the tree's remnants first, but she hadn't lingered long. Though the tree itself was gone, though she'd ripped it out by its roots with her power, the earth and air still soured in that space, and the notes in her soul vibrated with warning. Zussa's corruption had forever soiled this fissure between worlds, and Imari did not want to be anywhere near Zussa's infectious poison.

Nothing had been the same for Imari since she'd tasted the

power in the Divine Tree, when she'd accidentally freed Zussa. The world had opened up to her, overwhelmed her with its power and knowledge. It'd been enough to show her how to save Jeric, and even when that power had faded, the knowledge had not left her completely. Instead, it'd stripped every last barrier separating her from that well of Shah, and now she felt the power in *everything*.

She could *sense* the stars visible in her Shah sight. Feel their constant pulsing energy, the warmth of their light. And if she focused hard enough, she could hear their whispering vibrations, each and every pitch, humming steadily. A melody that played without ceasing, weaving through all of creation, singing in perfect harmony.

It was in these moments she began to understand the woman who had walked onto that battlefield over a hundred years ago and commanded men with a mere flick of her wrist. Fyri had not needed to slip into her Shah sight to manipulate the stars, as Imari had previously done. Fyri *had been* sound. Each and every interval, spanning the octaves. Individual, and all at once.

Imari thought it was too much power for one person.

"Are you all right?" Niá asked suddenly.

Imari glanced over to see Niá approaching.

Her strong and immediate connection to Niá had been unexpected. Imari had known her exactly three days, and yet she felt as though she'd known Niá forever. Maybe it was because Imari had been raised by Tolya, and Niá had been raised by Tolya's twin sister, Taran. Whatever the reason, Imari felt a deep and growing kinship to Tolya's great niece, and she suspected Niá felt the same.

"Yes...I was just thinking about what this place was like before." Imari glanced over the ruins, the weathered glyphs. "There is so much history here."

Niá stopped beside her. "I wish I could have seen it in its day."

"Tallyn showed me through his Sight."

*For Carly*

Niá looked at her.

"Ask him, when they return. I'm sure he'd be happy to show you too."

"I will." A second later, Niá looked to the dark hole in the earth, where the Divine Tree had once rooted. "But you weren't thinking about history just then."

"No," Imari admitted. "I was not."

Wind howled through the ruins, through the cracks and holes, promising rain.

"Don't fear the Shah, Imari," Niá said quietly. "It will not turn you into something you are not already."

Imari glanced at Niá, but Niá was staring absently at the middle distance. The rabid wind clawed at Niá's brown cloak and cropped hair. Niá had cut it short the day after they'd arrived. She'd gone quietly down to the bathing pools and returned with a knife and unevenly cropped hair. At the haunted look in Niá's eyes, Imari suspected Niá had gone to those pools with a very different intent.

Niá had set the knife on the table before Imari, and Imari had taken the knife, tucked it away, and neither had said another word about it.

"Oi, you two ready to head back?" Chez shouted, rounding a large heap of stones. Wind tossed his mop of brown hair and pulled at his tunic so strongly, it outlined his torso. "Storm's rolling in!"

Imari had gotten to know Chez better these past few days and understood why he'd become one of Jeric's chosen few. He possessed an easygoing nature that balanced the others well, spiced with Braddok's humor but tempered with a quiet sentimentality.

"Why don't you go on," Imari said to Niá.

"He's fine, Imari," Chez said, catching up to them. "Actually, you should be more concerned about Zas."

Imari eyed Chez. "How do you know he's not the one I'm

concerned about?"

"Smart woman." Chez grinned, then pulled something from his belt. "Found this." He held out a wedge of dark ore affixed to a tarnished metal hilt.

Imari recognized the ore at once. "*Nightglass...?*" It was what they'd used in The Wilds to defend themselves against shades. She was surprised to see it here.

"Thought that's what this was." Chez's gaze flickered to Niá before he held out the nightglass blade for Imari.

Imari took it and smudged her thumb across the dusty surface, leaving a clean streak of glossy night sky behind. "Where did you find this?"

"By the Mazarat...what remains of it, anyway."

Imari gave it back to Chez, who then offered it to Niá.

Niá looked at Chez, at the blade. Everything about her changed in that moment, as if sight of the knife brought upon a very recent and unwelcome memory. A muscle tightened in her jaw, and her gaze hardened as it flickered back to Imari. "I'll see you below."

Niá didn't wait for a response but walked on, back up the footpath that led to Av'Assi. Imari glanced at Chez, only to find him still looking after Niá.

He caught Imari watching him, then gave her a tight smile. "I'd offer it to you, but you've got a Wolf."

Imari arched a brow. "And I managed just fine on my own before him, thank you very much."

Chez chuckled.

"What did you find?" Jenya asked, walking up the sandy slope toward them. Her long ponytail swished behind her.

Chez tossed the dagger, which Jenya caught mid-air, then turned it over, scrutinizing it. "Where did you sniff this out, little pup?"

Chez smirked. "Secrets of the trade, Jenya."

Jenya grunted a laugh, then handed it back to Chez, who

slipped the dagger into his coat. "Are you ready to head back, Surina?" Jenya asked.

"You *might* need to convince your surina that her precious Wolf's gonna be okay first."

Imari gave Chez an annoyed look.

"She should be more worried about Zas," Jenya replied.

"That's what I said," Chez said. "Tell you what, Surina. You a betting woman?"

Imari eyed him. "Depends."

Chez looked pleased. He hadn't expected her to play along. "I bet you ten crowns that Zas comes back with something broken."

"And I bet you twenty it's his ego," Imari countered.

Chez laughed and smacked her on the shoulder. "Knew I liked you."

"*There* you are!" called a new voice.

They all glanced over to find Hiatt—Av'Assi's matriarch and leader of the elders—fast approaching.

Imari could not pin Hiatt's age, and the old woman would never say. Hiatt was old in a timeless sort of way, as if she'd been old for a very long time, and she most likely *had been* old for a long time because Liagé bore the effects of time differently. Shah power extended a Liagé's lifespan beyond what was normal, like it had for Tallyn, who had been on this earth for one hundred and forty-three years—long enough to live through Azir's first war. Imari suspected Hiatt had lived even longer.

Wind clawed at Hiatt's long black and silver hair, but one glance at the woman's face was enough to warn Imari that whatever had brought Hiatt to the surface was not good.

"The elders are gathering," Hiatt said, stopping before them.

Imari stilled. "*Now*?"

"Esaum called it."

Imari and Jeric had been pleading with the elders to join Corinth in the inevitable fight against Azir, but so far, the elders had given no answer. They'd promised to officially decide tomorrow, after evaluating Zas's findings today.

"But Jeric's not back, and without his account..." Imari's voice trailed, her gaze fixed on Hiatt's. "That's exactly why he's called it."

Hiatt looked at her in silent confirmation.

Esaum did not *want* to leave—he'd made no secret about that, which was why he'd nominated his son, Zas, as the leader of today's expedition. Holding the meeting now, without a Provincial king to influence their decision, gave little room for contest.

"Can't you hold them off a little longer?" Imari pleaded.

"I've done all I can, Surina, but Esaum will not wait, and you will not get another opportunity. Remember that I cannot show partiality in this. *You* must be the one to convince them."

# 4

---

"Uki, you need to drink." Ricón held the water flask to Gamla Khan's cracked and bloodied lips, but Gamla only sagged forward and slipped back into unconsciousness.

"I've got gurga in my pack," said Hoss, his saredd.

Ricón studied his uki and then splashed water into Gamla's face.

That did the trick.

Gamla flinched and sputtered, bolting upright as his eyes flew open. His gaze roamed wild, unfocused, his body clenched in habitual fear as he scrambled back against the wall.

"Uki, it's me." Ricón tossed the flask aside and reached for his uncle. "*Ricón.*"

Gamla's breath came quick and shallow, his eyes blinking fast as though he were trying to focus. To see. To be sure.

Ricón knelt before his uki and grabbed his face between his hands. "It's all right, Uki. You're safe now."

*Safe.*

The word tasted sour in his mouth. What did it even mean? Was anyone truly ever safe?

No, safety was an illusion. People might take precautions like bolting doors or storing grain, as if they had any control over their small little lives, but they could never stop evil, for evil was a power outside of themselves, and it did not follow any rules. It would take and take and take, forcing mankind to its knees, begging the gods for mercy.

Ricón had left Trier to investigate the Baragas a month ago, in search of the one who'd burned the holy temples at Bal Duhr. He'd taken three saredd and six guards with him, but they had not found any answers. Not until they'd journeyed home and intercepted tracks. Hundreds of them, rippling the sand—an army, marching straight for Trier.

Ricón had followed the wide trail to the valley's edge only to find Trier burning with white flame. Guardian fire, Hoss had said. Fear had seized Ricón's heart, and he'd started riding hard for home, but Hoss had caught up to him, grabbed his horse's reins and pulled him to an abrupt halt.

Ricón had nearly killed him for it and had left Hoss with a nasty bruise over his left eye.

"We can't fight that! Not like this!" Hoss had persisted through Ricón's best attempts at shoving him out of the way. "The best you can do for Istraa right now is to *stay alive*."

Ricón had eventually succumbed to the truth and fallen to his knees with his head in his hands.

They'd adjusted course, followed a narrow path deep in the Baragas, and headed north for Roi Naleed's protection and reinforcements. They hadn't gone very far before they'd stumbled across the pig carcasses and this cave, where they'd found his uki in a cage.

And his uki was in no condition to travel. He was hardly in a condition to live.

Hoss brought the lantern closer, and Gamla's gaze finally focused on Ricón. A crease formed between his brow, and relief filled his eyes. "Ricón."

The word was a whisper, a wish.

A prayer.

Ricón grabbed his uki's trembling hands and squeezed them tight so that he would know this was not a dream. But *sieta*, his uki's hands felt so frail when they were normally so strong. "I'm here," Ricón said. "And I am not leaving you."

"Where is—" Gamla was seized by a coughing fit, and Ricón let go of his hands to give him space. Blood splattered Gamla's filthy tunic, brilliant red specks against the dull brown.

Ricón exchanged a weighted glance with Hoss, who nodded once and strode off for their horses, where they'd kept medicinal supplies.

The coughing subsided, and Gamla sagged back against the rock wall, eyes closed. Ricón gazed at that wall, at the old blood and bat dung staining the surface. They should have carried Gamla out of this disgusting cave first, but Ricón had been too afraid to move his uki. He'd feared any drastic movement would kill him. Even now, each breath rattled with sickness.

How did one heal the healer?

Ricón glanced over to where Macai and Bett—two guards— stood at the cave's narrow entrance. The rest of his small entourage waited just outside with the horses.

"Either of you have water?" Ricón called out.

Macai jogged over and handed Ricón his flask, which Ricón unstoppered. He turned back to his uki. "You need to drink, Uki." He held the flask to Gamla's lips.

Gamla's breath shuddered, but this time, he took the water.

Ricón had so many questions. He wanted to know how long his uki had been caged here. How it had happened, who had done it, and *why*. But Ricón kept quiet, watching his uki closely and making sure he consumed enough water.

"That's probably enough for now," Ricón said after some time, taking the flask away.

Gamla understood; he was a healer, after all. Then he looked at Ricón with shocking clarity and asked, "Is little Imari with you?"

The question took Ricón by surprise. Gamla had gone missing *months* before the Wolf had written Ricón concerning Imari's whereabouts. "How did you know—"

"*Is she here*, Ricón?"

Ricón stared into his uki's eyes—his papa's same eyes—and he gave a slight shake of his head.

"*You left her?*"

"I wouldn't have if I'd known Trier would be attacked!"

Gamla stared hard at his nephew with that strength of will Ricón remembered, but that fury dissolved into pain, which etched lines at the creases of his eyes. He glanced past Ricón to Macai and Hoss, then to the cave entrance, where Bett stood with a few others who'd entered to see, and the fire left Gamla's gaze. Something much heavier had taken its place. "Are you all that's left?"

Ricón swallowed hard. "I don't know."

Gamla inhaled deep and closed his eyes.

"Who is it, Uki?" Ricón asked. "Who led the attack on Trier? The same one who kept you here? Was it because of Imari?"

But all Ricón received for his assault of questioning was a long, deep quiet.

"Uki."

Gamla's lids cracked open. "Then he has Imari." The statement was more for himself than for Ricón.

"*Who* has Imari, Uki?"

A beat. "Azir Mubarék."

Ricón frowned. He watched his uki, thinking he'd misheard. Behind him, Hoss and Macai exchanged a glance.

Ricón remembered Imari's story about the chakran. "Do you mean the chakran? Azir's spirit?"

"Not his spirit," Gamla said, sounding weary. "He is flesh now."

"That's not possible." Ricón shook his head, though he doubted even as he spoke the words. "Imari destroyed him at Skyhold..."

Gamla closed his eyes again, as if he could not physically look at the truth anymore. "Bahdra brought him back and gave him a body."

Bahdra...

Bahdra...

Why did Ricón know that name? It was at the edge of a thought, the thread of a memory, and yet when he followed that thread, it frayed into nonexistence.

"The Mo'Ruk?" asked Hoss.

One of the reasons Ricón had always preferred Hoss was because Ricón valued intellect over might, and Hoss had been gifted with both. The moment Hoss connected the name to the title, a very clear and terrifying picture came into focus.

"Yes," Gamla replied.

"But how is that possible?" Macai asked. "Bahdra is—"

"The one Mo'Ruk they never found," Ricón finished, exchanging a glance with Macai, then Hoss.

Bahdra had been alive all this time, hiding deep in the Baragas. He had been the one recruiting the Sol Velorians—for *sieta* knew how long—and, as of late, had been burning down Istraa's holy temples with people still inside of them.

Bahdra, Azir's Mo'Ruk necromancer.

*He* could have resurrected Azir and the other three Mo'Ruk, including the one renowned for guardian fire. The same fire Ricón had seen burning over Trier.

Oh, *sieta* have mercy on them all...

"I accidentally stumbled across this cave...on the pass." Gamla coughed into his arm. "It was a hot day, and the smell caught me. I went to investigate and found Bahdra. He threw some spell at me, and I awoke in a cage. He"—*cough*—"needed my help preserving and mending new bodies for the others."

For the Mo'Ruk.

"Isn't that *his* specialty?" Hoss asked.

"Yes," Gamla answered. "But apparently it takes a lot of stamina to pull four very powerful Liagé from the ground, and"—another cough—"he wanted me to use my talents where I could... so he could preserve his energy for the rest."

"What does he want with Imari?" Ricón asked. It was all he cared about just then.

"I don't know." Gamla paused and closed his lips against another cough. "Azir needs her for something."

"And you don't have any idea what that is?"

Gamla gave a subtle shake of his head. "I tried to listen, but they were...careful."

Ricón considered this and how this might change their path ahead. "We were on our way to Naleed's."

Gamla looked at him. "Why?"

"He has two thousand men, and we need—"

"More men are not your answer."

Ricón frowned. "I can't take Trier back with ten."

"And Branón couldn't save it with a thousand," Gamla said sharply. "Naleed's won't save you either."

Branón's memory hovered between them like a ghost, and though Gamla couldn't possibly have heard, he'd assumed Branón's fate.

Ricón neither confirmed nor denied; he could not, though he felt that answer deep in his soul, but now was not the time for grieving. It was a time to *act*.

"Well, I won't stay here," Ricón cut back. "If what you're saying is true, if Azir really has Imari, then I need to save her."

"I agree. But Naleed cannot help you."

"Then—*dashá*—*who can*?" Ricón was angry. Not at Gamla, but at everything. All of it. His own helplessness. That he was alive and his family, most likely, was not. The only reason his heart hadn't gone into a complete downward spiral was the knowledge that Imari was still alive.

"We need Liagé," Gamla said at last.

"*Liagé*? Need I remind you that they're the ones who just helped Azir destroy—"

"Not all Liagé followed Azir then, and not all are following Azir now."

"That doesn't mean they'll sacrifice their lives to fight alongside an Istraan sur..." Ricón's voice trailed as he studied his uki. "You already have someone in mind."

His uki grinned, albeit weakly. "I do. But the path won't be easy."

Ricón sighed as he looked to a sky he could not see. "I wouldn't trust it if it was."

## 5

The seven elders were already deep in conversation by the time Imari and the others reached Esaum's home, situated in the heart of Av'Assi. Conversation paused briefly as Imari stepped inside the large atrium, Esaum shot Hiatt an irritated glance, and then the elders proceeded debating involvement in this *Corinthian war,* or so Esaum kept calling it. Imari almost interrupted him on this point alone, but a sharp look from Hiatt held her tongue.

*Not yet.*

So Imari waited, listening intently while Niá translated for Chez—Jeric's only Corinthian representative, for Stanis had not come.

This fact particularly irritated Imari on Jeric's behalf. According to Jeric, out of all of his men, Stanis was the most experienced diplomatically; he'd been born to a line of emissaries, of a sort. He never minced words, and he was fiercely devoted to Corinth's gods—Imari had seen both of these qualities for herself. Therefore, Jeric had often entrusted Stanis with Corinth's more delicate matters when Jeric himself could not be present.

Like now.

Esaum argued that it was impossible to travel into Istraa without Lestra—Azir's seer—Seeing them, and Hiatt confirmed this point. Urri, an old restorer who'd opened her home to Chez, Aksel, and Tallyn, suggested investigating the old harbor at Liri, Sol Velor's former seaside city, but Esaum dismissed the idea, saying it was nearly impossible that any of their ships had survived these past one hundred years, and certainly not enough to transport *all* of them to Corinth.

"First and foremost," Esaum said, "this is not our fight, as the *sulaziér* would have us believe it is. Azir's grievance is and has always been against those rapacious Provincial kings. Even if he decided to turn his eye upon us—which I doubt—the powers that prevent our very own seers from Seeing *outside* of Sol Velor also prevent Lestra from Seeing *inside*, so we will remain protected, *as long as we stay here.*"

Many of the elders murmured in agreement, which was when Imari finally stepped into the conversation. "You're forgetting that Azir already *knows* you're here."

Everyone shifted their attention from Esaum to Imari—including Esaum, who looked thoroughly annoyed that she had spoken at all. Hiatt caught her gaze and nodded marginally in encouragement.

"No, Surina," Esaum condescended, taking back command of the room. "Azir knows that *you* and your *Corazzi* are here." Chez bristled at this slight to his king. "He's not particularly interested in the rest of us."

"If you truly believed that, you wouldn't have pressed for this meeting before *my Corazzi* returned. You're worried we're right about Azir, and you're worried King Jeric's testimony would persuade everyone else to agree with us."

The entire room fell silent. Even Niá stopped her translation mid-sentence, and Hiatt looked as though she were trying very hard not to smile.

Esaum's dark gaze speared her. He was all power, all affront. "And what would *you* know of Azir's nature, *Sulaziér*? You believe your title somehow gives you wisdom that evades those of us who actually knew him before?"

Ah, so Esaum *had* lived through Azir's first war, like Tallyn.

"And therein lies the problem," Imari pressed. "You knew *Azir*, but *Zussa* dwells within him now, and you cannot possibly predict what *she* will do."

"And you can? You're a *sulaziér*. Not a seer."

"I don't need Sight. Zussa herself showed me at the Mazarat." In that brief moment Zussa's spirit had filled Imari before moving into Azir.

"And you would trust the visions of the *Great Deceiver*?" Esaum scoffed, putting emphasis on those last two words. "Have you considered that she was only showing you what she *wanted* you to see so that you would do exactly what she wanted you to do?"

He had a point, and in Imari's hesitation, Esaum looked to Hiatt. "*Mi a'vorra*, this girl knows nothing of our history, and her bias prevents her from reaching an objective conclusion." He glared at Imari. "You might have crawled into a *Corazzi's* bed, but the rest of us need not join you."

Imari fumed, and Niá finished translating, but before Imari could find her words again, Hiatt said, "Enough." Her voice was low, the candles flickered, and a strange tingling infused the air.

Shah.

But it had the intended effect: Both Chez and Esaum drew back.

"You would do well to remember your place before our Maker, Esaum of Mumbar," Hiatt said darkly, and her voice filled the now silent chamber. "*He* is the one who brought her to us, and might I remind you that it did not go well for the last Liagé who claimed to know better than Asorai."

Her words settled, and tension charged the air.

Esaum's lips pressed into a hard and begrudging line. He did not wear rebuke well. "Forgive me, *a'prior*, I only meant—"

Just then, the door flew open, and Jeric stormed through. His cheeks were flushed, his eyes bright, and he was completely drenched. His sopping wet hair clung to his temples, and his cloak practically rained upon the dirt floor. Zas rushed in after, similarly soaked through, but also bearing a very visible bruise over his right eye. That was new.

"*A'prior* Hiatt," Jeric said, somehow managing to take complete control of this space, as he always did. He observed the room at a glance, and then his attention settled on Esaum, and he smiled, all teeth. "Sorry I'm late."

"The *dásh Corazzi* has something that belongs to us, and he will not give it back," Zas snapped.

"*He found it*, you piece of scat!" Braddok shouted from the door, where Zas's men would not let him inside. Imari could just see Aksel and Tallyn behind him, arguing with them.

"What did you find?" Esaum demanded.

"Absolutely nothing at all," Jeric said with a wolfish kind of mirth. "*Nothing* lives in this godsforsaken wasteland...except your skies, apparently." He gestured at himself, and Imari bit her bottom lip to keep from grinning. "There is no wildlife, hardly any cacti, and every rutting well is bone dry."

A few uncertain glances were exchanged, some murmurs. This was not the news Esaum had wanted them to hear.

"I *meant* what is Zas talking about?" Esaum said tightly, glancing to his son, who looked so small beside this Corinthian king.

"A talla." Zas glared at Jeric.

In that moment, the room seemed to inhale, and something within Imari stirred. A premonition, a warning. Her gaze snapped to Mazz, the enchanter, who was watching Jeric with unnerving intensity.

"You found a talla?" Esaum asked dubiously.

"I found *something*, yes," Jeric cut back.

"It *is* a talla," Zas argued. "A very old one, but I would stake my life on it. It bore all of the inscriptions—everything."

Jeric looked sideways at Zas, as if Zas were a little dog yipping at his heels.

"Well, let us have a look," said Gezze, a Liagé guardian and one of the seven elders.

A muscle ticked in Jeric's jaw, and the elders waited. Jeric's storming, blue-eyed gaze landed on Imari—for the first time since he'd stepped through that door—and her breath caught with its intensity. He reached into his coat, never breaking her gaze, and pulled something from his pocket.

A long and slender leather strip.

Glyphs had been etched all over its surface, where small golden spheres had been affixed—seven, to be exact, spaced at equal intervals. The spheres reminded Imari of bells, but these made no sound. Not to her ears.

But her soul heard them.

A bold chord blared in her mind with the force of a dozen horns, rattling her core as it knotted to her soul. It had bound to her; she knew it without question. This was what Mazz had been referring to, what he had been trying to conceive for her.

Imari noticed her hand was slowly reaching up, as if to take the object from Jeric, but she quickly stopped herself and forced that hand back to her side.

Jeric's gaze focused on her.

He'd noticed.

Zas snatched the strip from Jeric, and Imari felt a sharp pull deep in her gut.

"Is it truly a talla?" Urri asked Hiatt, who had gone stone-still.

*She recognizes it*, Imari thought.

But it was Mazz who answered, his warm, dark eyes fixed on Imari. "Yes. It is Fyri's talla."

Fyri's talla.

The very object that had destroyed this land and irrevocably changed the course of the Sol Velorian people, sending them here, trapped beneath the earth while scattering the rest.

And it had just bound itself to Imari.

A chill swept over her, head to toe. The room around her seemed to constrict and squeeze to a point with the talla at its center. Like a single pin, holding the fabric of this world together.

Jeric still hadn't moved his gaze, and now Mazz was eyeing her closely. Even Jeric's and Zas's men had ceased arguing at the door, all of them intrigued by this new and unexpected information.

"You're certain?" Esaum said, frowning at the leather strip now dangling from his son's fingertips.

"Yes," Mazz replied simply. "I made it."

Imari's heart pounded hard and fast. How in *all the stars,* in all the vastness of Sol Velor, had Jeric stumbled across *this*? How had it even *survived*? She supposed it wasn't too far a stretch that Fyri's talla could have been preserved in the sand all this time, in the place she had perished, but for Jeric to find it?

Imari remembered her flute. How it had always found her even when she'd tried disposing of it, but that flute had broken, and Imari did not believe in coincidences.

Right then, she wished she did.

"Then you should have it," Zas said, offering it to Mazz.

But Mazz did not take it. "It does not belong to me."

"But you made—"

"It belongs to Surina Imari."

Every face turned to her, and she felt the sudden urge to shove past them all and out the door, far away from that talla.

Away from fate.

"With all due respect, Prior Mazz," Esaum said, "but considering how Fyri used this device, do you think it wise to entrust it to another *sulaziér*?"

"It does not matter what I think," Mazz said. "It belongs to Surina Imari."

"I don't want it."

The words came from Imari, firm and unyielding.

Mazz regarded her, his expression inscrutable, while Zas looked...surprised.

But through Tallyn's Sight, Imari had seen how Fyri had used those bells, how men had fallen at a mere snap of Fyri's wrist. Imari wanted no part in Fyri's past—no physical contact with the one responsible for destroying *everything*.

"You don't have a choice," Mazz said somewhat sadly as he studied her.

"There *has* to be something else," Imari pleaded.

"It does not work like that, child. Tallas can take months to create. *Years*, sometimes, to find the right match. But more importantly, a talla can never be fashioned for one who is already bound. You must take this."

The room fell quiet as the others caught on to Imari's predicament, and then Esaum was not the only one voicing objections. Hiatt, however, remained quiet. Jeric too, as he watched her from just a few paces away.

But Imari remembered the verses. She remembered what they had said about every *sulaziér* before her, how they had succumbed to darkness, and this talla already possessed a dark past.

"I *will not*," Imari persisted, looking only at Mazz. "Do not ask this of me."

At last, Mazz sighed and took the talla from Zas. All objections ceased as everyone watched Mazz slip Fyri's talla into his robe. His gaze lingered on Imari a moment longer, with disappointment, then he turned and started for the door. The elders parted in silence, watching the old enchanter pass through the door, past Jeric and Zas's men, and out of sight.

Imari ignored the strong pull she felt as the talla moved farther away.

"I believe this meeting is formally adjourned," Esaum said at last.

"We have not voted," Hiatt reminded him sharply.

Esaum's eyes narrowed on Imari. "Those in favor of accompanying Surina Imari and this Provincial king to Corinth?"

Hiatt raised her hand, and...no one else.

No.

One.

Not even Urri, who looked tortured by her choice even as she stood there gazing apologetically at Imari.

"Those in favor of keeping to Av'Assi and rebuilding Sol Velor?" Esaum continued.

Ishaq, an elder and a restorer, raised his hand even before Esaum finished, then Habback, and Gezze, and—finally, regrettably—Urri followed.

Even if Mazz had stayed, his vote would not have made a difference.

Esaum looked at Hiatt and bowed his head. "Now I believe this meeting is adjourned. King Jeric. Surina." He flung their titles with an edge of distaste. "May the Maker give you strength for the path ahead. As for me and my house, we will worship Asorai *here*."

·⌒·

"WELL, THAT COULD HAVE GONE BETTER." Braddok professed later, once they were all seated around Hiatt's large table. Hiatt herself was not there; she'd gone immediately to speak with Mazz in private. So Imari and the others had returned to Hiatt's, where—in anticipation of Jeric's return—Imari had made a huge pot of bone broth, filled with a variety of mushrooms and spiced balls of grain and root. However, Imari quickly realized she'd failed to anticipate just how much four grown wolves could eat, and she grabbed more flatbread to help fill the spaces.

Still, Stanis did not join them.

"Hey, Surina," Chez said, raising his flagon of mead. "You owe me ten."

Jeric, who had been leaning back against Hiatt's counter, deep in thought, suddenly glanced up.

"*Twenty*," Imari shot back. "That's much more than a broken nose, and you know it."

All of them were now staring openly at her—Jeric most of all.

"She's right, little pup," Jenya said when Chez did not concede, and then he set his flagon down with a thunk and a sigh.

Jeric's lips parted in a rare display of stupefaction.

Imari smiled and opened her palm. "Time to pay up, Chezter."

Chez grumbled something incoherent, slipped a hand into his coat pocket, then withdrew two silver coins, which he tossed at Imari.

Imari snatched them from the air—Braddok whistled, impressed—and then she made a show of testing their weight before slipping them into her coat.

Jeric's mouth pulled into a slow smile.

"Well, well, well..." Braddok chuckled, beaming like any proud father.

"You bet that I would hurt Zas?" Jeric asked, a wolfish gleam in his eyes.

But Imari only winked at him and walked over to the stove.

"Oi, Brad. Pass the bread," Aksel called from farther down the table. Braddok made no such move, so Jenya pushed the plate down, despite Braddok's garbled protest, and Chez plucked a wedge from the top as it passed him by.

They were like a pack of starved cubs, all pouncing on the feast laid before them.

"You mentioned you have access to a ship?" Jeric asked Tallyn suddenly.

"Yes," Tallyn replied. "Or, more accurately, I have a means of contacting one."

"Iththith the thame thip that took us to thappor?" Chez asked, then swallowed his bite.

"*Manners.*" Aksel chucked a hunk of bread at Chez's head, but Chez ducked, and it sailed past. "There are *ladies* present."

"Braddok doesn't mind..." Jenya said from the end of the table.

Braddok gaped at Jenya in open wonder. "I can't believe it. Did Jen...just tell a joke?"

Jenya glared at him.

Imari chuckled as she scooped the last of the broth into a clay bowl.

"It is the same ship," Tallyn replied.

"You're certain he'll come?" Jeric asked.

Tallyn met Jeric's gaze. "I am certain."

"Well, look at the bright side," Aksel interjected. "There's no longer any need to worry if there's enough room..."

Chez groaned and drowned the sound in his flagon.

Imari crossed the room to Jeric, who still leaned against the counter, arms folded and long legs stretched before him.

"Eat." Imari urged the bowl at him.

He looked down at the bowl, and then back at her. "Where's yours?"

"I had a late lunch and probably too much flatbread dough."

His lips curled into a smile that made her heart skip its next beat.

"Take it." She pushed the bowl at him.

His fingers brushed hers as he took it, and then Imari dangled a wedge of flatbread.

His eyes found hers and rested there. "Thank you."

She nodded once, gave him the bread, and then hoisted herself upon the counter to sit beside him, her legs dangling over the edge.

Jeric tilted the bowl and sipped. "This is actually quite good."

"You sound surprised."

"I *am* surprised."

She whacked him on the back of his head.

Jeric chuckled softly and nudged her with his shoulder. "So violent for a healer..."

"Says the one giving out black eyes."

Jeric looked down at his bowl, and a shadow crossed his face. "He's lucky that's *all* I gave him."

She was about to ask what Zas had done to earn that black eye when Chez said suddenly, with all seriousness, "Hey, Wolf... did you still want to leave tomorrow?"

Jeric swallowed his next bite and slowly set the bowl down, while the others awaited his reply. But rather than answer, he looked to Imari.

He wanted her answer first.

And as much as it pained her, Imari said, "We can't afford to wait any longer."

Jeric studied her, as if needing to be certain. As if needing *her* to be certain.

"Each day we wait, Azir grows stronger," Imari continued. "*Zussa* grows stronger. And who knows how long it will take us to convince the elders, assuming that's even possible. Either way, we still need your numbers to overwhelm Azir's forces, no matter how many Liagé we have."

*Unless you use the talla,* said a small voice that Imari squashed immediately, but she could not sever the longing she still felt for the little object. Not completely.

"Then we leave tomorrow," Jeric said, pulling his gaze from

Imari and pinning it on the alta-Liagé. "As long as you're able to contact our transport."

Tallyn inclined his head. "That will not be a problem, Your Grace."

"But how long will it take our transport to arrive at...what was the name of that port again?" Chez asked.

"Liri," Tallyn replied. "And depending on where he is currently, and assuming he doesn't intercept poor weather, I imagine it'll take one to two weeks."

"And from Liri to Felheim?" Jeric asked. Felheim was the Corinthian harbor closest to Skyhold.

"Three weeks, potentially four. Again, it depends on the weather."

Jeric's brow furrowed. That was clearly longer than he'd hoped.

"It's the best I can do," Tallyn continued. "But this is our safest route."

"Lestra would be able to See us if we crossed through Istraa, correct?"

"Once we pass the border, yes."

"Can you just See anything you want to See, whenever you want to See it?" Chez asked.

"Not necessarily," Tallyn answered. "With proper training, we may learn to control what we See, though it's often erratic and difficult to piece together. However, if we have physically touched something or some*one*, it opens a direct channel, so to speak, and it is far easier to See the world as it relates to that person or thing. So while you"—he gestured at the others—"might not be an easy target for Lestra, Imari definitely is. As am I."

Chez clucked his tongue. "Ah."

"Are there any spells to block it?" Aksel asked.

"True seers are generally the best equipped at hiding from other seers, but there are some enchantments that might work...?" Tallyn looked to Niá, who had been sitting quietly upon a stool in the corner, eating.

Niá lowered the bowl from her mouth and set it upon her lap. "Potentially yes, but remember that Lestra hid an entire army from Rasmin, who *is* a seer. I doubt anything I could do would stop her."

At mention of Rasmin, Jeric's former Head Inquisitor, Imari recalled the last time they'd seen him—in Trier, fighting Astrid to give them time to escape. She wondered if he were still alive.

Jeric unfolded his arms to squeeze the counter instead. "How far to Liri?"

"Four to five days," Tallyn replied. "Hopefully."

Jeric studied him. "Is something out there, Tallyn? Is the elders' fear of this land grounded?"

At Jeric's question, everyone looked up from their bowls.

"I don't know," Tallyn said at last. "Between Niá and me, we should be able to create wards strong enough to keep us safe should we cross paths with any creatures of Shah. Regardless, I would rather face Sol Velor's wild unknown than risk capture by Azir and his Mo'Ruk. At least until we have Corinth's army behind us."

"I'll toast to that." Braddok raised his flagon, which Chez clanked with an "Aye."

Jeric, however, did not look satisfied, and his fingers tapped the counter's edge as his thoughts churned.

"I'll speak to Byri about the camels," Jenya said, standing.

"I'm coming with you," Braddok said, scrambling off of the bench so fast, he knocked over his flagon and spilled mead all over Chez, who cursed.

Jenya didn't turn as she threw the door open. "Just don't get in my way, *Rasé*, or I'll saddle you up beside them."

*Rasé* was the Istraan word for Red, which Jenya had taken to calling him.

Braddok waggled his brows. "You can saddle me up whenever you like."

Jenya stopped at the door.

Chez and Aksel laughed. Even Tallyn fought a smile.

"Sorry, Jenya, but you set yourself up for that one," Aksel drawled.

Jenya glowered at Braddok and left, and a smirking Braddok followed, calling after her.

"I should go as well," Tallyn said. "I'll contact our transport, and...Niá?"

Niá looked over from the washbasin, where she was setting her emptied bowl.

"Would you mind joining me at Urri's in the next hour? I'd like to visit Mazz and see what he has in the way of wardstones, so that you and I can fill in the gaps. It shouldn't take long if we work together."

"Of course," Niá replied.

Tallyn and Niá were walking out the door, when Aksel said, "Oi, Chezter. Let's go. Might as well check on Pissin' Stan and let him know we're leaving tomorrow. Maybe it'll improve his mood."

"That'll be a cold day in hells..." Chez said, then looked to Imari as he stood. "Don't keep our precious Wolf up *too* late, Surina. His tracking's scat when he's tired."

"Chez," Jeric said then.

"Mm?"

"Shut the hells up."

Chez chuckled then headed out the door with a grinning Aksel, and then Jeric was standing right before her, his hands on either side of her, boxing her in. As thrilled as she was by his sudden proximity, his expression was deadly serious. "Are you sure you're ready to leave tomorrow?" Jeric asked.

"No," she admitted, gazing into that storming, blue-eyed gaze. "I'm not sure about anything. Except you."

His expression softened a little, and his eyes deepened. He still smelled like rain. "Don't make this decision because of me."

"It's not *just* because of you," Imari said. "Jeric, you know I can't go to Istraa like this. It's too dangerous, and I'm not enough. *We* are not enough. Your army is our only chance, as far as I see it." A thought struck her then. "Unless *you* have changed your mind."

Two days ago, Jeric had proffered Corinth's force of five thousand men to help fight this war, though Imari knew that force would not come without resistance. Jeric couldn't know what state Skyhold was in, given the haste and manner in which he'd left, and she could tell that he worried how this request would be received by his jarls. Still, Jeric had been adamant that this war would find Corinth regardless, and he'd said that he would rather engage this fight offensively. His men had readily agreed.

Except for Stanis.

Stanis had accused Jeric of "sacrificing Corinth to fight Imari's war," stormed out of the room, and made himself scarce ever since.

All that to say, Imari would have understood if Jeric had changed his mind.

But Jeric did not break her gaze when he said, "My decision has not changed, Imari. The war will find Corinth, whether or not Stanis or any one of my jarls can admit that. I am asking you if you're ready because of your brothers."

Her brothers.

That had been the most painful part in all of this. "What other option do I have? I can't save Kai on my own. Even *with* a talla. And I'm no help to Ricón dead."

She wondered if Jeric would bring up Fyri's bells, and the immediate connection she'd felt to them. She wondered what he thought, if that connection had terrified him as it had terrified her, or if he would try to persuade her to use them regardless.

Instead, he pressed a palm to her face. His calluses scraped a little against her cheek. "I will do everything in my power to help you find them."

Imari placed her hand over his and inhaled deep. "I know. Thank you."

His gaze fell to her mouth, and he trailed a thumb over her bottom lip. "I missed you today."

"Did you?" Imari grinned against his thumb. "You have an interesting way of showing it, getting into fights while—"

He dipped his head and caught her mouth with his, stopping her words. His lips were warm and soft, and chapped from the desert, and her entire body sighed with relief, with pleasure. He had become such a comfort, a place her soul found rest. His lips kissed away her worries while his touch anchored her in what mattered most—this love they shared—and Imari could never get enough.

His hand slid into her hair while the other slipped around her waist, pulling her to the counter's edge and opening her legs so that they rest against either side of his narrow waist.

A little thrill moved through her body.

"I have strict orders to let you sleep, Your Grace," Imari said against his mouth.

"And here I thought you weren't one to follow orders."

"Who said I planned on *following* them?"

Low laughter escaped him, and he kissed her deeply—so deeply, a soft moan escaped her.

"Jeric?"

"Mm."

"You're getting sand in my mouth."

Jeric pulled back and looked at her. His eyes were huge and dark and predatory. "You're right. How thoughtless of me. I should clean up first." Without warning, Jeric scooped her up in his arms. Imari let out a soft yelp in surprise, then laughed as he carried her through Hiatt's back door and onto the dark porch.

"Where are we going?" Imari demanded through her laughter.

"To clean up."

"You can't carry me all the way to the springs!"

"Watch me." He smiled viciously and carried her down the darkened path, all the way to the most private of hot springs, and it was a very long time before they emerged.

---

## 6

*I*n the middle of the Yellow Sea, far beyond Istraa's shores, a small schooner raced. It charged the waves and ate them up, cutting through them like a blade. Seawater sprayed and spilled on deck, and *The Lady's* crew worked fast to secure the sails. This squall had trapped them for a little over a week, stubbornly blocking the way north and preventing them from returning to The Wilds.

Survak couldn't help but think that the Maker had something to do with it.

After Survak had dumped the Wolf and his pack at Zappor's docks, he'd lingered a few days for confirmation from Tallyn that the boy had survived.

No, not boy. *Man.*

But to Survak, he would always be a little boy. A little smile full of overlarge teeth, a little face splattered with freckles, and wild hair bleached blond from too many hours on deck beneath a brilliant sun.

That confirmation *had* come, and two days later, after they'd gathered enough supplies to cover their journey to Hiddensee, and after Survak had finally dragged his crew from Zappor's warm beds, they'd set sail.

Only to cross paths with this rutting storm.

Survak could not wait any longer. He'd heard what'd happened in Trier, thanks to the old alta-Liagé, and he needed to get the hells out of this place before Azir captured Zappor and the entire Pyrigian Bay.

Given the choice between the two, Survak would rather face the storm a thousand times over.

Overhead, a rope snapped, and a sail whipped violently. Men ducked and shouted as they fought to secure it.

"Cut it free!" Survak yelled from the wheel.

"But that's the spare!" Rikk yelled back as rain poured over his face.

Survak cursed. *The Lady* lurched, and seawater spilled on deck. "Cut it free anyway!" he shouted, and then the stone pendant upon his sternum warmed.

Survak barely noticed at first because he was so focused on holding that wheel, but then the stone began searing his skin.

"Godsdamnit, not now..." Survak grumbled. "Paz!" he yelled.

Paz secured a rope around a cleat then ran toward his captain.

"Take this." Survak stood aside, and Paz took his place. "I'll be back in a second."

Paz looked confused but didn't question as Survak shoved past the men, jogged down the steps and across the flooded deck, and shoved through the door to his quarters, slamming it shut behind him. None too soon, either, because the moment the door closed, Tallyn appeared.

Of course, it wasn't *actually* Tallyn, but a projection of him. Tallyn had explained that as long as Survak wore this wardstone, Tallyn would be able to communicate with him over long distances because Tallyn wore the stone's twin. Both had been cut from the same rock, Tallyn had further expounded, along with a list of other Liagé technicalities Survak didn't really care to remember. Survak's main concern was that it worked, though he didn't use it in front of his men. While they didn't despise the Liagé, Shah power still wasn't something any of them were accustomed to on the regular, and Survak didn't want distraction to divide his men.

"Good," Tallyn's projection said. "You're still wearing it."

"I don't really have time for this." Survak wiped the water from his face and squared his feet for balance. "We're in the middle of a rutting storm, and I'm trying to keep us alive."

Tallyn's projection glanced about Survak's quarters, though Survak still wasn't certain how much of these quarters Tallyn could actually see.

"Where are you?" Tallyn asked.

"North of the Pyrigian bay."

Tallyn looked pleased and not at all affected by Survak's urgency. "So you have not passed Felheim."

"*No*. I just said I'm stuck in a rutting storm—"

"I need you to go Sol Velor."

Survak stopped. He thought he'd misheard. "What?"

"The old port at Liri. The docks are rotten, but the delta is good, and you should be able to draw—"

"What in the actual hells, Tallyn?! I'm not going to Liri—"

"The tyrcorat are gone, thanks to Surina Imari."

This drew Survak up short, but just then a large wave crashed against *The Lady's* hull, and he pressed a hand to the cabin's low ceiling to steady his legs. Tallyn, however, stood perfectly still and at ease.

"Wait. You're in Sol Velor?" Survak demanded, one hand still on the ceiling as he rocked with the ship.

"Yes," Tallyn answered. "And we need transport from Liri to Felheim."

Survak stared at the alta-Liagé.

"There is so much to discuss, and I will tell you everything, but there's not much power left in these wardstones," Tallyn continued. "The Wolf King has agreed to help fight Azir, and he will supply whatever men Corinth can spare, but he needs your help getting home."

Survak dragged a hand over his face. "Wards, Tallyn..."

"You know I would not ask this of you if I were not desperate."

"Why can't you go through Istraa? It's not like you're trying to sneak an army through—"

"Lestra."

Ah.

*That* was why.

Survak ground his teeth.

"Please. We need you," Tallyn said. "*He* needs you."

Survak barely heard the storm raging beyond, barely felt the ship rock. Tallyn's words tangled up inside of him and piled into heavy knots, dragging him down the unforgiving road of memory. Survak silently cursed the day he'd given transport to a girl named Sable, because—once again—it had entwined Survak's life with *his*.

Yes, this was definitely the Maker's doing. It had his rutting omniscient name all over it.

"He is not the same boy you left, Captain Vestibor," Tallyn said quietly.

Survak felt an old flare of fury. "I didn't leave him."

"Then come back."

So many words crowded behind Survak's tight lips—so many *years*—but none of those words would fall. He wouldn't allow it, because then he would have to look at them.

"We will arrive in Liri in four to five days, and we'll wait one week," Tallyn continued. "If you do not show, I will assume you've gone north, and then we will try for Istraa."

"You can always just appear and ask me yourself," Survak snapped, gesturing at the stone.

"It could only be used three times. I made it in haste, and in haste it will end. Our time is up, old friend."

Even as Tallyn spoke, Survak felt the stone grow hotter and hotter—uncomfortably so. It burned his skin, and Survak jerked the leather cord. Leather snapped, and the stone came free. The ward on the surface shone white, and Tallyn's image flickered. Distorted.

"One week," Tallyn said, though his voice grew distant. He was like a memory, fading.

The stone flashed blinding white, and Survak let go just as it disintegrated completely. Ash drifted to the floor, and his quarters fell to darkness.

·⌐⟩·

NIÁ STOOD at the end of the path and gazed upon Gezze's home, where she, Jenya, Braddok, and Stanis had slept these past three nights. Where she had lain wide awake each night, staring at the ceiling, at all the cracks and bits of plaster peeling from the surface.

Lantern light flickered within. She knew Jenya and Braddok hadn't returned from Byri's; she'd seen them at the stables as she'd passed by. Jenya had waved, despite being in the middle of yelling at Braddok, so Niá had kept walking, and she hadn't stopped until she'd reached Gezze's.

Though she'd traveled into Ziyan, though she was deep underground and away from the world, her life at Ashova's followed her like a disease she could not shake. Specifically, Kahar Vidett. He terrorized her dreams, both sleeping and waking. It was always the same, him bursting through the door, bloodied as she'd left him on the steps with a knife wound through his heart, except that in her dream, he was still alive. He called her all of the horrible names he had called her in life as he overpowered her and stripped her bare, taking as he had always done. Sometimes his face would change into one of the other countless men who had visited her chambers—never Kai, though, strangely—but it was always Kahar Vidett at the end, right before he stabbed *her* through the heart.

Niá would wake gasping and trembling and clutching her chest, where her heart ached. She knew Jenya heard, but Jenya never said a word. Neither had Imari, the day Niá had returned from the pools with a knife.

Niá turned down a path that squeezed between two wattle and daub homes and stepped onto a different street, away from Gezze's home. Sleep could wait, but also Niá still needed to decide if she was going to leave with Jeric and Imari.

There was nothing for her in the Provinces. Nothing but pain and regret. She loved Imari—yes. Imari was already like family to her, and Niá felt a sharp stab of guilt even at the idea of telling Imari that she wouldn't be accompanying them tomorrow. But there was still another and very loud voice that was tired of doing what everyone else demanded of her, and it refused to be guilted into service ever again.

Though when Niá allowed her brain to rule over her heart, logic insisted that she couldn't equate the two. Imari was not *demanding* anything. She would be disappointed, but she'd respect and support Niá's decision to stay.

Niá found herself standing before the magnificent tree that grew from Av'Assi's heart. Its crimson leaves threw prisms of red light over the ground, its vast network of rich brown branches stretched in all directions, and its thick roots anchored defiantly to the rock—unshakeable.

All her life, Niá had believed there to be one tree: the Divine tree, which had been guarded by the Mazarat. The one Imari had destroyed when she'd unwittingly pulled Zussa out of it.

*"Though the binding of the Great Deceiver overwhelmed the Four Divines, their power rained back to our soil—untouched. From this, we received the tree of wisdom, the tree of life. A gift from Asorai*

*himself so that we would still know the perfect way he intended and find comfort in his promise to deliver us from the evil one."*

Niá had always believed the tree of wisdom and life to be one and the same, but they were not.

She gazed upon the enormous oak, the one that had brought Imari back from death. The people of Av'Assi called it Asorai's tree.

Niá had stopped believing in Asorai the day she'd been dragged into Ashova's, because certainly a good god would not allow such suffering. And furthermore, a good god would not have taken Saza away from her so cruelly.

*Why?* Niá cried in her mind. *Why do you let evil men triumph when you alone have the power to stop them all?*

It was why she'd followed Bahdra. She'd had her suspicions about him, but in Asorai's continued silence, she'd seen no other way. Bahdra had promised her freedom—Bahdra had simply *been there*—and so she'd shoved those suspicions aside and buried them deep.

*This is* your *fault. If you'd been there...if you'd helped...*

Niá stood there, glaring at that tree, and a flood of emotion engulfed her. Her legs trembled, her eyes burned, and Niá found it suddenly difficult to breathe. Her chest clamped down against the pressure, like a dam holding back the sea.

She could not let that dam break, or that sea would crush her.

Just then, soft voices echoed behind her. People often came to pray before Asorai's tree, but Niá was in no mood to see anyone just then, so she wiped her eyes and hurried off.

But the flood of emotion swelled.

And swelled.

She shoved it down, keeping to the shadows, though emotion made her steps unsteady. She stumbled a little along the path toward Urri's, where Tallyn stayed with Chez and Aksel. Twice, she stopped to gather herself, to breathe, and when she finally arrived and cracked open the door, Chez was the only one inside.

He knelt before the wood stove, his back to her, and he poked at the glowing embers. Niá decided she would wait outside and started to close the door.

"Hey, Niá," he said.

She stopped, one hand on the door.

Chez set down the fire poker. "Tallyn still isn't back."

"I'll come back later—"

"Please stay," he said, startling her. He'd startled himself too, judging by the awkward quiet that followed. He stood, a bit stiffly, and rubbed the back of his neck. "I mean, do whatever you like, but you're more than welcome to wait here. I was just packing up." He crossed to the table, where an assortment of swords and clothes had been laid out. Not all of them were his.

Niá didn't want to be alone with him. Not that she feared Chez. Actually, she liked him best of all the Wolf's pack.

But he was still a wolf, and she was in no mood for conversation.

Chez picked up a cream tunic that looked like it'd seen better days. The pits were grossly stained, the hem frayed, and the elbows were worn through.

*I can fix that,* Niá thought, but she didn't offer.

"Think Aks'll notice if I toss this in the fire?" Chez asked.

Niá looked at him, and despite the emotion churning inside, she felt the smallest smile twitch at her lips.

Chez didn't sense her dark mood, or he chose to ignore it. "I'd better wait. We might need it for kindling later." He shook out the shirt, folded it, and tucked it away into a leather satchel.

He picked up another tunic, folded it, and Niá realized she was still standing in the doorway. Chez, however, didn't say another word about it, and Niá found herself slowly stepping inside and closing the door behind her.

She crossed to the wood stove and sat upon the stool, her

back to the wall so that she could see both the stove and Chez simultaneously. Niá bent forward and held her hands to the stove. Her body wasn't cold, exactly, but there was comfort in the warmth, and she appreciated the distraction of those little dancing flames.

"You all packed?" Chez asked, shoving more items in satchels.

"Yes," she lied.

Quiet.

"You ever been to Corinth?"

Niá turned her hands over. "I've never left Trier."

In the corner of her eye, Chez stilled, a wad of fabric in hand. He shoved it into the satchel a second later.

"Well, it's cold," he continued easily enough. "The food's scat, and the people aren't much better."

At this, Niá glanced over at Chez, who winked and turned back to the table.

She wanted him to stop talking to her, but she also appreciated the distraction from her thoughts. Niá slid from her perch, picked up the iron poker, and stabbed at the embers.

"There's some kindling in the..." Chez's words trailed as Niá spoke a word—the Liagé word for the symbol she'd just carved into the dying embers. Power tingled through her chest, her symbol flared, and the embers ignited anew.

Chez cleared his throat. "Well, that's handy."

Niá knew he wasn't used to watching Liagé cast spells or how, exactly, he should feel about it. Which was precisely why she'd done this. To remind him of what she was.

Niá set the fire poker down. "How long have you hunted with the Wolf?"

Chez considered her a long moment, and then he turned back to his satchel and shoved another garment into it. "About three years. I was training to be a guard. Unfortunately, not everyone appreciates my sense of humor, and I got whipped for insulting the Wolf's brother. Jeric recruited me immediately after."

This surprised her. "He recruited you...*after* you insulted Prince Hagan?"

Chez threaded a strap through a buckle. "Hagan was furious, which only made Jeric more stubborn about it. We weren't at Skyhold very often, so it worked out."

"Right, because you were so busy hunting my kind."

Chez stopped, and when his gaze met hers, his humor was gone.

Niá stared right back in challenge. She didn't know what made her goad him, whether it was bravery or foolishness, but she suddenly felt the need to drill deeper. To find that hostility she was so certain he carried within. The faster she uncovered it now, the easier her decision would be.

But Chez simply turned back to the satchel and started tying another strap. His motions were sharp, quick. "You wanna know why I joined the guard?" he asked.

"No, and I really don't—"

"My parents were killed when I was a boy. During Saád's war," he continued anyway. "We lived in a small village not far from Fallow's Pass. You've heard of that pass, I'm sure." He didn't wait for her answer. "It was the one Saád used to sneak into Corinth. How he murdered Jeric's mother. That same band of Sol Velorians stopped by our village first. Their Liagé burnt it to the ground in the middle of the day. Men—women—children." He tugged a leather strap, tightening it.

Niá wanted him to stop.

But he didn't. "I was fishing with Aks when we heard the screaming. Pissed ourselves, we were so scared. Spent the night by the river so we could get away quick if they came. They never did. I don't know how long we waited, but by the time we went back, they were gone, and so was the village. Just burnt wood and broken stones and lots of charred bones and crows."

He moved around the table and stacked the three satchels he had packed.

"Then why on earth would you want to help us now?" Niá asked.

He met her gaze. "I don't."

Niá frowned.

"It's difficult for me too." He looked to the door, and a muscle ticked in his jaw. "But I trust Jeric. And I like Imari. And I want...*better*."

Niá didn't know what to say. She wanted to call him a liar, but there was conviction in his words that no lie could ever paint.

Chez looked back at her, gave her a tight-lipped smile, and said, "Goodnight, Niá. Thanks for helping Tallyn. Even if you don't come along tomorrow."

Niá froze. How did he...?

Chez winked again, though this time it lacked humor, and he ducked through a doorway and out of sight. Leaving Niá alone with her thoughts.

## 7

*I*mari opened her eyes to a dark room. To be fair, it was always dark in Av'Assi without the sun to light the morning, but Imari found it increasingly disorienting. Day and night blurred together, abbreviated only by moments of exhaustion and sleep. Time seemed nonexistent, an idea rather than reality, compounding the complications of her present circumstances. Because like time, down in this cave, Azir was more idea than reality. Most of Av'Assi was too far removed from the outside world, and she—a stranger—was asking them to abandon this and risk everything for that idea.

Imari sighed and turned her head toward Jeric, who slept deeply beside her. It was too dark to see him, so she slid her hand beneath their shared blanket and placed her palm gently against his back, between his broad shoulders. Not to wake him, but to touch him. To feel his solidness beside her. His skin was fire-hot —it always was—and his back expanded with each slow breath. She curled closer to him and tucked her legs behind his. He didn't wake, not completely, but his body shifted just a little, and he settled back against her.

Imari remembered the time they'd huddled naked together

after nearly drowning in the Kjürda. How proximity had been necessary for their survival. Now that proximity was necessary for her soul.

And yet...

She couldn't help thinking on the uncertain path ahead, Jeric's return to Corinth, and what awaited them there. Jeric's throne had been unstable when he'd left, and that had been nearly two months ago. Jeric had professed hope in Hersir, his Lead Stryker, who was intrinsically tasked with keeping Corinth's throne secure. Still, a chair without an occupant was an open invitation, and Jeric couldn't know for certain if one of his jarls had seized this opportunity or if Kormand Vystane of Brevera would finally launch an attack, presuming Corinth weak without her king. There was also the issue of how Jeric's jarls would react when he returned with Imari.

It didn't help that one of his own men could not come to terms with it.

Jeric had insisted she not worry, but she did, and she was pretty sure that deep down, he worried too.

These thoughts held her mind captive from sleep, so Imari decided to get up and start packing. She slid away from Jeric, careful not to wake him, but then he grabbed her thigh and held her firmly and decidedly in place. "Stay," he whispered in the dark.

"We need to pack," she whispered back.

Jeric didn't let go. "It's still dark."

"It's always dark here."

"Exactly."

Imari grinned then leaned forward and kissed his bare shoulder. "I thought wolves were nocturnal."

"I never said I wanted to go back to sleep," he drawled, all sleepiness now gone from his voice, and his hand slid slowly up her thigh, making her pulse quicken.

Imari smiled. "I love you." She kissed his shoulder again. "But those bags aren't going to pack themselves." She grabbed his hand and—regrettably—started pulling it off of her thigh. Jeric finally released her with a groan, and Imari slid out of bed.

The cold air shocked her bare skin, and she snatched a blanket off the chair, draped it around her shoulders, then padded around the bed to the nightstand and lit the small lantern. Warm, amber light filled their room. The bed creaked as Jeric slid his long legs out and stood—completely naked—beside her. He dragged his hands over his face and through his hair, wiping the sleep away.

Imari still found herself marveling at him, at his impressive shape and collection of scars. At all those magnificent lines of self-discipline and years of training. He crossed the room, completely at ease in his nakedness, and snagged his breeches off the chair.

"It's not polite to stare, darling," Jeric said languorously.

She blushed. "Well, it's a good thing I've never really been concerned with manners."

Jeric smirked at her over his shoulder, eyes searching and a bit hopeful, but she quickly turned around to grab her own clothes—a blouse and loose breeches. They were simple garments, but well-tailored, and Imari particularly liked the embroidery at the neckline. It was a pattern of Liagé symbols, repeated over and over again: protection, health, well-being.

Imari tossed her blanket upon the bed, and she was just pulling the tunic down over her head when Jeric's hands slid around her bare waist and drew her back against him. He'd put on his breeches, but his chest was still bare and warm against Imari's skin, and a fluttering filled her chest.

"Jeric, we need to leave," Imari reminded him, though her body had a very different idea of what they should be doing.

"I know," he said lowly. His fingertips brushed the hair from her neck, while one hand rested upon her hipbone. "But you slid out of bed so fast, I never got to say good morning."

"That's probably because you decided it wasn't morning."

Jeric chuckled and planted a kiss at the bend in her neck. His lips lingered there, sending shivers all over her body, and Imari seriously began reconsidering her current objective.

She was about to say as much when Jeric said, suddenly, "But you're right." He let go and stepped away. "We need to pack."

Imari glared back at him, but he only smiled, all mischief.

"Also, our dear matriarch is awake." He pointed at the bottom of the door, where a crack of open space revealed light beyond.

*Ah*, Imari mouthed.

Jeric winked at her then snagged his tunic off the chair.

Imari took a deep breath and dressed, somewhat unsteadily, and when she finished tying her sandals, Jeric said, "I'll handle this." He gestured at their few belongings, which consisted mostly of his weapons.

Imari slipped out of their bedchamber and into the front room and closed the door behind her.

Sure enough, Hiatt was wide awake, and it looked as though she'd been awake for some time. She sat at the table, wrapping something in a bundle of burgundy fabric, and an assortment of supplies were piled all around her.

"You're awake early," Imari said, slowly approaching.

"I'm not sure I ever went to sleep," Hiatt said, and Imari caught a bit of sadness in the matriarch's voice. "While I can't come along, I *can* support you in this way."

Imari stopped beside the table and scanned all the items Hiatt had spread upon it: breads, cheeses, extra clothing...

Nightglass.

"They were first manufactured here, you know," Hiatt said, noting where Imari's attention had settled. She finished tying a knot around the bundle of fabric and stood.

Imari picked up a nightglass blade. It was different from those Ventus had distributed throughout The Wilds. This was of sleek design, with a narrow blade and an elegant skal-black hand guard that curled at the ends, making Ventus's seem almost crude.

"These have been in Mazz's care for a very long time," Hiatt said, thoughtful. "He asked me to give them to you for your journey."

Imari met Hiatt's gaze.

Hiatt looked steadily back. "He wished to go too."

Imari's chest expanded with a breath. "He is not angry with me?"

"No, child," Hiatt said, and her gaze slid back to the table. "We might not always understand Asorai's ways, but we *do* understand that we must each walk our own paths in our own time. If you are not ready, then you are not ready, and we must trust Asorai with the rest. That holds for the people of Av'Assi too." She paused, thoughtful. "Anyway, this should be enough food to hold you over in Liri until your ship arrives...assuming you monitor Braddok's rations."

Imari's lips quirked into a grin. "I'll put Jenya on it."

"Wise."

Imari gazed upon the old matriarch, at those deep lines carved by life and experience, at eyes that had seen so much time. "Thank you for this, Hiatt."

Hiatt nodded once, then, "Oh, and this is from Mazz." Hiatt handed her the small bundle of tightly bound fabric, which she'd fastened with a leather strap.

Imari took the bundle. It was much lighter than she'd expected.

"It's your flute," Hiatt explained, "plus a few additional artifacts Mazz thought might come of use to you and Niá."

Mazz's generosity humbled her. Especially since she'd so adamantly refused him in front of everyone.

Just then, Jeric opened the door and strode into the room. He was covered in weapons, and he'd slung the full satchel over his shoulder.

"Good morning, Provincial King," Hiatt said, her tone clipped with a special edge of irritation that she reserved only for Jeric.

Jeric noticed but flashed her a wolfish smile like he always did. "Good morning, Prior Hiatt."

Jeric stopped beside the table, and his gaze fixed and narrowed on the nightglass. "Where did you find this?"

"It's from Mazz," Imari explained. She'd already told him about the nightglass Chez had found in the ruins, and her suspicions.

Jeric picked up a blade, flicked the edge, and looked sharply at Hiatt.

"There *are* those who still remember," Hiatt answered. "These are for you and your men. Just in case."

"Thank you, Hiatt," Jeric replied with sincerity.

Hiatt regarded him. She bowed her head a second later. "I hope you will not need them."

"I hope so too," Jeric said then began tucking them into the satchel, though he strapped one to his belt for easy access.

Hiatt handed Imari a second satchel, which Imari stuffed the food into, and when she finished, Jeric took that one as well.

"I'll walk you to the tunnel." Hiatt headed for the door. "Tallyn wanted me to tell you that he'll meet you just outside. He went to Gezze's to fetch the others."

"What about the camels?" Imari asked.

"They're staying."

Jeric and Imari looked to each other, to Hiatt.

"I argued for you," Hiatt continued, one hand on the front door, "but I was overruled. The fact of the matter is that our resources are extremely limited, and so those we've kept are very dear to us. The elders decided it wasteful to lend the beasts when you would only be leaving them behind in a few days."

Hiatt wasn't wrong, and Imari couldn't fault them.

"So we walk, and Byri has just earned two more camels," Imari said, looking to Jeric. There was little use in taking the two camels if only half of them could ride. The camels could carry their gear, but Hiatt was right: They had extremely limited resources. "Consider them a gift for taking care of us."

Jeric considered and jerked his head in a nod, though Imari could tell by the set of his brow that he didn't like this.

The three of them left Hiatt's and walked Av'Assi's streets, Imari and Hiatt in front, Jeric trailing a little behind. Most of the people still slept, though Imari spotted a young girl feeding the goats, and a handful of lights flickered in front windows. They hadn't gone very far before Imari spotted movement in her periphery, down an adjacent path.

At first she dismissed it, thinking it a rodent, but then she spotted it again at the next intersection, and the one after, and when they passed Asorai's great tree, she caught sight of a little boy darting beneath those thick and reaching boughs, trying to catch one last glimpse.

"Who is that?" Imari asked.

"Little Ishaq," Hiatt replied quietly.

"The elder's son?"

Hiatt tipped her head.

And, to Imari's surprise, Jeric started for the boy.

Hiatt looked as though she were about to intervene, but Imari placed a hand upon her arm. "Jeric means no harm, *mi a'prior*."

"Whether he means it or not, he is causing it."

Jeric stopped a few paces before the boy, who stood partially behind the tree's wide trunk, peering out and looking ready to bolt, but wonder kept him planted.

Jeric knelt beneath the reaching boughs, dug into one of the satchels, and withdrew a small object carved out of dried cactus wood. He held it out to little Ishaq.

Little Ishaq froze, his gaze darting from Jeric to the object in Jeric's hand. He wanted it—Imari could see it plainly on his face—but he was also afraid.

Jeric waited.

Slowly, the boy took a step, then another, and another, until he stopped before Jeric. He reached out, snatched the little wooden object, and then took two quick steps back.

But Jeric took no offense. "I made it for you," Jeric said in Sol Velorian.

The boy turned it over in wonder.

"It's a wolf," Jeric said.

The boy's eyes widened with understanding. Imari realized this boy would never have seen a wolf before, having spent all his life in this cave.

"So that you remember me," Jeric added.

Beside her, Hiatt fell very still and very quiet.

The boy grinned. His two front teeth were still too big for his face, and others still hadn't grown in yet.

And then he took off running.

Jeric grinned after him and stood. He glanced back and caught Imari's gaze, and her heart skipped a beat.

Hiatt continued on, quiet.

"Did you really carve that for him?" Imari asked as she and Jeric fell in after Hiatt.

He nodded. "I'd considered giving him a dagger but thought his parents might appreciate this more."

"Strangely, I think your little carving will leave a much deeper mark."

Jeric's brow furrowed as he gazed ahead. "I think so too."

They eventually ascended the path that led out of Av'Assi, but at the platform, Imari paused. She gazed down at this underground sanctuary, at all the little homes and paths and pools and floating lights, at the crimson tree glittering from its heart, and Imari found it suddenly difficult to leave.

This had been a respite from the chaos, a salve to the pain wrought by the outside world, and Imari didn't think she'd ever know such peace again.

Jeric had stopped beside her, and she glanced at him to find him studying her. Trying to see if this was still what she wanted.

She nodded once, and together, they turned away from the sanctuary and faced the tunnel, where Tallyn, Jenya and the rest of Jeric's pack waited at the opposite end. Stanis was there, standing ahead of the rest, as if he could not get away from this place fast enough.

In contrast to Chez, Imari found Stanis to be the most intimidating of Jeric's men. He was built like a bludgeon and had a face carved of hard, unforgiving lines, which undoubtedly aided him in his unofficial role as Jeric's emissary. Stanis's long, sandy hair had been pulled tightly back, and his shrewd gaze narrowed on her before he looked sharply away.

"Wolf," Braddok said to Jeric when they joined, then added, "Mornin', Surina."

"What's in there?" Chez pointed at the bulging second satchel.

"Provisions," Jeric answered.

"Great, put some of that in mine." Braddok started opening his much emptier satchel.

"No, I want them to last."

Aksel snickered.

About a dozen people had come to see them off, in addition to Urri and Gezze. She didn't see Mazz, and she wondered why he hadn't come to say goodbye in person, but she was presently more concerned by the fact that Niá wasn't among them.

"Where's Niá?" Imari asked.

Tallyn and Jenya exchanged a long look. Braddok rubbed the back of his neck, and Chez's features tightened as he looked to the horizon.

Oh.

She wasn't coming.

Imari's heart sank. "Did she say why?" Imari asked Tallyn.

Tallyn didn't answer immediately. "It was not an easy choice for her. That much I do know."

Imari met Jeric's gaze briefly, then looked back at the group. At Hiatt. "Please tell her that I understand. And...I love her."

"I will," Hiatt replied.

"And these are for you two," Tallyn said, holding out two small stones, one for Imari and one for Jeric. They looked exactly like the wardstones atop Skanden's wall—flat discs with wards etched onto the surface—but these were small enough to fit in Imari's pocket. "The others already have theirs."

Imari took hers, and the moment Imari's fingers grazed the surface, she felt the power humming within. It rang throughout her body like a chord spanning all octaves, but with two different instrumental signatures: Tallyn's and Niá's.

"She helped you," Imari said.

"She did," Tallyn replied.

Imari slipped the stone into her pocket while Jeric took his and did the same.

"I hate to see you go," Urri said with a large sigh and placed her hands on her wide hips. Wind pulled thick strands of her black and silver hair across her round face.

"But you probably don't hate seeing all your mead go..." Aksel said, nodding toward Braddok, and a few laughed.

"Thank you for taking us in," Imari said, looking to Gezze, to Urri, and then—finally—Hiatt. "I won't forget you, or all you've done for us."

"I'm sorry we can't do more," Hiatt replied.

"You've already done more than I could have hoped."

Jeric looked to Imari and said, "Shall we?"

Chez adjusted the strap of his satchel and headed down the path after Stanis, who had already started walking. The others exchanged goodbyes and well wishes and followed after Chez and Stanis until Imari and Jeric were the last two standing. Most of those who'd come to see them off started back into the tunnel.

Hiatt extended a hand.

Imari took it.

"I will see you again," Hiatt said, with the certainty only a seer could possess, but before Imari could ask, Hiatt squeezed Imari's hand, let go, and added, "It is time."

Imari inhaled deep, casting one last glance at the tunnel before she and Jeric started walking after the others.

"Wait!" a voice yelled from behind.

Imari's heart stopped.

*Niá.*

Imari spun around to see Niá sprinting down the path toward them, a satchel slung over her shoulder.

Imari and Jeric exchanged a glance as Niá slowed to a stop before them, red-faced and winded. Her gaze flickered ahead, where the others had also stopped, before her gaze shot back to Imari. "May I still come along?"

Imari smiled broadly. "You know you never need to ask."

**8**
_____

They left the ruins behind, crossed into the wide valley, and followed a dried riverbed northeast. A cold wind snapped, and a woolen blanket of clouds stretched across the sky in all directions, though thankfully it did not bring rain. Braddok, Aksel, and Chez chattered on and off, sometimes joined by Jenya, but the rest remained quiet and contemplative as they followed Tallyn along this old thread of civilization.

Imari imagined the riverbed in its day like an artery pumping life into the once-vibrant Sol Velor, though all that remained upon its shores now were bones: the occasional crumbling wall, the footprint of a city, a broken tower half buried in the sand, still stabbing skyward as if it'd died reaching for the gods' mercy. Imari would have liked to investigate, to see if more Liagé artifacts were buried amidst the rubble, but Tallyn insisted they press on.

"Time is not a luxury we can afford," he said.

Imari wondered if he had other reasons too. The same reasons that kept the elders from haste in investigating what remained of their homeland. And being out here, out of the safety of that rocky dome, Imari began to understand. Shah power infused the air like some heady perfume, always present, everywhere and in all things, tingling as she breathed it in. It was a note ringing persistently flat in the background, singing in dissonance to the world.

Jeric did not hear it or smell it, not exactly. Not in the way Imari described it to him, but Jeric was a hunter to the core. Though he could not see his enemy, he *sensed* something there, and so Jeric never relaxed.

Imari might have stripped Zussa from this land, but Zussa's poison remained.

Still, their day proved uneventful. Sand wasn't easy to traverse, but it was soft on the bones, and it was late afternoon when Imari spotted an enormous black bird in her periphery. It struck her for two reasons: one, because they hadn't seen any other living creature since leaving Av'Assi, and two, because it seemed to be following them.

Its wings stretched wide as it rode the currents, and sometimes it would dive behind a high dune, out of sight, but it always reappeared, keeping the same distance.

"I've been watching it too," Jeric said. He walked beside her, as he'd done for most of the day. "It started following us not long after we left the ruins."

Imari shot Jeric a concerned look, but Jeric's shrewd gaze remained fixed on the bird.

"Well, there's no other godsdamned thing out here," Aksel said. "Maybe it's hungry."

"That's not a bird," Tallyn said from the rear. "It's Su'Vi."

Jeric and Imari stopped. Their entire group stopped and looked from the black bird to the alta-Liagé.

"The enchantress?" Jenya asked.

"Yes."

"She can turn into a rutting bird?" Braddok asked, eyeing that bird again.

Rasmin had the ability to do that. He could turn himself into an owl.

"Yes and no," Tallyn replied. "Su'Vi has the unique ability to transform into an entire flock of birds." This statement received a few surprised looks from Jeric's men. "And she is able to break one or two from that flock to dispose at her will."

"That is rutting creepy..." Braddok murmured.

"So she's spying on us," Imari said, understanding.

Tallyn's one eye met hers. "Yes."

"Gods, I feel so violated," Braddok added.

"And you're just now telling us this?" Jeric asked.

Tallyn looked to Jeric. "There is nothing we can do about it."

"We can kill it."

"She's too far to shoot."

"Then use your godsdamned magic."

"That's not how it works, Wolf King."

Jeric took a step toward Tallyn. "You took on all the Silent —*and lived*—and you expect me to believe there's nothing you can do about one rutting bird?"

"Unless she comes closer, that's exactly what we expect you to believe." It was Niá who had answered. She stood off to the side, as she'd done most of the day. Wind snapped at her clothes and short hair. "She's too far to trap with a ward, and our veiling enchantments are *clearly* ineffective."

Jeric considered her, his gaze flitted to Tallyn before shooting back to the bird. "Well, we'd better figure something out. I'm not leading her to Corinth."

"She won't be able to follow us at sea," Tallyn said. "Even Su'Vi has limitations."

Jeric studied him. "You're sure about that?"

"I would stake my life on it."

Jeric didn't look convinced, but then he glanced to the sky and said, decidedly, "It's getting dark. We need to make camp."

Jeric was right. It was getting dark, and fast.

"What about there?" Imari said, pointing to the crest of a rise, where she could just see the flat table of a red plateau beyond. "I'd rather be on higher ground in case it rains."

"I agree," Jeric said, and they all hiked out of the dried riverbed, up a sanded dune, and to the base of the plateau. It turned out to be an entire community of enormous plateaus, which cut down the wind significantly. Jeric led them to the leeward side of one, where they set camp out of Su'Vi's avian view.

"Is it safe enough for a fire?" Aksel asked.

No one had brought wood for a fire, but Niá had brought a fire stone, which she had enchanted to ignite, if needed.

"Su'Vi already knows we're here," Jeric said dryly as he shook out a blanket and laid it down.

Tallyn's one-eyed gaze trailed the sky and the horizon. "Keep it out of direct sight. Just in case." He looked to Niá. "Shall we?" he asked. Niá nodded, and they both began establishing a perimeter using the wardstones they had made.

"What's that for?" Stanis asked sharply, his gaze fixed on the little stone in Tallyn's hand.

Imari looked to Jeric, but Jeric was studying his man with an expression Imari could not quite read.

"It's a barrier," Tallyn replied, setting down one stone, then another. The stones were about the size of Imari's hand, all shapes and colors, but many of the etchings were familiar to her. Some, because she'd seen them atop Skanden's wall. Others, because Niá had taught her. "It repels creatures of Shah."

"Like the symbols you were drawing in the sand on our way *into* Ziyan?" Aksel asked.

"Exactly like that." Tallyn placed another stone. "But these are much more reliable. Wind isn't a concern."

Stanis still looked as though he didn't trust whatever Tallyn was setting down, but he turned away, pulled out a blanket, and started arranging a place to sleep within their warded perimeter.

Imari exchanged a knowing look with Jeric, then knelt beside the satchel and started withdrawing a blanket for herself.

Jeric stopped her hand. "That's yours." He nodded toward the one he'd already laid upon the sand.

"I'm not helpless, Jeric."

"I'm not doing it to help. I'm doing it to honor." He grinned at her, then reached past, snagged the second blanket out of her hand, and began shaking that one out too.

"Well, thank you," she said, then sat upon the blanket Jeric had laid out for her, and *wards*, it felt good to sit. Her lower back ached, and her feet felt as though they'd been rubbed raw, so she unstrapped her sandals and set them aside. The leather straps had cut into her skin in places, and a blister was quickly forming upon her heel.

This did not bode well for the next few days.

Imari reached behind Jeric, grabbed the satchel, and lifted the flap, and then sifted through for the verraroot. She soon found the little root, grabbed one of Jeric's daggers to shave off a piece, and tossed it into her mouth.

"What is that, and can I have some?" Braddok asked.

Jenya looked at him with condescension.

"Verraroot," Imari said. "It dulls pain."

Suddenly, five open palms were before her. Imari chuckled, and she started shaving small pieces into each.

"That was in the riverbed?" Jeric asked. He'd been with her when she'd found the vibrant red root crawling out between two rocks.

She nodded as she carved a shaving into Chez's palm. "Chew and swallow."

Jeric sat upon the blanket he'd placed right against hers, long legs stretched as he held out his hand, and she cut another shaving into his open palm.

He eyed the fibrous red root then popped it into his mouth, and his face twisted with disgust. "Gods...this tastes like scat."

"Well, it usually grows out of it too."

Jeric stopped chewing and looked sideways at her.

Imari smiled, all innocence, then looked to Tallyn, who had set the last wardstone in place and was dusting his hands. "Would you like some, Tallyn?"

Tallyn looked as though he might refuse but approached her instead. Imari carved another shaving for him, then looked across the camp to Niá, who had withdrawn the little firestone she'd made. "Niá?" Imari called out.

Niá glanced over from the stone, then at the root in Imari's hand.

"I'm all right. Thank you." Her gaze caught Chez's before she frowned and looked back at the stone, then bent forward and spoke a word. The marking flared with moonlight, and white flame ignited. Imari already felt its warmth, even from six feet away.

"Huh. That's convenient," Braddok mused, impressed. Stanis gazed at the flame, his features tightened, and he looked away.

Niá stood, not making eye contact with anyone as she grabbed her satchel and moved it right to the edge of their warded circle.

Imari wanted to talk to her. They hadn't had a moment since leaving Av'Assi, but there was no privacy here, and Imari sensed that whatever gnawed upon Niá was not something she wanted to discuss in front of...well, everyone. Imari was considering walking over to her anyway when Jeric held a piece of bread right before her eyes.

"Eat," Jeric whispered.

Imari met his gaze and took the bread.

"You said three days to Liri?" Aksel asked Tallyn.

"Assuming the weather holds."

"Well, if it doesn't, maybe that flying demon will get struck by lightning," Braddok said, and both Aksel and Chez chuckled. Stanis remained quiet.

"How well do you know Su'Vi?" Jeric asked Tallyn.

At his question, everyone fell quiet and looked to the alta-Liagé.

Tallyn snagged a piece of bread from his satchel. "I wouldn't say I knew her well, though we were acquainted."

A beat. "She helped Rasmin create you and the other Silent, didn't she?"

How Jeric pieced information together, Imari would never understand, but the moment he said the words, she knew he was right. Su'Vi was an enchantress, and a powerful one. Rasmin was a seer, and though he might have Seen how to create Tallyn, he would have needed an enchanter's talents to bring that vision to life. Imari remembered the stone chamber Tallyn had shown her through his shared Sight and all the figures standing around the stone altar where Ventus's body had lain.

"She did," Tallyn replied. "However, Su'Vi did not have any more to do with me than that. Actually, I believe my—*our*—existence offended her, though she wouldn't dare admit that to Azir. Su'Vi was always a purist. Extremely talented, but merciless."

Imari remembered something the legion had said through Astrid. "Was she as talented as Niá's oza?"

At this, Niá fell very still.

A small, sad smile touched Tallyn's thin lips. "No, she was not. Taran of Bassi was the greatest enchantress of our age. Your Tolya was a close second."

Niá's gaze faltered, and she glanced away.

"I never knew," Imari whispered.

"You know now," Tallyn replied.

They all sat quiet for a bit, eating and drinking as night swallowed the land beyond Niá's little halo of light. Eventually, conversation resumed, and Imari remembered the little bundle from Mazz that Hiatt had given her. Imari reached for the satchel and withdrew the bundle of fabric. She untied the leather straps, unwrapped the fabric, and found her broken flute inside.

Right beside Fyri's bells.

Imari froze, and a wave of tingling washed over her, head to toe.

"Sonofabitch." Jeric sat upright.

"Oi, what's going on over there?" Braddok asked, looking over.

Imari stared down at the bells as her heart pounded hard and fast. The tingling persisted, but it was not coming from her flute. No, her flute still felt as lifeless as ever, like a body without a soul. A long crack split the glossy black bone in half, splintering through every hole, every inscription, from mouthpiece to end. Seeing it beside those bells, she suddenly understood Mazz, because a new fire burned in her soul—fire from the bells lying so still and innocent beside her broken flute—and that fire was growing fast.

"I...take it you didn't know that was in there," Chez said.

Imari glared at Tallyn, very aware of everyone, especially Jeric, watching her while she struggled to ignore the crescendo of heat in her soul. "Did you know about this?"

But Tallyn looked just as shocked as she felt. "I did not."

Just then, her thumb brushed the leather, and that one small touch was like oil to flame. The heat ignited, engulfing her completely, and her head filled with sound—every pitch, all at once. Without thinking, Imari threw the bundle. To get it away, to make the fire and noise stop, as if she could sever whatever connection had just been made. The bundle landed in the sand, just at the edge of Nia's light, but the strip did not stop glowing, and the sound would not cease.

Imari did not know how long she stared at those shining glyphs, grinding her teeth as that chord blared painfully in her skull. Seconds, minutes—it felt like an eternity—and then, finally, it quieted. All of it. The light, the fire, the song. Fyri's bells fell silent and dark once more, Imari's brow glistened with sweat, and everyone was staring at her.

Imari opened her mouth, but no words came. She did not know what to say, did not trust herself to speak.

She did not trust herself, period.

Jeric stood suddenly, took two steps, grabbed both her flute and Fyri's talla, and shoved them deep into his satchel, out of sight.

But Imari still felt its pull.

"Best get some rest," Tallyn said, addressing them all. "We've got another long day tomorrow."

A long and awkward beat passed.

"I'll take first watch," Chez said, slowly pushing himself to his feet.

"I'll join you." Tallyn looked to Niá and added, "Unless you would rather. I think it would be wise for at least one of us to be watching at all times."

Niá's glaze flickered to Chez, who'd gone to the edge of their camp, which opened to the valley beyond. "I'll take second."

Tallyn nodded and joined Chez, while everyone settled in for the night. Jeric, however, moved back to Imari's side and sat down, then slid his arm around Imari's waist and started pulling her down onto the blanket beside him.

"I'm not tired," she said.

"I'm not either," he whispered in her ear, still dragging her down until she lay in the crook of his arm with her head on his chest. He began rubbing his thumb against the small of her back, pushing out all the knots that walking had tied. "You're afraid," he said lowly, only for her, and his rich cello warmed away some of the cold terror that had taken residence.

"I'm terrified," she whispered.

His hand pressed to her back, his fingers splayed. "I'm not."

"You should be."

He moved his hand from her back to her chin and tilted it up as he craned back to look down at her. "I am not afraid of you,

Imari." He let his words anchor deep as his storming blue eyes bore into hers. "Do you understand? I do not fear who you are."

His words broke her heart and put it back together again.

"Jeric, I *can't*," she managed. She would not use Fyri's bells, but she *could not* use her flute, and though she did not explain further, Jeric understood it all anyway.

He pressed his thumb over her lips as if to silence all of those unspoken fears. "I know," he said instead, then settled her head back onto his chest, where she lay curled into his warmth, his arm wrapped securely around her while his heart beat a steady rhythm into her ear. She soon found herself hypnotized by the sound, by his constant drum, and eventually her weariness caught up, her body relaxed, and she fell asleep.

"There is inherent temptation in the receipt of power, for power belongs first to Asorai, suited for Asorai, but we of creation are fallen, forever inclined to taint what Asorai made pure. So how much more temptation did Zussa face, being the most powerful creation of all?"

~ Excerpt from the teachings
according to Moltoné,
Liagé Second High Sceptor.

## 9

*You are mine,* Sulaziér.

Imari's eyes snapped open to a dark world. A broad slice of night sky was visible from where she lay, camped with the others between plateaus, and yet that voice echoed.

Zussa.

It was *her* voice—Imari recognized it now. The one from her nightmares and the tree. The voice had belonged to Zussa all along, though the words rang stronger now. Clearer and more commanding, and Imari's power stirred despite herself, as if answering Zussa's call.

It terrified her.

Imari's gaze drifted to the little satchel where Jeric had buried the tallas. Even now, she could *feel* Fyri's bells like a soft and persistent tug on a lure.

*Tallas can take months to create,* Mazz had said. *Years, sometimes, to find the right match. But more importantly, a talla can never be fashioned for one who is already bound. You must take this.*

Jeric shifted behind her, draped his arm over her waist, and drew her close, and Imari instinctively settled into him. Moments before she'd fallen asleep, Imari had suggested, out of respect for the others—specifically Stanis—that maybe they should not sleep together. It wasn't that the others hadn't already suspected Jeric and Imari's sleeping arrangements back at Hiatt's, but showcasing it felt slightly discourteous.

When she'd said as much to Jeric, he'd promptly dragged her on top of him.

Braddok had waggled his brows and then made a similar offer to Jenya, who countered with a death threat.

But with the night had come the bitter cold, and Imari found herself very thankful for Jeric's insistence. Still, his warmth and solidness could not chase away the cold fear that had settled deep in her bones.

*Don't fear the Shah, Imari,* Niá had said. *It will not turn you into something you are not already.*

To which Imari thought, *I am a thief and a murderer.*

Imari wondered who Fyri had been before she'd known Azir. Had she always valued power over human life? Had she been a purist, like Su'Vi? The woman in the storm had begged her to leave Ziyan and told Imari not to speak Azir's name.

Imari could still see the hate twisting Fyri's features, but that hate had not been directed at Imari. It had been directed at Azir.

*I can hold off the tyrcorat to give you time,* Fyri had said, *but you must promise you'll leave and never come back to this place.*

Because she had known what was in that tree and what Azir had truly been after.

None of it made sense. Hadn't they been lovers? Wasn't Fyri the one who'd first tried to free Zussa for Azir one hundred years ago? And hadn't that very act inevitably destroyed her and all of Sol Velor? So why, then, had Fyri been hellbent on stopping Imari from helping Azir reach his goal?

All of these thoughts tangled in Imari's mind until her head ached and night softened with the pre-dawn. Jeric withdrew his arm from her waist as he rolled onto his back, though his breathing remained slow and steady. Fabric rustled nearby as someone else shifted.

They would all wake very soon, and Imari *really* needed to relieve herself.

Carefully, she inched away from Jeric and climbed to her feet. Without Jeric's warmth, the cold cut through her thin clothes, and she shuddered, pulling her scarf over her head and wrapping her arms tightly around herself. She could just see Niá at the camp's edge—alone—keeping watch over the valley, so Imari strode in the other direction, deeper into the garden of plateaus. The moment she stepped over their warded circle, a tingling sensation washed over her skin.

Imari found a hidden spot behind a lip of rock, but when she finished up, she did not return to Jeric's side. She strode for Niá instead.

"Good morning," Imari whispered in Istraan, taking a seat beside Niá.

Niá's gaze fixed upon the sweeping stretch of shadows beyond their camp, where a knife of fire now burned upon the horizon. "Morning."

"Seen anything?" Imari asked.

Niá shook her head. "Your Wolf was not lying. Sol Velor is a graveyard."

Imari tucked her legs before her and wrapped her arms around them as she looked west, to the dark silhouette outlining the jagged mountains that provided a natural border to the lands beyond Sol Velor. This mountain range stretched all along Sol Velor's southern edge, cradling it, until it touched the sea in the east. Imari could not imagine the magnitude of power that could have decimated this entire land.

A power Fyri had possessed.

"Any signs of Su'Vi?" Imari asked.

"No." Niá looked as though she might say more, but her brow creased, and she closed her lips.

"You *feel* it," Imari said.

Their gazes met.

"You feel it too," Niá whispered.

Imari nodded and gazed back to the valley. "This place feels... sick. Soured. It reminds me of a rotting corpse. I don't know how else to describe it."

"I know," Niá agreed. "It's actually harder for me to draw upon the Shah here."

"Harder in what way?"

"It's like...it doesn't want to listen. I really had to focus just to get that firestone to ignite." A pause. "I don't see how they'll ever rebuild Sol Velor."

"Well. They don't seem very concerned with *rebuilding* it," Imari said dryly. "They're perfectly content hiding in a cave for the rest of their lives."

"I don't know. That might have been true before you showed up."

Imari sighed. "I'd like to believe that."

"Sometimes people don't recognize their own captivity until they've met someone who is truly free," Niá said quietly.

Imari looked over at Niá, but Niá's gaze was fixed determinedly upon the horizon, her thoughts far away—in a certain temple, if Imari had to guess. Niá did not speak much of her time at Ashova's, and Imari did not ask.

"Your brother Kai visited me often," Niá said suddenly.

Imari stilled, utterly and completely, and then her eyelids slid shut as a tide of emotion churned within.

*Oh, Kai...*

She'd known he'd frequented Ashova's, but Imari had not known any more than that. She'd never asked. And all that time he'd been visiting Niá.

"Oh, Niá...I am...so sorry. I had no idea."

"Don't apologize for him. And what could you have done? Made him stop?"

Imari didn't know what to say. Didn't know what to *feel*. She both loved and hated her brother in that moment, and she immediately wondered if Kai had been cruel to Niá, but then what kind of question was that? He'd taken something from Niá that Niá had not wanted to give, which was cruelty in and of itself.

Was this the reason Niá had not wanted to come along? Because every time she laid eyes upon Imari, she could not help but remember Kai?

"Your brother told me a lot of things," Niá continued. Her voice came out sharp and bitter as her gaze set on that distant horizon, and a single tear slid over Niá's cheek. Niá did not wipe it away. "Personal things. Things he never should have told anyone, but he trusted me because he...he thought he loved me."

Imari's gaze faltered as her chest squeezed.

"Saza is my fault," Niá said in a whisper.

"No, Niá, he isn't—"

"He *is*," Niá ground out through clenched teeth, and another tear fell. "So is Oza Taran. They were helping you while I was... with your brother." Her voice broke on that last part. "Trying so hard to commit to memory everything he had to say about you so that I could pass it on to Bahdra."

Oh.

Quiet settled between them as Niá's words filled the last hole in Imari's puzzle from that night.

It had been Niá.

Niá who'd reported Imari's arrival. Niá who'd informed Bahdra that Imari was powerless. Niá who'd shared all of Trier's weaknesses, making it an easy victory for Azir. Niá who'd probably also known that Imari had been sneaking off to E'Centro each night, though she would not have known whom Imari visited. Imari had never shared that detail with her brothers, and if Niá had known, things might have turned out very differently.

Imari's papa might still be alive.

Imari felt the sting of betrayal, but Niá wasn't asking for

forgiveness. She was telling Imari because this was the guilt she carried always, and she was tired of holding it—tired of carrying it alone. Imari could see how the weight of it was slowly crushing her, because Imari understood that burden very well.

The sun peeked over the horizon, baptizing them in golden light, and Imari reached out and grabbed Niá's hand. "If you want to go back to Av'Assi, I will understand. It's not too late."

Niá's jaw clenched, and another tear fell.

"Understand me, Niá: *I don't want you to go back*," Imari said fiercely, and her own eyes burned. "But if that is what you want, I will not stop you. I just ask that you allow me to check in on you from time to time, because...you are the closest thing to Sorai I've ever had."

Niá's bottom lip trembled, and more tears spilled down her cheeks. They were shining streaks of sorrow in the morning sun.

Imari heard a noise and glanced over her shoulder to see Jeric on his feet and heading for them. Jenya and Chez also began to rise.

Niá pulled her hand back to hastily dab at her face with her tunic.

"Take your time," Imari whispered, touching Niá's shoulder as Imari stood and intercepted Jeric halfway. "Morning," she said, reverting to Common.

He reached out and brushed a rogue strand of hair from her face. "Everything all right?" he asked lowly. His gaze cut to Niá.

"It will be," Imari said.

Jeric's attention lingered on Imari, but Imari shook her head and mouthed *later*. He cast one last glance at Niá, and they both started back toward camp.

"Any signs of Su'Vi?" he asked.

"None."

"Do you think she's gone?"

Imari's arm brushed his as they walked. "I don't know, but I imagine we'll find out soon enough."

The sun rose higher now, painting the sky in fuchsia and turmeric and lapis, and the clouds ignited like little tufts of flame. There was no color like this anywhere in the world, no sky so large, no sun so bright.

"There's nothing like this in all the Provinces," Jeric said quietly, mirroring her own thoughts.

"No, there isn't."

Wind tossed his bronze-streaked hair, and he looked sharply back at her. "Will you be able to leave it?"

Meaning: Will you truly be able to spend the rest of your life in Skyhold?

"Beauty alone won't keep me," Imari answered with a small smile.

Mischief glinted in his eyes. "Well, that's unfortunate. I suppose I'll have to find other ways to earn your eternal devotion."

Imari chuckled softly, though the sound was dampened by Niá's confession.

Jeric noticed, of course, and looked as though he were about to ask, but they'd reached camp, where Jenya, Tallyn, and Jeric's pack were shaking out blankets. Well, Jenya was specifically shaking her blanket over Braddok's sleeping form, and Braddok woke with a jolt and a curse.

"Thank you, Jenya," Jeric said. "Not sure why I hadn't thought of that before."

Braddok picked up a fistful of sand and chucked it at Jeric, but it dispersed into a cloud and blew right back into his face. Chez laughed, while Braddok grumbled more curses and shoved himself to his feet. Stanis crouched in silence, his back to the group as he packed his things.

"Morning, Surina. Wolf," Jenya said as they approached.

"Morning," Imari said, while Jeric strode right through camp toward Aksel, who—Imari realized—still lay upon the ground with one arm slung over his eyes.

"Is he still sleeping?" Imari asked.

"Mmhmm." Chez confirmed. "Aks could sleep through war."

"*Could*?" Braddok guffawed. "He *does* sleep through war."

Jeric snatched a flask from Braddok's pack, despite Braddok's colorful protestations, popped the cork, and dumped the mead over Aksel's face. Aksel gasped and jerked awake, arms flailing wide as he sputtered and cursed.

"Get up. We're leaving." Jeric shoved the top of Aksel's head.

Aksel groaned and wiped mead from his eyes. "Son of a—"

"Ah ah!" Chez warned, wagging a finger. "Remember, we can't call him that to his face anymore. He's the king. You gotta wait till he walks away now."

"He can kiss my—" Braddok started, still irked about his flask, but Jeric gave him a look, and he shut his mouth with a grumble.

"And these were the best Corinth had to offer?" Jenya drawled, glancing between them as she slung her satchel over her shoulder.

"I'd like to get going, if you all think you can manage," Tallyn said, eyeing each of them as if he were suddenly regretting his current life choices.

"Calm down, old man, we're coming," Braddok said. He snatched up his blanket and gave it a good hard shake—right in front of Jenya, who closed her eyes and pressed her lips firmly together—then shoved it unceremoniously into his pack.

Which was when Niá joined them. Niá's eyes were mostly dry, if not a little red, and everyone pretended not to notice.

Everyone except Chez.

His expression sobered, and he looked very much like he wanted to ask her what was wrong, but he didn't.

"Hey, Niá," Braddok said easily, shouldering his pack. Aksel also nodded in greeting.

Imari handed Niá her packed satchel.

"You didn't need to pack my things," Niá said quietly.

"I wanted to."

Niá looked at the pack, at Imari, then squared her shoulders and nodded once, decided.

She was staying.

Imari could have hugged her. Niá took the pack, immediately noticed its lightness, and opened the flap, frowning once she realized what was missing.

"Your books are with Chez," Imari explained, and before Niá could argue, Imari added, "He insisted."

And Chez—probably anticipating Niá's response—had already started down the hill after Stanis. Niá looked sharply at Imari, but Imari raised her hands and said, "Take it up with him."

Niá never did take it up with Chez as the days passed, and they passed slowly. Partially because they could not walk any faster, but mostly because the landscape was an unchanging, monotonous swath of brown. Imari's feet and body ached despite the verraroot she took each morning and night, and she was completely coated in sand. It was in her ears, her nose, and other places she didn't care to mention, and it turned into a glorious soggy paste when it rained their third morning of travel. The rain didn't last long, however, and by afternoon, the clouds slowly dispersed, and Su'Vi began trailing them again.

Imari did not like Azir knowing where they were; she hoped Tallyn was right about the sea.

Despite her discomfort and pervasive unease, Imari counted her blessings, such as the fact that they weren't walking in the dead of summer, and though the nights were cold, they were not unbearable. Especially since Jeric held her close each night, which was her favorite blessing of all.

On their fifth day of travel, salt tinged the wind's hungry

claws, and damp patches began to appear within the dried riverbed they'd been following.

They were getting close.

"Would you look at that," Braddok said, gesturing at a small and frothy puddle of brackish water. Sand caked his brows and beard, turning his vibrant red to rust.

Jeric glanced at the puddle then frowned at the eastern horizon.

"What is it?" Imari asked.

"We should have seen gulls by now."

Imari hadn't considered this herself, but now that Jeric had mentioned it, he was right. Especially since winter had arrived in the Provinces.

"We haven't seen one rutting creature in five days," Aksel chimed in, stopping on Jeric's other side. "So I would say it's true to form."

But Jeric wasn't satisfied. "Tallyn, how much farther?"

"Over that rise, about three miles," Tallyn replied. He'd been quiet since this morning. Truthfully, he hadn't spoken much since they'd left Av'Assi, but today he'd seemed particularly introspective, and it worried Imari. "We should arrive by sunset."

"Then let's camp over there." Jeric pointed to a cluster of rocks ahead of them. "We can head for Liri in the morning with a full day's worth of sunlight ahead of us."

"Normally, I would agree," Tallyn said. "However, our dear captain will not tarry."

A crease formed between Jeric's brows. Imari could see him weighing their options. "Can you See anything ahead?"

Tallyn looked as though he was about to object. He'd been trying—and failing—to See anything since they'd left Av'Assi, but then his eye shuttered closed. A breath. That pale eye snapped open, and he shook his head.

Nothing.

Jeric's lips thinned, and his steely gaze fixed upon the destination they could not presently see.

"I am wary as well, Wolf King," Tallyn continued, "but I fear more that we'll miss our window, and I am not keen on being stranded in this place."

A muscle ticked in Jeric's jaw, and then he gave Tallyn a sharp nod and kept walking.

Su'Vi followed them for a little while, but as they reached the base of that last rise, she dove behind a plateau and out of sight. She did not reappear, but Imari could still *sense* her. She was the only one who could.

Whatever Su'Vi had done to hide herself had not worked on Imari completely.

These past few days, Su'Vi had been a steady pulse in her periphery, a tainted star that flickered erratically, but Imari could never quite look at her directly, for every time she did, Su'Vi would bleed back into the land's canvas, indistinguishable. Imari suspected Su'Vi's power had something to do with it—some enchantment designed to hide her specifically from them—but it hadn't mattered, because Su'Vi had remained visible.

Until now.

"Is she gone?" Jeric asked as they walked. He knew she could sense Su'Vi; she'd told both him and Tallyn when she'd first realized it.

Imari looked at Jeric. "I still feel her."

Jeric frowned, his gaze fixed on the place Su'Vi had vanished, but he didn't say another word about it.

They finally crested the rise, where the wind snapped and clawed anew, kicking sand and whipping clumps of hair across Imari's face. The gust nearly stole her scarf, but she caught it just in time.

Jeric eyed her sideways. "Nice reflexes."

"Never steal from a thief," Imari replied.

Jeric's mouth curled, and then they both gazed upon their

destination in heavy silence. A wide sea stretched ahead, black beneath dark clouds, and nestled where that black water kissed the sand was the old port city of Liri.

Liri had been enormous, that much was apparent, but all that remained was a wide footprint of broken sandstone, as if the gods themselves had trampled upon this magnificent sprawl of mortal pride, crushing mankind beneath their feet. What struck Imari most was the quiet. The *emptiness*. Water always brought life, but here, even the sea was still. There were no white caps, no rolling waves, no movement—nothing. No seagulls, not one. No ship, either. There was nothing but wind, and it whispered foreboding in her ears.

"It appears your captain isn't here," Jeric said sharply to Tallyn as the others caught up. They, too, fell silent as they gazed upon this ruin of pride.

"He'll come," Tallyn said, his one-eyed gaze fixed ahead.

"Did he already leave?" Imari asked.

"No," Tallyn replied without hesitation. "He would have waited through tonight; however, it's possible he hit poor weather."

Cold wind punched through them. Overhead, the clouds collided and churned, promising rain.

"I don't like this," Imari said.

"I don't either," Braddok said.

"So, we have a choice to make," Tallyn said, "Make our camp here or find shelter in Liri."

Jeric gave Tallyn a very condescending look.

Tallyn's one eye narrowed. "We could not risk our window, Wolf King."

Just then, thunder crashed overhead.

"Rutting fantastic." Braddok grumbled.

"So Liri it is," Imari said, looking at Jeric.

Jeric's lips pressed firmly together, his nostrils flared, and he glared at Tallyn. "You had better be right about this, old man."

And then he started treading down the slope's other side, toward Liri.

A wide thread of compressed sand met them at the base of the dune. Tallyn said it had once served as the main road into Liri, and even still, Imari could see the faint lines of old wagon ruts.

Lightning flashed overhead as they reached Liri's outer fields, or so that's what Tallyn called them. They were nothing more than sand and the occasional tuft of dried grasses now, and as they made their way into the city proper, the air reeked of salt and fish. Liri itself was a giant maze of broken stone and dry waterways. The people had engineered a network of canals to serve like roads, then built bridges to connect buildings and paths, though most all of the bridges had collapsed. Rotten canoes huddled together, some on dry land, others half-buried in isolated pools of brown water. Walls had crumbled, rooftops had collapsed, and the occasional scrap of faded cloth still fluttered from a window, like a final and futile attempt at surrender.

But it was the shadows that kept drawing Imari's attention.

They stretched long and wide and thick, lining every broken path, filling every deep crevice. Imari could not shake the sense that they were being watched, and every string in her body pulled taut.

Tallyn led them through the rubble, backtracking twice as they found the way blocked by collapsed buildings. They eventually reached Liri's wharf, marked by a long, wooden walk that framed the sea, from which a line of docks jutted out like fingers. The docks themselves lay in ruin, many of them broken off and all of them rotten, while dozens of ship masts stabbed up through the dark water like spears. A single barrel bobbed amidst the masts, like a lure for whatever evil lurked below the water's surface.

Jeric's boots thunked along the wooden planks, and he

stopped near the edge to peer into the water at all the rubble buried within. "He can't dock here."

"We'll have to go out to him."

He looked sharply back at Tallyn. Rain had started to fall, and it was quickly turning Jeric's bronze hair a soft brown. "We're not getting in that water."

"We won't have to. There should be at least one dinghy still intact." Tallyn pointed farther down, where the wharf's stretch of wooden ramps ended at sandy beach. There, at the bend in the shoreline, dozens of small boats had beached, probably from treasure hunters who had been unable to dock properly.

"Right now," Imari cut in, eyeing both Jeric and Tallyn as the rain fell harder, "we need to find cover."

They all appraised the facade of broken faces—all that remained of Liri's once magnificent wharf.

"There." Jeric pointed to the top of an old tower they could just see behind the wharf. It looked to be leaning and was partially attached to a domed building, though only half of the tarnished bronze dome remained.

"There's only one way out," Tallyn said, frowning.

"There's also only one way *in*," Jeric said. "And without your Sight, we need ours. Preferably from higher ground."

# 10

---

Tallyn and Niá arranged the wardstones as they'd done every night, while the others attempted to make themselves comfortable. It had been an uncertain hike to the top of the tower. As it turned out, the tower leaned more than it'd appeared to from the outside, and ascending the spiral stair had proven a unique challenge. The uneven stair eventually ended at a round room with a slanted floor, peeling plaster walls, and arched cutouts for windows, giving vantage of sea and city, as well as the broken dome abutting their hasty refuge.

Despite the tower's crippled posture and questionable stability, Jeric had been right about the view.

There was a single, small hatch in the rooftop, which was miraculously still intact. Jeric pulled the hatch down and—with a quick lift from Braddok—climbed out to inspect. Ten minutes later, he dropped back through the hatch, landing easily upon his feet. Rain dripped down his temples and soaked his clothes, and when he ruffled his wet hair, droplets went flying.

"Looks like there really might be a functioning dinghy," Jeric said, flashing his teeth at Tallyn. "It won't get us to Corinth, but it should get us across the bay. Assuming he comes."

"He will," Tallyn assured him, placing another wardstone. "Any sign of Su'Vi?"

"None that I could see." Jeric looked to Imari. "Can you...?" He didn't have to explain.

Imari closed her eyes.

Her world instantly became sound and light and the dark spaces in between. Going into the Shah plane had become second nature to her; she hardly had to try. But the moment she slipped into that space, she knew that something was very wrong here.

There were no stars—nothing except darkness.

It was as though a thick, black fog had settled over everything, and a strange scent tinged the air. Something metallic and...*wild*, vibrating with energy she could not see, only feel, and those strings within her pulled taut again in defense.

*What is this?* Imari wondered.

She pushed through that wild and metallic darkness to where the city's perimeter should be. Out here, the darkness thinned, and she began to see little pinpricks of flickering light in the ground, though even these struggled to stay ignited. She pushed her power farther still, through those desolate fields, over sand and rock, to the plateaus. There were many more stars here, but not nearly as many as there should have been.

*There.*

Su'Vi's little star flickered, perched upon the edge of a plateau. Imari could faintly hear her song—that warped and dissonant high pitch—but just as she'd caught hold, the song ceased and Su'Vi's light vanished, leaving silence and darkness behind.

Imari opened her eyes and found herself staring into Jeric's dark blues. He stood directly before her, studying her with a hunter's acumen, while the others looked curiously on.

"She's perched atop the plateaus," Imari said.

Jeric's gaze cut to the window as if he might see Su'Vi across the dunes.

"How do you know that?" Stanis asked. His voice dripped with accusation.

Jeric's attention cut sharply back to his man, but Imari put a hand on his arm and answered, "I see the world in stars when I... access my power. Even when there's no one living, the landscape is full of them."

Stanis frowned. The rest of Jeric's men looked intrigued.

"Do people have...stars too?" Chez asked, somewhat cautiously.

"People always stand out because they are so much brighter, but here..." She paused, and her attention snagged upon one of those dismal little banners whipping in the wind. She looked back to the others. "There is no light."

"Has that happened before?" Aksel asked.

Imari met Tallyn's gaze. "Only once. With...Zussa. At the tree."

Unease charged the air.

"What does it mean?" Jenya asked.

Seeing that Imari had no answer, Tallyn said, "I do not know, but we should eat and try to get some rest." His gaze flickered warily to the ceiling, to the peeling plaster and spidering cracks.

No one moved immediately, but then Braddok plucked a fresh flask from his pack (earning himself a reproachful look from Jeric, which he predictably ignored). He made his way to a window—stumbling a little from the floor's disorienting tilt—where he glanced out and took a long drink. "So where the hells is this dinghy, Wolf?"

Jenya joined him at the window and pointed ten seconds later.

"Ah." Braddok took another drink.

"It's not very big," Jenya said, looking back at Jeric. "Do you think it will hold all of us?"

"Honestly, I'm a little more concerned about this *tower* holding all of us..." Chez ripped a piece of plaster from the wall, but a whole section came away with it, unveiling a startlingly large crack in the compressed sand wall.

"How comforting..." Jenya mused.

"You lookin' for some comfort, Jen?" Braddok waggled his brows.

She whacked him on the back of the head. "Thank you, *Rasé*. I feel better already," she said, and Braddok laughed as she took a seat across from Stanis and Aksel, who had begun breaking off pieces of hard tack. Braddok joined, with a huge, stupid grin on his face.

Tallyn and Niá continued arranging the wards around the room's perimeter, but Imari didn't feel like eating or sitting, so she crossed to a window and peered out into the night. Lightning flashed, bleaching Liri's bones white.

Jeric joined her, leaned forward, and rested his forearms on the windowsill. This way, they were nearly eye level and close enough that she could smell the rain on his skin. He scanned the ruins, his expression all sharp lines and hard planes. "There's something very wrong here," he whispered.

"I know," she whispered back and leaned against the window beside him. "Where's the boat you found?"

"Over there." His shoulder flexed against her as he reached out and pointed. "Where the shore bends, near those rocks."

Her eyes strained, and then sure enough, she spotted a single dinghy on its side, resting upon the sand. They wouldn't have been able to see it from the wharf because it was hidden behind all the other boats. "Ah." Then, "Good eye." It appeared to be mostly intact, or at least more usable than anything else she could see, but she agreed with Jenya: It looked small. "I guess we can always take two trips."

"We can fit."

Imari looked at him, at the shadows beneath his eyes. "Go eat,

Jeric," she said. He hadn't eaten much since they'd left. He hadn't slept much either—none of them had—but Jeric had also taken watch each night with Tallyn, except for those few early hours just before sunrise, when he held her close.

"I'm not hungry."

"Liar."

He glanced sideways at her, his lips curled, and he leaned close, his mouth at her ear. "You're right. Actually, I'm *starved*... but not for food." And then he pulled away, a gleam in his eyes.

Imari felt suddenly flush all over. "Well, you won't be holding much down once we climb aboard that ship, so you'd better get your fill now."

"Oh, gods...don't remind me."

She chuckled then pushed at him. "*Eat.* I'll keep an eye out."

He didn't fight her this time. In fact, he looked a little appreciative and took a seat with his men and Jenya while Tallyn and Niá continued warding their perimeter.

A cold wind pushed against their tower, and the walls groaned. Stars, she hoped Survak arrived. They couldn't sneak through Istraa now, not with Su'Vi following them, but thinking on Istraa made her mind drift back to her brothers. Truthfully, they were never far from her thoughts, and Kai...

*Kai, you rutting, selfish idiot*, Imari cursed in her mind. *I could kill you.*

But she found it hard to hate him, remembering how she'd left him in Trier naked and chained to a demon. Remembering the deep well of agony in his eyes.

*Maker, keep him*, she prayed. *Keep them both. Give Kai the chance to make it right.*

Which was when Niá joined her.

"Finished?" Imari asked.

"Yes. We added a few other enchantments to the walls too. We wanted to...make sure they hold."

This made Imari laugh, and Niá smiled as both women

looked to the ruins. There hadn't been a moment for them to continue their conversation from that first early morning, but Niá's confession was always there, following them both as if Kai were here now, a part of every glance, every word.

The others' chatter murmured lowly through the whispering rain.

"You were closer to Ricón?" Niá asked quietly.

"Yes," Imari answered. "We always understood each other." Or, at least, they used to. The Shah had become a wall between them.

Niá stood quiet a moment, then said, "He was jealous of that, you know."

She meant Kai, and Imari wondered how much Niá actually knew about their family and her past.

"Saza was my only sibling," Niá continued, "but we had that too."

Little Saza.

Imari could not shake the image of him writhing on the street as he was consumed by Astrid's darkness.

"I never told you how we met, did I?" Imari asked.

Niá shook her head.

"Sebharan brought me to the Qazzat to visit his sick and injured guards," Imari explained. "Saza was carrying water, but when he saw me, he tripped and dropped the pails." A beat. "It was like he'd recognized me, but I'd never seen him in my life."

"He felt your power," Niá said.

Imari nodded; she understood that now. Imari explained what had followed and how she'd later gone to find Saza in the middle of the night, only to discover he'd stolen the herbs she'd left for the sick guards.

Niá's eyes glistened.

Imari hesitated, then, "How...did you end up at Ashova's?" Imari had been wanting to ask that question for some time, but she also didn't want to cause Niá more pain.

Niá stared out at the night, her gaze unseeing, and just when Imari didn't think Niá would answer, she said, quietly, "I was working the fields." She stopped. Took a breath. "One of the kahars had come to collect tithes from my master and took me instead." She took another breath and trembled slightly. "Oza found out later, when I never came home. She even went to Ashova's and begged the kahar to let me go, but he..." Niá swallowed. "He made *me* suffer for it, so Oza never came back again."

Imari started to reach for Niá, but Niá closed her eyes and turned her face away as she whispered, "Please, don't."

So Imari did not.

"Do I remind you of Kai?" Imari whispered after a moment.

"No," Niá said at last. "You don't remind me of him at all."

A clatter sounded behind them, and Imari glanced back. Her gaze locked on Chez's.

He sat just a few paces away, and he quickly looked down as he hurried to pick up the nightglass blade that'd slipped from his hands.

He'd heard everything.

Niá realized it too.

Imari was opening her mouth to say something—to change the subject—when a wardstone by the window began to glow.

It was just a flicker, a blip of light in this ever-darkening world, but even as Imari's gaze caught hold, that flicker grew steadily brighter—and held firm.

Behind her, Aksel chuckled at something Braddok had said, but his laughter stopped abruptly as his alpha jumped to his feet.

Jeric already had a nightglass blade in his hand.

Imari caught Jeric's lethal gaze, then Tallyn's, as everyone looked to each other, to the walls. Jenya and Braddok stood and peered out a window.

"I don't see anything; do you?" Imari asked, looking from window to dark window.

"No..." Jenya strained to see.

Suddenly, Niá fell stone-still.

"Niá...?" Imari asked, following Niá's horrified gaze.

To where a child stood in the middle of the street.

Imari's blood went cold.

It was Saza.

And yet it wasn't Saza at all. The figure below bore his small shape and child features, but these eyes were blank and empty and fully black, shimmering like obsidian. A shrill, dissonant tone rattled through Imari's soul.

Saza took a step forward, though his foot dragged oddly, as if it were difficult for him to move his body.

"What in the hells...?" Jeric said from right behind them.

"Tallyn, what is that?" Imari asked.

Tallyn had moved to the adjacent window, his posture rigid as he studied the figure below. "I do not know what that is."

Niá trembled, eyes wide and fixed on the thing that was and was not Saza. Her breathing came quick and frantic.

"Niá, look at me," Imari demanded.

Niá did not—could not—and started for the stairs instead.

Imari grabbed Niá's arm and jerked her back. "Niá, it's not him. I don't know what this is, but it is not Saza."

Niá was panic-stricken, her expression tortured with indecision.

"Niá, help me..." Saza cried out, but his voice felt wrong, its edges warped and echoing strangely. "It hurts, and I'm so scared, please, Ni...help me."

A second ward suddenly flared to life.

Then a third.

Imari caught Tallyn's gaze.

"Niá!" Saza's voice wailed. Niá was sobbing now, trembling violently in Imari's grip. "Niá, don't leave me!"

A fourth.

"Imari..." Jeric warned.

Because he needed her help. He needed her *power*. But she could not leave Niá alone.

Suddenly Chez was there. "I've got her," he said and—without waiting for approval—took Niá from Imari's hands and clamped his arms tightly around her. But the second Chez clamped his arms around Niá, Imari saw her mistake. Niá's entire body went rigid, her eyes flew wide open, and then a handful of things happened at once.

Niá's features twisted, and she screamed, "*Let go of me!*"

Chez, who'd been listening to Niá and Imari's conversation, heard the sheer terror in Niá's voice, also realized his mistake, and immediately let go. His arms dropped in the same moment that Niá bucked, throwing him off balance. Chez stumbled back, tripped over a satchel and a carefully placed ward, and tumbled into the wall, which already had a large fracture. Chez's body weight was more than it could take.

A splintering crack sounded, the wall gave, and he fell right through, taking plaster and chunks of sandstone with him. More wood crashed, Chez cried out, Imari heard a thud as his body hit the ground, and then...

Silence.

## 11

"*S*cat," Jeric cursed and bolted to the gaping hole in the wall.

Imari rushed after him, terrified of what she'd find, but when she looked out, all she could see was the adjacent rooftop and the fractured dome abutting their tower. A second later, Tallyn produced a tiny, white-blue light and sent it flying past them all and down into the dome's exposed bowels, where it hovered above the ground floor.

Chez lay nearly three stories below them, atop fragments of wood and stone, his skin silvery white in the glow of Tallyn's light. He wasn't moving.

Braddok cursed.

"He's still alive," Imari said. She could feel the pulse of his star, though weakly.

Everyone looked at her and collectively sighed with relief. Niá put a hand to her chest and whispered something Imari could not quite make out.

"I'll take the stairs—" Aksel started for the doorway.

Jeric grabbed his arm and yanked him back. "Not with that *thing* out there, you won't."

Aksel jerked his arm free. "We can't rutting leave him there!"

With quick decision, Jeric started digging through a satchel, withdrew a rope, and looped it around his shoulder.

"That's not long enough," Braddok said.

"It will be from that rooftop."

Imari appraised the adjacent spine of stone, an architectural joint connecting their tower to the dome like a ligament. It was about ten feet long and frighteningly narrow. Chez must have struck the spine first, then tumbled over the edge, into the open dome, but that break in his fall had probably saved his life.

Jeric begun testing the bottom ledge of the hole Chez had unwittingly made, checking its strength.

"I don't think this is a good idea, Wolf," Jenya warned.

"We don't have time for a better one." Jeric gripped the base of the hole and swung one long leg over. He lowered himself down the side of their tower until he was hanging, his body completely extended, then dropped the last ten feet onto that narrow spine of stone.

Tiles broke and stone fell away, clattering to the ruins below, and Imari held her breath.

Jeric stood perfectly still, waiting to be sure the spine could support him, then slowly and carefully walked forward.

Imari's heart pounded as she watched him walk that ledge like a tightrope. Beside her, Niá stood pale and frozen in shock. But Jeric moved like a mountain cat, steady on his feet, all the way to the dome's edge, where he crouched.

But Imari's attention had shifted from Jeric to the thick and pervading silence.

"Tallyn," Imari said suddenly.

Tallyn met her gaze, they both rushed for the window and found an empty street.

"Can you fix the wards?" Imari asked Tallyn, her nerves humming.

Because their warded circle had gone dark. Not because the

thing had fled, but because Chez had taken out a ward when he'd fallen and broken the enchantment.

But before Tallyn could answer, Aksel yelled, "He's moving!"

Imari and Tallyn crossed back to the hole in the wall and peered down into the wreckage. Sure enough, Chez was rolling onto his side, and he looked to be in a lot of pain.

Jeric was busy securing one end of the rope to a slab of wood jutting out of the roof like a broken rib. "Brad, get down here. I need your help."

Braddok cursed beneath his breath but did as his Wolf commanded. He climbed through the hole in the wall as Jeric had done, taking a few more chunks of plaster with him, then landed not nearly as graciously as Jeric had done before starting across the spine. Imari almost couldn't watch. Each step was a test of balance. Even Jenya went rigid beside her. Eventually, Braddok made it to Jeric, where that spine fanned out like a joint against the broken dome.

"Stay here and make sure the rope doesn't slip," Jeric said. "I'll climb down and get Chez."

"Like hells you will," Braddok started to argue, but Jeric was already lowering himself down the rope. Imari scanned their surroundings, the shadows, listening and reaching out with her senses, but there was no life, no stars—save their own.

Jeric hoisted Chez to his feet and handed him the end of the rope, but Chez was shaking his head. He couldn't lift his left arm. Instead, Jeric began wrapping the end of the rope around Chez's armpits like a sling. He was going to send Chez up first.

"Pull!" Jeric called up to Braddok, who promptly started pulling the rope, feet braced on that small platform while Chez held on with his one good arm.

Something tugged at the edge of Imari's senses, a discordant pitch against her thrumming nerves.

"Hurry..." Imari murmured, bouncing on her toes while her gaze flicked to the surrounding shadows.

Braddok had just pulled Chez onto that narrow ledge beside him when a shadow dripped from the dark recesses of the room below. Its shape was nearly humanoid, but it crouched upon all fours like a shade.

But this was not a shade.

This creature bore a flat face and eyes pure black, with two slits where a nose should have been, and its mouth was marked by a round opening full of needle-like teeth.

What in all the stars...

"*Tallyn,*" Imari warned.

"I see it," he replied, just as Braddok yelled Jeric's name.

But Jeric had already spotted the creature, and he was turning a nightglass blade in his hand as he watched that shadow slink closer.

Braddok worked fast to untie the knots, to throw the rope back to Jeric, but it was taking far too long.

"Tallyn, *do something!*" Imari said.

"I can't," Tallyn replied. "If I blast it, the rest of the dome will collapse. That wardlight should hold it off for now. That's what took me a bit longer. It does more than just illuminate."

Sure enough, the creature did not press any closer to Tallyn's little dome of white-blue light. It kept to the perimeter, slinking along the edge like a predator while Jeric watched, waiting for Braddok to drop the rope back through.

"Come on..." Imari murmured, rubbing her hands together and feeling trapped in her skin.

And then the thing...changed. Its features morphed into a sick sludge of color, and its body compressed and shifted.

Into Hagan.

It was Hagan on the night Astrid had attacked. Three black lines carved into each of his pale cheeks, though, like the Saza in the street, this Hagan's eyes were pure black. Soulless.

No, this was definitely *not* a shade.

"The hells...?" Stanis hissed, while Aksel said, "*What is that?*"

Meanwhile, Braddok seemed to be struggling to get the rope off of Chez, and the creature morphed again. Its features shifted, settling and unsettling between Hagan and an older version of Hagan—Jeric's father, perhaps?—and then the creature solidified into a woman.

The woman had a plait of long hair—Jeric's hair, soft brown threaded with gold—and a dark stain marked a hole in her chest. Her features were striking and well-structured, like Jeric's, though her pure-black eyes turned beauty into a nightmare.

Jeric's entire body went rigid, and Imari knew exactly who this was, even though she'd never seen the woman in her life.

"Jos...my darling," Jeric's mother spoke in a voice that echoed strangely, warping as Saza's had done. "Help me."

"Jeric, don't listen to it!" Imari yelled. "It's not her!"

But even from here, she could see the struggle in Jeric's face.

"Wolf!" Braddok yelled, then tossed the end of the rope down.

Right then, a massive black bird flew out of nowhere, shot across the night, and collided with Tallyn's wardlight.

*Su'Vi.*

Imari cursed as light exploded. A deep, sonorous bass shook their tower, and that light rained like a million shards of glittering glass before it landed upon the rubble and flickered out like dying embers.

Gone.

Plunging the world into complete darkness.

A horrible snarling sounded below, and Niá produced a new light this time, just as Jeric's mother leapt impossibly high into the air, fingers morphing into claws.

"Jeric!" Imari screamed, and the thing landed directly on top of him, knocking him to the ground.

Imari hardly had a moment to react because the thing—now some sick, amorphous stew of limbs, claws, and human skin—reared back with a horrible, otherworldly wail, like a dozen trumpets blaring in dissonance. It rattled Imari's head, and she covered her ears—they all did—as the sound blasted the quiet.

Jeric kicked the creature off of him and shoved himself back to his feet as the thing stumbled and collapsed, clutching the nightglass blade sticking out of its chest.

Imari could have cried in relief.

"Wolf!" Braddok yelled.

Jeric jumped up, grabbed hold of the rope, and pulled himself up, hand over hand, while Braddok simultaneously dragged him up and onto the narrow ledge.

And then the night erupted with wailing. From all corners of the city, yips and howls echoed, and a great pit settled in Imari's gut.

Stars, there had to be dozens of them.

"*Dashá*," Jenya cursed as Aksel growled, "Scat."

Imari looked at Tallyn, and in that glance, she knew that even if he had time to fix their wards, those wards would never be enough.

"We need to get out of here," Imari announced.

"To *where*?" Stanis snapped.

"The water," Imari answered and then yelled to Jeric, "Can you get to the dinghy?"

He looked to the night, the shadows, then back to her. "Take the stairs," he yelled back. "We'll catch up."

Imari hated splitting up, but she knew he was right. They simply did not have time to pull Chez all the way back into the tower. Jeric needed to find another way down for them, and fast.

"*Go!*" Jeric yelled as he and Braddok guided Chez farther along the dome's narrow perimeter, looking for a way down.

"Surina." Jenya waved at her from the doorway as the night howled. She was holding her and Braddok's satchels.

Imari pried herself away from the hole in the wall, snatched her and Jeric's packs, and ran down the winding stairs after the others.

Yelps and howls filled the night as they followed Tallyn through the ruins, sprinting through the rain and maze of looming silhouettes, until they reached the wharf.

There was no sign of Jeric.

"Imari, hurry!" Jenya yelled from just ahead.

But Imari stood watching for Jeric, praying he and the others had made it down in one piece.

The howls drew closer, and still he did not come. Imari reached out with her senses and caught hold of Jeric's brilliant star right when he, Braddok, and a stumbling Chez ran around a corner and onto the wharf.

"Oh, thank the Maker..." Imari sighed, but then one of those shade-like creatures tumbled out between buildings and onto the wharf behind Jeric's group. "Jeric, behind you!"

Braddok glanced back, pulled something from his belt, and threw.

Nightglass.

It cut across the distance in a streak of obsidian and sank into the creature's chest.

The creature shrieked as it toppled forward, skidding along the wooden planks to where it crashed into a huddle of broken fishing crates, but Imari hardly felt a moment's relief before three more tumbled out of a break between buildings farther down.

They skidded to a halt upon the wharf and sniffed the air. One by one, they turned their hideous, flat faces in Jeric's direction and started bounding after his group.

Desperate, Imari was opening her mouth to sing—to do *anything* to help—when she felt a pulse of air and a tingling of Shah from behind. Suddenly, a sphere of white moonlight arced high over her head and collided with the two creatures in front. White light jolted through their bodies, electrifying their forms, but the third creature merely bounded over their collapsing bodies, still determinedly on course.

But Tallyn did not send another light.

He stumbled and staggered and braced himself against a post. Between setting their perimeter, illuminating the dome, and this, he had spent all the Shah he could give tonight.

And the creature was now thirty paces away from Jeric and the other two, thundering upon the wharf's wooden planks.

Twenty-five.

"Take Chez," Braddok said, untangling himself from Chez and Jeric.

Twenty.

Without another thought, Imari began to sing. Her Shah sight was immediate, and in this dark city, she easily spotted the stars belonging to Jeric and his men. Heat bloomed in her gut, as it always did, but this time she had no talla to pour it into.

So it swelled inside her chest instead.

Still, she pressed on, ignoring the heat as she pinned the thing bounding after Jeric and his men, because she realized it *did* have a star, just like Fyri's tyrcorat. Like an eclipsed sun, fully dark but limned in light. It had been a person once—perhaps a resident of Liri or a wanderer making berth in a futile hunt for treasure—but its soul had been perverted out of tune by the corruption infusing in this land.

Imari just needed to tune it back to purity.

Her notes trilled over intervals despite the liquid fire now flooding her veins, and the creature's eclipsed star shone brighter —*louder*. She'd caught its tone, its soul, and wove it into her song. She augmented her tonic, turned its minor major, and the night filled with the creature's screaming.

Its light stopped moving, and with her human sight, she could just see it thrashing upon the planks, where it screamed and gnashed its teeth, but she did not stop her song. Not even as fire scorched her limbs and burned down her throat. A final note squeezed out of her, but she held it firm. There was a burst of power, a wave of heat and light, and the creature's eclipsed sun exploded into a million tiny stars. They rained down upon the wooden planks and fizzled out.

Imari didn't realize she'd collapsed until Jeric grabbed her shoulders and hoisted her up, dragging her along the wharf after him. Her vision swam, her insides twisted painfully, and she thought she was going to be sick.

"Don't do that again," Jeric said, holding her as they ran onto the beach after the others. But without Jeric to help him, and without solid footing, Chez tripped in the sand and brought Braddok down with him.

"Aks!" Jeric yelled.

Aksel glanced over his shoulder and sprinted back to help. Together, he and Braddok hoisted Chez between them and kept running.

"There's a ship!" Jenya yelled from ahead.

At first, Imari thought Jenya was talking about the dinghy, but Jenya was gesturing wildly at the water.

Where dim lights flickered in the middle of the bay.

Survak.

Imari held tight to Jeric and forced her legs forward in that too-forgiving sand, though her consciousness began to fade. Just a little farther—

There was a low growl, followed by a startled cry.

She glanced back to see a shadow seemingly drop from the night and land directly on Aksel, Chez, and Braddok, knocking all three to the ground.

*No.*

Braddok fought to get out from under Chez while the creature clamped its rounded jaws around Aksel's ankle and dragged him through the sand, back toward the docks. Aksel screamed and kicked and scrambled for purchase.

"*Aks!*" Jeric let go of Imari and bolted after him.

But the creature already had Aksel on the wharf, where more of those things now waited, crouched upon all fours and snarling. Aksel screamed and screamed as his captor dragged him through the horde, out of sight, and his scream suddenly cut short.

*No...*

It had happened so fast, Imari could hardly grasp hold of it, and Jeric stood there on the beach, heaving, his expression murderous as he looked at the horde scrambling on the wharf like rabid hyenas.

"Get to the boat!" Tallyn yelled.

The monsters on the fringe glanced over then turned from the wharf, from their fresh feast, and loped after them.

"*Jeric!*" Imari yelled, fighting her dizziness. Farther down the beach, Stanis and Jenya were shouting at them to run. To hurry.

Furious, Jeric turned away from the wharf and started running. He caught up with Braddok and Chez and started for the dinghy.

But the monsters jumped onto the beach after them, and they were gaining ground fast.

Another bolt of light arced over Imari's head, this time from Niá. Her blast struck the creature in front, punching a hole through its chest, and it went flying from the sheer impact. It careened into the two behind it, but the rest continued sprinting down the beach, undeterred, drawing more attention from the creatures still on the docks. More and more started running after them.

Too fast, too many.

They could never outrun this. It had to be stopped, and only Imari could stop it.

Imari shut her eyes tight and sang again. Someone yelled at her to stop, to run instead, but she did not—*could not,* or they would all die here. Fire ignited in her bones, as if her very marrow were aflame, and her stomach lurched with sickness, but she did not stop.

And then—suddenly—her vision flickered, warped and

distorted. The beach was gone; she was standing in a room she knew well.

Trier's great hall.

It bore the scars of battle, its shadows deep despite the glowing braziers, and at the center stood a robed and imperial figure—like a deity having descended upon the mortal world. The figure turned around.

Azir Mubarék.

Just as he was before, but also more. Fuller, sharper, an imposing figure of contrasts. His raw power was staggering —*crushing* as it pressed against her body, beckoning and seducing and tugging upon the well of Shah power within her.

How...how was this possible?

He looked at her as she gaped at him, and his lips curled into a vicious smile. He gazed about her edges, as if trying to make sense of a setting he could not quite see, and then those black eyes cut back to hers, and he approached. "You would use your Shah without your talla."

His voice was close. *He* was close, and he took a step even closer.

"It will kill you," Azir said, stopping right before her. He did not touch her, but Imari felt him everywhere, like a heady toxin impregnating the air. She did not move; she could not, because wherever she was, however this was possible, her body was still trapped in the desert and drawing upon the Shah to stay a horde of nightmares.

Azir's black eyes glittered, his palm rested upon her cheek, and *she could feel it.* His touch was a shock of ice against her skin.

"There is too much fire within you," he said, and then her consciousness became acutely aware of that fire. Of that searing, unbearable heat that was currently burning her up from the inside, and suddenly she couldn't breathe.

It was going to kill her.

"Use the bells," Azir demanded.

Imari's lungs clamped down, and her knees gave.

Azir gripped her arms and held her firmly upon her feet, his expression a flicker of madness and fury and complete adoration. And then he leaned forward and breathed upon her lips. So soft and bitter cold, like winter's kiss. "Live, *Sulaziér*," he said in that breath, "for I am waiting for you."

A rush of cold swept into her, dousing the flames on impact.

Filling her with strength anew.

Azir and the great hall melted away, and she was on the beach once more, kneeling in sand, straining to finish her song, which she now had the strength to finish. "From dust you were born. To dust you shall return."

The last word tingled as it passed over her lips. Imari collapsed upon all fours, heaving, and a deep bass rumbled from the center of the earth.

The ground trembled violently with sound. It pulsed through the wharf, through the horde of nightmares, vaporizing them as it burst through the ruins. Stone cracked and splintered, and a massive hole opened at Liri's heart, as if hell itself had opened up. The ruins collapsed into it, swallowed by hell's hungry teeth, but it did not stop there.

The hole was like a mouth slowly yawning wider, eating up everything in its path. Imari felt an overwhelming surge of heat and debilitating pain, and then her world went black.

JERIC DROPPED to Imari's side as the ground shook.

Scat.

Scat, scat, *scat*.

And Aksel...

Jeric didn't have time to consider his loss, because the city was collapsing around them.

What had Imari just done?

"Get to the boat *now*!" Tallyn yelled.

"But Aks—" Braddok was starting to say when a line of buildings along the harbor broke off into the water like shale sloughing off a mountainside, and Braddok nearly dropped Chez.

"He's gone," Jeric growled, scooping an unconscious Imari up into his arms.

Jeric gave Tallyn a look, and they all sprinted and stumbled along the sandy shoreline for the boat Stanis fought to steady as new waves pummeled into him. Jeric splashed into the seawater and dumped Imari into the boat, and Niá climbed in to secure her.

Once Jeric ensured everyone else was aboard, he pushed the boat off and climbed inside. Braddok and Stanis grabbed his arms to help him in, just as the rest of Liri—every stone, every bone, every memory—fell into that great chasm. And then the ground closed up like sutures sealing a wound, until all that remained of Liri was a patch of pale dust upon the earth.

## 12

*I*mari.

The voice echoed from the deep, as though drifting from the bottom of an ocean, calling through the fathomless dark—for her. She knew the voice, though she could not place it. It beckoned her heart, made it ring.

*Imari.*

She tried to go to it, to find the source, but she could not move. She had no body, only consciousness as she drifted in a vast, white nothingness, riding invisible currents. A thing caught in the in-between.

*Yiatén*, commanded the voice.

Light flashed—blinding white.

There was heat, and there was pain—oh, Maker, have mercy! —as every muscle in her body pulled tight. Finally, her muscles relaxed, and she opened her eyes to find Jeric's dark blues right in front of her, his features razor sharp. Beside him, Niá sat illuminated by the small light hovering above Tallyn's open palm. It cast a pale glow over their small dinghy and everyone huddled within—all of whom were staring at her.

Imari opened her mouth to ask what had happened, but then

her stomach twisted violently, she gripped the hull's edge, bent over, and vomited into the water.

Again.

And again.

Jeric gathered her hair and pulled it back. She couldn't stop. Her insides clenched, and her throat burned with bile.

Then blood.

Jeric's hand tightened on her hair, and he murmured something behind her. A second later, Imari felt cool fingers at the nape of her neck, and Niá spoke a Liagé word of power. A wash of tingling swept over her, and the need to vomit ceased. The nausea was still there, but—thank the wards—the urgency was gone.

Still, Imari gripped the hull's edge, trying to calm both heart and breath. Jeric combed his fingers gently through her hair, letting her know he was there, and then her body began quivering uncontrollably.

Jeric whispered something else, to which Tallyn responded quietly, and then Jeric was dragging her into his lap while the others moved aside the best they could in this cramped space. He wrapped his arms around her and pressed her head to his chest, holding her tight as she trembled. A moment later, he held a flask to her lips and said, "You need to drink."

Imari knew he was right.

He helped her sit a little straighter, but when she reached for the flask, they both saw that her hand was shaking too much to hold on to anything. "Here. Let me," Jeric said.

Imari didn't argue.

He held the flask to her lips, which proved a challenge in the rocking boat, and much of the water spilled over her chin, but she managed to swallow some before Jeric pulled her shivering body back against his and held her tight.

The rain fell in a thick curtain of whispers, water lapped against the hull, and the others sat quiet. Water was also begin-

ning to seep in through a small hole beneath Jenya's bench, but
Jenya noticed it too, said as much to the others, and then Niá
sealed it shut with an enchantment.

"Do they know it's us?" Braddok asked.

"They know," Tallyn replied.

"Then why all the rutting bows?"

"I imagine it's because they did not know if it was going to
be us."

Imari lifted her head and looked up to see a ship's silhouette
was just visible through the rain, marked by dozens of glowing
lanterns.

*The Lady.*

She had come, and she was close, but Braddok was right: It
seemed *The Lady's* entire crew had gathered on deck, and most of
them were armed. Heavily.

Imari turned her gaze to the shore, and her heart stopped.
There was no sign of the city—not one. No leaning towers, no
broken domes. Nothing. The rain made her view hazy, but Liri
was undeniably gone, wiped from the face of the earth as if it had
never been. And as she stared in wonder and horror, she remembered Azir. She remembered the raw press of his power, the ice of
his touch, and the noxious tingling of Shah that he had breathed
into her body from another reality. A breath that had saved her
life, she knew. Imari did not know how Azir had reached her—
how it had been possible—but it terrified her.

It was then she realized Jeric was watching her closely.

"Did I do that?" she whispered, still staring at the place Liri
had stood.

A beat. "Yes," he said quietly. "And it's fortunate you did;
otherwise, we never would have made it out alive."

A longer beat. "I'm sorry I couldn't save Aksel in time."

"He's not your fault."

"He's not yours either."

Stanis glanced over at them, ire in his eyes. He looked like he had a few pointed words to say on the subject, but then Jeric stood abruptly.

*The Lady* was upon them. They were close enough now that Imari could see—and recognize—*The Lady's* crew, but she didn't see the captain anywhere.

"Tallyn," called Rikk, *The Lady's* first mate, as he peered over the hull, appraising their drenched and motley crew. "I knew you were talented, but I sure as hells didn't know you had it in you to level an entire city."

Rikk's words were full of praise, but his tone was not. What had happened to Liri had frightened the crew—and it should have. The last time something of this magnitude had happened had been with Fyri, and Imari had no idea how the crew might react if they realized it had been Imari's doing. Imari wondered if Tallyn would correct Rikk. She hoped he wouldn't, because the chances of this crew accepting this terrifying display of power from Tallyn were much higher, considering Tallyn's long history with them.

To Imari's relief, Tallyn placed a hand over his stomach and gave a small bow, taking the weight of Rikk's accusation. "It is amazing what is possible when one is desperate enough."

Rikk smirked, but there was nothing friendly in it. "You're lucky the captain's fond of you."

"I know."

Rikk appraised him a moment more, and then the end of a roped ladder flew over the hull.

"I don't like this," Jeric murmured.

"It's a little too late for that," Tallyn replied, grabbing hold of the ladder's end.

"This won't work for Chez," Jeric said.

Tallyn stopped and looked back at Chez, who slumped against the hull while cradling his left arm, his features tight with pain.

"One of ours can't climb," Tallyn shouted to the crew.

There was some discussion on deck, and then someone tossed a fishing net over the rail.

"That'll work," Braddok mumbled, and he and Jeric secured Chez inside of it. Jeric gave a sharp whistle, the crew hoisted Chez aboard, then one by one, the rest of them began climbing the rope ladder.

"Are you ready?" Jeric asked Imari, once he, Imari, and Braddok were all that remained.

Imari stood but waited a moment to make sure her legs could hold her, then started up the ladder with Jeric close behind.

The ladder swayed more than she'd anticipated, which normally wouldn't have been a problem—she'd climbed in situations more dangerous than this—but her limbs were weak, so she took her time, rung after wobbly rung, as old rope bit into her palms. Finally, hands reached over *The Lady's* hull and dragged her onto a slippery deck, where *The Lady's* crew stood all around, eyeing them in silence. Imari received nods from Rikk, and Pazz, and another short, stocky man with a name Imari couldn't remember, but for the most part, *The Lady's* crew did not look thrilled to have a Wolf and his pack on board.

"Where's your captain?" Tallyn asked.

Rikk's attention slid to Tallyn. "Engaged, at the moment. He said to make yourselves comfortable below. Eat. Sleep. He doesn't give a scat, just stay out of his way. Those are my orders." Rikk turned and yelled, "To oars!" And then, glancing at the night, he added quietly, "Let's get the hells out of this place."

The crew scattered like sand beetles, skittering across the deck and up masts, manning oars and turning sails. They didn't speak; they didn't need words for this dance. The sails snapped full of wind, and *The Lady* lurched as she pulled out of the bay.

"Come on, Chezter," Braddok was saying to Chez, who leaned back against a barrel, eyes closed and face pale.

"Let me set his arm first," Imari said.

Braddok looked like he might argue, but Jeric gave a quick gesture, and Braddok helped Chez sit.

"There we go...easy now," Braddok said as Imari knelt at Chez's side. Her world rocked, but that tingling swept over her skin again. Niá's enchantment was still working very hard to hold her nausea at bay. Imari's mouth watered, and she swallowed, pushing around Chez's shoulder, trying to understand the angle it had slid out so that she could roll it properly in. Meanwhile, Chez winced, and the muscles in his neck pulled like rope.

She looked at Chez. "This is going to hurt."

He clenched his teeth and set his jaw, bracing himself.

Imari rolled his arm and popped the joint back into the socket. Chez sucked a curse through his teeth, his body tensed, and his eyes squeezed tight.

"Do you have something I can sling his arm with?" Imari asked Braddok, who pulled a spare tunic from a satchel.

"That'll work." Imari took it, then looked at Jenya. "Your scim."

Jenya handed Imari her scim, and Imari made a small cut in the front of the tunic, gave the blade back, and used her hands to tear the front in half completely.

Giving her one long piece of fabric.

Imari adjusted Chez's arm across his chest. "Hold it here."

Chez used his right arm to support his left while Imari wrapped the torn tunic across his torso and around his left arm, then tied a knot at his shoulder to secure it to his body.

"How long do I need to wear this?" Chez mumbled.

"At least three weeks," Imari said. "But I don't want you lifting your arm for six."

"Can you do anything for his ankle?" Niá whispered. She'd been standing behind Imari the entire time.

Imari moved to Chez's foot and picked up his boot, and Chez hissed. She untied the laces and slipped the boot from his foot while he sucked in more curses. "Well, it hurts. That's a good sign."

Chez made a face.

"Sometimes you don't feel pain with a break." Imari inspected the ankle, which was already as large as a grapefruit. She hummed too softly for anyone to hear over the wind and sea, using her power to inspect the things unseen, though her stomach turned again. "Luckily for you, it's just sprained. Stay off of it, and keep it elevated."

"I can help with the pain," Niá said, then looked to Chez. "If that's all right with you."

Chez gazed at her through half-lidded eyes, his lips thin. "Fine."

"Leave some of it," Imari suggested, and at the marginally offended look from Chez, she added, "If you don't feel *any* pain, you won't remember to take it easy."

Chez looked doubtful.

Jeric rested a heavy hand upon her shoulder then, and she looked back. He jerked his chin to the hatch, gesturing for her to follow him.

"We've got Chez," Braddok said, and Imari stood, then followed Jeric across the deck. The rain had stopped, but thunder echoed in the distance as the two of them skirted the rowers and ducked beneath the sails. Jeric stopped before the wide-open hatch that led below deck and held out his hand.

"You're not taking no for an answer, are you?" Imari said.

Jeric smirked and helped her onto the steep wooden stair that led into *The Lady's* belly. Wood groaned as she climbed down, and the steps shook as Jeric joined her. The stair ended at a narrow corridor, like an artery through *The Lady's* belly, and lantern light danced upon the wooden planks. Imari had never been down here. When Survak had transported them from River-wood to the Black Cliffs, she'd slept in his quarters, on deck. That journey had been quick, and she'd never had cause to go below where the rest of the crew ate and slept.

"Shouldn't you stay above?" she asked.

"Probably." He nodded for her to keep walking.

The boat rocked gently, lanterns swayed, and Imari trailed one hand along the tight corridor as she walked. Chatter echoed dimly from above, and down here, in *The Lady's* bowels, Imari could clearly hear all of her creaking joints. Little doorways opened to a kitchen, a small dining area, storage, more storage, and a few rooms with hammocks bolted to the ceiling and walls.

Jeric peered into one. "This one's as good as any," he said, then ducked inside.

Imari followed.

Stars, it was tight quarters. There was just enough room for her to stand without hitting her head on a hammock. Jeric, however, hunched over with one palm pressed to the ceiling.

"Take your pick." He gestured benevolently at the hammocks.

"I saw Azir," she said suddenly, needing to get this off of her conscience.

Jeric froze, his posture tensed—coiled—all levity gone. "What do you mean, you *saw* him?"

Imari's mouth felt suddenly dry, but he needed to know; she wanted no secrets between them. "I don't know how it happened, but I saw him when I was...singing."

He searched her with unnerving intensity. "Through the Sight?"

"No." Imari bit her lip. "This was different. I could...*feel* his touch."

Jeric took a small step toward her, his expression predatory. "He *touched* you?"

"It wasn't like that..." Was it? "He grabbed my arms and held me on my feet while I finished my song." She didn't say the other part, that he'd breathed his power into her—not yet. Not with Jeric looking at her the way he was right then. She didn't want to hide it from him, but she needed time to process, and right now, she didn't want to scare him further. Especially when she was already terrified.

The silence stretched, and Jeric still hadn't moved, though she could see him fighting for calm. For control. "Did he say anything to you?" His voice had, thankfully, lost some of its fervor.

"He told me to live. That he was waiting for me."

A deep crease formed between Jeric's brow.

"I think that when I opened myself to the Shah, it opened me up to him. All of a sudden I was standing in Vondar's great hall. I could see him, and he could see me."

Jeric's gaze sharpened on her like the point of a blade. "So he knows *exactly* where we are."

"If not from me, he will from Su'Vi," Imari cut back, feeling a little defensive.

Jeric's eyes slid shut, his shoulders expanded with a long breath, and the silence stretched, knotted with tension.

Imari hated it, but then she noted how dispirited Jeric looked standing there, and it struck her that perhaps the reaction he'd given might be more related to his *very* recent loss.

"Look, Jeric..." Imari sighed. "I have no idea how it happened, and I'm sorry if I've—"

"*No.*" He opened his eyes, reached out, and pressed his palm to her cheek, and Imari fell utterly still beneath that tender touch. "You did nothing wrong, and I'm sorry if I made it sound that way. I'm just...concerned, as you are. Clearly." His gaze flickered over her face, and the storm in his eyes calmed. "Has he ever done this before? Contacted you in this way?"

Imari shook her head. "Never."

Jeric considered this, then said, "You need to tell Tallyn."

"I'm planning to."

Jeric regarded her a moment more, seemed to make up his mind about something, and pulled his hand from her face to grab her hand instead. He guided her to a hammock near the floor and helped her into it. Imari meant to refuse, but the moment she sat in that hammock, in the dark and rocking chamber, she felt suddenly very heavy and very tired.

Jeric crouched at her feet.

"What are you doing?" she asked.

He grabbed her sandal and started unlacing the ties.

"Jeric, I can take off my own shoes..."

"I know." He slipped her sandal free, set it down, then started on the next.

Imari touched his chin and gently lifted his face. His movements stopped; his gaze met hers.

Yes, his recent loss was definitely to blame. The pain in his eyes nearly broke her heart. "I'm so sorry about Aksel."

His features strained, and he glanced down.

The silence expanded, but Imari didn't fill it. She let it sit, gave him space. She didn't reiterate that Aksel's death wasn't his fault. It wouldn't matter. Jeric would add this to the list of wrongs he'd written for himself, and it was a list he carried always, one that weighed upon him like a millstone around his neck. And, as Imari had recently discovered, that millstone liked to choke him in the middle of the night when he was sleeping.

Jeric slipped off her second sandal and set it beside the first, tucking both under her hammock.

"How many have you lost?" Imari asked.

Her question might have been considered insensitive, but she didn't think Jeric would see it that way. Mentioning the items on his list was also acknowledging their sacrifice, and when he looked up at her again, she knew she'd been right to ask.

"Nine. In three years."

That was a lot, especially when one realized how much time Jeric spent with these men.

"That's why I never get close," Jeric added quietly.

She remembered Gerald. "That's a lie."

His expression fractured just a little, giving glimpse of the fathomless well of regret and pain he carried always. "You're right. Because here you are, this magnificent, beautiful woman who means more to me than my own life, and I don't deserve any of it."

This time, it was Imari who reached out and rested her palm against his face, feeling the stubble tickle her palm. "Don't say you don't deserve it—"

"But it's true." His eyes were so blue, so tortured. "If you really knew all the things that I've done..." His voice trailed, crushed by the weight of his past—the sins that never ceased haunting him.

Imari grabbed his face between her hands. "I love *you*. *This* man. The one before me right now. Nothing changes that."

"It would, if you knew."

Stars, what she wouldn't give to take this burden from him. To help him see what he meant to her and how she saw him. "None of us are perfect, Jeric. Not you. Not me. But maybe together, we can form one...*partially* decent person."

His lips quirked at this, alleviating some of the heaviness that had settled upon his broad shoulders. "That equation is definitely weighted in my favor."

Imari grinned, then leaned forward and kissed his lips so softly. He still smelled like rain and sea, and as his warmth enveloped her, suddenly she didn't feel tired anymore. He seemed to sense this. However, to her swift disappointment, he pulled away to help her lie down instead. She meant to put up a fight, but as she settled into the hammock, overwhelming fatigue dragged her down.

And down.

Jeric bent over her, his lips at her ear. "*Sleep.*" His warm breath brushed against her skin like some command infused with Shah power. He kissed her temple so softly, but Imari didn't feel it, because his magic had worked, and she'd already slipped into dreams.

· ᴄᴇ꜋ ·

JERIC STOOD THERE A MOMENT, gazing down at her. Gods, she was beautiful. He brushed the hair from her face, but she didn't move. She was already deep in sleep.

Jeric didn't like that she'd seen Azir—that he'd *touched* her. He didn't like it at all. He sensed there was more to it that she hadn't voiced, more she didn't want to admit—not even to herself.

He knew all about that.

But Imari was right about one thing: Jeric cared more about his men than he'd ever admit, and every time he lost one, a part of him died. He wanted it back. All of those parts, all of those lives.

Again, he saw that rutting nightmare grab hold of Aksel's foot and drag him away. Again, he heard Aksel's screams.

He would hear those screams for the rest of his life.

Jeric dragged a hand over his face and through his hair, then left Imari to the dark and quiet of her hammock and strode back into the tight corridor. He didn't like leaving Imari alone, but she needed sleep and he needed to talk to Survak, and he reminded himself that he needn't worry for Imari here. The world was scat, but not everyone rolled in it. There were still men like Survak who stayed the hells out of it.

It was unfortunate Jeric didn't like sailing more.

As if to remind him, the ship rocked and his stomach rolled, and Jeric thought it was going to be a long few weeks.

He reached the bottom of the stair to find his men trudging down it.

"Where's Imari?" Braddok asked.

"Sleeping."

"She okay?"

Jeric nodded.

"Well, we're gonna eat," Braddok said. "Wanna join?"

"I'm going to have a word with our captain first."

"Good luck with that." Braddok snorted, then smacked Jeric's shoulder and ducked into the kitchen. Stanis caught Jeric's gaze but looked away as he followed.

Stanis was angry, and Jeric couldn't blame him.

He passed the others on his way up the stairs, then stepped out through the hatch. The savage wind shocked him after being in *The Lady's* warm bowels. Jeric breathed hot air onto his palms and rubbed them together as he scanned the deck for *The Lady's* captain. He'd break down Survak's door if he needed to.

The darkness was thick, but the lanterns kept it manageable. A handful of rowers remained at the oars, while others busied themselves tying rope. A few of the crew stood off to the side, drinking as they looked to the ominous, black water, but Jeric could not see *The Lady's* captain anywhere—

There, by the bow.

Jeric strode straight for him. A few of the crew glanced over as he passed, eyeing him warily, though none said a word. They didn't stop him either.

"It seems I find myself indebted to you yet again, Captain," Jeric said, stopping at the rail, right beside *The Lady's* captain.

Survak did not turn toward Jeric. He simply pulled his pipe from his mouth and breathed out long and slow. Smoke curled about his lined and weathered face as wind tossed his salty hair.

"There is no indebtedness," Survak said at last. "I didn't do it for you."

"I know."

Survak glanced sideways at Jeric, and his eyes narrowed. "Since when?"

"I suspected the last time you gave us transport. Tallyn confirmed it."

Survak looked back to the sea, reached into his pocket, and

withdrew more hash. He pushed it into his pipe and tamped it down upon the rail. "Does *he* know?"

"Not yet. But he will."

Survak shoved the pipe into his mouth, pulled flint and steel from his pocket, then struck them together over the bowl. Once. Twice. But his hands were trembling, and he couldn't make it catch. Then the flint slipped from his hand.

Jeric caught it.

He met Survak's gaze, then held out the flint. "Yes, you don't care at all, do you?"

Survak's lips pressed together, and he took the flint. He tried again, and sparks flew. The wind snatched most of them away, but a few landed in the bowl, and Survak sucked quickly to pull them in. Once settled, he slipped the flint and steel back into his pocket.

"You can't hide in your quarters all the way to Felheim," Jeric said.

"I can do whatever the hells I want, Wolf King. You don't command this ship."

"No, I don't," Jeric agreed. "Trying to command this ship was the mistake my father made."

Survak's gaze flickered to Jeric but then settled on the distance. "You're different from Tommad. I'll give you that. But you're still an Angevin."

"By that measure, you're still Corinthian."

Survak glared at the dark.

"Look." Jeric leaned against the rail beside Survak. "I am grateful for your passage, and I wish no quarrel with you, but godsdamnit, man, that's *your son*. Whatever he feels, whatever history you mourn, do not ruin a future because you're drowning in regret. Stanis is struggling with all of this. With *me*. I don't want to lose him, but I can't get through. *You can*."

"He doesn't want to hear a rutting word I have to say—"

"You've never *tried*," Jeric cut him off bitterly, thinking on his own father, who had acted the father in name only. "You are still Stanis's father. Take ownership of it, like you take ownership of this ship and this crew, for *how much more* is your own son?"

Survak stood perfectly still, though the wind tossed his short hair and snapped his coat. Then, "What if he won't hear it?" Survak's voice was low, as if the question came out against his will.

"Then at least you'll know you tried."

Quiet settled between them, and the wind raked at them with greedy fingers. Finally, Survak snatched his pipe from his mouth and dumped the still-burning tobacco into the sea. "My quarters. Ten minutes."

Jeric sighed with relief and started to turn.

"And, Wolf."

Jeric looked back at Survak.

"There's a special place in hells for you."

Jeric smirked. "Probably. Until then, there's a world to save."

# 13

Survak nervously picked up a book and set it down. He pushed papers around atop his desk, stacked them. Set the bronze paperweight—a gift from a Davros merchant—on top of them. Then looked at the door.

Footsteps stomped on deck, and his breath caught, his chest tightened, but the footsteps did not stop. They continued along the starboard side toward the stern.

That wasn't him, then.

Survak dragged a hand over his face and through his hair.

Gods have mercy.

He slumped down onto his chair just as a knock sounded on the door. He bolted back to his feet, smoothed back his hair, and pressed down the wrinkles in his coat. "Come in."

The latch turned, and the door cracked open.

Jeric Angevin peered through the crack. For a second, Survak saw only Tommad. It was the eyes, the deep set of them, and that square, Angevin jaw. But there was a warmth to the Wolf that Tommad had always lacked. A...humanity.

Which, considering, Survak found ironic.

He nodded at Jeric, and Jeric pushed the door open wider, holding it there as he stepped aside.

Survak froze.

He'd seen Stanis just two months ago, for the first time in...he didn't know how long. But Stanis hadn't been awake. He'd hardly been breathing, and now he was standing there, filling the door to Survak's quarters. A fully grown man, a mirror image of Survak himself—the Survak of his twenties. Survak was a good bit older now, and the sea had weathered the likeness right out of him. At least to everyone else.

Not to Stanis.

Stanis had been about to step through the threshold, but his eyes locked on Survak, and he went perfectly still.

Survak didn't know what to say, but his chest ached suddenly as a gulf of emotion overwhelmed him, and Stanis...

There was shock at first. Denial and confusion. Stanis looked at Jeric, and Jeric looked steadily back in silent confirmation. Stanis's confusion morphed into fury, and that gaze snapped back to Survak. "*You.*" The word was barely a whisper, but it strained like sails during a storm.

Survak meant to respond, but he'd been struck mute.

Stanis whirled on Jeric, his face swollen and crimson with rage. "You rutting asshole," he snarled, then stormed off out of sight.

Leaving Survak alone with Jeric.

Jeric gazed after Stanis a moment, then looked back to Survak. "I'll be back."

He didn't give Survak a chance to respond. Truth be told, Survak didn't know if he *could have*, but Jeric took off after Stanis, closing the door behind him.

For a long moment, Survak stared at that place his son had stood. Suddenly, he saw the path he hadn't taken and the life he hadn't lived. The one including a little boy who had worshipped the ground his father had walked upon.

A little boy Survak had left, not because he'd wanted to, but because he'd been unable to come home. Not without putting that boy's life in jeopardy. All of his choices had made so much sense to him then, but looking into the eyes of that man, of the boy he had abandoned, he knew his mistake: He should have fought harder. He should have done better.

He should have *tried*.

Survak slumped into his chair, buried his face in his hands, and cried.

JERIC FOUND Stanis in the shadows, standing amidst a stack of barrels that'd been secured to the hull. Jeric stopped beside Stanis and leaned against the rail as both men looked to the black sea. Much of the crew had gone below deck to eat, and at Jeric's request, Jenya had gone to stay with Imari, who'd still been sleeping soundly when he'd gone to retrieve Stanis.

Waves lapped against the hull, and the silence between them stretched. Jeric didn't fill it. He didn't know what to say. He wasn't sorry they'd solicited the help of Stanis's father; he couldn't see another way to Skyhold. Jeric didn't know the details surrounding Stanis's estranged relationship with his father, only that he'd had a father, and that father had betrayed Corinth and then abandoned Stanis at a very young age. Stanis had spent the rest of his life trying to build a new legacy of devotion to Corinth, untainted by his father's treachery, which had made him the perfect emissary.

It was also why—Jeric had long deduced—Stanis had joined Jeric's pack in the first place and fought harder than any of them, save Braddok. He'd always fought like he was trying to right a wrong. To prove that he was not his father. That he would defend Corinth to the death, no matter the stakes. On those points, Jeric had always found common ground with Stanis.

Until Imari.

Their relationship had strained since she had entered Jeric's life. Jeric didn't know what to do about that, if there was anything to be done, but bringing Stanis's father into the picture did not help Jeric's case.

Stanis shifted his weight onto his other foot and leaned forward to rest his elbows upon the rail. Lantern light gilded his back, leaving his face in shadow, but Jeric could see the lines, the rigid set of them.

"You know, I used to tell myself he was dead," Stanis said suddenly, breaking the silence. "When the years went by and he never said a word."

Stanis's hands flexed upon the rail. "I could have forgiven him for it. For turning traitor. I never understood it. I wanted to, but he wasn't there to ask, godsdamned coward. Then you had to go turnin' to them too."

It was the reason Captain Vestibor had left King Tommad's fleet: He'd stopped using his ship to capture Sol Velorians and started using it to smuggle them out of Corinth instead. Jeric had never understood the change, which had been sudden and complete, until he had begun to know Imari. And now, to Stanis's acute frustration, Jeric was choosing the same path.

"Why, Wolf?" Stanis snapped. "Why would you risk all of Corinth for one rutting Liagé?"

Jeric leaned his forearms against the rail as the cold wind tossed his hair. "You've seen The Crossing. You've been to Sancta Mai—hells, you've spent nearly all your life at Skyhold. *Liagé built that*. With *our* resources. With skal. Because we *used* to work together." He looked at Stanis, but Stanis did not look back. "I want that world, Stanis. I will die for it."

"How can you say that after what they've done to our people —*your own mother*, Wolf!"

"Because I stopped qualifying all by the actions of some. Imari saved your life, Stanis."

"That's her mistake."

Jeric's anger flared. "You can't discard a fact just because it doesn't support your beliefs."

"Why not? *You* are."

Jeric clenched his teeth to keep his words in check. "Stanis. Understand me. I am not excusing the things they've done, but if things are to change, the cycle must stop somewhere, and I will do everything in my power to stop it if I can."

"This is rutting scat..." Stanis growled and pushed off the rail.

Jeric grabbed his arm.

Stanis stopped and glared at him. "Let go of me, Wolf."

"Stanis, I will die for you too," Jeric said fiercely. "I am not saying their lives are worth more. The difference now is that I've realized *I* am not worth more."

"It doesn't fix what they've done!"

"No, and it doesn't fix what we've done either."

Stanis bristled. His jaw flexed.

Jeric let go.

Stanis rolled his shoulder and looked away. He started walking away too.

"Stanis."

Stanis stopped, but he did not look back.

"The mission has changed. I recognize that," Jeric continued. "And I understand if it's not one you want to fight for. The choice is yours."

For a moment, Stanis stood there, his silhouette illuminated by lantern light. And then he walked on, leaving Jeric at the rail, staring at his back.

## 14

*I*mari opened her eyes. *The Lady* creaked like old bones, and Imari's hammock swayed gently in a constant, soporific motion that kept coaxing her back to sleep. The room was dark, though lantern light spilled in from the corridor, and she spotted Jeric's satchel tied to a cleat on the wall just over the hammock beside hers.

Imari didn't know how long she'd been asleep, but judging by the deep ache in her lower back and shoulders, and the numbness in her right leg, she thought it had probably been a while.

Footsteps thudded on the deck above, and voices echoed softly. Imari forced herself to sit, but then her head spun, and she gripped the rope and waited. Breathed. She could still taste vomit on her tongue, and for a second, she thought she might be sick again. Imari closed her eyes.

Maker have mercy.

How was she going to survive this? Jeric was counting on her to use her power in their inevitable fight against Azir. But stars...if she was going to be this sick every time she used the Shah, she'd be more liability than help.

*Use the bells.*

It was the Maker's voice this time, though distant and murky, as though his words could not quite reach her. Still, they brought courage and comfort, as they always had.

*Then show me how, because I am terrified*, Imari thought.

Nothing.

Imari sighed, slid out of the hammock, and landed with bare feet upon the wooden floor. Her right leg was still numb and unsteady, and when the ship rocked, she barely caught herself. Her world spun again; she waited, then slipped on her sandals and stepped out into the tight corridor.

To her left were the stairs to the deck. To her right were a few more doorways and the ship's stern. Just then, Paz—one of the crew—trudged down the steps, and seeing Imari, he winked and said, "Morning. There's food if you're hungry." He gestured toward an open doorway, where more light and voices spilled out.

Imari didn't feel hungry, though she knew she needed to eat. "Thank you."

He touched his temple and ducked into the doorway.

Imari padded down the hall, using the wall for balance, and when she reached the doorway Paz had entered, she peered inside. A few of the crew huddled about a small table. They'd lit a fire within what appeared to be a skal-forged firebox, and a kettle sat upon the embers. Chez was there too, seated beside Niá at the end of a bench. Imari was glad to see his arm still in a sling and his sprained ankle stretched before him.

Chez noticed Imari first. "Hey, Surina."

The others stopped talking and glanced up.

Niá promptly stood. "You're awake. Come. Sit." She waved Imari over to the bench. Many of the crew nodded at Imari in greeting.

Imari was almost too embarrassed to ask. "How long have I been asleep?"

"About twelve hours," Niá replied.

Not as bad as Imari had expected, but not as good as she'd hoped.

"Here..." Niá gestured at the table to an assortment of moldy cheese, nuts, and legumes they'd most likely softened in that kettle. "Eat something."

"I will in a bit. Where's Jeric?"

"On deck with Tallyn."

Jeric probably needed the fresh air. Imari nodded and started to leave.

"At least take some bread," Niá urged, holding out a hunk of hard bread.

Which Imari took with gratitude. "Thank you."

Niá resumed her seat, and Imari proceeded up the stairs, munching on the hard cracker as she went. It did help settle her stomach, and she was grateful for it.

Cold and salty wind snapped at her as she stepped on deck, and a layer of woolen clouds blanketed the sky, making it impossible to tell the hour. A couple of the crew scrubbed the deck, and a few more tightened ropes and adjusted sails. It was a stiff wind, and *The Lady* glided swiftly across a black and white-capped sea. Imari didn't see signs of land anywhere, though she did spot a curtain of rain behind them.

Braddok stood near the mizzen, talking with Jenya and one of the crew. Stanis crouched a few paces away, mending a fishing net with Rikk. She looked toward the helm, where Jeric stood, speaking with Tallyn and Survak.

Jeric leaned back against the rail, arms folded over his chest as the wind tossed his bronze-threaded hair, and by the sharp set of his features, Imari surmised Jeric didn't like whatever Survak was saying.

Imari was halfway to them when Jeric glanced over. Seeing her, he unfolded his arms, pushed himself off the rail, and strode toward her. The other two looked over and trailed behind.

Jeric intercepted her and grabbed her wrists, holding her steady as he gave her a once-over. "How are you feeling, my darling destroyer?"

"Better," she said with a grin. He looked a little pale, but not green. Not yet. "How are *you* feeling?"

He gave a noncommittal grunt and released her wrists. "Have you eaten?"

She raised her left hand.

He frowned at the cracker. "You need more than that."

"I'll get there."

"Good morning, Surina," Tallyn said with a slight bow of his head.

"Morning," Imari replied, then looked at Survak.

The captain seemed...different. More haggard, wearier, and there was a shadow over him that hadn't been there before.

"It's good to see you, Survak," she said.

"Glad to see you're feeling better, Surina."

"*Imari*," she corrected. "We're not so formal as that, Captain."

Survak gave her a tight smile, but it did little to lift his heaviness.

"Survak says that if the wind holds, we'll arrive at Gilder in two weeks," Jeric said.

Two weeks. It was the best they could hope for, and yet she found it hard to feel very grateful just then. With Kai and Trier captive to Azir and with Ricón somewhere only the Maker knew, every second felt like an eternity.

"That's good news," she said instead, because it was good news, considering their alternative. "I noticed you're making a wide berth." She gestured toward the western horizon, in the direction of Istraa's shoreline, which none of them could see.

"Perhaps a little *too* wide..." Jeric mused, disapprovingly.

"We need to stay out of Lestra's range," Tallyn said, giving Jeric a very pointed look that Jeric ignored.

"Have you seen Su'Vi?" Imari asked, searching the clouds for that little winged spy.

"Not since Liri," Jeric said.

"Could she send another?"

"She could try," Tallyn replied. "But even enchantments have limitations. The farther her crows fly, the greater the strain on her person, and the more she must rely on the power in the physical world for support, and oceans are not known for being stable."

"Until she turns herself into a godsdamned fish," Jeric said, and Imari chuckled.

"Oi, Captain!" one of the crew—Vorrah—yelled from above. He was sitting at the crow's nest atop the mainmast, his legs dangling through the net's loops, spyglass in his hand. "We've got company." He pointed west.

In the direction of Istraa.

Jeric strode for the port-side rail, eyes narrowed on the horizon. Imari followed, but she couldn't see a thing.

"How many?" Survak called out.

"Three ships," Vorrah yelled over the wind. "Heading this way, about twenty knots."

Survak pulled a spyglass from his coat and held it to his eye. The deck chatter ceased, and Jenya and Braddok were quickly making their way over. Stanis and Rikk had set down the nets they'd been mending and started for them too, though Stanis trailed behind.

"Who is it?" Jeric demanded.

"They're Istraan ships, but they aren't waving the Istraan flag." Survak lowered the spyglass and looked to Tallyn, a silent question in his gaze.

Tallyn nodded, then his one pale eye rolled back, showing whites. He stood that way for only a moment, and a stillness settled over him before his gaze returned, now full of fear. "Kazak."

Azir's Mo'Ruk guardian. The one who'd destroyed Trier with guardian fire.

"You're certain?" Imari asked.

"I would know him anywhere."

Braddok let out a string of curses as they all gazed in the direction of the approaching ships, which they currently could not see with their naked eyes.

"I thought you hid us," Jeric snapped at Tallyn.

"I did," Tallyn replied.

"Then how the hells does he know we're here?"

"We're too much together," Imari answered, understanding. She wasn't talking about the crew; she meant Liagé, specifically. Their combined power—hers, Niá's, and Tallyn's—was too much to hide from a Mo'Ruk.

"They're gaining quick, Captain!" Vorrah yelled from above.

Survak pressed the spyglass to his eye again and cursed.

"How are they gaining *against* the wind?" Braddok asked.

"The benefit of having a guardian on board," Survak said with the bitterness of experience. "They can harness wind."

"So we can't outrun them," Jeric said, eyes fixed on the distance.

"No." Survak pulled the spyglass down. "We've got to lose them."

"Well, no scat, genius," Braddok mumbled, and Survak glared at him.

Imari looked around, but all she could see, stretching in all directions, was wide-open sea. However, an impressive thunderhead obstructed view of the sea northeast behind a thick sheet of rain.

Which was exactly where Survak's gaze had settled.

"Turn the sails for that storm!" he shouted.

Rikk looked toward the thundercloud, and his expression turned uneasy.

"Godsdamnit, *move!*" Survak yelled, and this time, the deck came alive. Rikk scrambled up the mizzen, and more crew climbed the fore- and mainmasts, and sure enough, three dots now sat upon the horizon.

*Wards*, they were moving fast. Vorrah had not been exaggerating. Imari hadn't spent abundant time at sea, but she'd visited Zappor enough as a child, and she'd never seen a ship cut water like that.

"Can you give us speed?" Survak asked Tallyn.

Tallyn considered, his one eye fixed on those ships. "Perhaps, but I'll need Niá."

"I'll get her," Jenya said and jogged off.

No sooner had Jenya ducked through the hatch than Rikk yelled, "Fire!"

Imari looked back at the Istraan shoreline to see a familiar sphere of flaming, white-blue light arching toward them like a cannonball.

Guardian fire.

"Scat," Braddok cursed, while Survak yelled commands at the crew to move *The Lady* out of the flame's path.

The flame reached its apex and began its descent of certain destruction.

And then Imari felt the pull. That draw on Shah power, the ripple down her own line as Tallyn thrust his palms forward and spoke a word.

Imari heard Tallyn's command more with her soul than with her ears. She heard its *meaning*—felt it to her core—and when his power pulsed forth, she knew what he was doing, what he was *creating*, even before it manifested.

And she knew it wouldn't be enough.

A sheet of warped air thrust forth from his hands. It shot through the air like some flying, transparent veil, intercepting Kazak's flame as it arced down, but the fireball sailed right through, burning a hole through its center. The rest of Tallyn's veil ignited, dissolved into thin air, and Kazak's fireball continued on its path.

Straight for them.

Jeric grabbed Imari's hand and pulled her back from the rail as someone yelled, "Look out!" And that cannonball of flame crashed into the sea.

Water sizzled and sprayed, hosing *The Lady's* port side, but some of the flame had landed on *The Lady's* deck, where it was now burning holes into wood and eating up rope. The crew scrambled for buckets.

"You can't put it out with water," Imari yelled, but they tried anyway and quickly learned Imari was right.

Which was when Niá and Jenya scrambled on deck, with Chez stumbling out of the hatch after them.

"The fire!" Imari yelled at Niá, who immediately understood and got to work putting out flame with enchantment. She and Tallyn had barely snuffed out Kazak's fire when Imari felt another pulse of power in the direction of Kazak's small fleet.

"Niá! I need your help!" Tallyn shouted.

Niá looked up from a pile of burning rope, spotted the second ball of flame now arcing over the sea, then sprinted for Tallyn. She joined him at the rail, grabbed hold of his extended hand, and together, they chanted. A much stronger wall of warped air shot forth, soared over the sea, and intercepted Kazak's ball of flame, just like before, but still, it wasn't enough. The abominable flame tore through, burning up their invisible net as it headed straight for *The Lady*.

This fireball landed even closer, rocking *The Lady* as it pushed a wave of scalding water on deck. Crew cried out and scrambled away as more flame caught rope and wood.

With sudden decision, Imari bolted for the hatch.

"Where are you going?" Jeric yelled after her, but she didn't stop. She ran down those stairs two at a time, sprinted down the hall, and burst into the room where she'd slept. She yanked Jeric's pack from the wall, tore open the flap, and rummaged through.

There.

Fyri's talla illuminated at her touch, and a wash of power tingled up her arm.

"You're going to help me stop him," Imari demanded of that little strip.

Above her, crew yelled, and she was sprinting back down the hall when *The Lady* rocked dangerously far on her side.

The talla slipped from her hands, and she slammed into the opposite wall. Wood groaned, and seawater spilled through the cracks, and she was pretty sure she'd heard one of *The Lady's* ribs snap.

But *The Lady* leveled out—still afloat—and Imari snatched up her talla and stumbled her way up the stairs like a drunkard, out the hatch to find the deck glowing with too much fire. Niá and Tallyn were overrun, and the crew, Jeric, and his pack scrambled to put out the flames, but seawater could not douse them completely.

Across the deck, Jeric spotted her. He noticed the talla in her hand, and his eyes cut through her.

*Do it,* those storming blue eyes said. *I believe in you.*

Imari wrapped the long strip around her wrist, over and over, up her forearm and toward her elbow. Curiously, six of the bells lined up, and though the leather's glyphs shone with silvery light, the bells remained dark. Hollow.

Silent.

The seventh bell rested on the underside of her wrist, and she noticed a small slit at the end of the leather, to secure the strip. She pushed the seventh bell through.

A shock of heat jolted down her arm and through her body, like flame eating up a wick, and suddenly her world came alive.

The bells shone bright, as if they held the moon, and they

were no longer silent. They rang out in song, one perfect span of chords breaching all octaves, all intervals—finally given breath.

Awakened.

Imari stood at the rail with those ships in view. Even without a spyglass, she knew which belonged to Kazak's. She could *feel* him like a tear in the world, sucking all light and joy into it. It pulled on her power, on that line of Shah, as if he might pull her into himself.

Imari gripped the rail and closed her eyes as seawater sprayed into her face, and before she'd even loosed a note, her mind slipped into that Shah plane. That world of light and dark. There was so much light around her on this ship. It was brilliant against the ocean, like some constellation of a ship floating through a black cloud. She was surprised to find that she could identify each and every star and who they were by their particular song.

Jeric's was always so bright, his cello loud in her mind.

And at the edge of that world of stars, across the vastness separating her from Kazak, she felt that draw on Shah power— much stronger now that she was in this plane. Much stronger than anything she had ever felt from Tallyn or Niá.

As she stood there marveling at the magnitude of Kazak's draw, he gathered energy for another fireball.

Imari knew this one would not miss.

But before Imari could intervene, Azir was there again, standing beside her on deck as if he'd stepped through a tear to enter *her* reality. He watched her with those black and hungry eyes.

*Leave me alone!* Imari growled in that plane. In that mess of reality and contrasts.

*I cannot,* he said. *For, you see, we are bound together, you and I.*

*You can go to hell,* she said and threw all her focus across the sea, blasting through the canvas of stars like a meteor. She saw the ships as clusters of stars all gathered over an undulating sea of black, and at the center of it all, where the light clustered, was a mass of writhing, inky darkness.

Kazak.

His darkness drew upon all the stars around him, as though he were ingesting their light into himself, distorting the tones of those nearest. And from that darkness, from that fathomless, writhing chasm, Imari heard a deep and powerful bass. The sound wasn't pure; it warped and grated against her ears, more reverberation than tone. It rattled through her bones and drowned out every other note—even the bells.

He knew she could see him.

Somewhere in the visible world, Imari's ears registered voices and shouts. Her body rocked hard, and she pitched forward against the rail, but strong arms wrapped around her tight, keeping her feet firmly planted.

She knew it was Jeric. His song rang through her body with a timbre that made her heart sing.

In the Shah plane, Azir noticed, and his face distorted with rage.

Imari focused back on Kazak, on the contorting mass of ink, and then suddenly Kazak was before her, as though the gap had closed between them, and they were standing face to face.

Strangely, Azir's rage morphed into a look of awe and wonder. *You* are *magnificent*, he said.

Imari ignored him, focusing on all the little stars around Kazak's dark and writhing mass, just like she'd done with the legion inside of Astrid. She picked out every surrounding pitch and hummed to each one in turn. Heat seared her wrist, and in her Shah sight, her bells burned as bright as miniature suns. Seven, each ringing a different pitch, for each bell represented a single tone in a natural scale—Imari understood that now. And each pitch Imari hummed, the respective bell reflected back, amplifying the sound before throwing it back into the stars, louder than Imari could possibly sing on her own.

The bells blared her song across the chasm, and all the stars surrounding Kazak's darkness flared blinding white. As before, Imari began weaving them together, mending the pure and beautiful song that Kazak's darkness had corrupted.

Imari sang on, letting her heart guide the melody, drawing those stars closer and closer together as she tuned them back to truth.

Finally cutting Kazak out.

*You are far more capable than I could have hoped.* Azir's words floated to Imari right as she felt a wave of hot fury from Kazak. His darkness slammed against her starlit restraints, those stars expanded and stretched like sails too full of wind, and then the air exploded.

Imari cursed as the force threw her back. Her normal vision returned as she toppled into Jeric, knocking them both down. They tumbled across *The Lady's* deck, and *The Lady* rocked again, sending them—and much of the crew—sprawling. Imari crashed against the hull, her head struck wood, and pain splintered her skull. She rolled back on deck, wincing as she tried to push herself up, and Jeric was beside her, gripping a rope as he pulled himself to his feet.

Thunder rumbled overhead, and fat drops of rain splattered the deck.

They'd reached the storm.

"No, keep them open!" Survak yelled as some of the crew started to draw the sails.

Imari knew he was trying to give them more distance, take them deeper into the storm, but Kazak was still too close, and he was livid.

Imari shoved herself to her feet as Kazak pulled on the Shah again—stronger than before. So strongly that the well of Shah power audibly groaned from strain.

"Imari..." Jeric started, but she was humming again, eyes

closed as her vision returned to stars and all the spaces in between.

Again, she saw Kazak's black mass. Again, she saw him drawing all the surrounding stars into himself, swelling with their light, their power.

Imari sang louder, nearly screaming into those bells, letting them magnify her sound across the chasm. The stars surrounding him flared bright, and she wove them quickly together with her song and pulled tight. Closing Kazak out once more.

But this time, she did not stop singing.

The writhing darkness roared in her mind, a furious and trembling bass. It pushed and shoved against her light, her song, until those little points of light shook and strained, and her thread began to fray.

*Hold*, Azir said beside her, though his outline bled into the darkness. She wondered why he would encourage her. Why he would not aide his Mo'Ruk instead.

Kazak shoved, and her lungs clamped down.

*Hold*, Azir demanded again as Kazak thrashed and snarled, tearing at Imari's threads of light. Pain lanced through her chest and belly, and Imari felt as though she were slowly being torn in half.

*Hold, my dear sulaziér.*

Imari couldn't breathe.

*Hold.*

The stars faded with her consciousness.

*Hold.*

Air exploded in a blast of sound and light, knocking Imari back across the deck.

*Truly magnificent*, Azir said with a wicked smile, fading completely, while Imari flew through the air. She landed hard on her back, tumbling and tumbling—

Jeric caught her in his arms. They both collided into a stack of crates, but Jeric did not let go. She was distantly aware of Jeric saying her name, and she tried to answer, but her mouth wouldn't move, and she could not stop shaking.

"Get below!" Survak yelled from somewhere.

Imari could hardly see. Hardly think.

Jeric managed to stand, dragging her up with him, but her legs gave, and she collapsed. He caught her just before she fell, scooped her up in his arms, and hurried across the deck toward the open hatch.

And her world fell silent.

## 15

Niá was still staring, awestruck, at the place the ships had been when a wave slammed into *The Lady*. Niá stumbled and grabbed hold of a rope for support as seawater spilled on deck, and just when she'd regained her balance, another wave slammed into them. Lightning crashed, thunder roared, and the torrential downpour blurred the world.

This storm was going to tear them apart.

"Tighten those sails!" Survak yelled through the wind.

"Bowline's burnt," Paz yelled back. "Kiers's trying to fix them."

*The Lady* tilted again, and more seawater spilled on deck. The sea was a sweep of massive black dunes, rising and falling in all directions.

"Niá!" Tallyn yelled at her from near the hatch, where Braddok, Jenya, and Chez were climbing below.

Niá looked up at the collapsed sails, then ran, stumbling and sliding, grabbing onto a mast for support, all the way to the bow, where crew struggled to mend lines of rope that should have been attached to the bowsprit. Only one line remained connected, but the rest had been burned right through, thanks to Kazak's fire.

They were fortunate to have the one intact.

There was no climbing masts or getting out on the bowsprit in this storm, so the men were trying to tie the loose ends together, but their knots kept slipping, the boat kept rocking, and they couldn't work fast enough.

"I can help!" Niá shouted.

The men ignored her.

She shoved right through them. "*Give me your blade,*" she snapped at one.

It was a testament to their desperation that he gave her the blade in his hands without hesitation. Niá cut a quick line in her palm and handed back the blade. She rubbed her slick palms together, smeared the blood with rain and seawater, then grabbed the rope's two ends and said, "*Evoré.*" Join.

The ends flared with moonlight and fused back together, like hot metal in a forge. All that remained of the break was a bit of char and discoloring.

The crew gaped at her and rushed her to other loose ends while *The Lady* dipped and rose. Niá mended all the rope she could, but some had been burnt too badly or too close to the boom, and with these seas, there was no retrieving them.

"Pull!" Rikk yelled, and one of her mended ropes pulled taut.

The staysail drew upright and snapped full of wind, but it held. And *The Lady* lurched.

Niá sagged against a mast and sighed with exhaustion as the crew rushed to draw the other lines, bringing tension back to the foresail. Survak barked commands, and rowers pulled in the oars. Seawater ran across the deck as Survak strained to turn *The Lady* into the wind.

"Hold on!" Survak warned from the wheel, and *The Lady's* nose dipped down a large wave so suddenly, Niá lost her footing. She pitched forward, toward the bow—

A strong hand grabbed the back of her tunic and yanked her back.

Chez.

He held on to her like an anchor, keeping her from falling into oblivion. Their gazes met, held. Finally, *The Lady* leveled, and Chez released her tunic to extend his hand before her instead.

Niá looked at his hand as the rain and sea sprayed, drenching them both. And she took it.

His fingers wrapped around hers, nearly swallowing her hand completely, and together they ran across the flooded deck and toward the hatch. It was closed now, but Chez let go of her hand to throw it open, and they both crawled through. Niá tried pulling the hatch shut after them, but the wood was too heavy with water, and she was still exhausted from her spells, so Chez moved in beside her upon the narrow stair and helped her lift and draw it closed.

There, cramped together in the shadows of that narrow stair, soaking wet and freezing, Niá realized how close they stood. She could feel the heat of his body, hear his breath.

Neither of them moved.

Niá glanced up.

Chez's eyes shone with ambient light, and then her heart raced for an entirely different reason.

He wanted to kiss her.

Niá had seen that look a hundred times. She knew it well. She knew every carnal twist and turn, all the way to its futile climax. Her clients returned to Ashova's again and again, thinking this time the path might be different, this time the end might provide something it had not before, but it always ended the same: empty, meaningless. It satisfied a moment but chipped at the soul, leaving a hole larger than before.

But something about the way Chez was looking at her felt... different. And Niá did not know what to do with it—not at all— and it made her feel suddenly ashamed.

"I'm not what you think I am." Niá wasn't sure why she said it, but she wanted him to know.

"I'm not what you think I am either," he said at last, then strode on down the stairs and ducked into the galley without looking back.

A moment passed, and Niá descended, her hand trailing the wood for balance. Wind howled and the boat rocked, and she tried not to think about Chez. She reached the hammocks and found Jeric sitting upon the floor beside an unconscious Imari, his long legs folded, his head tipped back against the wall. Sensing her, he cracked his lids open a fraction.

"Not one for the sea?" Niá asked.

Jeric's lips curled, and he looked back at Imari.

Niá had never seen such devotion, and she certainly hadn't expected it from the Wolf of Corinth. "How is she?" Niá asked, ignoring the twist of envy she felt. No one had ever loved her like that.

"Well, she's asleep," he said.

Niá stepped in and knelt beside Imari's hammock, which swayed gently, despite the tortured seas. Niá leaned forward; there was still blood on her palm, mixed with rainwater, but it was enough. She drew a symbol upon Imari's brow, spoke a word. Energy pulsed, Imari's features relaxed, and she settled into the hammock with a sigh.

"Thank you."

Niá glanced back at Jeric; their gazes met. He nodded at her once, appreciatively, then looked back at Imari.

"I might be able to help your seasickness," Niá said. "I'm no healer, but I do know a few tricks."

He eyed her.

"If you don't trust me, I understand."

"I do," he said. "I was just wondering why Tallyn never offered the first time we sailed on this godsdamned boat."

Niá arched a brow. "Do you really not know?"

Jeric smirked, then pushed himself upright as Niá turned toward him. Again, she wiped her finger across her palm.

"Turn your face to the wall," she said, and he did. She drew a small symbol just behind his left ear. "Turn back." He did, and she drew another small symbol behind his right. She whispered a word, felt the familiar tingling of Shah.

Jeric's brow furrowed. His gaze roamed and then settled on her, much clearer than it'd been a moment ago. "That's already an improvement."

"Good." She stood and dusted her palms. "My oza taught me that one. I used to get sick in the wagons." At the questioning look on Jeric's face, Niá added, "I worked in the fields...before. I helped deliver grain."

"Ah."

"Your men are in the galley," she said, before he could ask more. "Go. Eat. I'll watch her."

Jeric hesitated.

"She'll be fine. And if you're worried, you can always bring food back here."

Jeric considered, then stood. He was much too tall for this space, and he had to duck to keep from hitting the ceiling.

At the threshold, he stopped and looked back at her. "I don't know what your plans are when all of this is over, but I want you to know that you are welcome in Skyhold."

Niá's gaze faltered, and she stood in silence as the Wolf of Corinth walked out the door.

mari opened her eyes to *The Lady's* sleeping quarters; however, this time, she was not alone. Jeric sat near the door, one leg folded, the other stretched before him as he whittled at something in his hands. A lantern sat on the floor beside him, warming his light skin, and everything seemed peaceful. There was no storm, at least none that she could hear, nor any waves battering the hull. Just a gentle, soporific rocking as *The Lady* softly creaked.

Imari closed her eyes with relief. Thank the Maker, they'd made it.

For now.

Imari opened her eyes again and looked back at Jeric. His tunic hung loose, the top ties left undone, and his bronze hair fell forward over a brow made sharp by focus. It struck her how long his hair had grown since she'd cut it, and then her thoughts moved further back, to when she'd first met him. The day he'd stepped through Tolya's front door, and how she'd warned herself to be careful with him.

Never—not in a thousand years—could she have predicted *now*.

He shifted in his seat, stretched his bent leg and folded the other, completely unaware that she watched him. He propped his elbow upon his knee and held the little figure to the light, studying it with a hunter's acuity. Imari couldn't tell what he was carving from here—a wolf, perhaps?—but it amazed her that a man she'd initially found so callous and abrasive could be so concerned about the delicate subtleties of craftsmanship.

He went back to work, carving at one end with the point of a dagger. Every motion was thoughtful and decisive and careful, so careful.

Suddenly, he stopped carving, and his gaze lifted to hers. A grin played at his mouth. "There you are."

She was glad to see that he seemed in better spirits than before.

Imari grinned back and pushed herself to sit. Her head spun, only briefly, but she felt infinitely better than before. "Kazak's gone?"

"We haven't seen him since the storm."

Imari was almost afraid to ask. "Which was...how long ago?"

Jeric smiled at her, all mischief. "Only three days this time."

Imari closed her eyes with a sigh.

"It's better than two weeks," he reminded her.

"And it's worse than none at all."

He chuckled lowly. "After what you just did, I half expected you to sleep all the way to Gilder."

At the way he said it, Imari opened her eyes and asked, "What did I do, exactly?"

Jeric set his blade and project down beside the lantern, then rested his elbow atop his knee again. His tunic pulled, hugging his shoulder. "Tallyn says you put so much pressure on Kazak's line—or however it is you draw from the Shah—that his connection snapped and his power...rebounded. Those ships didn't follow us into the storm, and we haven't seen them since."

Imari thought back on what had happened and what she'd

done. On Azir, telling her to hold. He had not stepped in this time, not like before. He had not lent his power, only advice, and she had done all the rest.

With the aid of Fyri's talla.

The air had exploded with power, sending her flying, and she probably would have flown right into the sea if Jeric hadn't caught her.

"Thank you. For catching me," she said.

"Well, the alternative was jumping into raging waters to save your life, but that's sort of *your* specialty."

Imari smiled.

"Tallyn also mentioned he's never seen anyone stretch their power across a distance like that." Jeric paused, studying her. "Not even Fyri could do it."

Imari hadn't thought much of it at the time, only that she'd wanted to stop Kazak, but Jeric was still studying her, and she couldn't read the look there.

"So is that good or terrifying?" she asked.

His lips cracked a small smile. "All I can say is thank the gods we're on the same side."

Imari gave him a small smile in return then asked, quietly, "Did we lose anyone?"

Jeric shook his head. "Our only major casualty was *The Lady*, but Niá has repaired most of the broken lines, and Tallyn's been helping the crew mend the fire damage."

Imari was relieved to hear that.

Jeric pushed himself to his knees then moved to her bedside, or hammock-side. He rested a hand on each side of her legs as he looked at her. "How are *you* feeling?"

"Good, I think." She had the sudden urge to run her fingers through his tousled hair, so she did. She brushed it back from his temples, and he leaned into her a little.

"You seem like you're faring better," Imari continued.

"I am. Niá did something to my ears."

Imari trailed her fingertips behind his right ear—there. She felt a mark of power, a resonant tingling. "Smart."

Jeric placed a hand over hers. Imari's gaze slid back to his, and the look in his eyes held her captive.

"You were incredible to watch," he said, looking between her eyes. "I almost *didn't* catch you because I was so transfixed by your song."

"I hope that's not all you're transfixed by," Imari said wryly.

Jeric's lips curled, and his head bent closer. "Hardly." His mouth caught hers, there in the quiet, in the calm of that small space, and for a moment, Imari could pretend it was theirs. That they were alone as he slid his hand to the small of her back and kissed her deeply. He tasted gloriously like the sea, like salt and freedom, and she wanted to drown in his depths forever.

But forever came to an abrupt halt as footsteps echoed down the hall.

Jeric pulled back just as Tallyn appeared in the opened doorway.

"Ah, you're awake," Tallyn drawled, as if he had known very well what he'd just interrupted. Also, he was glaring at Jeric.

"Only just," Jeric said simply, unaffected by Tallyn's subtle reprimand. He slipped his hand from Imari and jumped to his feet, though he couldn't stand fully, so he bent his head.

Tallyn's cutting, one-eyed gaze slid back to Imari. "When you're feeling up to it, I'd like a word."

"Could we have that word outside?" she asked. "I've had enough of this rutting hammock."

Tallyn's scarred features tightened at her word choice, and then he looked sharply at Jeric, who smirked.

"I'll be on deck." Tallyn gave Jeric one last pointed look and then vanished down the hall.

Imari slid out of the hammock, but she had been in that hammock for so long, her legs weren't ready to support her. Her knees gave, but Jeric caught her.

"Should I have Tallyn come back?" he asked.

"I'll be all right."

Jeric looked doubtful, but Imari was resolved. She stepped away from Jeric.

"You'll want this," Jeric said, snagging a long, woolen coat and a pair of boots off the floor, where he'd been sitting. "Those northerly trade winds burn."

Jeric held the coat open for her.

The coat was enormous, composed of panels of wool stitched neatly together. The hem had been reinforced with leather strips, and large canines served as buttons—bear teeth, perhaps?—and thick fur lined the hood.

"Survak gave you this?" she asked as she slipped into it.

"He got it from a trader in The Fingers."

"Bought it or *got* it?" Imari asked, adjusting the heavy wool over her shoulders.

"He didn't specify."

Imari laughed.

The coat was much too big and very heavy, but it would do the job fantastically well. Actually, she was beginning to feel a bit hot. She slipped on the boots, which fit well enough, as Jeric grabbed a second coat and put it on. The coat would have fit him perfectly if it hadn't been a little too short at the wrists.

Jeric grabbed her hand and gave it a light squeeze before leading her into the hall. Light and voices echoed from the galley, and some of the crew ducked in and out of doorways, trudging up and down the steps. They nodded as they spotted Imari. Some waved, and she smiled back.

"I never get this kind reception," Jeric mused.

"I wonder why..."

Jeric chuckled softly.

Imari stopped in the galley's doorway, where some of the crew drank at the table. Surprisingly, Stanis was with them too, playing Spades with a man named Arik. He glanced up from his game, his gaze flickered from her to the man directly behind her, then his features tightened, and he looked back at his game.

"Morning, Surina," said Gortch, a squarely built man with a rope-like scar along his left cheek.

A few more "mornings" went around the table.

"Someone get the surina some water," Jeric said.

"*Please*," Imari hastened to add, then cast Jeric a sideways glance that he ignored.

Vorrah produced a water flask and passed it around the table to Imari.

"Want somethin' to eat?" Arik asked.

"This is perfect for now." She raised the flask. "Thank you, gentlemen."

They nodded, and she left them all in the galley.

"Where were these fine manners when we first met?" Jeric said dryly as they ascended the narrow and creaking stairs.

"I don't waste manners where they're not appreciated. Also, I distinctly remember wanting you to leave."

"That worked out well."

Imari chuckled.

The hatch had been left open, and a blue sky stretched beyond, dotted by puffy clouds. Despite the cheerier weather, Jeric was right. That bitter cold northern wind snapped, and Imari clutched her coat tight as she stepped on deck. An indigo blue sea lapped at the hull while a quiet crew swabbed the deck and steadied the lines, but there was no sign of the storm anywhere, or Kazak.

Imari spotted Braddok, Jenya, and Chez seated near the bow, all facing the sea. She found Tallyn standing with Niá and Survak upon the quarterdeck. Survak was talking and gesturing at *The Lady's* top sails, but seeing Imari and Jeric, he stopped and waved them over instead.

Jeric put a hand on the small of her back as they crossed the deck. The sun slipped behind a cloud, casting *The Lady* in shadow and stealing what little warmth remained. It would be a cold week at sea.

"Surina," Survak said, pulling his pipe briefly from his lips as she and Jeric ascended the quarterdeck's short stair.

Niá gave her a small smile in greeting.

"How are you feeling?" Survak asked.

"Well, thank you," Imari replied. "Hopefully your *Lady* didn't suffer too much."

"She'll be fine." Survak patted the rail like an adoring father. "Thankfully, you gave her time to slip away, and Tallyn and Niá have been kind enough to expedite repairs. We were just discussing our trajectory."

"Yes, where are we, exactly?" Imari asked, gazing at the empty horizon.

"East of Hüdsval." Survak took a long draw from his pipe.

Imari had heard of Hüdsval. It was an enormous port along Corinth's southern ridge, near Istraa's northeastern border.

"But we're not heading to Hüdsval," Imari said, looking between them.

Jeric's eyes narrowed upon the horizon, as if he might see Hüdsval from here. "My father moved the bulk of Corinth's fleet to those waters during Saád's war. Berret oversees them now, and he's Stovich's man through and through."

Meaning, Jeric did not have much faith in a warm reception from Hüdsval. Stovich was Jeric's most powerful jarl, and—Imari suspected—the largest reason behind Jeric's eagerness to return home. Stovich had not hidden his disdain of Jeric's father or his opinions that Corinth needed new blood occupying the throne.

However, to avoid Hüdsval completely...

"Are you really that worried about Stovich?" Imari asked.

Jeric's storming gaze landed on her. "Yes. What I need in Stovich is also what makes him the most dangerous. He knows it. Always has. Ironically, my only present consolation is knowing he's more than capable of keeping Kormand from launching a full-fledged attack in my absence."

"You don't honestly believe Brevera would attack Corinth *now*?" Tallyn asked.

Jeric's condescending gaze slid to Tallyn, and Imari suspected they'd already argued over this while she'd been asleep below. "You're right, Tallyn. How silly of me. Kormand's only sought after Skyhold for the last twenty years, but what would I know? Sometimes I forget your erratic flickers of Sight are more accurate than my entire life's experience in dealing with a person."

Tallyn's expression flattened.

"Anyway, we are *not* berthing at Hüdsval." Survak puffed irritably on his pipe. "Tallyn and Niá have kindly put a new veil over *The Lady* to keep us from being sighted by scouts, and, assuming the weather holds, we should reach Felheim's harbor within the week."

Something about the way he said this prompted Imari to ask, "And we have enough supplies?"

Survak released a plume of smoke, which was quickly snatched by the wind, and his brow furrowed.

"That's...what we've been discussing," Niá answered this time. "I believe I can enchant the nets to increase yield."

"We *hope*," Survak corrected without looking at anyone. "Hope you like fish."

"I definitely prefer it to starving," Jeric said, and Survak grunted.

The sun emerged from behind the clouds again, and light and warmth returned.

"Might I have a word, Surina?" Tallyn asked, gesturing toward the stairs.

"Of course." Imari exchanged a quick glance with Jeric, then followed Tallyn down the steps, across the deck, and all the way to the captain's quarters, where Tallyn pushed open the door and ushered her inside.

But Imari did not go in. "Survak's all right with us using his quarters?"

"Yes. This way we can have a bit of privacy. Also, it's warmer."

Imari couldn't argue that. She glanced back and spotted Jeric on the quarterdeck, leaning forward with his forearms against the rail, watching her as she ducked inside.

Tallyn closed the door after them, shutting out the wind.

Stars, this room. It brought back so many memories of a time not so long ago, though it felt like another age. When she had been Sable, Jeric had been Jos, and they'd been on their way across Hiddensee, fleeing from Ventus, his Silent, and the shades.

"The Wolf has informed me that you've seen Azir," Tallyn said without preamble.

Imari stilled. She looked at Tallyn, who had taken a seat at Survak's desk.

"I did." A part of her was irritated at Jeric for telling Tallyn, but she *had* promised to tell the alta-Liagé. Jeric would have only mentioned it out of concern for her.

Still.

"Would you care to elaborate?" Tallyn said.

Imari took a seat on the edge of Survak's narrow bed. She explained what had happened in Liri, at least from her limited perspective, and when she finished, Tallyn was quiet for some time.

"You saw him again on *The Lady,* didn't you?" Tallyn asked.

Imari shifted beneath his stare. She hadn't even admitted this to Jeric yet. "I did."

"Did he touch you again?"

So Jeric had told him this too. "Not this time."

"Could he see where you were?"

Imari thought over his question. "I don't know if he could in Vondar. He kept looking past me, like he was trying to make out where I was, but I have no idea what he could see. This time, when he appeared on the deck, he knew I was using the bells—

that much I can tell you—and he...noticed when I used my power against Kazak."

Tallyn's eye was like a pale crystal orb, staring at her, unblinking, and his scars pulled tight.

"Is it real, Tallyn?" Imari asked in frustration. "Or is this some trick of my imagination?"

"It is no trick of your imagination, Imari."

"Then how is this happening?"

Tallyn considered her a long moment, then leaned back against Survak's desk. "I do not know why this is happening. It is possible that when you touched Zussa at the tree, it formed a connection to her."

"Then how do I stop it?"

"I don't know if you can."

Which was precisely what Imari feared. "Then I am a danger to all of you."

Tallyn regarded her. "You just saved this entire ship and everyone on it from resting eternally upon the sea floor. You are no danger, Imari."

"But this ship would not have been compromised in the first place had I not been aboard."

"And the Provinces would not be so vulnerable had Azir not been resurrected." A pause. "It does not do to dwell on what-ifs, Imari. There is only *what is* and how we respond to it."

Imari sighed and chewed on her bottom lip.

"Azir has appeared to you only these two times?" Tallyn asked.

"Yes."

"And only when you were drawing upon the Shah?"

"Yes."

"I'll need to think on this a bit more," Tallyn said, then paused before asking, "Was he the one who told you how to stretch your power across the sea?"

"No," Imari said, and Tallyn looked unconvinced. "I swear to the stars, Tallyn, he didn't explain anything other than telling me we were *bound together*, and I told him that he could go to hell."

Tallyn coughed and looked very much like he was fighting back a smile. "Truly, he did not explain it?" At the annoyed look on Imari's face, he added, "I am only asking because in all my one hundred and forty-three years of life, I've never known someone who could stretch their power in that manner—and that's with years of Mazarat training. Not even Azir had figured how, though believe me, he tried, so you can understand why I need to be sure. If he had discovered how, that war could have fared very differently. I do not say any of this to frighten you but so that you're acutely aware of every piece in this intricate design. To deny one's vulnerabilities is the surest way to fall down upon them. So how did *you* do it?"

Imari's gaze flickered to the porthole, to the gray sky beyond. "I didn't know how to stop the fire, so I thought to stop the man himself. I remember...wanting to get closer to him, so I pushed my power out farther, and it was like...the world folded. All of a sudden he was standing right there before me."

Tallyn studied her very quietly. "You are telling me that you performed something generations of Liagé have tried and failed to do...by accident."

Imari didn't like the way he was looking at her. "*I don't know,* Tallyn. I tried, and it worked, but if you have some other idea, by all means, please share."

If he took offense to her tone, he didn't show. "It's the tree, isn't it?"

Imari stopped.

Tallyn's features opened a little, as if he suddenly saw something in her he hadn't before. In that moment, Imari remembered the verses. She remembered all the questions she had wanted to ask Taran, but Taran had departed from this world before Imari had been able to get answers. About how the *sulaziérs* of old had all fallen. Imari had literally held Zussa inside of herself when

Imari had freed her from the tree, and ironically, Imari had Azir to thank for not being Zussa's permanent vessel. Still, had that momentary possession irreversibly tainted her? *Bound* them, as Azir had said and Tallyn suspected?

Imari wrung her hands within the folds of her coat. "Is something wrong with me? Am I...doomed to Fyri's same fate?"

Tallyn sat spine straight as he folded his inked and scarred hands upon his lap. "No, child, and nothing is wrong with you. I'll admit that I initially worried a piece of Zussa had stayed with you. I do not believe so now."

"Why?"

"Because I know you," he said so simply.

"And what if you're wrong, Tallyn? What if all of you are wrong about me? What if a piece of Zussa *did* stay with me, and now you've given me this...this weapon that Fyri used to destroy all of Sol Velor—"

Imari realized she was standing and breathing hard, her hands curled into fists. She didn't know why she felt so angry, only that she was.

Tallyn regarded her, but Imari could not read the look there. "Imari." He said her name firmly, as if he could calm her down with one word. "All of us have the potential for evil. It is in our nature. What sets you apart is that you do not choose it as Azir and others have. Do not fear what you are because others have taken your gift and used it for ill. You have been given a great gift, Imari. Use it well."

# 17

allyn's words hovered like a dark pall the days that followed. The air turned colder too, as if inspired by Imari's own misgivings, and the sunlight dimmed. For three days straight, Imari didn't see the sun at all. Just a blanket of woolen, gray clouds that turned this endless sea a deep cobalt blue. The water *looked* cold, like the Kjürda in winter, and that northern wind burned.

And one by one, Jenya and all of Jeric's men succumbed to seasickness. After so many days at sea, it was impossible to avoid, so as they took ill, Niá enchanted their ears in the same way she'd enchanted Jeric's.

Except for Stanis. He stubbornly refused any Liagé assistance, instead preferring to vomit over the rail at regular intervals and sleep all the moments in between.

Seasickness didn't hit Imari, so she spent the time helping the crew where she could. Anything to keep herself busy, because physical labor was the best distraction for an unwieldy mind.

And she needed a distraction from the talla that called to her constantly like a melody she could not shake.

"Arik will do that," Survak said when Imari grabbed the

bucket and broom to swab the deck after Stanis had vomited all over it. Survak whistled at Arik, who started jogging over to them.

"I can do it," Imari said.

"It's *his* job."

"Let it be mine today. Please."

Survak studied her. She wondered what he saw, if he heard the desperation in her voice, if he'd seen these signs before. Whatever he saw, Survak redirected Arik to the sails.

Imari nodded her thanks and got to work. Once she'd finished scrubbing away all evidence of Stanis's most recent bout of vomiting, she dragged her bucket and broom to the starboard side, where they dumped the fishing nets, and soon after caught sight of Jeric emerging from *The Lady's* belly. He'd been helping Rikk and a man named Cleats mend a couple of internal boards that'd rattled loose, which Cleats had noticed this morning when water seeped onto the storage room floor.

Jeric had thrown a long coat over his creamed tunic, though he didn't bother buttoning it as he stepped on deck.

Imari couldn't help but watch him and his long and powerful stride as he crossed the deck toward Braddok and Chez, who stood with Survak at the helm. Jeric was taller than all the crew, and though he tried to keep out of their way, they moved before he did, giving him a direct path to Survak.

People always moved for Jeric.

His hair was long enough to tie back now—which he had—though the wind tugged a few sun-kissed strands free. His facial hair had filled in too, giving frame to those sharp lines and hard planes.

He stopped before Survak and his men, exchanged a few words, and then his keen gaze caught on her.

She realized she was still watching him, and she got back to work.

A few moments later, Jeric's boots thudded back down the helm's steps, and he crossed the deck, moving toward her.

"Is it fixed?" Imari asked as he approached.

"Mostly." Jeric leaned against the rail and faced her. His dark facial hair turned his eyes to sapphires. "Tallyn and Niá are enchanting it now. To be safe."

"Good." Imari bent over and slopped more seawater onto the deck.

"What did you do to piss him off?" Jeric asked wryly.

She smirked as she resumed scrubbing fish entrails from the planks. "I asked to do this."

She could feel him watching her.

"You *asked* to do the worst job on the ship."

"It's not so terrible. Maybe you should give it a try."

"I have self-respect."

"Too much, I'd say."

Jeric chuckled lowly, but then bent forward and tipped the bucket over the planks, spilling more water out for her.

"Why thank you, Your Grace," Imari said.

Jeric inclined his head. "My sincerest pleasure, Surina."

Imari continued scrubbing, and Jeric leaned back against the hull, hands planted on the rail.

"Gods, I almost feel guilty standing here while you do this."

Imari eyed him. "Not that guilty, apparently."

"Or I just prefer *watching* you." He flashed his teeth. Imari gave him a look, though her cheeks flushed. But then Jeric's expression sobered, and he said, "Truthfully, would you like help?"

"You already did." She nodded at the bucket. Just then, Stanis strode past them, toward *The Lady's* aft, and vomited over the rail.

Imari exchanged a long and frustrated look with Jeric.

Jeric had explained Stanis and Survak's connection once Stanis had fallen to seafaring misery and refused to let Niá help. Imari suspected some of his crew had figured it out too, like his first mate, Rikk, whom she had caught watching Stanis on more than one occasion. But whatever he thought of Survak's

Corinthian past—if he'd figured that part out or already knew—Imari had no way of knowing. He still followed his captain's orders without hesitation, and he ensured the rest of the crew did the same.

Stanis finished, wiped his mouth, and turned away from the rail. His gaze landed on Jeric, then Imari, at the broom in her hands. His brows pinched together, and then he proceeded to the hatch and climbed into *The Lady's* belly, where he would undoubtedly go back to sleep.

Imari looked at Jeric, but Jeric was still gazing after his man.

"So we arrive in Felheim tomorrow," Imari said, drawing Jeric's attention back.

He inhaled deep and settled back against the rail again. This time, he looked out to sea. "By nightfall." He opened his hands, flexing his fingers. "I'm trying to decide whether or not to have Tallyn enchant *The Lady*."

It was what Tallyn had done the first time, when Survak had brought him to Felheim so that he could warn Jeric about the two Silent heading south from The Wilds.

Imari scrubbed at a particularly hard spot of fish grime. "So Corinth's king aims to sneak into his own home."

She didn't look up, but she felt his eyes on her.

"I've no way of knowing what awaits me there," Jeric replied sharply. "Surprise has always been my greatest ally. For all I know, Stovich could have proclaimed himself king."

"Hm."

A beat. "You disagree."

Imari bent over and emptied the rest of the bucket. "How can I? If you'll recall, that's exactly how I survived in The Wilds. By surprise and sneaking." She set the bucket upright, used the back of her hand to wipe the hair from her forehead, and then looked straight at him. "But sneaking is for thieves. You're a king. I say let them know you've returned. Let *Stovich* know you've returned.

Let everyone see you, healthy and strong, and let them tell the world their king has come home."

He stared at her, then, "There are eight of us. Possibly seven." He glanced toward the hatch, where Stanis had gone.

"And there are far more than *possibly seven* who are loyal to you."

Jeric tapped his thumb against the rail. "It takes time to find those people, Imari, and time is not something we have."

"Exactly. So let the good people of Corinth spread word that their king has returned. And if we get to Skyhold only to find your throne occupied, then *your people* will know you're still alive. When my papa was gone for over a year during Saád's war, the only thing that kept Roi Naleed from taking over was that the people of Istraa knew my papa was alive. He wouldn't let them forget; he constantly sent supplies from all over the world as a reminder, or so my uki Gamla always said. How much more will those loyal stand for you once they've actually *seen* you?"

When she finished, Jeric simply stood there studying her, though she couldn't read the look there. His facial hair covered so many of those subtle shifts in his expressions that she'd only begun to understand. But his eyes...they were deeper than the sea just then.

"I will not have Tallyn enchant the ship," he said at last.

Imari smiled. "Good."

AT DUSK THE FOLLOWING DAY, as Jeric had projected, Corinth's shoreline came into view. White-capped water lapped at *The Lady*, wind snapped her sails, and Jeric's men gathered at the hull to see that stretch of earth from the land they loved so dearly. Even Stanis stomped on deck, eager to see a horizon that might help steady his belly.

It didn't.

He bolted to the starboard side and vomited his dinner over the edge.

"Rutting stubborn ass," Braddok said, then looked to the horizon and sighed. "Gods, I thought I'd never see her again."

"Bjorn's gonna be so disappointed," Chez drawled, and Braddok chuckled.

"Who's Bjorn?" Imari asked.

"Owns the Barrel," Braddok answered, and at her questioning look, Chez further explained, "It's our local tavern."

"Ah." She should have guessed.

"I'll take you there tonight," Braddok said to Jenya with a waggling of his brows.

Jenya slid an annoyed gaze to the horizon.

"We're heading on to Skyhold tonight?" Imari asked, a little surprised.

Braddok shrugged. "Don't see why not. It's only about an hour from Felheim—"

"*Two*," Jeric cut in, joining them. "On foot, in this climate." He nodded toward the mountains they could all now clearly see, which were draped in pristine white.

Braddok grumbled and made a very disrespectful face that Jeric chose to ignore.

Chez glanced at Braddok. "Bria's pa still keeps those stoliks?"

Braddok tensed. His gaze flickered awkwardly to Jenya. "I think I might have heard something of it."

Imari wondered who this Bria was.

"How many?" Jeric asked.

Braddok shifted. He wrinkled his nose, and his big beard twitched. "Nine, but one's a foal, born last sowing season."

Jenya's gaze slid to Braddok, where it narrowed. Imari tried very hard not to smile.

"What are stoliks?" Niá asked, either not reading Braddok's sudden awkwardness or ignoring it. Imari sensed it was the latter.

"Corinthian horses," Chez replied. "They're bred for our winters and rocky terrain. Rode one once along Fallow's Pass through four feet of snow. Didn't slow him down one bit, but I was a godsdamned block of ice by the time we reached our destination."

"Is he good for them?" Jeric asked Braddok, who still looked uncomfortable.

"For you, he will be," Braddok replied, then cleared his throat.

Jeric considered this, then nodded once.

"You don't wanna take the sewers?" Chez asked, gazing curiously at his alpha and king.

Jeric's gaze met Imari's briefly before he looked back to the ever-approaching shoreline. "No. We use the main gates. I want all of Corinth to know we've returned."

Eventually, the shore split in half where seawater carved into the sound. Survak barked commands at his crew, some sails were drawn, and the rowers took over. Imari had never been to Gilder Sound, though she'd heard of it before. Still, she had not been prepared for such dramatic beauty.

The mountains huddled right up against the water's edge, touching both sea and sky. Thick and heavy clouds nestled between jagged peaks, which were cloaked in snow and pines. A thin fog settled over the water, not so thick to make it blinding but just enough to set a haze over everything, and all the crew fell quiet as *The Lady* glided in between the shore's open arms and into the sound.

Where they were intercepted by a small schooner.

The schooner waved a brilliant Corinthian-blue pennant, and about a dozen men stood at the helm, all dressed in heavy wool coats and bearing long skal swords. One—their captain, Imari deduced by the elaborate, Corinthian-blue coat—stood before the rest.

"Rowers, stop!" Rikk yelled, and the rowers ceased rowing.

A palpable tension settled over *The Lady's* crew, and they eyed that Corinthian vessel as one might regard an approaching shark. Imari didn't see Survak anywhere.

The schooner glided nearer, and up close, Imari could see the captain was an older man with a stern expression and salty hair tied back at his neck. His attention fixed entirely upon Jeric, who stood near the bow.

She could see the moment realization struck.

"King Jeric!" the captain shouted, and he immediately dropped to one knee and lay a long, slender skal sword flat across his leg. One by one, his startled guard followed suit.

Imari thought this was a good sign, though *The Lady's* crew still looked on with misgiving. Vorrah observed from the crow's nest, holding a small crossbow.

"Captain Boratta," Jeric called across wind and wave. "Is this normally how you welcome Corinth's guests?"

Imari heard the edge to Jeric's voice.

The man—Captain Boratta—stood, though the rest of his guard remained prostrate. "My sincerest apologies, Your Grace. I did not recognize the ship, and these are uncertain times." He *did* sound sincere, despite the fact that he was yelling, but the wind had picked up, so there was no other way around it.

"That they are," Jeric replied. "Are we clear to port?"

"Aye, Your Grace. We'll provide escort." Captain Boratta's gaze slid over *The Lady's* many occupants, who were gathered along the rail—Imari included. His gaze lingered there a moment, sharpened, and then he looked back to his king. "Who captains this ship?"

"That'd be me," Rikk said to Imari's surprise, but even more surprising was Rikk's Corinthian accent. It was so fluid, Imari wondered if Rikk had been part of Survak's original crew when Survak had served the Corinthian crown under another name.

Rikk strode briskly to Jeric's side, and the "captains" studied one another.

"Follow us in," Captain Boratta shouted at last. "Don't get too close to The Rock. It's wider than you think. This is a fine ship, and I'd hate to see her gutted."

"Thanks for the warning," Rikk said, though Imari suspected he was already well acquainted with the sound's maritime topography.

The captain saluted Rikk, bowed his head to Jeric, then gave orders to his crew that Imari could not hear. Soon, the Corinthian schooner turned around, the men hoisted a white flag beside the Corinthian-blue, and the ship pulled back into the sound.

"To oars!" Rikk yelled, and *The Lady's* rowers resumed position, dropping their oars back into the water and pumping with impressive synchrony.

"Do you trust him?" Imari asked Jeric as *The Lady* glided after the schooner.

"Boratta never liked Hagan much. So, yes."

Imari smirked.

"He used to take me out to sea," Jeric continued thoughtfully. "When I was a boy. I always like the idea of sailing."

"What happened?"

Jeric looked sideways at her. "I sailed."

This time, Imari chuckled. "That's a very sad story."

"Aye, it is. It's unfortunate I wouldn't have entertained Niá's little enchantment back then."

"Yes, and who knows? Perhaps they would have called you Shark instead."

Jeric laughed.

They soon sailed through the sound's outstretched arms and out of the sun's last rays. The air turned suddenly colder, the world darker, and lights from the Sunguard—Gilder's marine defense—flickered up ahead. They glittered from a high tower rising from an enormous rock—*The* Rock, the people called it. It stood at the sound's center, attached to the world by an impressively high bridge that had been anchored to the side of a mountain. Imari spotted silhouettes in The Rock's lantern light, undoubtedly from the guards watching *The Lady* as she glided into the sound.

From the bridge, Imari trailed her gaze along a precarious road that sometimes ducked inside the mountain only to appear out the other side, winding all the way down to the village of Felheim, which sat wedged between mountain and shore. How they'd built that impossible road, Imari could not fathom. She'd never seen tunnels so long and wondered if—like Skyhold—Corinthians of old had worked with Liagé to build this.

The village itself was a sprawl of wood and stone structures, all shapes and sizes. Buttery light flickered inside murky window-panes, and smoke curled from chimneys, mixing with the fog that had settled. Wooden docks lined the shore, most of them empty, and a layer of snow blanketed everything. Dense fog had nestled into the mountains' deep crevices, but with the night, that fog slowly seeped down the cracks to where it began stretching across the black water.

Snowflakes began to fall as Rikk directed *The Lady's* crew to the docks, and within the hour, with Captain Boratta's help, *The Lady* was drawn and anchored and ready to sleep.

Still, Survak did not emerge.

"How else may I assist you, Your Grace?" Captain Boratta asked from the docks.

Rikk had ducked into the captain's quarters, Imari noted.

"I'll take it from here," Jeric answered the Sunguard captain, then added, "However, you might warn Otten he's about to have company. Don't mention my name."

"Of course, Your Grace." Captain Boratta bowed. "I am here should you have need of anything else." He strode off, with two of his crew following.

Which was precisely when Rikk emerged and exchanged a quick word with Jeric.

"Is Survak coming?" Imari asked Jeric as they gathered their things from below.

Jeric shook his head. "He's worked with Boratta."

"Ah," Imari mouthed.

They trudged back on deck with the others. Many of the crew had already left *The Lady* for Felheim, and the little schooner was now halfway to The Rock.

"You told Boratta to warn Otten...that mean we're staying the night?" Braddok asked. The snow was falling harder now and coated his thick beard and brows.

"Yes." Jeric's attention settled on the village. "Can you See anything, Tallyn?"

"I would rather not alert anyone to my presence," Tallyn replied quietly.

Jeric nodded fractionally, and then looked to Braddok. "See if you can secure stoliks for tomorrow morning."

"Aye." Braddok shouldered his satchel and started for the ramp, then paused. He glanced up at the drawn sails, at the rigging. "I'm gonna miss her."

Imari's gaze trailed the deck and the simple life they'd lived these past two weeks. "I am too."

Braddok sighed, patted the rail, then started down the ramp. Stanis followed after without a word.

"Ready?" Chez asked Jeric.

Jeric considered, then said, "I'll meet you there. I'd like to have one quick word with the captain first."

# 18

*J*eric did not bother knocking, and he did not find the door locked. He knew it wouldn't be.

Survak sat at his desk by candlelight, his quill scratching furiously across a sheet of paper. He did not look up as Jeric entered, nor when Jeric shut the door. He simply dipped his quill in ink, signed his name, then dusted the paper with sand.

"I want to make you an offer," Jeric said.

Survak plopped the quill into the inkwell, shook the excess sand from his paper, and folded it crisply in thirds.

"Fight for me. Command my fleet at Hüdsval, and I will grant you full pardon."

Survak held black wax over flame, let it drip upon the paper's fold. He pulled something from a drawer—an old signet ring?— stamped it in the wax, returned the ring to the drawer, and stood, facing Jeric.

Those eyes—Stanis's eyes. Gods, Jeric still couldn't believe he'd never connected the two before. And he'd seen that look in Stanis too.

He was a man who did not know how to deal with his pain,

and so he fell back on anger. Anger was safe; anger kept him in control.

Survak stepped forward. He stopped one pace away from Jeric and presented the sealed letter. "Will you give it to him?" His voice was low, and it trembled with emotion.

Jeric looked at the seal—an anchor set inside a wolf head's outline—and then back at Survak. "You kept it."

It was the Sunguard's crest, and this particular ring had belonged to the Sunguard's High Captain.

"Will you?" Survak persisted.

Jeric regarded the old captain and plucked the letter from his grip. Survak stalked back to his desk, sat down, and pulled another sheet from the drawer.

Jeric watched him a moment, then strode to the door and opened it a crack, letting the cold, wintry air slip inside. Survak's candle flickered, and he looked over at Jeric, annoyed.

"My offer stands, Captain Vestibor," Jeric said. "Let me know when you change your mind." He slipped the letter inside his coat and left, closing the captain's door behind him.

IMARI, Tallyn, Jenya, and Niá followed Chez slowly through Felheim's quiet and snowy streets. The hour wasn't late, but the wind had gained force and was flecked with ice, and Imari was very grateful they weren't heading on to Skyhold tonight.

Also, she found the ground a bit unsteady after spending two weeks at sea.

Eventually, Chez approached the door to a building with two stories, a steep roofline, and a lot of windows. Smoke rose from multiple chimneys, carrying the scent of cooked meat. There was a sign too covered in snow to read over the door, but Imari guessed this was the place called Otten's that Jeric had mentioned.

"Are you sure it's a good idea for us to walk through that front door with you?" Imari asked Chez. Though they were huddled in heavy wool and hoods, two Istraans, one Sol Velorian, and a very scarred man would definitely not pass unnoticed. Jeric's pack might have softened to them, but the rest of Corinth had a long road ahead.

Chez seemed to remember where they were, and who was in his company, and said, "Wait over there, behind those stables." He pointed to a small structure attached to Otten's side. "There's a back entry. I'll let you in. But let me have a word with the master first." He hurried off through the snow, up Otten's front steps, and shoved through the front door.

For a moment, there was light and cheerful noise and...music.

A lute.

Fingers danced over strings, plucking a song Imari had heard once from a troubadour that had ventured into Skanden—

The door closed, muting the song, and the night returned to snow and wind.

"Imari."

Niá was waving at her from nearly halfway to the stables. Imari clutched her coat and hurried after them. They slipped around the wooden stables and into a small courtyard, where they moved beneath an awning and waited.

And waited.

"Do you think he's okay?" Niá asked when half an hour had passed. Imari could hardly see her face for all the wool and fur.

"Ten more minutes, and I'll go inside," Tallyn said.

But five minutes later, Chez appeared around the corner and flagged them over.

"Sorry about that," Chez said, glancing furtively about them. "Lots of people in the hall, and all of them were pretty excited to see their king returned."

"That's promising," Imari said as she stepped through the smaller door in back that Chez was holding open.

A narrow hall lay beyond, lit by two glowing lanterns, and the air smelled like cedar and smoke.

*Wards*, it felt good to be out of the wind and cold.

Doors lined the walls, and the opposite end opened to a great room with hearth, light, and loud cheer. Imari could just see two men seated at the end of a table. One of them chuckled as he lifted a chalice to his lips.

"This way." Chez gestured to a dark and wooden stair to the right.

Imari ascended as quietly as she could, though the boards groaned and creaked like an old man's bones. The stair ended at a second level with another corridor lined with doors and lantern light.

Chez led them down the hall, and Imari heard voices behind a few of the doors, while laughter echoed from below, sometimes punctuated by clattering dishes. Chez handed out keys and pointed to corresponding doors. "Last door on the right," he said to Imari.

Imari was expecting a key, but he gave her a wink instead.

Ah.

Imari left the others, reached the door on the end, and knocked softly.

Quiet.

She knocked again.

"Try the handle," Chez said from farther down the hall just before ducking into his own room.

Imari frowned but tried the handle.

The door opened.

She glanced back down an empty hall, then slipped into the room and closed the door behind her.

The room was far more comfortable than what Imari had been expecting. A large, four-poster bed stood off to one side, plush with pillows and thick, woolen blankets. There was a writing desk in one corner, where Jeric had dumped their satchels and three daggers—where had he been keeping those? A hearth filled the wall across from the bed, though no fire burned within, and a great, bear-skin rug warmed the wooden floor. Imari thought the skin probably belonged to a gray, though she'd never seen one herself. Grays were native to Corinth, especially the Gray's Teeth Mountains, and that skin was much larger than any bear she'd ever seen.

This was definitely a room kept for important patrons, like Corinth's king.

Heavy draperies covered the window adjacent to the bed, shielding their room from eyes and drafts, and there was a small doorway in one corner where warm lantern light spilled through.

Imari heard a soft splash.

She smirked, peeled off her coat, and tossed it over the bed as she tiptoed for that small doorway and peered inside.

Jeric's clothes were scattered on the washroom floor, and he sat in a round, wooden tub full of steaming water. His head was tipped back, his long arms draped along the tub's rim, and his eyes were closed.

It reminded her of another time, another place, when he'd asked her to cut his hair. When she'd made sure the water was deep enough, when she'd done her very best not to look.

She allowed herself to look this time, and she drank in the sight of him. Every line, every scar. And her heart beat faster.

"Did you lock the door?" he asked quietly, without opening his eyes.

"Of course I did. What idiot leaves a rented room unlocked?"

His lips curled, and his eyes opened to slits. "One who was given only one key and didn't want to get out of this bath once he got into it."

Imari raised a brow. "Oh? Then what am I supposed to do with myself for the remainder of the evening?"

He looked at her in a way that made her feel flush all over. "I might have a few ideas."

"Hm," Imari replied flatly, then stepped into the washroom and rounded the tub.

His gaze followed her until it could follow her no more, because she'd stopped directly behind him, out of view.

She pulled her shirt up and over her head and tossed it to the floor.

"You're not going to ask about my ideas?" he said, his voice dropping lower.

She slipped off one boot, then the next, and started untying her breeches. "No."

"Why not?" Jeric had gone completely still, his head tipped slightly, listening.

Imari slipped out of her breeches, then moved back around the tub and stepped over the lip, into the hot water with him. There was plenty of room for them both, and the water felt divine. Jeric's gaze slid over her body, devouring her with his eyes. Her cheeks burned and her pulse raced, and she climbed into his lap, tucked her legs on either side of his—straddling him—then reached forward to the nape of his neck and untied the leather strip. His glorious hair fell free, and she let the strip fall to the floor. "Because I'm not really interested in talking to you right now."

Jeric smiled viciously, then pulled her mouth down to his, and Imari forgot all the rest.

·⌒⌒·

UPON A ROOFTOP, a black bird perched. It had watched the ship dock and followed the passengers as they'd walked these streets.

For she had been waiting.

She had watched the Corinthian king walk through the door and later watched the others slip through the back.

The night matured, and still they did not emerge.

The black bird pushed off of the roof with a cry, into the snow and fog, and was gone.

## 19

_N_iá stood at the window, peering out into the dark and snowy night. A few of Felheim's lanterns had been lit, but they did little to illuminate the village obscured by the heavily falling snow.

Niá had never experienced a snowstorm before. She'd never expected it to be beautiful, though she suspected she would not think it so had she not been admiring it from behind a window with a fire burning right beside her.

"Is something wrong?" Jenya asked from where she sat at the small table.

Niá scanned the shadows. "No. I thought I...sensed someone."

It had been what had drawn her to the window in the first place. That pulse of Shah power, that fleeting strain of energy, but when she had gone to look, there had been nothing.

"Could it be Tallyn?" Jenya asked.

Which was what Niá had first suspected, only this had felt... different. Also, Tallyn had been adamant about not using his power, at least until they were settled at Skyhold, which was also why Jenya had been forced to start their fire the old-fashioned way.

"Maybe," Niá replied. She stood there a minute longer, then closed the drapery and joined Jenya at the table.

Their room was comfortable, but the chill would not leave, despite the fire Jenya had started in the hearth. Winter still slipped through the cracks like an unwanted guest, and neither Niá nor Jenya had taken off their heavy coats. Niá was glad to see plenty of woolen blankets upon the two small beds. There was also this table, two chairs, and a washroom down the hall that was available to all patrons. Niá desperately needed a bath, but she wasn't so desperate as to take a public one in Corinth. She imagined Jenya felt similarly.

Niá picked up a roll, tore off a bite, and slipped it into her mouth.

Which was when someone knocked on the door.

Niá and Jenya exchanged a look. Jenya withdrew her scim as she stood and crossed to the door while Niá prepared to throw an enchantment. Jenya gave Niá one last, readying glance, then cracked the door open, but her posture immediately relaxed, and she opened the door wider.

Chez strode in.

Niá felt herself tense.

They hadn't spoken since that moment on *The Lady's* dark steps, and Niá felt that silence. She hated that she felt that silence, and yet it ate at her, little by little each day. That wasn't to say Chez was rude; he wasn't. He just wouldn't talk to her, didn't try, and generally kept his distance.

Niá felt that too.

Chez took quick inventory of their room. His gaze snagged on Niá briefly before settling on Jenya. "Do you need anything?" he asked.

Jenya shook her head then looked to Niá.

Chez looked to Niá too.

"No. Thank you," Niá replied.

Chez nodded once. "I just came to tell you that the Wolf

wants to leave at dawn," he said, then ducked back through the door and started closing it.

"Did they secure the stoliks?" Niá asked suddenly.

Chez stopped and looked back. "They did." His gaze lingered on her a moment, and he closed the door.

Niá realized she was still staring at the door, and she looked away. Right into Jenya's dark eyes.

Jenya raised a brow, then reached forward, picked up the ampoule of Corinthian akavit, filled a chalice, and pushed it at Niá. "Drink."

Niá eyed the chalice. She'd never had akavit before; she didn't enjoy spirits in general, but she picked up the chalice and brought it to her lips. Jenya raised her own with an "*A sieta*"—to the saints—downed the contents, and slammed her empty chalice on the table.

Niá eyed the amber liquid, and then she, too, tipped the chalice back, feeling it burn all the way down.

JERIC'S EYES flew open to dim lantern light, his heart pounding. He'd had the dream again. Of drowning in blood, in screams, as shade poison burned through his bones.

He sighed and dragged a hand over his face.

Imari's hand rested on his chest, and her thumb absently rubbed circles upon his skin. It was a habit she'd formed; she wasn't even aware she was doing it. But she had become his line and his anchor, always drawing him out of the dark despair that night relentlessly threw him into—like now.

He turned his head toward Imari.

She lay curled against his side, one leg entwined with his. Her thumb had ceased moving upon his chest, her breaths came slow and steady, her features relaxed with sleep.

Gods, he didn't deserve her.

*She has need of you. Serve her well*, that voice had said.

But it was Jeric who'd had need of *her*, over and over again. Jeric who needed her *always*.

He reached out and brushed the hair from her face. Her dark lashes fluttered, and she rolled onto her other side with a sigh, taking her hand with her.

Jeric sat up a little, leaned forward, and kissed her bare shoulder, then—very carefully—slid out of bed.

There was still something he needed to do. He hoped he wasn't too late already.

He dressed quickly, not bothering overly with ties, then tucked two daggers into his coat and slipped out the door. The hall was empty and dark but for one lantern at the end. Jeric didn't know the hour, though it had to be late, because most of Otten's occupants were deep in sleep. He used the key to lock his and Imari's door, tucked it into his breeches, then strode down the hall.

Only to stop before the door nearest the stairs.

Even before he opened it, he knew its occupant was gone.

He tried the handle. Unsurprisingly, it turned, and Jeric pushed the door open to a dark room. Light from the hall spilled into that space, just enough so that Jeric could see that the bed was still made, though the bedding had been slightly rumpled.

Stanis had come here, but in the end, he hadn't stayed.

Jeric closed the door and crept down the stairs, pausing at the bottom. Light flickered from the hall at the end of the corridor, and then a man came into view mopping the floor. Jeric ducked back into the stairwell, counted to ten, and glanced back. The man had moved on, and Jeric slipped out the back door.

Gods*damn*it, it was cold.

Jeric rubbed his hands together as he strode through the snow and to the stables, where he found Stanis saddling one of the stoliks Braddok had secured.

Jeric stopped a few paces away, watching Stanis adjust the bit's shank. Stanis finished, rubbed the stolik's nose, and stepped around to the saddle.

"Here to stop me?" Stanis asked, not bothering to look back.

"No, I came to give you this." Jeric took two steps forward and produced the sealed letter.

Stanis looked at the letter, at Jeric, then back to the saddle. "I don't want it."

Jeric regarded Stanis, and then he walked to a stable post and used a dagger to stab the letter to the wood. He dropped a small bag of coin upon the stool.

"I don't want your money, Wolf," Stanis said sharply.

"It's not mine. It's yours. Our contract was through winter. This is what I owe you."

"I'm breaking contract. You don't owe me scat."

"That's your anger talking. Don't be a rutting fool."

Stanis looked at him. His lips parted, but then he closed them and shook his head instead.

"Best of luck to you, Stanis," Jeric continued. "I hope you find whatever the hells you're looking for." Jeric walked on across the courtyard and through the back door.

He didn't see Stanis standing there, staring long after him. He didn't see Stanis struggle as he looked from coin to letter.

He didn't see Stanis lose the battle.

Stanis jerked the dagger from the wood and took the letter with a trembling hand. He knew that stamp. He *hated* that gods-damned stamp.

He used the dagger to break the seal. The paper shook as he unfolded the stiff creases, and then he moved beneath the stable's lantern so that he could read.

*Stanis,*

*No mission was worth more than what I lost with you.*

*I am sorry.*
*For all of it.*

*Pa*

Stanis read it again.

And again.

He sagged back against the stable wall as his teeth clenched and his eyes burned. With a pained growl, he shoved off the wall, crumpled the paper in his hand, and chucked it into the night. He watched it land in snow, watched it sink, and then he climbed onto the stolik, nudged it with his heel, and rode off into the storm.

---

## 20

*W*armth brushed Imari's cheek, and she opened her eyes to find Jeric standing beside the bed, fully dressed and leaning over her. The lantern burned softly in the corner, illuminating him from behind.

Was it morning already?

"Time to go, love," he whispered.

Imari groaned, rolled away from him, and nobly pulled the blanket over her head.

"Now you know how it feels." He squeezed her waist lightly through the blankets. A few seconds later, she heard Jeric rummaging through what she presumed to be their satchels.

She dragged the blanket from her face to see him strap a dagger to his thigh, then two more to his waist. "Are you expecting a fight?"

"I'm always expecting a fight."

Imari grinned, then begrudgingly slid out of the blankets and the bed. The cold air shocked her bare skin, but Jeric was there with her breeches and tunic, which were both dry, thank the Maker. After their...bath, she and Jeric had both washed their salt-crusted clothes and spread them out to dry by the fire.

"Thank you," she said, taking her clothes. She dressed quickly, tugged on her boots and coat, then strode to the window and peeled back the draperies to peer outside.

Winter burned through the windowpanes, and the sun had yet to rise, but thankfully, the snow had stopped falling. A thin fog had settled over Felheim, obscuring the sleepy seaside village, though she could just see *The Lady's* silhouette in the cracks between buildings, floating like a ghost in the clouds.

"Were they able to secure horses?" Imari asked. Her breath fogged the glass.

A beat. "Yes."

Imari glanced back, but Jeric wasn't looking at her. He hoisted one satchel across his chest, adjusting the strap.

"Stanis isn't coming," she said. She'd sensed when Jeric had left, just as she'd sensed his return, and he had come back much heavier. She'd wondered then but had been too tired to ask. Looking at him now, she knew for certain.

Jeric stopped. His nose twitched, and he lifted the other satchel. "He is not."

Imari felt a prick of guilt. Though Stanis's departure wasn't entirely her fault, she marked the beginning of their contention. She was the root of it, invading every moment after, and Survak had simply been the one to set fire to it all. "I'm sorry."

Jeric hoisted the other satchel over his head so that one rested on each side of his waist and their straps crossed his chest. He did not look at her.

"Where will he go?" Imari asked.

"I don't rutting know." His anger snapped—not at her, but at the situation. Still, he caught himself, sighed, and then looked at her. Emotion churned in those dark blues. "I'm sorry."

"You don't owe me an apology for that, but I *will* take one of those satchels..." She gestured at both satchels. She knew which contained the talla (the one resting upon his left hip).

"I'm just carrying them outside," he said, his tone softer. "And then they'll become our stolik's burden."

Imari joined Jeric at the door, but he did not open it. He looked at her, and a crease formed between his brows. "I don't know what we'll find," he said at last.

He meant at Skyhold.

And *this* was the worry Imari had suspected, despite his fervid attempts at hiding it. This vicious, ravenous thing that would not let him alone—and hadn't since he'd first left Skyhold in search of her. Now that he'd lost another good man, that worry cut much deeper.

Imari saw him waver, she saw him doubt, but she did not tell him everything would be all right. She would not say what she could not possibly know, but there was one thing she *did* know for certain.

"Then anchor yourself in what is constant," she said. "Anchor yourself in what's true, and you can weather whatever storms come your way." She grabbed his hand, squeezed it tight. "We are not alone, Jeric. We never have been."

His expression cracked a little, and he raised their entwined hands to his lips. "I will never understand why the good Maker saw fit to give me you." He strummed his thumb over her knuckles, setting song to every string in her heart. His gaze flickered to her lips, and he pulled her in, kissing her mouth so softly. He pulled back much too soon, taking her breath away with him.

"Ready?" he asked.

"No," she said. "I don't ever want to leave."

A sad sort of smile touched his lips. "I know the feeling."

They made their way down a dark and quiet hall. Imari heard the occasional clatter from the kitchen, probably the cook readying for the day. Jeric opened the back door, holding it for Imari, and she stepped outside.

*Wards,* it was cold. The air burned her eyes and nose, especially after the warmth of their room, which she already missed.

She hadn't been this cold since The Wilds—not even aboard *The Lady*—and Imari balled up her hands and tucked them into the pits of her arms while her boots crunched through the courtyard's deep snow. In some places, it reached halfway to her knees.

Braddok and Tallyn were already at the stables, standing alongside five enormous stoliks. She'd seen the Corinthian stoliks before, but they were still impressive to behold, nearly equal in height to an Istraan camel, with long, shaggy manes, thick coats, and muscled legs.

"Good morning, Braddok, Tallyn," Imari said.

Braddok looked over as they approached. "Morning. Was just about to come an' getcha."

Tallyn nodded and resumed securing his things to one of the smaller stoliks.

"The others are on their way," Jeric said, rubbing his hands together and breathing hot air upon them. He'd drawn his fur-lined cowl, and his eyes looked startlingly blue within.

"Stanis?" Braddok asked.

Jeric caught Braddok's gaze and shook his head.

Braddok exhaled a cloud of hot air and dragged a massive paw over his face. Then, "Survak still here?"

"Aye," Jeric said as he strode for one of the larger stoliks—a rich chocolate brown with a cloud of white upon its nose. "But I'll be surprised if he's still here come nightfall."

Braddok and Tallyn were quiet at this.

Imari approached Jeric and the chocolate brown stolik. This stolik was so tall that his—for it was definitely a *he*—mandible rested an easy five inches above her head. He was thoroughly enjoying the nose-rubbing Jeric was giving to him, but once Imari caught up, the stolik turned his head toward her instead, dipped his nose, and nudged her shoulder.

Jeric eyed her sideways, and one edge of his lips curled.

"Beast likes you," Braddok said.

She put a hand on the end of the stolik's nose, right between his nostrils, and he nudged her again. "Beast. Is that your name?"

The horse snorted wisps of hot air and studied her through its long, thick lashes.

"That's what they call you when you're the biggest," Braddok said. Then added, "Or at least that's why all the ladies call me beast...mornin', Jen."

Sure enough, Jenya was striding across the courtyard, though her pacing slowed significantly at being thus addressed by Braddok. Niá was right behind her, both of them buried in wool and fur, and Chez trailed them.

Chez did a quick scan of the courtyard, frowned, then caught Jeric's gaze. Jeric shook his head a fraction, and Chez's features tightened.

"Where's Stanis?" Jenya asked.

"He's not coming," Jeric answered in a tone that did not invite further questions. "There are enough stoliks for all of us, but four will have to double. Imari and I will share him." Jeric gestured at Beast.

"Jen and I can share that one." Braddok gestured to the second-largest stolik, but Jenya promptly trudged through the snow to the stolik nearly as small as Tallyn's and hoisted herself into the prepared saddle.

Chez clucked his tongue. "Denied."

Braddok placed a hand over his heart. "You wound me, Jen."

"Keep it up, *Rasé*, and I'll make it fatal," Jenya replied, to which Braddok only chuckled then strode to a stolik.

Leaving the last for Niá and Chez.

Imari half expected Niá to object. There had been a palpable tension between the two that Imari did not quite understand, but to Imari's surprise, Niá trudged right up to the other large stolik, grabbed hold of the saddle's horn and—with a bit of a strain—pulled herself up. But the saddle was higher than she'd anticipated, and she soon found she could not pull herself up all the

202 | BARBARA KLOSS

way. Chez stepped forward, grabbed her foot, and gave her a boost, which was a bit awkwardly done since Chez could still only use one arm.

Niá scrambled onto the saddle, which had been designed for two to ride tandem, and she scooted to the front.

"It's better for his back if I sit forward," Chez said. "I'm heavier."

Niá scooted to the rear.

Imari caught Jeric's gaze a brief and curious moment, then walked around Beast to mount, and she was just reaching for the horn when Jeric grabbed her waist and lifted. She swung her leg over, scooted to the back, then leaned out of the way for Jeric, who climbed in easily.

Just then, the back door opened, and a middle-aged man stepped through. He was so buried in furs, he looked like a small bear.

"Morning, Your Grace," the man said with a bow of his head. He took in their group at a glance as he trudged toward them, sack in hand. "Thought I heard you."

"Mornin', Ott," Braddok said.

Imari assumed this was the man who owned this place.

"Brought this for you." Ott stopped beside Beast and held up the cloth sack. His gaze flickered briefly to Imari. "It's yesterday's bread, but that's all I've got this early."

Jeric took the sack. He pulled open the drawstring, peered inside, then nodded at Ott. "Thank you."

"'Course." Ott's attention slid back to Imari again. His eyes were curious but not unfriendly.

"Thank you again for your hospitality," Jeric said, tying the sack to his saddle.

Ott looked back to his king. "It is my pleasure, Your Grace."

And Jeric urged Beast on.

"Your Grace," Ott called out.

Jeric stopped their horse and looked over his shoulder.

"Corinth has always needed you. May the gods grant you speed." Ott bowed his head, then went back inside.

·⟨⟩·

"WHAT WAS THAT ABOUT?" Imari asked Jeric once they'd left Felheim and ridden into the Blackwood.

Their road was winding but empty, save for the deep snow that'd buried it during the night. Their stoliks didn't seem to notice; they simply raised their knees when the drifts piled high, maintaining a steady pace as the morning matured. The fog had lifted, though a thick blanket of clouds blocked the sun. They passed no other travelers, though they did spot a jackrabbit bounding through the pines.

"Ottenback has...seen a lot of things," Jeric answered at last.

"That is an awfully vague reply for a man who's spent his entire life obsessing over details."

She sat pillion, so she couldn't see his face, but she could tell by the way his cheek pulled back that he was smiling.

"Let me guess," she continued. "He never liked your brother either."

"Father, actually. He didn't care much for me either. He just liked me *better*."

Imari chuckled and rested her head upon Jeric's broad back, swaying in rhythm with him as their stolik walked. The others rode in line behind them, with Braddok bringing up the rear. Imari sometimes overheard him and Jenya arguing—or, rather, Jenya arguing at him. But right then they were quiet, as though this solemn, snow-covered forest had naturally lulled them all into somber reflection.

"I used to visit Felheim with my mother," Jeric continued quietly. His deep cello rumbled against her ear, and the song within her resonated in response. "She loved the Sound."

"Is that where you got your unrequited love for the sea?"

Jeric chuckled lowly at this. "Well, it was definitely in *her* blood. She was a Stykken."

Imari sat upright. "As in Brom Stykken? The man who rules The Fingers?"

"Brom's her cousin."

Imari's lips parted. "I had no idea."

"It isn't widely remembered," Jeric continued quietly. "At the time, the Stykkens wanted an alliance with Corinth."

"Because of the mines?" The mines had been the largest point of contention between Corinth and The Fingers for as long as Imari could remember.

Jeric's head turned so that she could see his profile. He looked pleased. "You know their history?"

"Just what I've picked up over the years. I know those mines were originally shared between your two Provinces, but your father assumed ownership of them after the war." Imari looked to Jeric for confirmation.

Jeric tipped his head. "*Assumed* is a nice way of putting it."

"But I never knew how your mother factored in," Imari said, and now the depth of animosity between nations made more sense. "So why isn't Stykken going to war for it now?" Because the sole motive that would have stayed Stykken's vengeful hand—Jeric's mother—no longer lived.

Jeric appraised the wall of solid mountain rock to their left. "I don't think he can. Prolonged poverty has stolen much of the strength and gristle that once made their people great. They're mostly simple seafarers now."

"*Simple seafarers.*" Imari grunted. "Have you actually met one?"

Jeric turned his head back to look at her out of the corner of his eye. "More than you have, I'm sure."

"Five crowns says you haven't."

Jeric's features flattened. "You've been spending too much time with Brad."

A smile danced on her lips.

"And when would *you* have spent *any* time in their company?"

"At least twice every year, when sowing season starts and at last harvest, from the time I was nine until quite recently, when they'd sail to Riverwood to barter herbs from Tolya. How else did you figure I'd learned about your mines?"

Jeric looked sharply back at her, his eyes narrowed irritably. Mostly at himself, because he should have known better. He should have remembered.

Imari leaned closer to him. "And sometimes, when they were very desperate, they'd travel all the way into Skanden to seek her out. So call them what you will, but they have a loyalty to their kin and king that would put a saredd to shame. You should be prepared."

Jeric sat quiet, studying her in his periphery.

"So. About my five crowns..."

Jeric flashed his teeth. "I've got a better idea."

"Oh...?"

His eyes danced with mischief, and he leaned back a little. "How about I show you tonight?"

Imari smiled, though her cheeks suddenly felt flush. "Your people have been without their king for three months. I don't believe you'll have a moment to spare."

His expression turned suddenly wolfish, making her heart pound. "For you, I will spare every moment."

Imari held his gaze, her breath forgotten as he reached back and squeezed her thigh, and then he faced forward.

They fell into a companionable silence, though it took Imari a moment to regain her composure, because her thoughts had happily run away with various ideas of Jeric showing her what he'd meant.

"Did Otten know your mother?" Imari asked after some time.

"Yes." He paused. "Back then, Felheim used to see a lot of travelers from all over the world, especially from The Fingers. After Saád, they stopped coming."

"That's not good for business."

"No, it is not," Jeric said in a way that led Imari to believe that Otten's was just one of many Corinthian livelihoods that King Tommad had strained.

Again, she considered the strenuous road ahead of them—the one that had nothing to do with Azir but everything to do with Jeric's own people. She hoped her presence did not make that road more difficult for him.

"Stykken will work with you," Imari said.

Jeric laughed darkly.

"I'm serious. Return to him what is owed, and you'll find yourself a fierce ally."

"Try telling that to Stovich."

"Certainly Stovich will cooperate, given the circumstances."

"Mm."

"You don't think he will?"

Jeric sat quiet. A clump of snow fell from a high tree branch to their right. "He might. But it'll come with a price I'm not willing to pay."

"Such as?"

"*Such as* his daughter, the Lady Kyrinne," Braddok cut in, drawing his stolik alongside them.

Jeric's attention landed on Braddok, and there it stormed.

Braddok rolled his eyes. "She was gonna hear about it one way or another. Better to hear it now."

Imari got a sinking feeling as she looked between the two men who were currently in the throes of a silent standoff. And suddenly Imari wondered something she hadn't wondered before but absolutely should have wondered. He had been a prince, after all.

"Are you betrothed, Jeric?" Imari asked.

Jeric's gaze remained fixed on Braddok. "Unofficially," he said at last, turning that one word into five.

Imari felt a stab of jealousy she knew she should not feel. Betrothals—or whatever unofficial agreement existed between Jeric and this Lady Kyrinne—were built on station, not feeling, just as her papa had threatened her with a betrothal to Fez. And yet...

"Stovich's probably there now," Braddok continued, defending himself. "You've been gone almost three months. There's no way that greedy bastard left your chair alone for that long; I don't care what Otten says."

Jeric stared at the road ahead. His entire demeanor had changed, and Imari couldn't help but wonder: How well-acquainted was Jeric with this Lady Kyrinne?

"Well, if Stovich *is* there, that makes your task significantly easier," Imari said instead.

"What task?" Braddok asked.

"Giving Stykken back his skal mines," Imari replied.

Braddok looked from Imari to Jeric, then tipped back his head and laughed.

Imari felt the strange and sudden urge to punch him. She found herself looking back to Jenya, who gave her a long, commiserative glance.

It was then that the Blackwood's wall of pines opened to the Valley of Kings, and for the first time in months, Imari laid eyes upon the place that had both imprisoned her and set her free: Skyhold.

The enormous skal wall encircled the city, while the great fortress towered over all from its precarious perch high upon the mountainside.

Jeric stopped their horse, waiting as the others drew along-side them, and all fell to quiet reverence as they gazed ahead.

"She looks all right," Braddok said, his eyes fixed on the wall. "Just buried in snow."

"Try this." Imari held out the spyglass that she'd dug out of her satchel.

Jeric looked at it, then her, and laughed.

"Where the hells did ya get that?" Braddok asked, dumb-founded.

"Well, do you want it or not?" Imari asked.

Jeric took it.

"Hey, godsdamnit...she offered that to *me*," Braddok said as Jeric put the glass to his eye.

"And what's yours is mine," Jeric said. "I am your king."

"You're a godsdamned piece of—"

"Ah ah! Remember what I said...?" Chez warned.

"Yeah. I *am* behind his rutting back, the cocky sonofabitch."

Jenya pinched the bridge of her nose and closed her eyes.

Jeric pulled the glass away, then held it out to Braddok. "Here, peasant."

Braddok snorted, but curiosity took him, and he put the glass to his eye. He immediately pulled it away to admire its assem-blage. "Five hells, Surina? You take this from the captain?"

Imari smiled, all innocence.

Braddok laughed, looked approvingly at Jeric, then raised the glass back to his eye.

"There are eleven guards over the gate and one Stryker," Jeric said while Braddok peered through the glass.

Braddok frowned. "I only see eight...oh. There's the little squatters." He paused. "Where's the Stryker?"

"North tower. By the stair."

"I don't...ah."

"Do you usually keep so many on watch?" Tallyn asked, his one eye fixed on the wall.

"After what happened in Trier, I'm sure Commander Anaton isn't taking chances."

"I think that Stryker sees us," Braddok said, holding out the glass.

Jeric took it and peered through but pulled it away two seconds later. "Let's hope they recognize us before they shoot."

Niá paled. Jenya's eyes narrowed on the wall, her hand on her scim.

"He's kidding," Braddok said. "Mostly."

Jenya turned her narrowed eyes on Braddok, who winked.

Jeric leaned back, reached around Imari, and slipped the spyglass into the satchel alongside her talla. "Hold on tight," he whispered to her, then gripped the reins and snapped them tight, and their stolik took off at a gallop.

Imari barely grabbed on to Jeric in time.

They thundered across the open lawn, and the others filed in behind. Imari fixed her attention to the top of that wall. She could not make out any guards from this distance, but she prayed they would know their king.

So far, their arrows did not fly.

It could also be because they were not yet in range.

And that wall loomed nearer.

Her gaze slid to the place the crucifixes had stood: Tommad's macabre garden of dying Sol Velorians, where their flesh had fed the crows and their blood had watered the ground. The garden was gone now. Not even the wooden crucifixes remained. Jeric had cut them all down, and the newly fallen snow had buried the ugly stain of their unwilling sacrifices.

They were halfway across the lawn when she finally spotted the guards. She counted only seven, but then a few more appeared, descending the steps of the towers framing the gate, which was also when she noticed the scaffolding before the unfinished statues of Corinthian gods.

Sol Velorian laborers had been tasked to build them, but there was no sign of those laborers now, because Jeric had set them free and infuriated his jarls in the process. Now, the scaffolding stood like the bones of another age, preserved for all to study and judge.

Two dozen guards now stood at the wall, and half held cross-bows aimed straight at them.

Braddok and Jeric exchanged a long look.

They were two hundred yards away and eating up the ground fast. Still, the guards did not lower their bows. Imari slipped her hand into the satchel with the talla, and the moment her fingers grazed the leather, her power stirred.

One hundred yards.

The guards drew back their bowstrings, and Imari gripped the talla tightly. She was about to take to song when an unarmed guard with cropped hair and a deep Corinthian-blue coat suddenly raised a fist. "*At ease!*" he yelled to his men. "*At ease!*"

The archers lowered their bows and relaxed their bowstrings, and Jeric's posture practically sighed in her arms.

The man upon the wall yelled more commands that Imari could not decipher, but the ramparts came alive with guards scurrying about, the portcullis gears groaned to life, and the gate's large metal grate began to rise.

Jeric tore right through the open gate, through the short tunnel of black skal, and into the city proper, where many guards —and some citizens—gathered.

Jeric drew their stolik to an abrupt halt; he didn't have a choice. The crowd blocked their way forward, and that crowd was expanding fast, full of whispers and murmurs, all straining to see the source of disruption. For many did not recognize their king at first glance, with his facial hair filled in and his coat of The Fingers' design, but the guards nearest quickly caught on and dropped to their knees, swords flat upon them, followed by murmurs of *Your Grace* and *King Jeric*. Their deference rippled through the crowd until all whispers ceased and every knee and head had bowed.

Imari breathed in deep and exchanged a relieved glance with Jenya, who had positioned her stolik nearer.

"Where is your commander?" Jeric asked, scanning the crowd, the wall, and looking unimpressed by it all.

"I am here, Your Grace," boomed a man's voice—the man who'd shouted orders from the wall—and a figure pushed through the crowd. He barked commands at his guards, who promptly set to work, making a perimeter for their king while yelling at the crowd to back away.

"My king." The commander bowed deeply before Jeric. "I am relieved to see you've returned. When I learned what befell Trier, I feared the worst."

Jeric gazed down upon his commander. "Rise, my good man. Thank you for keeping Skyhold secure in my absence."

The commander stood and appraised their group, taking particular interest in their non-Corinthian members.

Especially Imari.

She had never met the commander herself, but she knew of him, and what she'd heard certainly befitted the man standing before her. No seam was out of place, no buckle out of line. Even his thick brows held together in rigid form.

Commander Anaton.

"All is well?" Jeric asked.

"Yes, Your Grace. Corinth is very well now."

# 21

---

*W*ord of Jeric's return traveled fast, and throughout the city, people scrambled to get a glimpse, to see with their own eyes the proof of those words they didn't dare believe. Many cheered, Corinthian banners waved, and all the while Anaton's guards fought to clear Jeric's way forward.

For Imari, hope burned bright.

Jeric's jarls might fight him at every turn, but to the people of Corinth, Jeric was blood; he was life. He signified Corinth restored to her best self, and Imari hoped this display gave Jeric hope too. And as they trotted down Corinth's cramped streets, beneath her cantilevered facades and crowded buildings, Imari remembered the last time she'd passed by them—with Ricón, heading home to Trier for the first time in ten years.

She felt a prick of sadness for the life that had been cut short before it had even begun. For her papa, for Taran, for Saza, and for her brothers. Now that she was safely behind Skyhold's protective wall, perhaps Tallyn could try to find Ricón.

Perhaps Tallyn could tell her if Kai was still alive.

These thoughts brooded like a cloud over their bright arrival, following Imari across the high bridge that stretched like a wide tongue over a deep canyon of rock and tree, giving entry into Skyhold's great fortress.

The bridge had been cleared of snow, or rather was in the process of being cleared. Guards and servants startled out of the way as Jeric's stolik clomped across those wide planks of Blackwood pine, past more guards, and right into the fortress's inner courtyard, where even more guards awaited them.

Jeric dismounted before their stolik had arrived at a complete stop.

It was then a few of the guards realized who stood in their presence, and three rushed forward to aid their king. The one in front was trimmed and middle-aged and nearly as tall as Jeric. He also looked to be of great import; Corinth's colors decorated his apparel and Corinth's pride shone upon his face, and Imari noticed a wide band on the middle finger of his right hand, set with Corinth's crest.

"Your Grace," said the man in an equally trimmed and important voice. "I barely recognized you."

"Hersir, am I ever glad to see you," Jeric said, clasping the man on the back.

Ah, so this was Hersir, overseer of Corinth's Strykers: the group tasked by the Corinthian gods to uphold Corinth's throne. The same group Jeric had been relying upon to secure Skyhold in his absence. It was also the group Jeric had joined but rejected soon after, promptly returning the Stryker ring given to him. A ring that probably resembled the one currently on Hersir's middle finger.

"As am I," Hersir replied, and then added more quietly, "I was beginning to worry, Your Grace."

"Is everything...?"

Hersir bowed his head. "As you left her."

Imari did not know if this was good news or not, but Jeric's posture eased.

Hersir exchanged a few quick greetings with Jeric's men, and then his attention settled on Imari. Jeric angled himself to fold Imari into the conversation and placed a hand on her back as he did so. The gesture was subtle, but Hersir noticed. He did not look bothered, but he also did not look pleased.

"I don't believe you two have met," Jeric said. "Hersir, this is Surina Imari Masai of Istraa."

Hersir bowed his head. "It is a pleasure."

Imari didn't detect any falsity, though his tone was not as easy as it'd been a moment ago. "I've heard much about you."

Hersir raised his head and his brow. "Good things, I hope."

Imari graced him with a smile. "The very best, and it seems you deserve it for keeping Corinth secured in his absence."

An emotion flickered across Hersir's face that Imari could not pin.

"Where's Dom?" Jeric asked, searching the courtyard.

"I believe he just rode off with an ornery foal," Hersir said, to which Jeric chuckled. Hersir appraised their stoliks. "These are fine breeds, Your Grace."

"They're Mattai's," Jeric answered.

"I didn't realize he was still breeding. Does he have more? A few of my men could use fine stoliks like these."

"You may have two of these after I pay for them."

A slight grin touched Hersir's firm mouth. "Thank you, Your Grace. My men will appreciate it." Hersir turned to the two guards who waited a few paces behind him. "Take His Majesty's stoliks to the stables, and make sure they're cared for."

The guards didn't hesitate. Hersir's attention returned to Jeric, and he gestured to the double doors in back. "After you, Your Grace."

Jeric grabbed their satchels from the saddle and led them all through the doors and into the fortress's great hall.

Imari's body clenched with old fear from the first time she'd set foot in this cavernous space, when she'd followed Jeric through that door *right there*, situated between two blazing hearths, on her way to meet Prince Hagan.

When Hagan had told Jeric who she really was.

She could still see Jeric's face when he'd put the pieces together.

The hall wasn't empty now, either. Men and women of considerable wealth—judging by their finery—stood about chatting near the enormous hearths, and one servant tended the fires while another offered platters of food to the guests, but all of it ceased the moment Jeric strode through that door with Hersir. Every word, every motion, as though the entire room had been enchanted into complete stillness. It was the long breath between symphonic movements, the semibreve rest between musical themes, filled with silent anticipation for what part came next.

Three heartbeats later, one man stepped forward from the rest. Imari took him to be in his late fifties, and he bore his age with pride, like a war medallion upon his breast. His hair was either straw or pale silver, Imari couldn't really tell in the fire light, and it'd been tied neatly back in a knot at the nape of his neck, not a strand out of place. He wore a fitted, Corinthian-blue coat trimmed in silver, polished black boots, and an authority that pushed against Jeric's own.

She couldn't decide if the man was happy to see Jeric or not.

"Your Grace," the man said with surprise, and his voice echoed in the silence.

"Stovich," Jeric snapped through his teeth. There was no affection in his voice, and he glanced sidelong at Hersir. "I did not realize you were here."

Stovich's features tightened subtly, despite the smile he put on, and then he dropped to one knee and bowed. Quick as the rolling tide, everyone else in the room dropped to their knees in subjection to their king.

Braddok and Chez appraised them all without humor, Tallyn

and Jenya and Niá gazed curiously on, and Jeric's attention remained fixed upon the man he'd called Stovich.

There was one particular woman kneeling behind Jarl Stovich who lifted her face to look upon her king. There her gaze lingered, as if silently pleading for Jeric to look in her direction, but he did not acknowledge her.

The woman was beautiful, with long, honey-colored hair, exquisite features, and a figure shaped to an envy. Imari wondered if she was Lady Kyrinne, and her stomach squeezed.

"Excuse us," Jeric said to the room, his gaze still fixed on his most contentious jarl.

A beat.

The women gathered long skirts as all rose to their feet.

"Not you," Jeric said to Stovich.

Stovich's lips thinned, but he remained, staring at his king while the rest trickled out through the side doors.

Hersir also started to leave, but Jeric glanced at him and said, "Wait."

Hersir bowed his head and waited.

The woman with the honey-colored hair was the last to go, taking her time as she crossed the great hall. She paused at the door and glanced between Stovich and her king. Her pale gaze skimmed their ragged group then settled upon Imari.

Those beautiful features sharpened just slightly, and then she was gone, closing the door behind her.

Jeric turned to Hersir. "See that our guests have something to eat and rooms prepared for their stay. The skal suite should suffice for the surina."

Hersir hesitated, glancing from Jeric to Stovich, as if he were caught between two blades.

"Is there an issue?" Jeric asked sharply.

"The skal suite is occupied, Your Grace," Stovich said. He was still on his knee, upon the hard tile floor, and it appeared to be causing him some pain. Jeric either didn't notice or didn't care. Imari presumed it the latter.

Jeric's eyes narrowed. "Occupied."

"By my daughter and myself."

Jeric stared at Stovich.

Stovich shifted, and Imari could empathize. She knew what it was like to be the object of that scrutiny. "We will relocate ourselves immediately—"

"Give the surina my chambers," Jeric cut him off. He looked to Hersir, who blinked back in surprise, while Stovich flapped his mouth shut like a fish. "I will stay in the west wing."

"Yes, Your Grace," Hersir replied. He glanced at the others, at Imari. "Follow me."

Niá, Jenya, and Tallyn followed after, and Imari started to go, but Jeric grabbed her hand.

She was very aware of Stovich and Hersir watching them.

"I'll find you as soon as I can," Jeric whispered, then leaned forward and kissed her cheek. He pulled back and met her gaze, imparting something Imari could not quite read, and then he released her hand.

Imari left, feeling suddenly as though everything were about to change.

## 22

---

"**W**ant us to stay?" Braddok asked quietly.

Jeric considered, his gaze fixed on the squirming, old jarl. "Guard the doors."

Braddok nodded, then he and Chez exchanged a glance and took positions at the two major entry points.

Jeric strode straight to one of the high-backed leather chairs, situated before his favorite hearth—the one with a gray's head mounted above—and sat down. He stretched his legs before the fire and draped his arms along the rests. He'd prefer to lean back, but this was the only godsdamned chair in this godsdamned hall that actually fit him.

Aside from the throne.

But he wasn't in the mood to sit on a rutting slab of metal.

A log popped; the silence stretched. In his periphery, Stovich —who was still kneeling—turned his head to look over at Jeric.

"Have I caused offense, my king?"

"Have you?"

Quiet. "If I have, it was never my intention. I came only to—"

"Spare me your rutting platitudes, Stovich. Have a seat." Jeric gestured at the chair opposite.

A beat. Stovich stood, bracing his lower back as he did, Jeric noticed, then made his way to the chair and sat down. The wood creaked beneath his weight, and the old leather crackled.

Jeric eyed Stovich, who looked to the fire where it was safe.

"Why are you here?" Jeric asked without preamble, for Stovich liked a dance of words, and Jeric would not give him one.

Stovich considered him. Jeric had always been an enigma to Stovich; he knew that much. Never persuaded by gold, never falling for subterfuge, never impressed by power. And Jeric had always found that men who were persuaded by such things never quite knew what to do with him.

Stovich regarded his king, one finger ticking upon the armrest. "I am here because you were not, it is winter, and we are hungry."

"Fair," Jeric said. It had always been Stovich's loudest complaint: Stovichshold might oversee the bulk of Corinth's skal mines, but people could not eat skal, and Jeric's father had taken too much profit from Stovichshold's citizens for them to purchase much else.

But Stovich had not expected Jeric to agree, and not even years of practiced self-control could hide his surprise. His eyes narrowed on Jeric, as though he didn't trust Jeric's answer.

"Why else?" Jeric asked.

Stovich's expression was careful. "I am not certain I understand your meaning, my king."

"Am I?"

Stovich blinked. "Are you what?"

"Your king?"

"Of course."

"So when I tell you that I will need every single fighting man that Stovichshold can spare, you will send them to Skyhold without question?"

Stovich's finger stopped tapping. "So Azir really has returned."

Jeric regarded his jarl a long moment and tipped his head.

Stovich searched Jeric, his own features inscrutable. "And you would take us to war against him."

"No. Azir has declared the war. I am simply trying to defend us."

"Give him the Istraan bastard, and we won't have to defend any—"

Jeric drew a dagger and held the tip at Stovich's throat.

Stovich stilled, his lips thinned, and the fire reflected in his eyes. "You would risk all of Corinth for *her*?"

At this, Jeric leaned close. So close, he could see his own silhouette reflected in Stovich's eyes, with only Jeric's dagger between them.

"I would tear this world apart for her," Jeric said through his teeth. "But this is not about Surina Imari. This is about Corinth, which Azir will take, with or without her."

Stovich watched Jeric, unmoving, and—finally—Jeric lowered his blade, but he did not put it away. He held on to it, tracing the edge lightly with his thumb.

"I am not fool enough to presume fealty by killing a master and forcing my authority over his people," Jeric continued, eyeing the length of his blade. It was a fine dagger. "Your people are loyal to you. They listen to you, they always have, and men who believe in a cause are infinitely better fighters than any sellsword. So tell me, Stovich: What are your terms?"

Stovich regarded Jeric for a long moment as the fire crackled and popped.

"You know what I want," Stovich said lowly.

"Pretend I don't."

Stovich leaned forward and rested his elbows on his knees. "Appoint me head of your council. I want complete oversight of all Corinth's mines and forty percent of profits."

Jeric nearly laughed. "Ten."

"Thirty."

"Eleven."

Stovich's eyes flashed. "Twenty, and you will not break your betrothal to Kyrinne."

Jeric had been waiting for it; he'd been trying to decide how best to handle this matter ever since leaving Ziyan. No, even before. From the moment he'd first landed in Trier, after nearly two months apart from Imari, when she'd jumped into his arms at the sight of him.

He had known then.

"Twenty-five, and the *agreement* is void." Jeric knew full well he was playing a game of semantics. Stovich thought so too, but before he could object—and the words were already crowding in his mouth—Jeric added, "And I will also refrain from having you publicly stoned for treason."

Stovich stiffened. "On what grounds, Your Grace? For staying at Skyhold in your absence?"

"For stealing Corinth's ore and timber and selling both to Brevera for gold."

Stovich's own daughter had been the one to let this delicious morsel slip. Of course, Kyrinne hadn't known the full extent of her father's business dealings, and Stovich had easily gotten away with it, blaming his losses on the recent Sol Velorian raids—he'd had plenty of those. But Jeric had never trusted Stovich, and he'd meant to investigate but had been swiftly drawn away by multiple Sol Velorian attacks, followed by his father's illness, and...here they were, nearly a year later.

Anger and offense made Stovich rigid, though his face paled. "You have no proof."

Jeric eyed him.

Stovich shifted beneath his stare. "Who told you?"

And herein lay the piece Jeric needed to navigate with care. Though he did not desire a future with Kyrinne, he didn't mean to cause her harm.

Jeric flicked the tip of his dagger as he considered Stovich.

Letting him feel the edge of Jeric's judgement. "Suffice it to say that I know. So do we have ourselves a deal or not?"

Stovich's neck blotched crimson, and a thick vein pulsed in his temple. His lips clamped furiously shut, trapping a hundred fierce words behind them, but at last he sagged back in his chair in a posture of defeat. A single forelock slipped from its knot and fell forward over his face. He pushed it back, and his gaze cut to his king. "You will drag Corinth into civil war. The people will never accept her."

It was his final attempt. The flailing hand of a drowning man in a raging sea.

Jeric smiled wolfishly. "They will accept her if you do, my dear Stovich, and that is the *only* reason I am not dragging your traitorous ass into the square. Do we understand each other?"

Stovich gazed upon his king long and hard, then looked to the fire as he growled, bitterly, "Aye."

## 23

*P*er Jeric's instructions, Hersir escorted Imari, Jenya, Niá, and Tallyn to the kitchen. The five of them earned many long looks from both guard and guest as they walked the fortress's winding halls. Imari recognized two guards who had been there the night the legion—through Astrid—had attempted to take Skyhold. Those two guards also recognized Imari, casting cautious but not unfriendly nods of greeting her way. However, most of the glances were not kind, though with Jeric's Lead Stryker as their guide, none dared interfere.

They eventually made their way to the kitchen, which was a beautiful disaster of flour and chopped vegetables. It seemed that news of Jeric's arrival had reached the head cook, then struck this kitchen like a hornet's nest, and everyone scrambled to fashion a celebratory feast. Imari was taking her seat at a small table in the corner when a man carried in a fresh slab of raw meat and slammed it upon the wooden counter. The cook bent over it, examined the cuts, and then exchanged some quick and harsh words with the butcher.

"One moment," Hersir said, then approached the cook.

Both cook and butcher stopped arguing as Hersir quietly

addressed them. The cook suddenly noticed Imari and the others, and her eyes narrowed.

"It'll be a moment more," Hersir said when he returned. "A few of Mika's cooks have taken ill, so she's short of help today."

Imari wondered if this illness was something she could ease. "Where are they?"

Hersir frowned, not understanding her intent.

"The ones who are ill."

"You will have to ask Mika," Hersir said, then inclined his head. "If you'll excuse me, I need to have your chambers prepared."

"Of course," Imari answered, and as Hersir took his leave, Imari made her way to the cook—Mika. The butcher had left, and Mika fumed over the slab of meat. Sensing Imari, she glanced up. Her features tightened, and she immediately glanced back down again.

"I'm busy," Mika said curtly. She picked up a large mallet and begun slamming her frustration upon the bloody slab of muscle.

"Where are your ill?" Imari asked in Corinthian.

Mika did not respond. She did not appear to hear Imari through her own anger.

"Hersir mentioned a few of your cooks have fallen ill," Imari continued. "I would like to help, if I may."

Mika stopped, bloodied mallet in hand, and stared at her. The picture was marginally terrifying.

"I studied with Gamla Khan," Imari explained, and it wasn't a lie. She'd spent far more time beneath Tolya's tutelage, but Gamla's was a name everyone recognized. "He is my uncle."

Mika's gaze slid over Imari, but she didn't reply.

Imari waited a breath, then said, "My offer stands. Should you change your mind." She started to turn.

"What was your name again?"

Imari looked back. "Imari. Imari Masai."

Mika looked long at her, and then the ice in her expression

cracked. She wiped bloodied hands upon her flour-dusted apron and said, "Follow me."

Imari held up a hand to Jenya and the others while mouthing, "I'll be right back," then followed Mika through a door in back. The door led to a narrow stair and directly into the servant quarters. It was a dark space that smelled of burning oil and cedar, and they hadn't taken two steps before Imari heard coughing farther down the hall.

It was deep, and it was wet.

"Where do you keep your medicinal herbs?" Imari asked Mika.

"We don't have a special place for them," Mika said. "They're just with the regular herbs."

Which meant they didn't really have medicinal plants, and Imari was silently sifting through all of her options with basic vegetation when Mika reached a door and opened it.

The room was small and dark, with only one tiny candle to give it light. Imari thought first to open a window, but there was none. A young woman lay upon a small cot, her back to the door, and her body racked with cough. The woman wasn't in terrible shape, but she would be soon if this wasn't treated. These sorts of coughs rooted deep and strangled like nymroot.

Mika held the door open as Imari stepped into the room. The space didn't smell foul. Stuffy, but not like illness. She stopped beside the bed, leaned over, and pressed her cheek to the woman's forehead. The woman did not stir at Imari's touch, and her skin was fire-hot.

"How long has she been like this?" Imari asked, drawing upright.

"She took ill yesterday," Mika replied.

Imari pressed her lips together, considering. "Show me where you keep your produce, and I need to get a kettle going."

Within the half hour, Imari had made enough slightly modified medicinal tea for Mika's two ill and helped them drink it down. She sang a soft melody to each—too soft to draw questions, but not so soft that her notes could not find purchase and lend strength to those two weary souls. Imari left strict instructions for Mika, who immediately gave another servant the task of following those, and by the time Imari returned to the table, the others had finished their bowls of stew. Imari's sat untouched and no longer steaming.

"I can get you somethin' fresh," Mika said, much more gently this time, and reached for Imari's bowl.

"No, no, it's fine." Imari put a hand over her bowl. "Thank you."

Mika looked at her a moment, glanced about their table, and then ducked her gaze as she murmured, "Thank you, miss," before returning to her counter.

Niá, Jenya, and Tallyn all stared at Imari with a question.

"They'll be all right," Imari whispered.

Niá raised a brow, her gaze silently asking, *Did you use Shah?*

She wouldn't ask aloud. Not here. Not with so many ears. Imari pinched a little space of air with her thumb and forefinger, winked at Niá—who grinned—then brought the bowl to her lips.

After they'd finished, a slight, adolescent man named Farvyn showed them to their chambers.

"Does your former Head Inquisitor's suite still exist?" Tallyn asked after Farvyn showed him to his particular door.

"I believe so."

"If it's all right with you, I would like to have a look."

Imari hadn't even considered Rasmin's old offices and what intelligence they might have to offer them concerning Azir and his Mo'Ruk. "May I come with you?" she asked Tallyn.

"Of course," Tallyn replied, and they all followed Farvyn back through the halls, which turned out to be quite a walk. Rasmin's offices were on the opposite end of the sprawling fortress, which required passing back through the great hall.

Jeric was no longer there, however, and the guests had

returned—more than before—but their chatter turned to whispers, and one broke away and started for them.

The woman with honey-colored hair whom Imari had noticed earlier.

"Farvyn," the woman drawled sweetly. She extended her hand to the young man, though her blue eyes were fixed entirely upon Imari. "Who have we here?"

Farvyn took her fingertips and brought them awkwardly to his lips, as if this woman's mere bearing set him off balance.

"Surina Imari Masai of Istraa," Imari said before Farvyn could form the words.

Something shifted in the woman's gaze, though her features remained neutral. She smiled, but there was nothing sweet in it. "Lady Kyrinne Brion of Stovichshold."

Just as Imari had suspected.

"You must have had quite the journey here this time of year," Lady Kyrinne continued. Her gaze flitted over the others. "I have heard the most unfortunate rumor, and I pray it isn't true. Tell me, has Trier truly been taken?"

Imari considered Jeric's betrothed. It was like standing before a desert viper, with its cold eyes and forked tongue that constantly flicked outward to test the air for the vulnerabilities of its victim.

There were two choices when dealing with vipers: walk away or crush the head. Imari felt the sudden and inexplicable urge to do the latter.

"Yes, we have had quite the journey," Imari replied instead. "And we are all very tired, so if you will excuse me..."

Lady Kyrinne dipped her head but not her gaze. "Of course, Surina Imari," she said, all politeness and pleasantries, though Imari did not miss the fire deep within her eyes. "I welcome you and yours to Skyhold."

·⌒⌒·

IMARI CURLED in a chair by the fire and opened the little book of Moltoné's teachings. She'd found it in Rasmin's old offices, tucked away amidst a pile of ancient texts. Of course, it hadn't been out on display. She'd been rummaging through the stack—both Corinthian and Sol Velorian—flipping through pages, when she'd come across a thick mudbrick of a book that wasn't a book at all but an empty shell. Within, Rasmin had stashed this little book that Imari had never seen but Taran had mentioned aplenty. They were the teachings of a certain Liagé High Sceptor who had written much about Shah, specifically with regards to *sulaziérs*.

Imari had initially mistaken the book for Il Tonte—the Liagé verses—because of the tree embedded upon the face, but when she'd opened that soft leather cover, the text was entirely foreign to her. Further investigation brought her to a name: Moltoné.

Tallyn had stepped over then and said, "Ah. Moltoné's teachings. I haven't seen one of those in a very long time."

So Imari had taken the little tome in hopes of more deeply understanding her power, and how and why it had negatively affected all of the *sulaziérs* before her.

Like Zussa, and like Fyri.

Or why that talla would not let her alone.

She'd stashed the little talla in Jeric's wardrobe, behind a row of crisp tunics and rich wool that all smelled deliciously like him, and then she'd changed into one of those cloaks, wrapped herself in it, and curled up by the fire Jenya had started for her. Jenya herself had gone to stay in the little antechamber, leaving Imari alone to read.

Probably the most fascinating piece of her discovery wasn't the words at all but the man who had kept this hidden tome:

Rasmin. He had underlined so much of it, and his notes filled the margins. Thoughts and suspicions and interpretations that he had not wanted to forget.

She hadn't read far when she realized that this was the book that had led him to her.

*"Of all classes of the Shah, there is none equal to the Sulaziér. While all others act upon the physical world, the Sulaziér acts upon the spiritual. It is said to be the voice of Asorai himself, for it holds power over the living and the dead, and Asorai, in His infinite wisdom, will not give each generation more than one."*

She had heard that before, from Rasmin's own lips. She read on. About the first *sulaziér*, Asorai's first in command.

Zussa.

*"But such power corrupted Zussa. She saw herself a god and rebelled, leading others in that cause against Asorai. Still, she calls to her successors in hopes of raising them in defiance of Asorai's will, and each must face the temptation suffered by the very first—the Great Deceiver.*

*"And though the binding of the Great Deceiver overwhelmed the Four Divines, their power rained back to our soil—untouched. From this, we received the tree of wisdom, the tree of life. A gift from Asorai himself so that we would still know the perfect way he intended and find comfort in his promise to deliver us from the evil one.*

*Zussa's return has been Seen. We do not know the day or the hour, but she will walk upon this land once again to break the good Word that Asorai, in his perfect wisdom, established for us all. The people will languish and the land will cry out in tears of blood, and yet Asorai has again promised deliverance. His first shall be the last, in order to rewrite the first Word so that all may live."*

Imari read the passage again and again, piecing together what she knew of Rasmin, and what he had said to her. Rasmin had clearly taken this passage to heart; it'd been underlined with such firm pressure that grooves scarred the page, and he'd scrawled notes all around the text. He'd deduced that "first" referred to *sulaziér*, meaning a *sulaziér* had started and a *sulaziér* would finish.

Rasmin had not, however, answered the question of "rewrite the first Word so that all may live."

Imari wondered how many Liagé he'd caught and tortured to try to understand its meaning.

Regardless, his highlights and notes settled one thing: He had not sought her out because of anything special that Imari had done. He'd simply Seen the signs, gleaned them from those he'd tortured, and anticipated Zussa's arrival was near.

Imari just happened to be the present *sulaziér*.

She glanced over at the wardrobe where she'd stuffed Fyri's talla, where its song did not—would not—stop singing. She set Moltoné's teachings down upon the table, stood, and made her way to the wardrobe.

That song grew louder, bolder, as if it knew she was near, that she was coming. She took a breath, opened the door, reached inside, and retrieved the talla.

The bells fell quiet. Calm. Like a babe in her mother's arms.

Imari turned the leather strip over, tracing those glyphs and etchings with her gaze. "What happened to you?" she whispered to the woman who was no longer there. The woman who had sold her soul to Azir and torn a land apart with her power.

And yet...

Something nagged at Imari. A fact that didn't quite make sense: the hate in Fyri's eyes when Imari had mentioned Azir, but Azir had not spoken Fyri's name either. What had happened between them? What had made two lovers despise one another, and...

Why had Fyri tried to stop Imari?

Clearly, Fyri had known Zussa was tied to the Divine Tree, and if her original aim had been to free Zussa for Azir, then wouldn't she have aimed to *help* Imari?

Unless...

Unless Fyri had turned on Azir.

*"You do not know what you are doing,"* Fyri had said. *"I can hold off the tyrcorat to give you time, but you must promise you'll leave and never come back to this place."*

*"If I go, the man I love will die,"* Imari had said.

*"Better him than the world."*

Imari hadn't understood what Fyri had meant, but she understood now, and—stars—the more Imari considered it, the more she felt in her heart of hearts that it was true.

"You tried to stop him, didn't you?" Imari whispered to that little talla, as if she were talking to Fyri herself. "He never told you that Zussa was in that tree, and when you realized she was there, you tried to stop him." A beat. "Just as you tried stopping *me*."

Imari could have sworn the bells rang a somber melody in response.

Just then, the door to her bedchamber opened, and Imari shoved the talla behind her back. But it was not Jenya who peered in.

It was Jeric, and the sight of him made her heart stutter. He'd changed his attire since this morning, exchanging Survak's smuggled woolen coat for a tailored Corinthian-blue trimmed in rich gray fur with large bear canines for buttons. His coat hung open, and he'd traded his boots for a fresh black pair that stopped at mid-calf, fitted black breeches, and a crisp white tunic that was partially unbuttoned and tucked into a waist decorated by Lorath's sleek form.

His gaze found her, and his lips curled, but he looked weary.

"There you are," Imari said. "I was beginning to worry."

"So was I," he said with a sigh. "May I?" He gestured at the room.

"Of course. It is *your* room."

"Not now, it isn't." He winked as he pushed through the door and closed it behind him. He stood there a moment, glancing about his bedchamber. "Do you need anything? Blankets? More pillows? Water—"

"No, it's perfect."

His gaze skirted the closed draperies and settled on the fire, which he started for. "Are you warm enough?"

"Really, Jeric, I'm fine..."

He snagged a log from the small stack beside the hearth and tossed it upon the fire. Sparks flew as flames danced and wood popped. He grabbed the fire poker then crouched upon the balls of his feet and pushed at the logs, sending another shower of sparks upon the embers.

Something was bothering him.

"How did it go today?" Imari asked.

Jeric pushed at the wood a few seconds more, then dropped the poker upon the hearth, where it clattered against the flag-stones. He shoved himself to his feet. "Well, it—" He spotted the little book upon the table, bent forward, and snatched it up, then turned it over, eyeing the little embossed tree upon the cover. His gaze cut to her. "Where'd you get this?"

"Rasmin's old office."

Jeric frowned and turned the book back over. "I've searched those shelves...where did you find it?"

"Inside of a book that wasn't a book."

"Ah," Jeric mouthed. He flipped through the pages, and a crease formed between his brows. "I've never seen this one."

"It's a collection of Moltoné's teachings."

Jeric's expression opened a little in understanding.

"You still haven't answered my question."

Jeric closed the book and set it down, but then touched her elbow instead.

Because the talla was still behind her back.

Imari withdrew the little object.

Jeric glanced down, then back at her. There was no judgment. Only curiosity. "Practicing?" he asked.

"More like...wondering."

"About?"

Imari sat down in the chair. "I think..." She bit her lip. "I think we're wrong about Fyri."

He studied her. "Which part?"

Imari shared her suspicions while Jeric tracked every word, and when she finished, he asked, "Does believing she turned in the end give you more confidence to use that talla?"

A beat. "Yes, but that's not why I believe it."

Jeric held her gaze a long moment, then looked to the fire and rubbed his neck.

He wasn't concerned about the talla at all. His mind was elsewhere, sifting through the heavy things he'd hauled in behind him when he'd walked through that door.

"Jeric, what happened today?" she asked.

Jeric dragged that hand over his face, then pulled off his coat, tossed it over the back of the chair across from her, and sat down upon the chair. He leaned forward, elbows on his knees with his hands dangling between them. "All of Istraa is taken."

Imari's heart skipped its next beat. Of course, she didn't believe that Istraa could stand against Azir on her own—not for a second—but to hear it stated so plainly, and so certainly, made her chest ache.

*Ricón.*

"They met some resistance at Bizra Tai," he continued. "I am told Kazak made quick work of Naleed's army, and Naleed surrendered."

Roi Naleed, who had two thousand fighting men. It was the

entire reason her papa had betrothed her to Naleed's son, Fez. Bizra Tai was Istraa's most heavily fortified city—comparable to Trier. It was where Ricón would have definitely gone to set up a new stronghold to try to fight back against Azir.

"Any word on Ricón or Kai?" she asked quietly.

Jeric pressed his lips together and shook his head.

Well, that was good, she supposed. Azir hadn't proven to be the sort to keep his victories quiet. If he'd found Ricón, he would have put him on display, just as he'd done her papa. But then... where was Ricón?

"What of the Sol Velorians there?" Imari asked, for Roi Naleed had also employed the most slaves.

Jeric's fingers tickled the air. "Many of them joined Azir's ranks."

"Define *many*."

"One thousand. That's Hersir's estimate."

One *thousand*.

Which meant Azir now had nearly two thousand Sol Velorians at his employ, as well as four Mo'Ruk and at least two dozen Liagé.

Imari sagged back into her chair as a heavy weight settled upon her breast. How in the wards could she ever hope to find peace between their peoples when so many Sol Velorians had chosen to fight alongside that monster?

"STOVICH WILL RIDE out tomorrow to prepare his men," Jeric said.

Imari met his gaze.

He looked steadily back. "I renounced the betrothal."

His words settled in the quiet, in her lungs and in her heart. "That could not have been an easy conversation."

He didn't look away as he said, "For me, it was quite simple."

Her heart swelled, though she heard what he did not say. "Then how did you persuade him to fight alongside you?"

Jeric's sharp gaze slid to the fire. "Because I know things that he would rather I not share."

Imari studied his strong profile, the fire reflecting in his eyes, and she couldn't help but think how the real battle wasn't on the field at all. No, it lay in private conversation behind closed doors, where a small handful of men and women played god, directing people's fate as they deemed fit. It didn't seem right that so few could make fateful decisions for so many, and yet if they did not organize a defense, Azir would take the Provinces in one blazing sweep of guardian fire.

"How many men is he sending?" Imari asked at last.

"One thousand."

It wasn't enough, and they both knew it.

Jeric leaned back in his chair, his body angled toward the fire as he draped his arms along the rests and stretched his long legs before him. "Niá has agreed to visit the skal mines. She says she might be able to enchant our arms to deflect spells, and perhaps even embed them with more...offensive measures."

That would definitely help, and Imari was glad to hear that Niá was willing to do this, but, "Will your people allow it?"

Jeric's expression tightened, and those fingers danced. "I don't know. I think that enough of them know what's happened to Istraa, and they are afraid. Is fear enough....?" He shrugged. "But Chez has agreed to accompany her to make sure she's safe."

"Tallyn isn't going?" Imari asked.

"No. He's riding to our northern border with Grag."

"Your hunter?" she asked, and Jeric nodded. Grag Beryn had been the first one to discover the shade carnage in the Blackwood. "He found more shades, didn't he?"

Jeric tipped his head. "Brom Stykken contacted Hersir while I was away." Jeric dragged his teeth over his bottom lip and raked a hand through his hair. "First it was their livestock. Then...people. He'd heard what had happened here and thought to inquire."

"Are they coming all the way from The Wilds...?" Imari asked skeptically.

"So it seems, though I can't figure out how they'd get over The Crossing bridge."

Imari couldn't either, because The Crossing was heavily warded, and nothing had been able to cross ever since...

Azir.

Nothing of Shah had been able to cross that bridge since *Azir*, when the Liagé who'd sided with the Provinces had banished all of his vile creatures to The Wilds and enchanted that bridge to hold them there. Just like the wards surrounding Skanden—all of which needed to be maintained to hold their power.

Imari's lips parted with realization.

Tolya had maintained those wards, and twice every year, when Imari and Tolya proceeded along their circuits through The Wilds, they had gone near The Crossing.

Because Tolya had helped maintain it—Imari understood that now. Tolya was gone, yes, but only recently. Not nearly long enough for those wards to lose their effectivity, which is what'd happened in Sol Velor. No, The Crossing's enchantments must have been overwhelmed. Imari had seen it happen before. But it would take someone, or something, very powerful to overwhelm the entire bridge, and Imari happened to know just the one—a particular enchantress who also was not confined to travel on foot.

"Su'Vi," Imari whispered.

Jeric frowned.

"Su'Vi destroyed The Crossing's enchantments," Imari said.

Jeric's dark blue eyes focused on her, and she could see him now piecing all the facts together that she had just assembled.

Azir planned to weaken them from the north too.

"Have Niá enchant skal for Stykken," Imari said.

Jeric looked at her as if he hadn't heard her correctly.

"I'm serious, Jeric. We don't have nightglass, but we have Niá, and if she can enchant skal against Azir, she can certainly enchant it against shades—"

"We don't have any skal to spare, Imari," Jeric replied sharply. "If you'll remember, Astrid emptied my armory, and I let my skal miners go. Quite recently, in fact." He looked at her with emphasis, because freeing those miners had been the major point of contention between him and his jarls, many of whom refused to release the Sol Velorian slaves in their respective holds.

But Imari leaned forward and pressed on. "You can't afford *not* to spare it, Jeric. All the skal in the world will not save us from Azir, and you know it. Help Stykken in this, and perhaps *he* will help *you* when Azir marches upon Skyhold's gates."

Jeric laughed darkly and shook his head with irritating condescension. It was in moments like these that she understood Braddok's annoyance with his arrogant majesty.

"Stykken will cling immutably to his rocks as he's always done," Jeric drawled with bitter contempt. "He won't help Skyhold. He'll be glad to see her fall."

Imari glared at him. "Since when did you inherit Tallyn's gift of Sight?"

Her tone was not kind, and Jeric set his keen gaze upon her. But before Jeric could argue—and he looked as though he were about to—Imari added, "You keep saying you are not your father, Jeric, so stop making the same decisions. You might be standing on the same board, but if you make different plays, you might just find yourself a different outcome."

The Wolf's gaze cut right through her. "Different does not mean *better*."

"And *better* never has a chance if you keep following the same rutting path. You know your father was wrong in this. You said so yourself. *So—make—it—right.*"

She wondered if she'd pushed him too hard, but she stood by her words. Jeric studied her a long moment and then leaned back in his chair, his expression inscrutable.

"My council's going to have their work cut out for them with you," he said at last.

"I'm pretty sure that's why you invited me."

A grin cracked his lips. "Among other things..." he said, and her cheeks flushed. He continued studying her, almost thoughtfully, and then he looked back to the fire. "I'm walking the perimeter with Hersir and Anaton tomorrow to check Skyhold's fortifications. I'll...see what I can do."

"There. I knew you could see reason." She threw his own words back at him.

Jeric's gaze flickered to her with amusement.

Quiet settled between them, and then she added, suddenly, "I met Lady Kyrinne today."

She couldn't say what prompted her to share this, but there it was, out in the open, and she found herself watching for his reaction.

Jeric's posture tightened, which was enough to confirm her earlier suspicions: he and Lady Kyrinne had known one another, and probably better than Imari wanted to know. Despite herself, jealousy twisted like a knife inside of her.

"She intercepted us in the hall when we were on our way to Rasmin's chambers," Imari continued. Thankfully, her voice rang easy. "She made a point to introduce herself."

"What did she say?" Jeric's tone was careful.

"Nothing, really." Imari paused. "I didn't exactly give her the opportunity, because I excused myself. She...reminds me too much of a desert viper."

Jeric laughed. It was a rich laugh that rang from somewhere deep, and the sound of it made her heart sing.

"She is very beautiful," Imari admitted.

Jeric's laugh tapered, and leather creaked as he slid out of his chair. He crossed that small space between them and knelt before her. With him kneeling and her seated, they were nearly eye level. He grabbed her hands, laced her fingers with his, and looked straight into her eyes. "She is *nothing* compared to you, Imari."

Imari felt suddenly foolish for bringing it up. "I'm sorry, Jeric. I shouldn't have...you don't need to explain—"

"Yes, I do." He stared hard at her, as if he could impart his meaning and his heart in that one look. He also seemed to be fighting words. "I am...not proud of many things in my past, but I will tell you anything you want to know—I swear. *Anything*. Even if it means you finally see me for the wretch that I am, but I need *you* to know that you have my whole heart, and that is where it will stay until the day I die."

Imari gazed into his eyes, into those swirling blue depths, and suddenly none of it mattered. Not Kyrinne. Not his past. All that mattered was this—*them*. This was real. *He* was real, and he was still kneeling before her, patiently awaiting her decision and judgment.

"The past is for the Maker," Imari said, repeating those words Tolya had said to her so long ago. "And I love the man you are *now*. In the present."

A smile touched the edge of Jeric's lips. He released her hands and grabbed her hips instead, then dragged her forward to the very edge of the chair so that her feet rested on either side of his knees and her thighs rested against either side of his waist, and the way he looked at her then set her soul on fire.

"I can stay a little while longer," he said, his voice low. "It's entirely up to you. I know it's late."

Imari placed her palm to his cheek, gazing into that deep ocean as the dark hairs on his face tickled her skin. "Stay."

He smiled, then dipped his head and caught her mouth with his, and Imari let herself drown.

"In the beginning, there was the Word, and the Word was good. Asorai saw that it was good, and so he wove it into all creation, from the depths of the sea, to the stars in the heavens, though to mankind he gave part of himself. To guide them, he appointed five rulers to bear the weight of his Word in all its nuances and song, to keep it pure, to keep it right, so that all might know the perfect way Asorai intended."

~ Excerpt from Il Tonté,
As recorded in the First Verses by
Juvia, Liagé First High Sceptor.

## 24

*M*orning came too soon. Jeric had stayed as long as he'd dared—long enough that Imari had fallen asleep upon his chest. His side of the bed was still rumpled from where he'd lain, and in his place, upon his pillow, sat a little wooden wolf.

Imari grinned and picked up the little wolf he had carved.

She thought of his hands and the care in which they'd carefully tended this small piece. The same way they tended *her*.

She wrapped her hand around the little wolf completely. This bed felt much too large with Jeric not in it, though she understood why he'd left. They hadn't *officially* married before the public, and Jeric didn't want to complicate matters. Neither of them did. Technically, she should not have let him visit her, period, but she'd lacked the willpower for that.

She slid out of the blankets, and the cold shocked any semblance of sleep from her bare skin. Jeric had picked her cloak off the floor and draped it over the end of the bed, and Imari quickly changed into it. She slid the little wolf into her pocket, padded to the draperies where a line of soft light shone through, and peered outside at a pristine white world.

It had snowed in the night, dressing all of Skyhold in a thick, white veil. Imari could just see the town from her vantage, that huddle of jagged rooftops and winding streets. She didn't see many people out at this hour, but smoke rose from chimneys, casting a thin haze over everything.

Hazy, just like their future.

Imari did not know what lay ahead or how she could possibly stop the Great Deceiver, but she couldn't worry about that yet. She would move forward as she had always done: one day at a time, and today, she would check on Mika's ill.

Imari found her clothes neatly stacked and folded upon the chair, with her talla set upon them. She dressed quickly but didn't put on the talla, instead slipping it into her coat's inner pocket, just in case. Even so, the talla pulled upon her soul with startling intensity, and Jeric's faith in her did little to ease the sudden rush of anxiety she felt just then. Thankfully, that initial shock of power faded to a soft and distant hum, and Imari stepped into the hall to find Jenya waiting.

Stars, she'd forgotten Jenya had been just one room over, with only a door to separate them. Jenya looked at her, and Imari's cheeks burned.

"Good morning," Imari said in Istraan. "I...ah..." Embarrassment made her forget whatever else she'd been about to say. "I'm sorry," came out instead.

Jenya arched a brow. "It's not like I don't know."

It pained Imari to add, "Yes, but I forgot you were there."

"I wasn't. I waited in the hall until he left."

That should have made Imari feel better. It didn't.

"Sura Anja kept her kunari in her antechamber at *all* times," Jenya added.

Imari realized her mouth was hanging open, and she promptly closed it. "I won't ever ask *that* of you."

Jenya looked as though she were fighting back a grin as she said, "*Tama.*" Thanks.

Imari glanced down the hall. Windows lined one wall, and the draperies had been pulled back to let in the light, though they did little to dispel the shadows. Like the cold, they remained a permanent guest, taking up residence in the high arches and deep corners.

"I need to check on my patients," Imari said.

Jenya bowed her head. "After you, *mi a'surina.*"

They walked the fortress's winding halls toward the kitchen. However, Imari did not know the fortress well, and she made a few wrong turns before finding her way.

Unlike the fortress, the kitchen was wide awake. Flour coated the counters, where freshly baked bread sat cooling while new loafs were shoved into hot ovens. One woman stood over a bowl cracking eggs, while another arranged a platter of fruit, and Mika stood in the corner yelling at Farvyn.

Imari noticed the flour dusting his hands, and she fought very hard not to smile.

Mika caught sight of her, then stopped yelling at Farvyn to whack him on the head with an oven mitt.

Imari thought that Mika probably would've gotten on well with Tolya.

Farvyn ran off as Mika shuffled over to Imari, barking more orders at the other women along the way.

"How are they?" Imari asked Mika.

Mika didn't answer immediately, and for a split second, Imari feared the worst. But then Imari realized the look Mika was giving her was not one of grief but of wonder.

"I'll show you." Mika gestured at her to follow.

More servants—mostly Corinthian, though Imari spied one Sol Velorian—dashed out from behind narrow doors and squeezed past them in the hall, all of them casting Imari long and curious glances.

One thing was certain: Imari's presence here was secret no longer.

Mika pushed open the door to the first room, and Imari found the girl wide awake and still pale, though she was sitting up in bed.

"This is the one," Mika said to the girl, and the girl's soft brown eyes settled on Imari.

The girl looked uncertain, which was how Imari's patients had usually looked at her when they'd first registered the appearance of the one who had just saved their lives.

"How are you feeling?" Imari asked, stopping a few paces away from the bed. Jenya waited near the door.

"Better," the girl said in a small voice. "Thank you."

"You're most welcome," Imari replied, then looked at Mika. "She needs to rest one more day."

Mika did not look thrilled by this directive but didn't argue, and Imari visited the second girl to find her similarly improved. Imari made more herbal tea for both, left instructions for Mika, and then started to go.

"Surina," Mika said.

Imari turned to find Mika holding out a cloth pouch, drawn closed by a string, and it smelled deliciously of bread.

Mika urged it toward Imari. "It's...for you."

Imari took the pouch. "This smells wonderful. Thank you, Mika."

"Let me test it first," Jenya whispered as they left.

Imari glanced sideways at her saredd. "It's not poisoned."

"They're Corinthian."

Imari gave her a look, but Jenya held out a stubborn hand. Imari sighed, opened the bag, and withdrew a roll, but rather than hand it to Jenya, she took a large bite. Jenya glared as Imari swallowed, smiled, and kept walking.

Only to be intercepted by Commander Anaton.

He was alone, and he looked marginally uncomfortable. As if he still wasn't sure whether or not he should have sought her out.

"Surina," he said crisply, respectfully, giving her a sharp bow.

"Commander," Imari returned.

His brow furrowed. "I...wondered if I might beg your assistance this morning."

Imari waited for him to elaborate, and behind her, Jenya stepped closer.

Commander Anaton's gaze flitted to Jenya before settling back on Imari. "Some of my men have taken ill, and I wondered if you might help them."

This was...not at all what she had expected.

Mika passed by at that moment, exchanged a knowing glance with the commander, then cast a slightly more friendly glance at Imari before pushing on to the kitchen.

Ah. Word traveled fast.

And Commander Anaton stood there with the same look in his eyes that she had seen from so many: a desperation and a *hope* that she might be able to help where others had failed, even if her methods vexed his convictions.

"How many?" Imari asked.

Relief softened the commander's features. "Four. One is...in very poor condition."

Imari sighed. "Take me to them, and I'll see what I can do."

It was late into the evening by the time Imari returned to the fortress. As Commander Anaton had said, one of his men was very ill, and Imari had spent the better part of the morning with that man alone. However, just as she'd been leaving the barracks, another one of Commander Anaton's guards asked if she'd see to *his* family, who had also taken ill. And while she tended to them, another family had come asking for assistance, and so on and so forth, until she found herself walking all over Skyhold's snowy streets, tending the sick—and there were many, for winter's closest companions were cold and disease.

Thankfully, one of her patients owned a shop that sold root vegetables and dried herbs—some even imported through Gilder Sound—giving Imari access to many of the supplies she needed for only a few additional crowns. It wasn't much compared to Tolya's verdant bank of remedies, but it would suffice, and Imari found that her song filled in the gaps where herbs fell short. Though like before, she kept that song quiet, to not raise suspicion, and none were the wiser. Except, maybe, Jenya.

Imari broke only for lunch, when Jenya had shoved a loaf of bread in her face, and promptly returned to work.

At one point, she spotted Jeric from afar, standing upon the ramparts of Skyhold's great skal wall, walking with Hersir and pointing at something beyond the wall.

"Did you want to rest, Surina?" Jenya asked.

Imari dragged her eyes from the men, looked to Jenya, and gave her a tight smile. "No, no. I'm fine." And they continued on, though Imari felt a prick of unease she could not explain.

It wasn't until the moon had risen high and Imari's temples began to ache that Imari finally agreed to call it a day. But rather than head straight for Jeric's bedchamber, she turned down the hall that led to the kitchen and explained—much to Jenya's annoyance—that she would like to make some tea.

The kitchen was mostly dark and empty when they arrived, save one servant who swept the floors by the hearth's glowing embers. Jenya fed a stove while Imari rummaged through Mika's closet of food and herbs, and there, in the silence, the softest whisper grazed Imari's ears. It was a layered rush of words, too soft to decipher, like wind through pines.

Imari froze, hand gripping a jar of dried fellfew leaves that Mika had replenished. She glanced over her shoulder and into the kitchen where Jenya adjusted the kettle atop the stove. Jenya did not appear to have heard it.

Perhaps Imari was more tired than she thought.

She sighed, grabbed the jar, and was stepping off the stool when the whispers brushed her ears again.

A chill swept over her head to toe.

"Did you hear that?" Imari asked, walking out of the closet and into the kitchen.

Jenya glanced over and frowned. "Hear what?"

Imari appraised the dimly lit room, the wooden support beams, and the thick stone walls with mortar in between. The servant had left, and the broom had been propped in one corner.

"I heard...voices," Imari said.

A crease formed between Jenya's brows.

Imari's belly tingled suddenly, as if her power were responding to some inaudible command, and her attention slid —unconsciously—to the small door on her left.

The door to the cellars.

Where Hagan had kept her imprisoned, and where Astrid had snuck the legion into Skyhold through a hidden entry near the Muir.

Imari's heart pounded. She'd seen Jeric working with Hersir to fortify Skyhold's wall; certainly he had remembered to bury this little secret.

"Where are you going?" Jenya asked.

"I need to check something," Imari replied. Following a foreboding that she could not explain, she placed her hand upon the door, pushed it in, and stepped into darkness.

## 25

"*I*'ll get a light." Jenya appeared in the doorway, holding a lantern she'd plucked from the kitchen.

"Thank you," Imari said, and the two of them descended the stair while that pull beckoned her constantly forward.

"Do you know where you're going?" Jenya asked as she followed close behind.

"Not really, but I know where I am," Imari admitted. She eventually stopped before the door situated at the end of the cellar's long and cramped corridor.

A door that led to the dungeons.

There, Imari stopped, and her pulse panicked with old memory. With flickers of a very near and recent past. Images of Hagan flashed in her mind, and Rasmin too, and she felt a sudden and heavy weight settle upon her chest, as if her soul had been flung back in time, once again trapped in those dark moments of terror. When she'd thought she would die in this horrible place at the hands of a monster.

"They kept you here," Jenya said suddenly, quietly.

Imari pressed her lips together and nodded once. She touched the handle—it turned—and she pushed the door in.

The hinges groaned open to darkness, and the air smelled stale and dusty and old.

Imari held out her hand for the lantern, which Jenya grudgingly passed over, and then she started down another narrow stair.

Wards, this place. It was like walking back into a horror. Her heart pounded and her steps trembled, and her hand trailed the cold stone as she and Jenya descended into the fortress's unknown depths. Unlike the fortress with its carefully laid stone and impossible masonry, this had been cut right out of the mountain like a mine, but instead of mining for precious gems and ore, they'd mined for information.

But this time, there was more.

An acrid stench hung in the air, tinged with something foul and rotten, and there was a chill to this place that had not been there before. It pierced her heart and iced her soul, and Imari's nerves hummed with unease.

Imari's gaze slid down the dark tunnel where Jeric had kept Astrid. The end of that tunnel was black as pitch, and though Imari could not detect any life, a shudder rolled through her spine.

Imari felt Jenya studying her.

"That's where he kept Astrid." Imari looked down the narrow crack in the wall across from her—the entry to the sewers—but continued toward Astrid's old prison instead.

Water dripped in the distance, and shadows danced like demons upon the roughly hewn walls. They walked right past Imari's old door, which hung open. Imari glanced inside, remembering clearly what waited within, but she didn't stop to look.

She was far more interested in Astrid's cell, and she found it just as Jeric had described: that thick skal door bent in half like a book and discarded upon the floor, its wards charred like burnt paper, and though that fire had long since diminished, Imari swore she could still smell it burning. As though the wards' death had stained the air.

Behind her, Jenya fell silent.

Very slowly, Imari crept to the broken door, and there she crouched, her gaze skimming this thick skal canvas of destroyed wards. The wards were now illegible, their meaning and power lost. No, *incinerated*.

"Two Silent did this?" Jenya whispered.

"Yes." Imari stood, her gaze fixed on the black hole that had been Astrid's prison, and then she started for it, stepping carefully around the door. She stopped in the threshold, where the stink of feces and urine struck her at once.

Maker have mercy.

The walls were *covered* in glyphs, all drawn in old blood, but Imari had never seen these combinations before.

"Can you read it?" Jenya asked quietly, as if she, too, feared the shadows were listening.

"No. It's like she used Liagé symbols to make her own glyphs."

"What does that mean?"

"It would be like...using our letters to make her own words."

Jenya considered this. "So they're meaningless."

They should be, except Imari could *feel* the echo of their power, like some distant tone just beyond her hearing, and there was an unshakeable off-ness to it. Corrupted, as though the tone had been plucked on rotted strings and fetid wood to ring through nightmares and darkness.

No, Astrid's words were not without meaning.

But then what had she written? Or, rather, what had the legion written through Astrid's feeble hands?

It was the same set of six symbols, Imari realized, painted over and over again. Large and small. Horizontal or vertical or spiraling, but never deviating from those basic six. They were rearranged into every possible combination.

Premonition nagged at Imari. There was something about

those specific symbols, and yet she did not know any of the glyphs Astrid had written.

And then it suddenly struck Imari as to why those symbols bothered her: Together, they formed the glyph *ziermo*.

It was the one glyph she did not see upon the walls, the glyph her subconscious had been searching for—the glyph so common in the Liagé texts, because it was the first, it was the beginning, and it was Asorai's.

It literally meant: *The Word*.

And the legion had spent every moment in this cell using Astrid's blood to take it apart. To unravel it, to make it nonsense.

Behind her, Jenya cleared her throat and stepped back into the hall, farther away from the smell.

Imari cast one last glance about Astrid's cell, then followed Jenya back down the hall but stopped at the crack.

Where that strange pressure pulled again, but much stronger now.

"What's down there?" Jenya asked.

"Something I need to check," Imari said, then ducked through.

It was just as she remembered. This little storage closet, completely forgotten, stuffed with empty crates and cobwebs that were much thicker than the last time she'd passed this way. She batted them off and spit some from her lips.

Boards had been nailed across the hatch, but this did little to satisfy Imari's growing sense of unease.

"Is this how Astrid got out?" Jenya asked, suddenly understanding.

"Yes," Imari replied. "It was also how Jeric was going to sneak *me* out."

Jenya stood quiet as she studied the boards. "Is it enough to keep people from coming in?"

Imari opened her mouth to answer, but then set down the lantern and placed her hands on the boards, closed her eyes, and hummed. Her Shah sight came immediately. Jenya burned so brightly beside her, and throughout this space, Imari could see thousands of faint pricks of light. She easily found the hatch, the new boards, and those little points of light along the refined skal nails that had bound them in place.

She found their pitch on the first try.

Those little points of light trembled as she wove them into her song. They gave her no resistance, no fight, and she pulled them higher, weaving them into the tapestry of light all around.

Finished.

Her note ceased, her eyes opened, and the black nails lay scattered upon the floor.

Jenya stood silent, met her gaze, and a kind of fearful understanding passed between them.

"I'll ask Tallyn and Niá if they can seal this properly," Imari said.

"Good idea."

But that pull upon her soul did not cease, and so Imari pushed the nails aside and started lifting the boards.

"What are you doing?" Jenya asked.

Imari wasn't sure. "There's Liagé writing below, etched into the walls. I didn't know what it meant at the time, but I'd like to see if I can read it now." It wasn't a lie, but Imari couldn't bring herself to admit this overwhelming draw she felt to the sewers below. Perhaps it *was* the writing, since the last time she'd been here, she hadn't been fully opened to the Shah. But if it wasn't...

Imari continued lifting the boards and setting them aside. Jenya helped a second later, and once they'd moved all of the boards and opened the hatch, Imari said, "Wait here."

Jenya looked primed to object, but Imari said, "There's no danger to me down there, I promise you, and I'm not going very far. There's no reason for both of us to tromp through sewage." Imari slid her feet through the open hatch. "But if you don't see me in the next thirty minutes, feel free to come down."

Jenya's lips set as Imari lowered herself onto the roped ladder.

"What about the lantern?" Jenya asked, because they only had the one.

"Let me see if I can..." Her voice trailed into a note and a Liagé word of power that Niá had also taught. Her power stirred, tingling at the tips of her fingertips, where heat began to form and coalesce. Imari opened her eyes to see a tiny sphere of silvery moonlight hovering above her open palm.

She'd done it!

Jenya looked impressed.

"Keep the lantern," Imari said, and she descended the ladder as her little orb of light followed her into the darkness.

## 26

*I*mari dropped the last few feet, and her boots squished in muck. Jenya peered over the open hatch, her face bleached of color from Imari's light.

"I won't go far, I promise," Imari called out.

"Thirty minutes."

Imari touched her temple in acknowledgement, then looked back to the sewer. Her light made the rock silver, and the shadows were deep, and yet...

They *pulled* upon her. Coaxing her heart gently forward. Imari did not remember feeling this before. Of course, she'd been running for her life at the time, and she might not have noticed the sensation, but she did not think that was the case.

Imari started walking, her gaze fixed on those shadows as her little light floated overhead, illuminating the space immediately around her. She moved out of Jenya's view and deeper into the tunnels as her boots squelched in mud and muck.

In her mind, she saw her flight and remembered her desperation. She remembered rounding this corner and Ventus's inhumanly white face appearing, and then her world had gone dark.

She remembered her decision to run back into the fire, to warn Jeric.

All of these memories plagued her now, running relentlessly in her mind as that sensation drew her deeper.

And more insistently.

It became a burning itch she could not scratch, and her fingertips tingled anew, though it had nothing to do with the light hovering above her head. That unshakeable pull compelled her toward a narrow archway that she had not noticed before in the wall to her left.

Imari stopped and glanced back. She could not see the hatch anymore.

Still, that draw persisted.

Imari took a deep breath and ducked through.

It was another tunnel, though this was a capillary compared to the artery she had left, and yet, unlike the wide tunnel behind her, these walls were smooth. Imari's heart became timpani in her ears, her breath loud in the deep quiet. That tingling moved through her body, through each and every bone. It was similar to when the Shah stirred in her belly, when it would pour out and fill her limbs, but this was different. This time the outside was pouring *in*.

What was this place?

Imari pressed her hand to the smooth stone. A shock of tingling energy jolted through her palm, and she jerked her hand away.

And then her little orb went out.

Imari froze, heart pounding as she stood in total darkness, but before she had a moment to make the orb again, a flash of silvery light rippled through the tunnel. It rushed over the walls like water, pulsing outward from the place she stood. Whispers layered and crescendoed, pushing like the wind as it followed the light.

Deeper, out of sight.

Silence.

Imari's breath came hard and fast, and darkness swallowed her once more. Her nerves hummed; her body tingled all over as her heart drummed against her ribs.

*Do not fear*, said the voice from the heavens, reaching her even in the depths of Skyhold. *I am with you.*

And so she took a deep breath, made her little light again, and kept walking.

Deeper, into the tunnel.

The walls did not light up again, but she felt the energy in them. The air hummed with it, as if in that burst of light, the walls had come alive, radiant with Shah power. Coaxing and luring, drawing her forward as if desperate for her to find...

The pull stopped. She concentrated, making sure she hadn't lost it, that she hadn't gotten distracted somehow, but no. It had been there, pulling stronger than ever, and then it had simply ceased.

Imari looked at the space to her right.

It was a smooth piece of granite, though her little orb illuminated a few odd grooves in the stone. There was nothing remarkable whatsoever, and yet the air charged here like it did around a ward. She pressed her hand to it.

A flash.

Something hissed, then a distant, otherworldly scream filled Imari's head.

Shadows warped, distorted.

Suddenly every string in her body pulled taut, as though some invisible hand had tightened them to near breaking and strummed a single, loud chord.

Imari gasped from the strain of it—the *power* in this place—and every hair on her body stood on end.

Another flash.

It was Azir's face, though his eyes were pure black, no whites, and his teeth snapped. *Mine.*

Imari jerked her hand back, panting as she stared at that smooth stone bleached of color.

"Surina!" called a voice, giving Imari a start, but then she realized it was Jenya.

How long had Imari been standing there?

Imari took a breath, trying to calm herself, trying to unwind those strings that had coiled so tight.

"Surina, are you all right?" Jenya called again.

"Yes! I'm coming!" Imari yelled, then ran back for the entrance, wondering what in all the stars she had just discovered and hoping Jeric had returned so that she could show him what she'd found.

·⟨⟩·

IMARI RETURNED to Jeric's bedchamber in a bit of a daze, while Jenya kept stealing glances at her.

"Are you all right, Surina?" Jenya asked.

"I'm fine. Just exhausted is all." Imari did not want to share what had happened. Not yet. She wanted to speak with Jeric about it first.

Also, she wasn't exactly sure what to say.

Imari took off her coat, slung it over the bed, and sagged into the chair before the fire, which she didn't have any energy to start.

The next moment, Jenya was there. She grabbed the flint from the hearth and used her scim to start the fire.

"Thanks, Jenya," Imari said.

"You should sleep," Jenya said quietly.

"I will." She couldn't possibly sleep now, and she wanted to talk to Jeric first.

Jenya studied her a moment. She looked as though she

wanted to speak, but the words never came, and then there was a knock on the door.

It wasn't Jeric.

Jenya looked at Imari. "Shall I send them away?"

Imari considered the door. Stars, she didn't want to move. "No, no...answer it."

Jenya gave her a look. "You're not their servant, Surina."

"The moment I forget who it is that I actually serve is the moment I no longer deserve to be called Surina," Imari replied. "Please open the door."

Jenya regarded her a moment longer, then opened the door.

A woman stood on the other side, smartly dressed in a simple yet elegant Corinthian-blue gown, her light blonde hair braided upon her crown.

"I am sorry to interrupt," the woman said. "However, my mistress, Lady Kyrinne Brion, has fallen ill and has requested to see Surina Imari Masai, if the surina would be so inclined."

Imari went completely still, staring at that crown of braided hair.

And Lady Kyrinne's servant waited.

"What is the matter, if I may ask?" Imari asked carefully.

"A migraine that has kept my mistress in bed since midday," the servant replied.

"I see."

The quiet stretched.

Then Imari stood. "I'll go."

Jenya gave her a disparaging look, which Imari returned with fire. Visiting Lady Kyrinne was the very last thing Imari wanted to do, but a refusal might reflect poorly upon Jeric, and she did not want to strain any working relationship Jeric had formed with Lady Kyrinne's father, Jarl Stovich.

"One moment, please, while I gather my things," Imari said to the girl.

"Thank you, Surina," the girl replied.

And Jenya shut the door.

"Forgive me, Surina, but I don't think this is a good idea," Jenya warned.

"I don't either, but a refusal might be worse."

Jenya did not look convinced as Imari stood and threw on her coat, and Jenya followed Imari into the corridor in silence.

They followed Lady Kyrinne's servant through the fortress's sprawling halls, past guards and servants and guests. A couple of the guards nodded with familiarity at Lady Kyrinne's servant, the woman smiled in return, and Imari wondered just how much time Lady Kyrinne had spent here.

That knife of jealousy twisted.

The woman led them up the winding steps of a tower and stopped before a beautifully engraved door.

This was where Jeric had originally intended for Imari to stay.

The woman knocked lightly and then pushed the door in a crack. "My lady, Surina Imari is here to see you."

Imari's insides coiled. Perhaps Jenya was right. Perhaps this was a bad idea—

Lady Kyrinne's voice sounded on the other side of that door, and then the woman pushed the door wider, motioning for Imari to go in.

Imari strode through, with Jenya right behind her.

She spotted Lady Kyrinne sitting in a high-backed chair, and the first thing Imari thought was that Kyrinne was beautiful. Exquisite. Her long, blonde hair cascaded over her shoulders in elegant waves, and she wore a deep Corinthian-blue gown that matched her eyes and flattered her curves.

Imari ignored the sinking feeling in her gut and smiled instead. "Lady Kyrinne."

Lady Kyrinne smiled as she stood, showing no signs of significant pain. "Surina Imari Masai. Thank you for coming." Then to the servant, Lady Kyrinne said, "You may go, Istanza."

Istanza bowed and left.

Lady Kyrinne looked at Jenya next, expectant, but Imari did not send Jenya away. Instead, she said, sharply, "I see you are feeling better."

Lady Kyrinne's gaze slid back to Imari, and her composure did not falter. "I am, thank you. These migraines come and go so suddenly, one can never quite predict how long they'll last."

Lies. "Istanza says you've been in bed since noon."

"I have," Lady Kyrinne continued with a smile Imari didn't like. "So maybe the rumors *are* true."

"Rumors...?"

"That merely standing in your presence is enough to heal a person."

Imari eyed the Lady Kyrinne. "I wish that were true. It would make my task far less strenuous."

Lady Kyrinne regarded her, that smile still curling her lips. "Whatever your methods, you've left quite the impression in a very short amount of time. Anyway, now that you're here"—Lady Kyrinne sat back down in the high-backed chair—"why not have a seat, and let us get to know one another properly."

Like hells. "That is very kind of you, but I really should be—"

"Oh, I insist," Lady Kyrinne cut in. "I understand that we are going to be working very closely together through this war that seems inevitable, and...possibly *after*."

She was baiting, and the only thing that kept Imari from walking out the door just then was knowing Jeric needed this woman's father to supply fighting men.

"Who can possibly know what comes after?" Imari said instead, her tone clipped. "We might all die."

Lady Kyrinne's eyes glittered. "Well, you're certainly not here for your optimism, are you?"

"I've spent most of my life in The Wilds. Optimism wasn't a luxury I could afford."

Imari shouldn't have said it.

To Lady Kyrinne's credit, her features remained cool and calm and irritatingly beautiful, but Imari caught that fiery spark in her midsummer-blue eyes. Lady Kyrinne smiled then, all pleasantries, as she picked up a carafe half full of an amber liquid—akavit, Imari was certain—and poured it into two small glasses. "Then let us toast to what *is* certain, Surina."

Lady Kyrinne set the bottle down, picked up both glasses, and held one to Imari.

Imari did not take it.

"Do you not drink, Surina?"

"I don't care for it."

Lady Kyrinne considered her and then set Imari's glass down. "Jeric doesn't care for it either, though I never understood why."

She'd called him by his familiar name on purpose, and Imari's gut twisted despite herself.

"Cheers." Lady Kyrinne raised her glass, a gleam in her eyes. "To forging new and...very unexpected alliances." She tilted her glass toward Imari and then downed the liquid.

*All* of it.

"What do you want, Lady Kyrinne?" Imari asked, cutting right through this exhausting haze of false manners.

Lady Kyrinne pulled the glass away and looked at her. All of her friendly pretenses evaporated—finally—and in its place settled something deeply bitter. She stood, but metal scraped as Jenya drew her scim. Lady Kyrinne stopped, her features sharpened, and Imari raised a hand to hold Jenya off.

Jenya slid the scim back in place, but her hand remained on the hilt.

"What I want..." Kyrinne started in a low, trembling voice. Imari could smell the akavit on her breath. This wasn't Kyrinne's first glass, Imari realized. "...is to know why Jeric chose a *Scab bastard* to be his queen."

Jenya looked as though she were about to pull that scim free again, but this time Imari pushed her hand out and said, firmly, "*No.*"

"You used your sorcery on him, didn't you?" Kyrinne continued, her cold eyes fixed Imari. "*Didn't you?*"

"Lady Kyrinne," Imari said sharply. "I think you are tired, and I should go."

Imari gave Jenya a look and started for the door, but Lady Kyrinne grabbed her arm—hard.

"Let go of me," Imari warned.

But Kyrinne did not. Her fingers dug into Imari's arm. "The people of Corinth will never accept a Scab."

"Then it's fortunate you don't speak for the people."

Kyrinne's fury burned hot.

Imari jerked her arm free. "Good evening, Lady Kyrinne."

Lady Kyrinne's features sharpened, and she stared as Imari strode for the door and threw it open.

Only to find two enormous men standing on the other side, dressed in traditional Corinthian armor, blocking her path.

She might have thought they'd come asking for help like all the rest, but their expressions were not friendly.

Her pulse quickened, and the one with a full beard stepped forward, forcing Imari to take a step back.

"What are you..." Imari's voice trailed as three more men stepped into Lady Kyrinne's suite through a door in back.

These men were not wearing Corinthian armor but were buried in heavy wools and metal helmets with narrow cutouts shaped in a "T". The largest of the three leveled a crossbow at Jenya, who had drawn both scims, while the two in Corinthian arms closed the door, locking them all inside.

"What is this?" Imari demanded, but Lady Kyrinne only smiled like the desert viper she was. She had tossed the bait, and her little mouse had been caught.

"Drop your scims," snapped the man holding the crossbow. His accent wasn't Corinthian. Imari wasn't sure what it was, though it struck a vaguely familiar chord.

*Chord.*

Imari did not have her talla, but she had her voice, and she began to hum.

She heard a click.

Air whizzed.

Jenya cried out and dropped to one leg with a bolt sticking out of her thigh.

Imari's note turned into a gasp, and she lunged forward, but the second man grabbed her arms and jerked her back while the third helped the two Corinthians apprehend Jenya. Her blood was already soaking through her pant leg, and her features twisted with pain.

"Try that again, little songbird," continued the man in that strange accent, "and I will bury this bolt in her Scablicker heart."

His eyes were deep and dark and cruel through the narrow slit of his helmet.

The man considered her, clucked his tongue, and then the man dressed in furs, who stood with Jenya and the two Corinthians, approached. He stepped behind Imari, where her arms were being held firmly by another, and cold metal snapped around her wrists with a sharp *click*.

Ice immediately flooded her body and filled her head with sludge.

Liagé binds.

"She's secured," said the man behind her, in that same strange accent.

Jenya lunged against her captors with a curse, and one of her Corinthian captors slammed the hilt of his sword against her skull.

She gasped and collapsed.

Imari felt a swell of emotion press through her chest, but the binding's enchantments pushed back—squeezing the air right out of her lungs until she dropped to her knees, choking for breath.

"Breathe, little songbird," said the man, lowering the crossbow as Imari gasped and wheezed.

"Who...are you?" she managed through the gasps.

A beat. The man ripped off his helmet, and a coat of thick, brown hair spilled out, dusting his shoulders and framing a face that was battle hardened and shrewd. But it was the inked marking at the corner of his right eye that gave him away, one that stretched from temple to cheekbone—a symbol that was not Liagé but *Breveran.*

"I am Kormand Vystane," he said. "Corinth's new king."

## 27

*J*eric and Braddok stood together, watching Hersir climb the stairs of the main watchtower, illuminated by a line of flickering torches. They had accomplished all they could for one day, and it was time to retire. Night had fallen three hours ago, and with it had come the cold, and now snow.

Winter had arrived late, and she seemed to be making up for lost time.

They'd spent the entire day inspecting every inch of that godsdamned skal wall while taking inventory of the remaining skal arms, but Jeric felt no better than he had this morning. Corinth simply lacked the resources and the time to acquire them.

Which was why he had gone ahead and done exactly what Imari had asked him to do: He'd written Brom Stykken.

He looked at Braddok, who gazed upon that massive wall with a rare display of solemn sobriety. Because Braddok had come to the same conclusion: They simply did not have enough fighting men.

Gods, Jeric didn't even have enough wolves to qualify as a

*pack.* He had *two* when he'd started with five—eleven, if he counted all the men he'd lost over the years—and his small, sad number made him acutely aware of their losses.

His cruel mind replayed those last images of Aksel as he was dragged into the horde. Jeric would never stop seeing that as long as he lived. His mind shifted to Gerald next, lying dead in the snow, his skin stained black. And then his mind flipped through all the faces of the other men Jeric had always told himself he did not care about—he'd paid them, after all—and yet Jeric felt the sudden urge to steal one of Dom's stoliks and ride hard into the night. *Run.* Where, he didn't know. Just...anywhere but here.

Maybe he would never come back. Let all these godsdamned vultures destroy themselves, and let the world they'd created burn.

"I'm heading to the Barrel; wanna join?" Braddok asked.

Jeric hesitated. A bitter wind stirred his hair and burned his nose. He could use a drink, but he wanted to talk to Imari. He hadn't had a moment to speak with her, though he'd caught glimpse of her when he'd been atop the wall with Hersir. Considering what he'd overheard from Anaton's guards, she'd been busy.

And Jeric had never been prouder.

"I'll wait if you wanna grab your lady wolf first," Braddok added with a wink. "But do me a favor. Tell her to bring Jen."

Jeric smirked. "Maybe tomorrow."

Braddok realized Jeric was serious and groaned. "You're so boring now. I miss the old Wolf."

"The old Wolf didn't have a kingdom to manage."

"Didn't stop your father..."

"Which is why I am now drowning in his godsdamned scat."

Braddok chuckled, then asked, "You think Chezter's back yet?"

"I doubt it." Jeric started to walk on. Chez had left with Niá this morning to see what could be done with the skal at Westych, a nearby mine. "I'll see you in the morning...?"

"If you're lucky," Braddok said after him. "If not, means *I* got lucky."

Jeric shook his head, and both men continued on their separate ways through Skyhold's quiet streets. Jeric's breath clouded the air before him, and he shoved his hands into his coat to keep them warm. It was a good hike to the fortress, but Jeric didn't mind. It gave him time to think, to consider their next moves and all potential weaknesses, of which he had an abundance.

He eventually made his way into the great hall to find the hearths ablaze—they always were, this time of year—and a few people still huddled around them. He spotted Godfrey, his master of coin, speaking with Merya, an older woman of prominence who'd never technically held a seat on his father's council and yet always found herself a part of it because she somehow knew everyone and every*thing*.

Perhaps he should offer her a seat. With the Head Inquisitor and Jeric's entire family gone, his council had grown rather...thin.

At Jeric's entry, both looked over and stopped talking. "Your Grace," Godfrey said with a bow, and Merya followed suit. "I hope the day proved productive...?"

Bleak was a better word, but Jeric kept that happy thought to himself. "Do we have any responses?" Jeric asked instead. He'd tasked Godfrey with sending messengers to Corinth's jarls first thing this morning, requesting aid.

"Jarl Rodin will send arms and men," Godfrey replied.

Jeric did not show the overwhelming relief he felt. If Rodin accepted, that meant Vysr, Jarden, and Ulvich would follow. "How many?"

"Two hundred men and as many arms."

That left them about one thousand men short of matching Azir's numbers.

"I should also add that Rodin would like resources to see Yllis working again."

Of course he would, godsdamnit.

Astrid had freed all the Sol Velorian slaves at the Yllis skal mine in Rodinshold, right after she'd killed the guards watching over them. Rodin would need someone to work those mines, but Jeric wasn't sending Sol Velorians, so he would have to get creative. "Done. What of the others?" Jeric looked to Merya this time, because somehow she managed to hear things before they were actually said.

Merya considered him with that cool gaze of hers. "Ossbo will help. I cannot give you an exact figure, but I estimate he will supply around the same."

Good. Then with Rodin, Ossbo, and the other three, perhaps they were only four hundred short.

Jeric dragged a hand over his face.

"I understand the Istraan surina left...quite an impression on Skyhold today," Merya continued, still watching Jeric.

Godfrey was watching him too.

"I'm sure," Jeric replied. "Corinth has been without a healer for far too long, and there's nothing men value more than their own health and well-being."

"No, there is not, Your Grace," Merya agreed.

Jeric angled himself away from them, signifying an end to the conversation, and to Godfrey, he added, "Let me know if you hear anything else, no matter the hour."

Godfrey bowed his head. "Yes, Your Grace."

Jeric strode out of the hall and through a side door before anyone else could stop him. He took a roundabout way to his bedchamber so that his destination wasn't immediately apparent to anyone watching, though he hardly passed any guards, which surprised him. Perhaps Anaton had already assigned them to the wall and barracks.

Jeric finally reached the door to his bedchamber, but there he stilled. He did not hear voices on the other side. He didn't hear anything at all.

She could be asleep. She could be bathing. There could be a perfectly normal reason why the room was this quiet.

And yet...

Jeric tried the handle; it turned easily. He pushed the door open a crack and peered inside.

The antechamber was empty, though a lantern glowed upon a small table right beside a platter of food that had not been touched.

Jeric frowned and slipped inside, lithe as a cat, and closed the door behind him without sound. He crept to the bedchamber door and listened, but the silence remained complete. He cracked the door open to an empty bedchamber. Fire blazed in the hearth, and the bed was still made.

He couldn't imagine she was still out at this hour.

His pulse quickened as he strode to the washroom. Empty. He dipped his fingers in the water—ice cold.

A shadow passed over him, and Jeric whirled around to see Kyrinne standing behind him.

Gods, he hadn't even heard her come in. He must be more exhausted than he thought.

"What are you—" he was starting to say when she plunged a dagger into his thigh. He gasped in pain and staggered against the tub.

Kyrinne took a step back, startled as she gaped at the bloodied knife, at him with his blood now dripping onto the tiles. As if she couldn't believe what she had just done.

Jeric couldn't believe it either. She might have struck a major artery, considering the amount of blood currently pumping out of him. "The *rutting hells,* Kyrinne!"

"You weren't supposed to be here!" she said, as though she were trying to convince herself. To make an excuse for what she'd just done.

Jeric's mind reeled, but his thoughts wouldn't settle, wouldn't hold. His consciousness was already slipping. He stumbled forward, gripping the tub with one hand while his other clutched the knife's hilt, keeping the blade inside of him to staunch the flow. "Where's Imari?"

Kyrinne flinched, but she did not answer. She only backed away, staring in horror at his bright blood painting the tiles.

"*Where is she, godsdamnit!*?"

Just then, two Corinthian guards burst into the room, thank the gods above.

"Scat," one of them cursed in an accent that was *not* Corinthian, and he looked from Jeric to Kyrinne. "You were supposed to distract him, not kill him!"

Jeric blinked, not sure he'd heard correctly, or why he should know that accent, and his vision began to tunnel.

"Get Kormand," one of the guards said.

Kormand...?

But then Jeric's world faded.

## 28

*N*iá held tight to Chez as they rode the winding path back to Skyhold, though their way was slow. It'd snowed most of the day while she'd been enchanting arms at Westych mine. At one point, Niá had voiced her concern, fearing they'd be stuck for the night, but Chez had said simply, "We'll be fine. I could ride that road in my sleep. In fact, I think I did once."

Niá couldn't tell if he was serious, but they'd stayed, and Niá had kept enchanting. She hadn't enchanted this much since... well, ever. They'd left Skyhold at the crack of dawn with Murcare —Jeric's overseer of skal mines—beneath a cover of woolen clouds, but their path had been clear. The ride had taken a little over an hour before Chez pointed at the wooden tower marking the Westych Outpost. Votte, who oversaw its operations for Murcare and his royal highness, had greeted Chez and Murcare with friendly faces, but his expression had darkened when he'd spotted Niá.

Chez either hadn't noticed, or pretended not to, and proceeded to explain their dire situation, the state of Istraa, and King Jeric's orders, with some interjections by Murcare. At the end of it, Votte had looked mistrustfully back at Niá and asked, "So what's *that* doin' here?"

"*Niá* is going to enchant our skal," Chez had replied.

Votte and all the men beside him had gone stone-still, but before Votte could say a word, Chez added with an edge Niá had never heard before, "Kazak leveled Trier in a span of one *hour* with his guardian fire. We won't win this fight with skal alone."

Votte had stood quiet for a very long time as he'd looked from Chez to Niá and briefly to Murcare, who slowly nodded as if to affirm Chez's assertion. "And you trust that one?" Votte had asked, eyes narrowed on Niá.

Chez had looked straight at her and said with conviction, "I do."

Niá had felt something give inside of her.

Votte had eventually led them to a small, squat building, full of crude ore and refined pieces, then delivered a mallet and chisel. Niá got to work, carving glyphs into the hard metal, imbuing them with her words of power. Chez had guarded the entry while she'd worked, sometimes joined by Murcare, who had taken a distant curiosity to her process. He never liked to get too close, Niá had noticed, as if mere proximity might make him catch a spell.

She'd half considered casting one on him out of spite.

Around late afternoon, Chez brought hot food, but when she didn't eat it, he set it directly on top of the piece she'd been enchanting.

"Eat, Niá. You look a little pale, and we've got a long ride back."

He wasn't wrong. She'd been enchanting since mid-morning, and her entire body tingled with Shah and fatigue. So Niá took the bowl and ate but kept on enchanting everything Votte and his men brought to her: swords and shields and bows and arms. She enchanted until her head would not stop spinning and daylight waned.

"We're done for the day," Chez had said decisively, taking the last piece she'd enchanted and piling it on top of the others. "It's getting late."

There were still more pieces to be spelled, but Niá was grateful he'd called the day. She didn't know if she had the energy to enchant anything more.

Chez appraised the pile. "You've done a lot today."

"It doesn't look like a lot," she'd replied.

"It's more than we've ever had. At least since Tommad the First." He'd considered her, then extended a hand.

Niá had looked at his hand. At him. And then she'd taken it.

He'd pulled her to her feet, but he hadn't let go. The moment stretched, their gazes locked, and then he'd let go and turned away.

Niá still couldn't decide if she was glad for it or not.

Chez left to speak with Votte and Murcare, where they'd decided Murcare would stay to help Votte bring the wagons of enchanted skal to Commander Anaton first thing tomorrow, while Chez and Niá would ride back to Skyhold to debrief her king.

And it was a very slow ride.

The snow was thick, piled as high as their stolik in places, but Chez navigated their path expertly, skirting those thick patches and hidden depressions. He picked their way across a stream and frozen pond and never faltered, never lost his way.

Always steady.

"You told Votte you trusted me," Niá said suddenly.

Chez swayed with their mount, and Niá with him. He didn't answer.

Niá didn't want to ask. Didn't want to care. "Did you mean it?"

Chez turned his head and looked to the trees, the sky, and Niá caught a glimpse of his profile. The way his soft, brown hair curled at his temples, the crooked bend of his nose. He sighed and looked forward again. "Would you believe me if I said I did?"

Niá opened her lips, then closed them.

They fell quiet, and the wind howled through the pines. Boughs bent and swayed, dumping clumps of snow. One fell on their stolik's flank, startling their stolik forward a few quick steps.

"Whoa," Chez said, pulling on the reins. "Easy, girl." He patted her neck, and the affection seemed to calm her, but then she reared her head, her ears flickered, and she stopped decidedly in place.

Chez looked left then right, but he wasn't urging their stolik forward.

"Is something wrong?" Niá asked.

The world lay silent, the trees still, and trepidation needled in the back of Niá's mind.

"Wait here," Chez whispered, then dismounted. Here, beneath the trees, the snow was only ankle-deep.

Niá jumped down behind him, and Chez gave her a fierce look that Niá returned.

Chez's lips thinned, and he said, lowly, "Stay close." He started forward with Niá right behind. He stepped around a few enormous pines and halted suddenly.

It didn't take Niá long to discover why.

From here, the land sloped down, and in the middle of their path, a few hundred yards ahead, another stolik lay half buried snow. Its dark eyes sat wide open, unblinking and staring at a world it could no longer see.

Dead.

Wildlife had recently torn at its corpse, staining the snow in blood. And just beyond that, Niá spotted more shapes buried in the snow.

Her heart hammered in her chest.

"Scat," Chez cursed and ran down the slope.

Niá started after him. He didn't tell her to stay back. She followed him right to the edge of the scene, where she stopped and stared at the frozen hand reaching out of the snow.

Her stomach turned, and she swallowed hard.

"Maker have mercy..." she whispered in Sol Velorian.

She counted nearly a dozen bodies, all scattered, some in pieces with limbs dragged through the trees only to be discarded a few yards away from the scene.

Chez crept forward through the snow, body tensed and every sense on alert as he moved through the frozen corpses. Through this waste of life. He knelt before one—a man sprawled on his belly, arms reaching as though he'd been trying to crawl away at the time his head had been severed from his body.

Chez brushed the snow from the headless corpse's back and went still.

"You know this man," Niá said quietly.

A muscle flexed in Chez's jaw, and he looked at her.

In that one glance, Niá knew she wasn't going to like his answer.

"It's Stovich."

Stovich, the man who'd left for Stovichshold just this morning to assemble his men. The one upon whom Jeric was depending to help fight this war, because he had the most resources, and the most fighting men.

And he'd never reached Stovichshold. He never would.

Niá looked around at the others, at the bodies half buried in the snow. "So these must be—"

"His party. Yes."

"But who did this?" Niá asked in a breath.

Chez did not answer. He stood abruptly, features hard as he walked around the scene, eyes tracking the edge, the shapes, the bodies. Niá suspected he was searching for Stovich's head.

Could...Sol Velorian rebels have done this? They'd certainly done it before. Niá had heard all about the raids while she'd been at Ashova's, and a certain Wolf who'd done everything in his power to stop them. From a distance, it had been much easier to hate a Wolf while applauding her own.

When she didn't have to see how war involved real people, with real stories, and real families depending on them—on *both* sides.

But Niá did not think this had been done by Sol Velorians.

She crept through the scene, careful not to step on anyone, and then she stopped beside one man's body. He lay on his side, staring at nothing, and his Corinthian-blue jacket had turned black from all the blood. She noted the fatal wound in his gut, which had spilled his entrails into the snow.

Niá stumbled back, put her hand against a tree, and closed her eyes.

*Breathe,* she told herself. Waiting for the nausea to pass, for her breath to steady.

*Breathe.*

"Ni," Chez said.

Niá opened her eyes, and Chez tossed something to her. It hit the snow at her feet.

An arrow.

She picked it up and brushed off the snow. Niá hadn't seen many arrows in her life, so she wasn't entirely sure what she was supposed to be looking at or why Chez had tossed it to her.

"It's Breveran," Chez said.

She looked at him. Concern chiseled his features.

Brevera.

The land due east, whom Corinth had initially blamed for the Sol Velorian raids. The land Jeric's father had accused of hiding Sol Velorians and offering freedom in exchange for assistance fighting Corinth.

Of course, Niá had known better. Bahdra had planted that rumor to distract the Provinces from Istraa's southern border, where he'd been hiding and assembling *his* army.

"But why would Brevera do this?" Niá asked.

"I don't know, but we need to go. *Now.*"

Niá pocketed the bolt, and they both sprinted to their mount, climbed into the saddle, and galloped back to Corinth as fast as they dared.

## 29

*J*eric opened his eyes to total darkness. Someone had cuffed his hands over his head and then suspended him from the ceiling so that his toes brushed the dirt floor, but the pain digging into his wrists was nothing compared to the deep throbbing ache in his leg where Kyrinne had stabbed him.

Gods*damnit*, that woman.

He was surprised she'd had it in her.

Although, when he remembered the look on her face, it seemed she was surprised she'd had it in her too.

Jeric growled in a fury and jerked his body against his restraints, but the chains only rattled and set his body swinging. Strain pulled through his arms, setting his wound on fire, and Jeric clenched his teeth against the pain.

Stovich had lied. He'd never meant to send Jeric men. He'd just been biding his godsdamned time, waiting for Jeric's return. Waiting so that his daughter could get close enough—and she would, because Jeric was a rutting idiot—and end the Angevin line right in the privacy of Jeric's bedchamber. Kyrinne might not have cooperated with her father had Jeric given her what she'd wanted.

He had to hand it to Stovich: It was the quickest takeover Jeric had ever witnessed, and judging by the deep quiet surrounding him, there hadn't been much of a fight.

But where was Imari? And Braddok? Gods, if Stovich so much as put a scratch on either of them...

Voices sounded beyond his cell. Jeric strained to listen, but the sound was too muffled. He counted two speakers. No, three. One had a tone that struck Jeric oddly, though he couldn't place it.

Metal jangled, the door opened, and light spilled inside. A man's thick silhouette filled the doorframe, and Jeric blinked, straining against the bright intrusion.

"I finally leashed a dog," said the silhouette.

Suddenly, the voice clicked: It was Breveran.

What in the *rutting hells* was Brevera doing here?

The figure stepped into the cell, and two Corinthian guards trailed behind—rutting traitors. They carried a lantern, which illuminated the Breveran's face and the mark tattooed at the corner of his right eye.

Godsdamnit all to hells.

It was Kormand Vystane.

Jeric hadn't seen the Breveran king since he was a young adolescent, but he'd never forgotten. One didn't forget a person like Kormand. He was a beast of a man, all scars and rough skin. He looked like a gray, dressed in his pile of furs and leather, and a single sword hung from his left hip.

Jeric had previously suspected Kormand of being the Sol Velorian leader, offering amnesty in exchange for allegiance, working with them to weaken Corinth. Of course, that was before Imari, before he'd realized it had been his own rutting sister who'd been in league with Bahdra.

So what in the *five rutting hells* was Kormand doing here now?

And what had he done with Imari?

But Jeric didn't ask those questions. That would reveal far more about Jeric's priorities than it would ever reveal about Kormand's.

Kormand murmured something to the other two, who took position just outside the door but left the lantern.

And Kormand approached like a bear stalking its prey.

Jeric wondered who'd let him in, because Kyrinne could not have acted alone. It couldn't have been her father either, because he'd left this morning, unless that had been nothing but a ruse.

Kormand stopped one pace away, triumph on his face. "Have you gone mute, dog?"

"Go to hells, Kormand."

Kormand gave a little smirk, and then he punched Jeric square in the jaw. The force of it sent Jeric bouncing back on his wrists, and pain lanced through his arms and shoulders. Jeric didn't cry out. He flexed his jaw, tasted blood on his tongue, and when his body naturally swung forward, he spit into Kormand's face.

Kormand's features twisted, and then he struck Jeric again, right where Kyrinne had stabbed him.

This time, Jeric couldn't suppress his cry. The wound was too tender, his insides bruised, and they burned with new fire. He yelled through his teeth while Kormand wiped Jeric's spittle off of his face then grabbed the chain over Jeric's head, jerked him forward, and leaned in close.

"She almost nicked an artery," Kormand said through his teeth. "A hair closer, and you'd be dead. What a pity that would have been, because we'd never get to have this little chat. Seems you pissed off the wrong woman."

Understanding dawned cruelly in that moment.

All that time Kyrinne had been relaying information to Jeric concerning her father's secret business dealings with Brevera, she'd been developing her own alliances. However, Hagan had died, Jeric had ascended the throne, and her fortune had shifted, so she had not acted. But then Jeric had run off after Imari, and Kyrinne realized she would not be Corinth's queen, so she'd sent for Kormand.

*You weren't supposed to be here*, she had said to Jeric while holding that bloodied knife in her hands.

However. "Where's Stovich?" Jeric asked.

Kormand considered him a long moment, then snapped his fingers.

One of the Corinthian guards reappeared, sack in hand. The cloth was stained dark, and Jeric went very still. Fear settled in, anchored deep, and twisted his stomach as Kormand took the sack and turned it upside down.

A severed head rolled out of it.

Stovich's. Expression slack, eyes open and drooping and vacant.

Kormand looked at the head without emotion. "I gave him the choice. As it turns out, he's still your man through and through. Returning to his vomit, like a dog." Kormand's gaze cut back to Jeric. "His men are mine. Corinth is mine. You lost your prey this time, Wolf."

Jeric glared straight back. "You can kiss my ass."

Kormand gripped the chain over Jeric's head again and leaned in close. "I'm going to enjoy watching you burn."

Just then, someone else walked through the door: Hersir. Jeric's Lead Stryker and overseer of all the guard.

Unharmed.

Unbound.

God*damn*it.

"You rutting sonofabitch," Jeric snarled. "Is this about that godsdamned ring?"

Hersir's gaze flickered briefly over Jeric before settling on Kormand. "Skyhold is secure."

Secured, and entirely without a fight—at least none that Jeric had heard. Jeric didn't know how much of the guard had shifted allegiance for crowns, but clearly it had been enough. Hersir didn't have a rutting scratch on him.

And yet...

"Where's Anaton?" Jeric glared only at his Lead Stryker, but Hersir did not look at him—would not look at him—though his expression cracked just a little. And Jeric knew: Anaton was dead. A rock sank in his gut. "You killed him, you piece of scat."

"No, your ineptitude killed him, Wolf," Kormand said. "Though it does make one wonder how you Angevins held on to Skyhold for this long, considering two of your most powerful men were so easily dispatched."

Jeric laughed. He didn't know why he was laughing. Nothing about this was amusing, but the more he laughed, the more he couldn't stop himself, despite the pain it caused. Kormand and Hersir gazed upon him as though he'd gone mad.

Maybe he had.

Jeric's laughed tapered, and he looked straight at Hersir. "You've doomed us all."

But it was Kormand who replied, "I just saved us."

"By murdering my most talented commander and cutting off the head of Corinth's largest army?" Jeric looked pointedly at Stovich's severed head.

Kormand leaned in close, a gleam in his eyes. "No, that was just for you. For Corinth, I'm handing over your Scab bastard."

Imari.

Jeric's heart dropped into his stomach.

"To who?" Jeric asked darkly. He suspected the answer, but Kormand couldn't be *that* much of a fool.

Kormand smiled, confirming Jeric's suspicion.

"I will kill you for this," Jeric said.

"I'm not the one chained to a ceiling."

"If you think Azir will grant you amity, you're a godsdamned fool. And now you're giving him the only chance Corinth has at fighting back." Here, Jeric looked at Hersir, but Hersir glanced away.

Kormand grabbed Jeric's chains and pulled him in close so that their faces were a handbreadth apart. "No, Wolf. *I* am the only chance Corinth has to survive Azir, and now Corinth is going to watch you burn."

## 30

*I*mari sat upon the floor of Lady Kyrinne's chambers. Three guards stood watch, two near the door, one beside Imari. Imari didn't know where they'd taken Jenya, or if Jenya was all right, and when she asked, no one answered. They ignored her completely.

Fear squeezed her chest, given nowhere to go due to her Liagé bindings. They were like a cold compress, contracting her body and soul, seeping into her mind like thick syrup and turning her thoughts into sludge.

She hated these bindings.

But even as her anger flared, the bindings doused her passion like water over flame. Hot steam took the form of pressure, making it difficult for her to breathe.

Especially when she thought of Jeric.

*Maker, let him be alive. Please let him be alive.*

Imari listened, though there wasn't much to hear. The occasional cry reached her ears, sometimes from outside, sometimes from within. She gathered that Kormand's men were securing the fortress and the city—aided by many of Skyhold's own—and she was trapped here until everything settled.

And then...she had no idea what Kormand intended.

It could have been five minutes, it could have been five hours, but finally her door opened and Hersir strode through.

Totally unbound and unharmed.

"It was *you*," Imari said.

Hersir looked at her. Emotion churned in his eyes, but it was not remorse. Just determination and resolve, and suddenly, Skyhold's quiet takeover made absolute and terrible sense.

Hersir looked to the guards. "Grab the Liagé."

"You were one of the only ones he trusted!" Imari implored, but her words had no visible effect on Jeric's Lead Stryker.

"His mistake," Hersir replied curtly.

Her heart broke for Jeric, or at least she suspected it did. Cold sludge seeped from the bindings and tingled down her arms and into her chest, and she found it momentarily difficult to breathe again.

The guards looked at Imari and hesitated.

"She's bound," Hersir said. "She can't hurt you."

Imari glared at Hersir as if she could injure him with that one look, even as the guards hoisted her up. Hersir looked away and stalked through the door.

Imari had no choice but to follow.

The hall was quiet, though voices echoed from afar. They turned a few corners and passed many guards. Some of them wore Corinthian colors. Some did not. A few servants scurried and hid.

The fortress had been taken, and Imari had hardly heard a sound.

They reached the main hall, and there Imari spotted a few dead guards. Kormand's men were dragging them away and piling them together near the door. Hersir stopped briefly to speak to one of the men and then continued escorting her out the main doors and into the cold night air.

Snow flurried, dusting the drawbridge and outlining it in

white. Imari wasn't wearing a coat, and she knew she should be cold, but she was already frozen inside.

The city of Skyhold was wide awake. Her windows remained dark, but Imari could see all the faces lurking within, citizens who wanted to know what was happening but wished to stay out of sight. Imari followed Hersir past three more piles of dead Corinthian guards, but there weren't nearly as many as Imari would have suspected.

Hersir's reach must've gone deep. Or, perhaps, Angevin favor truly was a thing of the past.

Imari spotted some commotion near the gate, where a handful of Corinthian guards sat with their hands bound behind their backs. Hersir eventually led her through the doors of a long and low building that featured Corinth's wolf crest above its main door. Inside was a wide sparring ground and an assortment of weapons clinging to the walls. It reminded her of the Qazzat, where Istraa's saredd had lived and trained before Kazak's guardian fire had destroyed it. Imari expected this to be the residence of Hersir and his Strykers.

He led them down a stair in back, down an arched stone corridor lit only by a couple of burning torches, and stopped before a warded skal door.

A Liagé prison.

Hersir pushed it in. "In here," he said to the guards.

The guards shoved Imari inside.

She stumbled forward and nearly tripped but then spun around and glared at Hersir, who stood there, looking at her, his expression steel.

"How could you do this to him—" she started, but Hersir slammed the door shut on her words.

Her anger burned so hot and so fast, her bindings could not quench it completely, and Imari screamed as she ran at the door and kicked it hard. But in her anger, she'd forgotten the door was warded, and the moment her foot struck skal, glyphs flared and a jolt of energy shocked her body like lightning. Imari cried out and staggered back as that energy rattled through her bones. She slumped back against the wall and stayed there, using it for support as she tried to catch her breath, but she could not inhale fully. Her bindings had caught up, and it felt as though a heavy weight rested upon her lungs, preventing them from expanding completely. Her consciousness began drifting, and Imari closed her eyes to focus on her breathing.

In.

Out.

In.

Out.

She slid down to the floor and sat, legs folded, and tipped her head back against the wall, waiting for that wild energy to pass through. Waiting for the bindings to release their hold on her lungs.

Imari didn't know how long she sat there, but eventually, someone shoved a hunk of stale bread and a bowl of water through a slider at the base of her door. She didn't feel like eating, but she knew she needed to.

She scooted over to the food, but her hands were still bound behind her, so she lay very carefully upon her side and took a bite of bread directly off of the floor. It tasted like sand in her mouth, but she forced herself to eat the rest then moved on to the water. However, due to her fatigue and the Liagé bindings making her motions sluggish, in the process of scooting to the bowl, she knocked it over and spilled the precious water all over the dirt floor.

Imari cursed and managed to flip the bowl back over, but there was nothing salvageable. All the water was gone.

Imari sighed, closed her eyes, and waited.

And waited.

She hadn't realized she'd fallen asleep until someone was shaking her.

"Get up," a man's voice demanded.

Imari's eyes blinked open, and two guards dragged her to her feet. Hersir stood before her, and he wasn't alone.

A figure waited in the threshold, veiled in robes black as midnight.

Even through the haze from her bindings, Imari felt the surge of power. Like a charge in the air before a monsoon. The air sizzled with it, and Imari had the distinct impression that she had felt this particular brand of power before, but the bindings made it impossible to decipher any more than that.

Hersir gave Imari a once-over then stepped aside.

And the figure approached.

Lantern light danced across a face covered in inked glyphs and thin, silvery scars. The transformation was such that Imari didn't recognize her at first.

Su'Vi, the Mo'Ruk enchantress.

The one who had secured her in Trier when Azir had first taken it, and yet...she was so much more than Imari remembered. More...*alive*. As if Imari had only met Su'Vi's shadow that fateful day, and the archetype herself now stood before her.

Su'Vi's long, slender fingers grabbed the edges of her hood, and she lifted it from her face to let it rest upon her shoulders. A plait of black hair spilled out and fell to her waist, though the left side of her head was shaved smooth. A small, metal bar pierced her left brow, and there a charm dangled in the shape of a bird.

"Hello, *Sulaziér*." Even Su'Vi's voice was fuller. Richer. A complete chord where before it had been one single, thin note. "We meet again."

"What do you want, demon?" Imari snapped, though her voice came out weak.

Su'Vi crouched, her head cocked like a bird as those dark eyes stared.

Imari spit in her face.

Su'Vi's eyes flashed, and she slapped Imari across the face. Imari fell onto her back, cheek burning and eyes watering.

"I see you have not learned," Su'Vi said simply. "You will."

Before Imari could respond, Su'Vi pressed a thumb to Imari's forehead, spoke a word, and Imari's world went dark.

icón stood upon the edge of a cliff and gazed across the stretch of sand.

Ziyan.

He'd spent plenty of time in the Majutén, navigating the dunes' ever-changing paths, where civilization became a thing of memory and death was always one misstep away.

It paled in comparison to the unease he felt in this place.

From the moment Ricón and his men had stepped over the boundary, the air had soured and the wind had howled like some ill portent. This landscape was completely foreign to him, framed by a horizon he did not know. Red plateaus jutted out of the earth like the skeletons of a forgotten civilization—and they had passed many actual skeletons.

All of them were human.

Ricón did not know what infected this land, but being within its borders, he could smell that infection everywhere.

The sickness.

He could not understand what had propelled wanderers to test fate in this place. He would not be here himself had his uki not sworn to the *sieta* that Imari had come here with Azir. Still,

Ricón could not fathom what Azir sought in this wide stretch of desolation, or why he'd needed Imari to find it.

"What about there?" Hoss asked, pointing to a clump of rocks marked by a broken saguaro that had looked very much like a person from a distance.

Ricón nodded at Hoss, and they all made for the rocks to set camp. The sun hung low, and premonition tingled at the back of his mind. He recalled Imari's stories about The Wilds, about the coming of night and the urgency to wait behind warded walls to protect against monsters until the sun returned.

What he wouldn't give for a warded wall right then.

"Would you like help, Uki?" Ricón asked, noting his uki Gamla seemed to be hesitating to dismount.

"No," Gamla said at last, then swung a leg over and toppled right off the horse.

Ricón caught him; he'd been waiting for it. It had, unfortunately, become a tradition these past two weeks.

Gamla gripped Ricón's arms and steadied himself. "Thank you." He let go, dusted his knees, and walked on.

Ricón and Hoss exchanged a concerned look.

His uki had not been the same since they'd found him—there was no denying that. He was extremely malnourished, yes, and that'd greatly affected his energy, but it had also addled his mind. Ricón did not know if that was an effect of malnourishment or irreparable damage from the horror his uki had endured. Whatever the cause, Gamla had remained quiet as they navigated the Baragas—very slowly, due to his present physical state—and passed into Ziyan. Sometimes he would mumble, but Ricón could never make sense of the words. It was as if his body were here but his mind was somewhere else, having conversations with persons only he could see. Gamla did not exist in the present, seemingly unaware of where they were heading or what they were doing until, all of a sudden, he would voice strong opinions about what Ricón should do.

He was very unpredictable. In fact, Ricón was seriously considering tying his uki to a horse tonight, just to make sure his uki did not wander off.

Ricón's saredd and guard started unpacking and settling their horses for the night while the sun dipped lower.

It felt like a warning. He knew the others sensed it too.

"Fire?" asked Macai.

A beat. "No," Ricón said.

Macai did not look thrilled by Ricón's answer, but he did not argue, and they all sat in formation upon the sand, awaiting the inevitable night.

Except for Gamla, who stood before the saguaro, mumbling as though he were having a conversation with it.

Ricón sighed and strode for his uki. "Come on, Uki," he said, grabbing his uki by the shoulders and coaxing him back to camp.

But his uki stood firm. "*Flesh*, Ricón."

Ricón frowned. "What?"

"Cut his flesh."

Ricón exhaled slow. "This way, Uki."

"No, *no!*" Gamla insisted, shaking his head. "He is offering his flesh to you." He waved a hand at the broken saguaro.

Ricón shut his eyes and pinched his lips in frustration. "Why would I want his flesh, Uki?" he asked, because it was easier to indulge than to fight.

His uki gripped his shoulders with surprising strength, and Ricón opened his eyes, startled. The look on his uki's face was suddenly very clear, very intense. "Because its blood will protect you against *them.*"

"Them who?" Ricón asked.

Uki Gamla bent his head a little closer. "The others," he whispered.

"What is he saying?" Hoss asked, looking over.

Ricón considered his uki. Even if there were a shred of truth in his words, Ricón could not fathom what a saguaro spine could

offer that his scim could not; however, his uki Gamla was resolute. That fire was in his eyes, and Ricón knew that the only thing
left to douse those flames was to indulge him again.

So, very carefully, Ricón took his scim and cut into the
saguaro's green flesh.

"Deeper," Gamla demanded. "To the bone."

Ricón carved deeper until his scim struck that wooden bone,
all while Gamla watched with approbation.

"Each of you, come here!" Gamla said to the others.

"They will, Uki," Ricón promised.

Gamla did not look satisfied, but he did not press the issue
and instead walked right back to camp and sat down in the sand
with his back to the sun.

Ricón caught Hoss's gaze again. He knew what Hoss was
thinking—what they were all thinking: *We followed the promises of
a madman into Ziyan?*

Ricón wondered if he'd made a big mistake, but it was too late
to turn back tonight.

Ricón jerked his scim out of the saguaro and stopped when
he noticed the oily black substance now coating the blade.
Unusual. He looked at the saguaro, at his blade, then lifted it to
his nose and carefully wafted the air to his nostrils, but the oil
was odorless. He frowned at his uki and approached the camp.

"Don't you want to watch the sun set?" Bett was saying to his
uki, but his uki did not answer. His gaze fixed resolutely on the
darkening sky behind them.

Bett shrugged and tossed a bit of tack into his mouth.

They all sat quiet, watchful as they ate, as the sun sank lower
and night descended, and the full moon turned the sand silver.

Still, his uki had not moved from his position.

Ricón stood, snagged a blanket, and approached his uki, for
with the night had come the cold. He draped the blanket over his
uki's shoulders, though Gamla gave no reaction whatsoever, and
Ricón was starting to walk away when Gamla grabbed his ankle.

Ricón looked back.

Gamla was staring up at him now, fear in his eyes. "They are coming, Ricón."

Ricón's men fell silent, and Ricón felt them looking over at them. "Who?" Ricón asked.

Gamla squeezed his ankle harder, like some final act of desperation. "*They are coming.*"

"Uki, I don't know what you're—"

A horse snorted, a few whinnied, and their ears flickered. One stomped in the sand, and another began pulling on the rope Macai had tied, while Macai cursed and jumped to his feet. Bett stood too.

"Do you see anything?" Ricón asked Hoss, who had withdrawn his spyglass to scan the horizon.

Macai's horse was now dragging the rock Macai had tied it to.

"No, I don't see anything—" Hoss's words were cut short as a... spirit appeared out of nowhere, a hundred yards away. Ricón did not know how else to describe it, this blot of inky darkness drifting a few feet above the silver sand, and though the moon was full, it had no shadow.

Was this the tyrcorat so many had warned about? The skin eaters that haunted this forsaken place? Ricón had heard many stories, and all described them as demons of a kind, haunting this land since the day Sol Velor had been destroyed.

"Do you see that?" Hoss asked. He'd pulled his spyglass away then put it back to his eye.

"Yes...is that a tyrcorat?" Ricón asked.

"I don't know. Maybe."

*Sieta,* he'd been a fool to come here. Especially without the proper safeguards, though his uki had sworn...

Ricón glared at his uki, who sat on the sand, legs folded and eyes closed, murmuring.

"Uki," Ricón said.

Nothing.

"*Gamla Khan*, answer me!" Ricón tried again.

But his uki only murmured, and the horses were in a frenzy while Macai and Bett tried to calm them down.

"*Sacréb...*" Hoss warned.

Ricón turned back to see the thing moving closer. This midnight streak of tattered robes, with edges blurring strangely as it floated shadowless toward them over the sand.

His men fell silent, and Ricón flexed his fingers over his scim, heart pounding as he wondered if steel could penetrate a spirit. "We need your help now, Uki," Ricón growled.

But his uki did not respond, and the thing drew closer.

And closer.

And then, in a sudden gust of wind, the thing picked up speed and rushed at Ricón. It lifted a skeletal face, its jawbone opened unnaturally wide, and it screamed an inhuman sound.

On reflex, Ricón cut with his saguaro-oiled scim, expecting his scim to slide right through even as he did so, but to his surprise, it struck bone. The monster shrieked, twisting in a cloud of rotten robes and bone as it rose higher and higher.

Where it vanished in midair.

Silence.

Ricón heaved and glanced at his scim. The blade was now coated in a black, tar-like substance.

"*Sieta a'mon...what was that?*" Bett said just as another one appeared in the opposite direction.

And another.

And another.

Dozens of them, in all directions, now gliding toward them like the tide.

Ricón cursed. "The saguaro!" he ordered his men, and this time they did not hesitate, stabbing their blades into the saguaro's cracked flesh. A horse bolted, but he did not make it far before three of the demons descended upon him like vultures and tore him apart as he screamed.

*Sieta a'mon...*

The night erupted in shrieks and inhuman wails, and the demons swept nearer.

"Uki!" Ricón yelled, but Gamla did not rise from his seat, did not stop murmuring.

Ricón and his men formed a circle around him. Ricón wondered how in the stars they were going to survive so many.

And the horde descended.

Ricón fought, never breaking, never ceasing. Never giving those demons an inch. They shrieked and they screamed as poisoned steel pierced their bones. His uki had been right; whatever was in that tree was working, but Ricón did not know how long it would last, and there were so many of them.

And then a man screamed.

Ricón stole a glance back to see Joca lifted off his feet by two of the demon vultures, and Ricón was poising to throw his scim when a demon descended upon him instead.

There was a flash of light.

A keening, ear-splitting wail so loud the air shook with it.

Joca dropped in the sand, straining and coughing, and when the light faded, the monsters were gone.

Ricón panted, sweat dripping and heart hammering, scim trembling in hand.

"Where did they go?" Vizi asked in terror as everyone looked frantically around.

It was then that Gamla stood. Satisfaction lit his eyes, and he pointed south.

Ricón expected to see more of those demons, but instead he saw nearly two dozen silhouettes. *Human* silhouettes, *walking* upon the sand, toward them. These cast long shadows in the moonlight, and the one in front had a sheet of long, black and white hair.

Gamla smiled, his eyes completely present and aware. "They

are here." Gamla patted Ricón's hand and started toward the group.

"Who are they?" Ricón called after his uki, but Gamla only kept walking as the group slowly approached.

Ricón cursed, then started after his uki. "Uki, *wait*."

But his uki did not wait. He strode forward with purpose and strength of a caliber Ricón had not seen since finding him in that cave.

The silhouettes were close enough now that Ricón could see faces with normal *human* features, inked glyphs painted around them.

Liagé.

What in the stars...?

They did not look unfriendly, and they did not draw weapons, but Ricón knew well that Liagé did not need steel to pierce, and so he kept his hand steady upon his scim. Hoss kept stride beside him, his hand at his waist.

A half-dozen paces away from the other group, Gamla stopped, and so did they, and Ricón and Hoss stopped behind him.

Wind howled through that great divide, throwing sand and pulling at the old woman's sheet of hair. Ricón counted twenty-six in total, men and women aging from late adolescent to...he had no idea how old that woman could be. She looked as though she were in her eighties, but Ricón also knew that Liagé did not age normally. She could easily be one hundred and fifty.

The old woman looked at him with eyes sharper than any scim. "You are Sur Ricón Masai of Istraa?" She spoke in Sol Velorian.

Ricón blinked with astonishment. "I am," he replied in her tongue, though the dialect felt clunky in his mouth. Then, "You sent the tyrcorat away."

She regarded him, and the rest of her party watched, cautious. "Your sister defeated Fyri and her tyrcorat," the woman replied to Ricón's surprise. "Unfortunately, there are other creatures who plague this land. I do not know what those were, but many horrible things have come forth with the tyrcorat gone. It was foolish of you to have come."

She wasn't wrong.

"Well, I thank you for saving our lives," Ricón continued. "We will return to the Provinces at dawn."

"Then you can be our guide, for that is where we are headed."

Ricón's first instinct was to say no, but after what had just happened, he realized his uki had been right. They needed Liagé to help them fight Azir and his Mo'Ruk.

Assuming these Liagé would agree. They could be heading into the Provinces to join forces with Azir, but if that were the case, why bother saving Ricón and his men? It was clear this woman had already known who he was.

"What business have you in the Provinces?" Ricón asked.

The woman studied him. "We are not your enemy, young sur. The heart chooses evil. The Shah does not make one so. Your sister asked for our help against Azir, and we denied her. We were wrong."

Ricón was still skeptical. "So what made you change your mind?"

The woman did not answer immediately, as if she were deciding whether or not she could trust him with the truth. "Shortly after your sister departed, our Sight returned. Know that we seers have not been able to See anything outside of Sol Velor for over a hundred years." Here, she paused, studying Ricón as if to ensure he followed. "Now we all very clearly understand what is at stake, and we have come to make amends to Imari, and to our gracious Maker, and do everything in our power to put an end to Azir once and for all. As the Maker wills."

It was then Ricón noticed they all carried satchels full of supplies. They hadn't just happened upon Ricón's group because they lived nearby. No, they were here because they'd already been traveling, and Ricón was very fortunate they'd stumble across him and his people when they had.

"You never said your name," Ricón said at last.

The woman looked at him a long moment, and then she smiled. "I am Hiatt," she said, "And we are the Liagé of the Mazarat."

## 32

*C*hez rode them hard through wind and snow. Their stolik kept an impressive pace, as if he too understood the urgency and what was at stake, while Niá clutched Chez tight, hoping they weren't already too late.

*Keep her safe*, Niá prayed. *Please...if you're there. Protect her.*

Niá didn't pray often. She used to, when she was a little girl, but she'd stopped calling out to the Maker after her first night at Ashova's when she'd cried out, and he had not intervened. He'd abandoned her to monsters, and she had cursed his name ever since.

It was why Bahdra had been so easy to follow, despite Oza Taran's warnings. For why should Niá care about honor when her own creator had disregarded hers?

The problem, however, was Imari.

Because Imari had shown her what was possible. Imari had shown her what was *good*. She was the one Niá should follow—and *would*, for as long as Niá walked on this earth. It was upon Imari that Niá's fears now rested while Chez masterfully guided their stolik through the snowy Blackwood. He did not take the road; he'd said he did not trust it. But he navigated these woods as though he'd memorized the placement of each and every tree, every dip and stream, intent on the unknown ahead.

Eventually, he slowed, and Niá realized they'd reached the edge of the Blackwood. A wide lawn stretched before them, white with snow, and beyond loomed the imposing skal-black wall and the abandoned statues framing its gate. A few figures walked the ramparts, and more stood over the gate. Nothing looked amiss from here. There were no signs of battle, and the snow remained untouched.

"There's a spyglass in my pack. Can you reach it?" Chez asked.

Niá fumbled a little with the strap. They'd secured Chez's pack to the horse's flank, and the rope had twisted in their flight, but she finally got it open and withdrew the cylinder of solid brass.

She handed it to Chez, who expanded the brass into a jointed rod, then turned back to Skyhold and held it to his eye.

"*Scat.*" Chez went rigid. "Scat-scat-*scat.*"

Niá's spirits dropped on the first *scat.* "What do you see?" she whispered, trying to spot the source of his cursing.

He handed her the glass. She took it and—a bit awkwardly, because she'd never used a spyglass before—held it to her eye.

"Other way," Chez said.

Oh.

She turned it around and tried again.

"Past the gate, top of the watchtower."

It took Niá a moment to find the watchtower at this magnification. She swung the spyglass too high at first and found herself looking only at heavy gray clouds, but then she finally managed to find the topmost platform of the watchtower.

Where three men stood talking as the wind tossed their hair. She didn't recognize any of them, and only one wore the traditional Corinthian arms. "Who are they?"

"The one with brown hair is Kormand Vystane," Chez said, his tone grim.

Niá froze. "As in Brevera's king?"

Chez tipped his chin, eyes fixed on that tower. "And those are Breverans walking that wall."

This time, Niá pulled the spyglass away to aim before she looked through. She found the wall, moved the glass slowly to the ramparts—

Sure enough, she spotted two dressed in Corinthian arms, but the others were buried in brown leathers and thick furs.

Niá could not understand what this meant. Her first thought was that Kormand might be here to help Corinth, but Chez's reaction spoke to something else entirely. And as she considered the situation, even if Jeric had somehow reached out to Brevera for help and Kormand had agreed, Kormand couldn't possibly have arrived so soon.

Unless he'd already been here.

And *that* was who Stovich had unwittingly intercepted on his way home.

"Skyhold's been taken," she said, handing back the spyglass. Chez took it. "Aye."

"But *how*? There's no signs of any—"

The gate's double doors opened, and three riders exploded out of it. One wore Corinthian colors, the other furs, and the last was draped in a rich black cloak that billowed in the wind like a demon. It was a blot of ink against the stark white, as though it had seeped through a tear between worlds. But Niá's attention had been swiftly drawn to the figure hunched before it, the one tied to the saddle and propped up by the demon's arms.

Even from a distance, she knew it was Imari.

Chez held the spyglass back to his eye and cursed a second later. "You godsdamned sonofabitch."

Chez's words brought her back, and she looked at him in question.

"That's Hersir." Chez dragged his teeth over his bottom lip.

Niá looked from Chez to the one dressed in Corinthian blues.

The one who had escorted them to the kitchen. "Corinth's Lead Stryker?"

Chez tipped his head, too angry to speak.

No wonder there hadn't been a fight. Jeric's entire military had been compromised. Rulers were only as powerful as their constituents permitted them to be, and Jeric's had handed his throne to Brevera.

But *why*?

She looked at Su'Vi, and the answer settled in Niá's mind: Hersir had bartered with Azir. Imari for peace.

*Fools.*

Azir would never honor it; deceitful men did not recognize honor.

Suddenly, Niá felt a sharp jolt on that well of Shah power from the direction of the robed figure, but the strength in this connection startled her.

Because it pulled as strongly as Bahdra's had.

Niá realized then that the rider was slowing down, cowl turned in their direction.

In a rush, Niá pulled off her glove and picked the scab off her arm from her last enchantment, then wiped her finger in the fresh blood and prayed it would be enough as she drew a quick symbol on herself.

"Niá..." Chez warned as he gripped the reins, preparing to run.

But they would never outrun that rider.

"Look at me," Niá demanded, her tone urging him to hurry, and he did. He watched her, fear in his eyes, as she drew that same symbol upon his forehead, then spoke a word. Her glyphs flared faintly, power pulsing as the enchantment took.

Momentarily severing her tie to the Shah so that the rider would not sense her power. Niá hoped it would be enough.

Hersir and the other rider had slowed, but the cloaked demon holding Imari had stopped completely. Air pulsed forth in a sphere of contorted air. It pushed toward Niá and Chez like some localized gust of wind, kicking snow and carrying a whisper. A word; a command.

*Reveal.*

Niá reacted on instinct. She spoke another word, hoping and praying that there was still enough power left in her glyphs to activate this spell.

That burst of unnatural air slipped right around them, like water over rock, knocking snow from the thick boughs instead, and then...

Silence.

The figure sat inhumanely still, gazing in their direction. Chez's gloved hands flexed over the reins, and Niá placed her hand on his arm, silently urging him to wait. To trust her.

The cloaked demon made a gesture to the guards upon the wall, kicked the stolik, and finally rode on. Hersir and the other rider fell in behind, but it wasn't until the trees swallowed them and the guards at the watchtower turned away that Niá dropped her forehead against Chez's back and sighed with relief and exhaustion. Her second enchantment had left her winded.

That had been too close.

Chez shifted, though she didn't lift her head.

"That was a Mo'Ruk," Chez whispered.

"Su'Vi. And Imari was on that horse."

A beat. "I need to find Jeric."

Niá sat up. Her eyes found Chez's hard blues, and she was about to argue when another band of riders exploded from the gate. Niá counted five, some dressed in Corinthian arms, some not, and they were all galloping straight in her and Chez's direction.

So *that* was the meaning of the gesture Su'Vi had given. She'd ordered a search party.

Chez cursed. "Hold on." He wheeled them around.

Niá barely fastened her grip in time and looked behind her as

Chez guided them farther into the trees. He didn't dare urge their horse to run and give them away. Niá could no longer see the riders through the trees, but their thundering gallop grew louder as they neared, and Niá knew that no matter Chez's powers of evasion, they had one very real problem that he could not avoid: tracks.

Niá gripped Chez's shirt with one hand and used her other to wipe through her blood and draw another symbol upon her forearm. She closed her eyes and spoke the command, then pursed her lips and exhaled, as though she were putting out a candle. The breath tingled as it left her lips, imbued with Shah power, and Niá watched as it pushed the snow behind them like a strong and localized wind, smearing their tracks.

The thundering soon stopped, and a voice echoed. Their pursuers had entered the Blackwood and were probably searching for the tracks they knew must be there.

Meanwhile, Chez led them silently and steadily down an embankment, where a stream cut through the snow. They splashed along the bank, leaving no tracks behind, while Niá kept watch behind them. They rounded a boulder, and suddenly their stolik reared upon hind legs with a whinny. Niá fought to hold on.

"Whoa...easy..." Chez tried to steady their horse, to keep it from bolting, and a low growl sounded ahead of them.

A dark shape slunk out from behind a wide tree trunk a dozen yards ahead, and Niá's blood turned to ice. At first she thought it was one of the creatures they'd run across in Liri, the one that'd taken Saza's form. This bore the same inky black skin, the same elongated and sinewy limbs, but it was also different. Its snout was long and canine, its spine bowed, and its eyes were yellow with pinpricked pupils.

A shade. It had to be.

"Niá," Chez said, low and even. "My nightglass."

But she was already digging into the pack for it.

The shade slunk nearer, its eyes fixed on them as its thin lips curled back with a snarl. Razor sharp teeth gleamed.

Niá slipped Chez the blade, and Chez slid from the saddle. Behind them, Niá heard a splash; their pursuers had reached the river.

She jumped from the saddle and landed in the snow.

"What are you doing?" Chez snapped, though he didn't turn to look.

"They're at the stream."

And then three things happened very fast. Their horse bolted. The shade lunged at Chez. And a man holding a crossbow and wearing Corinthian plates appeared around the boulder.

However, the shade's presence caught the Corinthian off guard, and he stood in momentary bewilderment as Chez dove into an evasive roll. The man didn't see Niá until Niá was charging him with blood on her palms.

"They're over here!" the man yelled, then swung his crossbow toward her, but Niá was too close, and she rammed into him, throwing them both back against the boulder. He was much larger than she was, and stronger, and the moment he'd regained his balance, he threw her right off again.

But she'd managed to do what she'd needed.

Niá whispered the word even as she hit the ground. She felt that familiar tingling pulse of energy, and then the man started screaming.

Well, if his fellows hadn't heard him before, they certainly heard him now.

Niá shoved herself back to her feet to see the man clawing desperately at his breastplate, which was now glowing with heat, thanks to the mark Niá had drawn upon it. Chez was still trying to get an advantage on the shade, dodging and diving and swiping the nightglass. The shade charged and Niá cried out, but Chez dove aside again, twisting as he fell, and rammed the nightglass into the shade's belly.

The shade screamed a horrible, alien sound that all of Skyhold would have heard.

Niá cursed, then picked up the crossbow the man had dropped in his desperation to rip the burning plates from his body. She distantly noted the squared tip of the bolt as she aimed and shot him right in his exposed chest.

His body jerked as he gave a cry, and he collapsed. A split second later, Niá dropped the crossbow and ran to him, put her foot to his chest, and ripped the bolt from his body before turning to face a wide-eyed Chez. Behind him, the shade lay dead and bleeding black into the snow.

"If they find this, they'll know we did it." She held up the bloodied bolt.

Chez closed his mouth. He blinked.

"Oi, Gavis!" a voice yelled from farther down the river. "You all right?"

Niá and Chez exchanged a look. Without a word, they dragged the man's body closer to the shade. Chez plucked a dagger from the man's belt and wiped it in the shade's black blood. He cut quick on the dead man's jugular—three close incisions to resemble claw marks, but Niá glanced away as thick, dark blood burbled. Chez set the bloodied dagger just out of the man's reach so that it looked as though it'd slipped from his hands as he'd died, then Chez grabbed Niá's hand, and the two started running. Suddenly, Chez jerked her behind the twisted roots of a fallen pine, and two riders rounded the boulder.

Chez squeezed her hand tight as they crouched, still and silent. One of the men cursed and both dismounted, rushing toward their fallen comrade. Niá used the blood on her hands to draw a new symbol upon her forehead and Chez's, then spoke the word of concealment. Just in case. Chez might be able to take them on, but if none of these men returned to Skyhold, Kormand would send more.

But the effort made her dizzy, and she slumped against Chez.

"Rutting shade..." one said with a huff. Leather creaked. "Thought these bastards were supposed to leave us alone."

So they'd known shades were here. Interesting.

"Kormand will wanna know," said the other. Their accents were clipped and harsh.

"Aye."

"Hey, look at this..." said another with suspicion.

Niá's heart raced, and she and Chez exchanged a long glance as the men fell quiet. A second later, Niá heard them whisper.

They'd found the hole in the dead man's chest.

Chez squeezed her hand hard but drew a blade with his other. A twig snapped nearby, and one breath later, a large man with a full and bushy beard peered around the tree roots.

Chez's body flexed to move, but Niá squeezed his hand with a wordless and insistent *no*.

The man looked directly at them.

No, *through* them. He frowned, scanning the landscape all around while Niá's heart pounded against her ribs.

"See anything?" the other called out.

"Nothing," the man said with disappointment. He gave the forest one last glance then stalked back around the broken tree.

Chez stared at her with wonder as she closed her eyes with relief and exhaustion.

"What the hell did this, then?" the other man asked.

"Must've been the shade. There's no one else out here." A beat. "Help me pick him up."

There was grunting, a fair bit of cursing, and within a few minutes, the men continued on their way. Night had descended in full, and the trees shivered in the ice-flecked wind.

"Help me get Jeric," Chez whispered fiercely.

Niá didn't respond.

Chez grabbed her wrists. Not uncomfortably, but as one begging and pleading with everything he was. Niá looked at him —at the desperation in his eyes for his leader and his friend—

and she did not pull away. "Please, Niá. With you, I might actually be able to save him."

"Chez, he..." She hesitated. "We don't even know if he's alive."

"I know that." Chez didn't let go. "But if he *is*, I will never forgive myself."

Niá knew what that was like. She lived with that regret every day of her life.

She looked sharply away, but Saza was there too. Eyes vacant and black and empty. The wind snapped, and her eyes burned. Imari needed her help, but Niá wasn't naive enough to think she could take on Su'Vi all alone.

Niá looked back at him, into those clear blue eyes. In them, she saw her reflection.

"All right," she said at last. "How do we get in?"

# 33

Three hours later, by cover of night, Niá stood at the base of Skyhold's great skal wall beside Chez, who was throwing a metal cleat at the ramparts. He'd found the cleat amidst the abandoned scaffolding, nearly giving Niá a heart attack since the scaffolding was just beside the gate, where a handful of Corinthian and Breveran guards stood watch. The night was dark, the moon hidden behind a thick layer of clouds, and her concealing enchantments still hummed with power, but her heart clearly didn't trust either, because it was hammering against her ribs as if it were about to break out of them.

Chez had come back with a rope and a bent piece of skal, taken one look at her, and whispered, with a smirk, "Worried about me?"

Niá had pressed her lips together and glared, then started walking past him. He'd gently grabbed her shoulder and said, "That way."

She'd stopped. And then she'd turned around and stridden in the opposite direction.

They'd jogged along the wall's perimeter, pausing only when they heard voices above, and Chez finally stopped at a joint in the wall—a rectangular protrusion that rose from ground to crest like a spine. There, Chez tied the rope to the bent piece of skal and instructed Niá to stand back.

Niá had initially suggested they use the secret entrance to the sewers, but Chez had expected that entrance wasn't so secret anymore and didn't want to take chances.

"There are other ways to get inside the fortress," Chez had said, "once we're inside the city, and we also don't know for certain that Jeric is being held in the fortress."

Chez's third attempt took; he tugged hard once. Twice. But the cleat held. He looked down at Niá with indecision.

"I'll go first," she said, but he grabbed the rope.

"No, I'll go. I want to make sure it holds, and I can keep watch while you're climbing." His tone didn't leave any room to argue, and he also didn't wait for her answer. He grabbed the rope and started climbing, hand over hand, feet braced against the slick skal wall.

Niá watched him go, impressed by his speed and agility, though he still favored his right arm just a little, but the higher he climbed, the faster her heart raced. He soon reached the top, climbed over, and looked to the spaces she could not see before motioning at her to follow.

She did as he had done—or tried to. The rope was raw and frayed, and it cut into her already aching palms, and her bloodied hands kept sliding. She propped her feet as Chez had done, but she wasn't nearly as graceful or quick, and when she was halfway up the wall, she made the mistake of looking down.

Her breaths quickened, her palms sweat, and her vision began to swim.

"*Ni!*" Chez said as loud as he dared.

She looked up. Chez was bending over the wall, looking down, though she could not see his features in the darkness.

And he began to pull.

Niá ground her teeth, forcing herself to hold it together, to steady her breaths. To hold on. Her fingers ached from gripping so tightly, and her palms kept slipping.

And slipping.

A fall from this height would kill her. Just as she felt that she could no longer grip the rope, Chez caught her by the wrist.

A little gasp escaped her as her legs dangled over ground that was too far away.

"Give me your other hand," he hissed.

Niá shut her eyes. *Focus*.

She reached for him with her free hand, and he caught her and pulled her over. She tumbled right over the wall and onto Chez, sending them both stumbling back onto the walkway.

Voices sounded to the right, farther down the walk, and they both froze, her palms against his chest, his arms around her waist. Niá could just make out two silhouettes walking toward them. One of them was holding a torch, and there was nowhere to hide.

"Follow my lead," Chez said in her ear, then jumped to a stand, simultaneously kicking the cleat back over the wall and jerking Niá to her feet.

"Oi! You there!" a man called out in that same harsh accent.

"Don't say a word," Chez murmured, holding her firmly beside him as the men approached. "Hey," Chez called back to the men. His voice was surprisingly bright and even, if not a little winded. "Did either of you two see a Scab pass by on your end?"

The word made her insides squirm, but she knew what Chez was doing.

The guards were close enough for Niá to distinguish features: one was short and built like Majutén cattle, and the other was about Chez's height. Both wore breastplates, but not of Corinthian design. Niá spotted a crest over the short one's left breast: two crossed swords within a circle.

Breveran.

The men stopped. The taller one frowned as he looked from Niá to Chez. "Where the hells did you come from?"

"That ladder," Chez said, slow and deliberate, with a bit of patronization as he pointed to a break along the inner wall that Niá had not noticed until that moment. The top of a ladder was just visible through the opening. "Anyway, I caught her trying to escape." Chez jerked Niá's arm, but not painfully. "Her mate ran too, and I thought I saw him come up here. Have you seen anyone?"

The shorter one looked less interested in the situation than a moment ago, but the taller one was looking over Niá, then drew his sword and pointed the tip at Chez's nose.

Niá stopped breathing.

"Then explain to me why you're both covered in blood and neither of you are wounded."

A beat.

"It is my menses. My lord." It was the first thing that popped into Niá's mind.

She felt the slightest twitch in Chez's hand, but her answer was effective. The man's expression twisted with disgust as he looked her over.

"Everything all right over there?" called out a voice from farther down the wall.

Niá kept her gaze down and stood as though to diminish herself. It was easy enough to do; she'd had lots of practice.

"Fine," the taller guard barked back. He turned to Chez and added, "But I'd better not catch you up here again, or you forfeit the Scab."

Chez inclined his head then jerked Niá around with a fair bit of force—for show, she knew. Still, her nerves hummed with old memory, and her muscles tensed.

"Climb down before I push you down," Chez said roughly for the guards to hear, though his grip on her arm was tender.

Niá cried out as if in pain—again, for show—and started

down the ladder. Chez climbed down after her, grabbed hold of her arm again, and started dragging her away while the guards watched from the ramparts.

"What if they'd recognized you?" she whispered once they'd rounded a corner.

"Lucky they were Breveran," he whispered back. He pulled her into a shadowy niche between two cramped buildings, and there he leaned back against the wall and dragged a hand over his face before his eyes fixed on hers. "Sorry about that."

He meant the insult. And the force.

"Don't apologize unless what you said is true."

His gaze held hers, he nodded once, then looked to the street beyond. She could just see Skyhold's magnificent fortress looming over the city, though it was all silhouettes and torchlight at night. To Niá, it still wasn't initially apparent this city had been taken. There were no signs of battle or distress. The lanterns burned as they'd done just last night, though there were fewer, and the city lay quiet. But therein lay the difference—the quiet. The absence of life, of motion and sound, and most of the city's windows sat dim and dark. Skyhold's citizen were here, but no one wanted to be seen, for no one knew what to expect from this new Breveran master.

Just then, a handful of men stepped onto their street. Chez and Niá ducked back and waited for them to pass, then Chez motioned for her to follow.

She hurried after him, staying in the shadows, and Chez was careful to keep a good distance from the guards ahead of them. Chez eventually stopped at the end of an alley, where a wide and open square unfolded before them, and at its center stood an enormous pyre marked by three prominent posts.

Wood for a sacrifice.

Niá looked at Chez, whose eyes lit up for perhaps the first time since they'd found Stovich's headless body.

Because that pyre meant Jeric was still alive.

Chez watched the men pass through the heavily guarded double doors of a low, squat, and windowless building on the other side of the courtyard.

"Stryker quarters," Chez said, answering Niá's unasked question. "That's where they're keeping Jeric."

"You're sure?"

"I bet my life on it."

"Now what?" Niá asked, for there was no obvious way to sneak inside.

But to her surprise, Chez grinned. "Now, we follow the rats."

## 34

The door to Jeric's prison opened, and a very familiar silhouette filled the space within.

Kyrinne's.

He should hate her, and he did; however, it paled in comparison to the hatred he felt for himself right then.

Kyrinne said something to the guards beyond his door, then grabbed a lantern and brought it with her into Jeric's prison. She closed the door, but not completely, leaving a crack for safety.

Jeric almost laughed.

Kyrinne looked at him, and her expression settled into righteous triumph, though anger swam in her eyes. Rejection was pride's greatest vulnerability, and he had exploited Kyrinne's completely.

"My lady," Jeric said with all the charm in the world.

Which only stoked Kyrinne's anger. "You will burn tomorrow."

"Then I'll see you in hells."

Kyrinne marched forward and slapped him across the face.

Jeric swung in his chains, wincing as metal carved into his wrists, and he flexed his aching jaw, surprised he tasted blood.

"I *loved* you," she snapped.

"Right, so at which point did you start rutting Kormand? Is this a recent development, or have you been rutting him for a while?"

Emotions were so easy to extort, and Kyrinne's features twisted. "Don't you *dare* judge me."

"I'm not judging. I'm impressed," Jeric said, then spat blood on the ground. "You took my throne without a fight. I'd appoint you head of my army if you weren't a godsdamned traitor."

"*Traitor?*" she hissed, leaning close. "This coming from the man who abandoned Corinth to chase after a *Scab*. You've been gone for three months!"

"It was when your father started his business dealings with Brevera, wasn't it?" Jeric continued. "You were forging your own alliances in case you and I didn't work out...but I'll admit: I definitely underestimated how much you wanted the throne if you were willing to bed that ugly sonofabitch and sacrifice your own father—"

Kyrinne punched him right in the stab wound she'd given him. Pain lanced through his body, and Jeric hissed through his teeth as he bounced upon his chains.

"You're such an ass," Kyrinne snarled.

"That's the only honest thing you've ever said to me." Jeric managed.

Kyrinne glared at him, and Jeric laughed, which further inflamed her anger.

"We'll see who's laughing tomorrow when you and the rest of your pathetic mutts are burning in the square."

Jeric's laugh tapered, but his smile stretched wide, all teeth. "Go to hells, Kyrinne."

She pressed her lips together, fuming, then gathered her skirts and picked up her lantern. "I'll enjoy watching you burn."

"No, you won't."

She turned on her heels.

"I'll give your regards to your father," Jeric called at her back.

She flinched at that but slammed the door shut, and Jeric sagged in his chains with a sigh.

Gods*damn*it.

His wound was on fire again, his head felt dizzy, and *by the gods,* if he hadn't been chained, he might have killed her just then. Gods, for all he'd accused his father and brother of weakening Corinth, he'd practically handed Corinth over on a silver platter named Kyrinne.

Jeric didn't realize he'd passed out until a thud sounded against his door. He woke with a sudden gasp, chains rattling, and his door flew open.

Light spilled in, and Jeric blinked, certain he was hallucinating. It was a man dressed in Breveran clothes but wearing Chez's face.

"Oh, thank the gods..." Chez rushed forward.

Jeric closed his eyes and opened them again, but Chez was still there. "What the hells..."

Chez chuckled as he reached above Jeric's head to unfasten the shackles. "Ni, can you open these?"

And then Niá was there—also wearing a Breveran coat—reaching over Jeric's head as she spoke a word. A breath of tingling air whispered over his wrists, and the bindings clicked open.

Jeric collapsed.

Chez cursed, barely catching Jeric in time before he hit the ground. "I've got you."

Jeric leaned on Chez, and together they stood while Niá hurried to the door and peered out to keep watch.

"How"—Jeric grunted—"in the hells did you get in?"

"The old cistern. Found Braddok and Jenya first, and they helped us find you."

Braddok was alive. Jeric felt suddenly overwhelmed with relief.

And Chez had used Skyhold's old waterways, which Jeric's father had literally barred after people had begun taking residence within them. But those bars would not stop an enchantress like Niá.

Jeric looked at Chez. "Stovich is dead. Anaton too. Hersir—"

"I know," Chez replied solemnly, and then Braddok appeared in the doorway.

Braddok's left eye was swollen shut, and he had a nasty gash along the left side of his face, but he was *alive* and wearing Corinthian armor that was much too small for him. The men exchanged a long glance, and Braddok nodded once.

"We stuffed the bodies in storage," Braddok said, and Jeric suddenly understood where they'd acquired their new attire. "Jen's keeping an eye on the stair."

"Good," Chez replied. "And you grabbed clothes for—"

"Where's Imari?" Jeric cut him off.

They all fell quiet, and Jeric's blood pressure skyrocketed.

"Su'Vi took her," Niá answered.

Jeric ground his teeth and shut his eyes, feeling that pressure rise and rise. It made his chest ache. "When?"

"A few hours ago," Chez replied. "Niá and I saw them ride off."

Jeric opened his eyes and looked at Niá. Her anguish mirrored his.

"We need to get moving," Braddok said from the door, gesturing sharply down the hall beyond.

"Can he walk?" asked a woman's heavily accented voice, and then Jenya appeared just outside the door, also wearing a Breveran coat. Her left thigh had been bandaged, her leathers were stained with blood, and she was holding out a large pair of boots and a fur-lined Breveran coat.

Jeric took a step, but his leg gave, and Chez caught him again. Chez exchanged a quick glance with Niá, who then turned to Jeric and said, "I'm no healer, but I know a trick to dull the pain."

"I'd take her up on it," Jenya said, gesturing to her own bandaged leg.

Jeric clenched his teeth and nodded once, then Niá wiped her finger in his blood, painted a word upon his leg, just beneath the wound, closed her eyes, and spoke a word. Jeric felt that rush of tingling air again, and the pain in his leg subsided. It wasn't gone, just quiet. A dull ache where there had been fire.

"Thank you," he said.

"You're welcome." Niá wiped her bloodied finger upon her coat. "Be careful with it though. It's not healed."

"Did Kormand do that?" Braddok asked as Jeric shrugged into the coat Jenya had brought.

"Kyrinne," Jeric replied.

Braddok guffawed. "Didn't think she had it in her."

"That makes two of us." Jeric pulled on the boots with Chez's help, and they all stepped into an empty hall. Chez snagged a sleek and well-engineered crossbow he'd propped against the wall, and Jeric noticed the Stryker emblem branded upon the tiller's underbelly.

Jeric looked at Chez, who winked then tossed a sheathed sword and belt at him.

"Couldn't find Lorath," Chez said as Jeric took the blade. It was of Breveran design. A little crude and lacking artistry, but better than nothing at all.

Jeric slung it across his torso, and then Chez led them to the other end of the hall, through a doorway, and into a storage closet, where a crate lay on its side. The grate beneath it had been removed and set aside.

Braddok took a whiff, and his nose wrinkled. "Why is it always godsdamned sewers..."

"Would you prefer your cell, *Rasé*?" Jenya asked.

"Only if you're in it with me." Braddok waggled his brows.

Jenya rolled her eyes then slid her legs over the edge and

propped her hands against the rim. "How far's the drop?" she asked Chez.

"Eh, not far. I'd say Wolf here could reach the grate from the floor."

Jenya slid through and landed with a squelching sound. Braddok groaned and slid through after, and then Jeric sat down on the edge, taking care with his leg.

"You okay?" Chez asked, but Jeric waved him off and lowered himself through.

Gods, he was thankful Jenya had given him boots.

He landed on his one good leg, but his body was weak, and he tumbled sideways, right into Braddok, who barely caught him in time.

Niá dropped down after, then Chez, but then Chez grabbed Niá's waist and lifted her up while Niá slid the grate over the hole and spoke a word. The rim flared white-orange, and the grate melted back into place.

Braddok snorted.

Chez set Niá gently back on the sewer floor, and Niá opened her palm and spoke another word. A soft light appeared, illuminating a long, arched tunnel with a few inches of sewage for a floor.

"Where does this let out?" Jenya asked.

"A few places, but we snuck in through the old armory." Chez motioned for them to start walking. "This eventually joins the main tunnel."

"Which ends where...?" Jenya asked.

They walked mostly single file, boots squelching in the mud and sewage while Niá's little light threw a silvery glow upon the rough stone walls. Somewhere, water dripped, and Jeric kept a hand lightly upon the walls for balance. Though the pain was manageable, he'd lost a lot of blood, and his steps were unsteady.

"Technically Gilder, but the way is barred along multiple joints, and there's a waterfall."

"How did you get through the wall?" Jeric asked.

Chez explained how he and Niá had first escaped Su'Vi and Kormand's guards, then climbed the wall and snuck through the city for the armory.

"You're smarter than you look, Chezter," Braddok said.

"Wish I could say the same..." Chez replied. "But I'm glad you were at the Stryker quarters, because I had no rutting clue how we were gonna get all your asses out of the fortress proper."

Jeric considered the way forward. With Niá's skills, they could try for Gilder, but Gilder could not help them now. What Jeric needed was more men, and a lot of them. Gilder did not have numbers, not like Stovichshold, and maybe...

Maybe.

Yes, they needed to go north, not east, and Jeric remembered what Chez had said about how they'd climbed the wall.

Jeric glanced back at Niá. "Niá, are you able to conceal *all* of us?"

"Not all of you at once," she replied. "With Tallyn's help, perhaps, but I...don't have the strength left to hold the enchantment for each of you simultaneously."

Jeric wondered if Tallyn was still with Grag Beryn up north hunting for shades. If Tallyn had Seen what had happened here, and if he would come. They could certainly use his help now. Regardless, they couldn't afford to wait for the alta-Liagé.

"Do we know how many Breverans are here?" Jeric asked.

"My guess is around fifty," Chez said.

Jenya stopped in her tracks. "That's *it*?"

"You don't need numbers when your own rutting guard sells you out," Braddok murmured.

Jeric didn't doubt there were others among Skyhold's ranks still loyal to him, but there was the matter of sniffing them out. He didn't have that kind of time, and even if he did, there was no guarantee those guards *would* stand, because many had families. As loyal as they might be to Jeric, they would not risk the lives of their families if they believed Kormand had already won. Hence tomorrow's very public burning: a warning to those who might rise against.

Fear was a man's most powerful weapon. Brandish it well, and entire nations would fall to their knees without shedding a single drop of blood.

Their tunnel dipped slightly, following the land's topography, and Chez eventually stopped beneath another grate. He lifted Niá as before, she spoke a word, the metal rim glowed then melted, and she pushed the grate aside. Chez lifted her a little higher, and she peered out, looked around, and then said, "All clear."

One by one, they helped each other out of the hole, and...

Out of a privy.

"I don't even wanna know how you knew this was here," Braddok said, flicking a suspicious mass from his tunic.

Chez waved at them to continue, and they all followed him out of the privy closet and into an empty, dark corridor that opened into a cavernous room that'd once stored an impressive collection of skal weaponry and arms.

Skyhold's armory, which Astrid had depleted while Jeric had been in The Wilds searching for a healer.

"This is your armory?" Jenya murmured with condescension, arms akimbo as she gazed upon the empty racks.

"*Was*," Braddok said. "Until Wolf's dear sister plundered it all and handed it to Bahdra."

Jeric made his way to the large door opposite, listened for a heartbeat, then pushed it open to an empty guardroom. This was traditionally where Commander Anaton's men had kept watch over Corinth's stockpile of arms, but with nothing left to watch, there was no longer any reason to keep it guarded. Jeric ascended the dark and narrow stair to the left, which ended at the third story landing, where the guards had slept. This space was eerily empty now, left to the cold and shadows, though a tall window

324 | BARBARA KLOSS

permitted diffuse light from the outside world. Jeric crossed to that window and peered outside.

His city was quiet and miraculously still intact. In fact, one might never know she'd been taken had one not been intimately acquainted with her usual sounds, the way she breathed and the rhythm of her heart. But Jeric was. He knew every turn, every pattern and sound, and Skyhold was not herself. She was a prisoner in her own home, withdrawn and quiet and far too dark, as though trying to hide from the monster who had taken her away from her rightful master.

Godsdamnit, that woman.

Godsdamnit, his own rutting ego.

Winter air cut through the window and bit at his skin, but Jeric hardly felt it. His gaze landed on three guards patrolling the street perpendicular to the square before them. Two wore Corinthian arms, and the third he recognized as one of Hersir's Strykers.

Maybe Jeric should've kept that godsdamned ring.

The men continued on toward the main square, where Jeric could just see a large pyre and three posts.

*I'll enjoy watching you burn.*

"Think we could sneak through the gate?" Braddok asked, joining him at the window.

"Too many guards."

"I bet my life some of 'em are still loyal to you."

"Perhaps. But we can't risk it."

"Mm." Braddok paused. "If we could just draw them off somehow..."

Braddok's words gave Jeric an idea. He shoved away from the window and hurried back down the steps with Braddok right behind, and he looked straight at Niá. "Can you start a fire from a distance?"

A gleam lit her eye. She'd made the connection.

"Not from a distance—no," she said. "But I could enchant a

projectile, and I happen to know a trick to keep the fire from going out."

Jeric's lips curled. "Perfect."

"And where are we supposed to find a projectile...?" Braddok asked, glancing pointedly about the empty armory.

"We could always throw you," Jenya offered.

Niá pulled a crossbow bolt from her pocket. It was used, judging by the bloodstain soaked into the wood.

"Where'd you get that?" Braddok asked.

"Off the Breverans that followed us into the Blackwood," Chez answered.

Jeric took a closer look, noted the square tip, and smirked. "And it's Breveran."

"Aye," Chez replied with a mirroring smirk.

Jenya caught on and asked, "But will it be enough to distract them?"

"Guess we'll find out soon enough," Braddok said.

"I need your blade," Niá said to Chez, who promptly pulled a dagger from his belt. Niá took it, picked off a scab, and wiped fresh blood upon the edge. The act still startled Jeric, though not as much as it used to. Niá carved the bloodied blade along the arrow's shaft, engraving small Liagé characters. Once finished, she handed the blade to Chez, and Jeric held out his hand for the bolt.

"I don't think so." Chez pushed Jeric's arm away. "Stick to your nose, Wolf. Archery is *my* world."

Jeric eyed him. "Don't miss."

"Please." Chez grunted and took the bolt, and they all ran up the stairs to the window.

"That's a long shot, Chezter," Braddok drawled, and it *was* a long shot, but Chez was exceptional. Almost as good as Gerald had been.

Chez snapped the bolt in place, raised the crossbow, and

gazed down the barrel, all determination. He closed one eye, flexing his fingers, his expression set.

The night breathed.

Chez pulled the trigger.

String snapped, air whizzed, and Jeric hardly heard Niá's whisper as that bolt shot straight for the pyre. The bolt ignited midair, burning like a shooting star, and they all watched in silent apprehension.

Scat.

The bolt wasn't going to make it. The shot had been too short, and Chez cursed the moment he realized it too.

The bolt struck the cobblestones, then bounced and tumbled across the square.

And tumbled, and tumbled...

Right into the pyre.

Jeric held his breath, watching the little flame struggle in the snow.

The fire caught.

A single tendril of flame reached higher, slowly stretching and arching, as though the Maker himself had breathed life onto it. Within five seconds, the entire pyre ignited, casting that quadrant of the city in a brilliant orange glow.

Someone in the square began to yell. Guards shouted. The streets startled awake, and already, Jeric noticed figures moving frantically atop the wall, but there was no space for relief. Not yet. They still had to get through the gate, and he prayed to the Maker that this diversion would be enough to give them a chance. They just needed time to get into the Blackwood, and once there, they could lose any pursuers.

"Let's go," Jeric said. He bolted down the stairs, still favoring his injured leg, and stopped at the main door to listen. He heard distant shouting, but nothing close, so he opened the door a crack and peered into the night.

The square before them lay dark and empty, but to his left, the sky was aglow and flames now reached above the rooftops.

Behind him, Braddok whistled through his teeth. "That was quick."

"Should we climb the east side?" Chez asked.

"We are going through the gate," Jeric answered.

They all looked at Jeric.

"You're serious?" Jenya asked.

"We need horses, or we won't get far."

No one argued, and Jeric threw on his fur-lined cowl, ducked outside, and plunged into the cold night while the others followed. He led them down dark alleys and side streets, stopping only twice as Breverans and Corinthian guards ran past, heading for the unexpected inferno. They finally reached Skyhold's stables, which were wedged against the inner wall. Beyond stood the main gate that Jeric was glad to see hanging wide open, with only one man currently standing guard.

Gods, this might actually work...

The horses whinnied and brayed when Jeric entered the stables, and a young stable hand appeared, only to be knocked unconscious by Braddok a split-second later.

"No time to saddle," Jeric said, running down the line and opening all the gates. Braddok realized what he was doing— Jenya too—and clapped hinds to get the horses running while Chez hoisted Niá atop a large stolik, then climbed on after.

Jeric mounted his own stolik, while Braddok and Jenya climbed on two others.

The guard, who had been futilely chasing after the bolting horses, suddenly stopped when he noticed Jeric and the others galloping toward them.

"Lower the gate! Lower the— " the guard was screaming when a blade sank between his eyes. His words stopped, his knees gave, and he collapsed in the street.

"That's my girl..." Braddok beamed at Jenya.

A few men shouted atop the wall, metal creaked and groaned, and the portcullis began to drop.

*Scat.* "Chez!" Jeric shouted.

Chez aimed his crossbow at the watchtower and fired. There was a sharp cry, and a body fell from the night and landed on the hard ground below, but the portcullis did not stop falling. Chez hurried to snap a second bolt in place as another guard appeared, standing before the gate with a bow raised. However, this guard did not take aim at Jeric. He aimed high, toward the slowly turning gears of the portcullis. He fired, another cry sounded, and the portcullis stopped.

The guard tossed the bow aside and looked at Jeric, who was now upon him.

"Hit me, Your Grace!" the guard yelled at Jeric.

Jeric understood. It needed to look like the man had at least tried to stop them.

"I won't forget this," Jeric promised, then struck him over the head with the hilt of his dagger. The man collapsed as Jeric and the others galloped past, through the gate, and across the open lawn. More men yelled from the wall, arrows zipped by but none struck, and finally the Blackwood's dark shadows swallowed them.


"MY LORD."

"Hurry!" Kormand barked at his men, who were frantically trying to extinguish the inferno that simply would not go out. "It's climbing the rutting wall!"

"*My lord*," Vost repeated, louder this time.

"The hells...put yourself to use, man, and help them carry that trough!"

"The Wolf has escaped."

Kormand froze. He whirled on Vost so fast that Vost flinched and stepped back. "*What?*"

"The Wolf is gone, my lord."

Kormand barreled right to Vost, grabbed him by the collar, and hoisted him to his toes. "What do you mean, *gone*?"

Vost's throat bobbed as he strained to breathe. "His...cell is empty."

Kormand stared hard at his man and then set Vost back upon the ground, grabbed his face between his hands, and twisted. Spine snapped, Vost's body went slack, and Kormand shoved him aside with a growl.

And then he started for the Stryker quarters.

Kivo, Hersir's second-in-command, who'd noticed the exchange, jogged over to him, covered in soot and drenched in sweat.

Kormand did not slow, did not speak. He shoved through the quarters' front doors—now unguarded, as all efforts had gone into putting out this hells storm—and strode down the stairs and to the cells that were holding a Wolf, his dog, and the saredd.

They were empty.

Every. Rutting. One.

He found the men he'd placed on duty shoved into a closet, all dead and stripped of their weapons, boots, and armor.

Kormand picked up a footstool with a yell and chucked it against the wall. Wood exploded.

"I'll send a search party at once," Kivo said.

Which reminded Kormand that Kivo was still there. Kormand whirled on the Stryker. "You had one task!"

A muscle ticked in Kivo's jaw.

"You will find him, or you will not set foot in this city ever again, do you understand?" Kormand snarled.

"Yes, my lord."

Kormand started off.

"What about the execution?" Kivo asked.

Kormand ground his teeth together and dragged a hand over his face. The people needed to see the Wolf King dead, or some would still hope, and he'd sworn that he would handle the Wolf King.

"Burn these until they're unrecognizable and hang them in the square." Kormand gestured at the dead guards as he stormed off.

## 35

*I*mari opened her eyes to a crackling fire. She was lying on her side upon a wool blanket, her wrists still shackled by Liagé binds, and on the other side of that fire sat two figures, one man and one woman, eating and sharing a flask between them. Imari did not know the woman. She was buried in wool and fur, and her hair was a soft brown, threaded with silver, and plaited over one shoulder. The man was angled away from Imari, his head turned from the fire, though his hair was cropped close, his figure trim, and he wore a heavy coat made of rich wool.

"—you think?" the woman was saying in a thick Breveran accent.

"I *know*," the man replied. His voice sang a full bass chord, and Imari was surprised to find she recognized it. He set the flask down beside the woman. "I've word there's over a thousand in those mountains."

The woman took a long drink. "I don't believe it. A group like that can't stay hidden for long."

"They did in the Baragas."

Imari's mind finally caught up. The pair was referring to the Sol Velorians that'd been hiding deep in the Baragas before they'd assembled behind Bahdra's cause, and they seemed to believe another large group existed in a different mountain range.

"Yes, but Branón didn't hunt like your Wolf." The woman said 'wolf' like 'welf.' "He would've sniffed them out."

"He tried," the man said, "but he could never devote enough time due to all the raids."

The woman took another drink. "Then one of his prisoners would've talked. He certainly gave enough to his inquisitors."

The man turned his face back to the fire. It was Hersir.

"Our Head Inquisitor was more concerned about finding her." Hersir gestured in Imari's direction. "There is no knowing what other information he dismissed."

The woman shrugged. "I still find it hard to believe."

"We'll find out who's right soon enough."

The woman tipped the flask toward him, and then her attention flickered to Imari. Their gazes met, and Imari cursed inwardly. The woman froze, flask in hand, and a vicious smile curled her lips. "Well, well, well, looks like our little desert bloom is awake."

Hersir looked over, caught Imari's gaze, and promptly looked away again.

"You rutting coward," Imari snapped at Hersir, but the Liagé binds drained the strength from her voice.

"He's not the one chained and lying on the dirt," the woman answered instead.

"Did you give up your voice too, the day you gave up your honor?" Imari continued, glaring only at Hersir.

The woman set the flask down, stalked toward Imari, and shoved her onto her back. Imari winced as the bindings dug into her wrists and spine, and the woman pressed her boot atop Imari's throat, cutting off Imari's air.

"Know your place, bastard," the woman spat while Imari gasped for breath.

"Karra."

But the woman—Karra—did not relent, and Imari began to see stars.

"*Karra*, that's enough." Hersir stood, ready to intervene, but Karra lifted her boot with a smirk.

Imari wheezed and curled onto her side, and Karra spit on Imari's face with a curse Imari couldn't quite decipher. She was too busy sucking down air.

"What are you doing?" said a voice that cut like the winter wind, ice cold and bitter.

Hersir went rigid. Karra stopped in her tracks.

Imari followed the sound to where Su'Vi stood at the camp's edge, as if she'd simply appeared out of nothing. She stood with impossible stillness and a terrifying calm, though there was nothing calm in those fathomless black eyes.

"We were checking on the girl, *a'prior* Su'Vi," Karra hastened to say, though her voice trembled with unease.

Su'Vi watched Karra. "Whatever harm is done to her will be repaid to you a hundred times."

Karra swallowed, head bowed. "Yes, *a'prior*."

And then Su'Vi's gaze fell upon Imari.

That pale, inked face struck a powerful, dissonant chord within her, and the bindings at Imari's wrists pushed cold sludge through her veins, diffusing whatever emotion had begun to rise.

Su'Vi's attention cut back to Hersir. "You were to inform me at once."

"She only just woke, *a'prior*," Hersir said quietly. His entire bearing seemed diminished beside this powerful Mo'Ruk.

Su'Vi regarded him a moment and then approached Imari. Her boots made no sound upon the frozen earth, nor did her velvety black robes stir, as if the elements themselves could not touch this horrific wonder of the spirit realm.

Su'Vi stopped over Imari, then crouched before her, those black robes pooling upon the ground. Without warning, her hand whipped out, and she grabbed Imari's chin hard, squeezing until Imari's eyes watered.

"Feed her," Su'Vi said abruptly then released Imari and stood.

"I will not help you!" Imari said at Su'Vi's back. "Whatever it is you're planning, I will die first."

Su'Vi walked on as if Imari had not spoken, and then Hersir was there, crouching before Imari with a bowl and ladle.

Imari glared at him, though her body trembled. Her anger was too much, forcing the bindings to filter more sludge into her veins, and she could not stop shaking.

Hersir scooped the ladle into the bowl. He did not look at her.

"What will they do to Jeric?" Imari asked.

Hersir held the ladle to her lips and said, "Drink."

But Imari pressed her lips firmly together and glared at Hersir with all the fire left in her body.

His gaze met hers. Hard. Defiant. Cold. "Drink it, Surina."

Imari spit in his face.

Hersir flinched as her spittle trickled down the side of his cheek, and he looked very much like he might wrap his hands around her neck and squeeze the life from her body. But he appeared to remember Su'Vi's warning and instead dropped the ladle back into the bowl, set it on the ground before Imari, and stood.

"You think that handing me over to Azir will keep Corinth safe?" Imari said after him. "That he'll let you keep your rutting gods? You don't have a—" Heat seared upon her forehead, right between her eyes, and Imari's words cut off with a gasp.

But there was no flame. Just heat—searing, unbearable heat —and then it was gone.

Imari heaved and caught Su'Vi's intense gaze across the fire. Su'Vi's hand was outstretched, her fingers curled. Seeing that Imari understood, she lowered her hand and started to walk away.

"I won't help you!" Imari yelled after her, but her words came out raw and ragged.

Su'Vi paused and glanced back, her expression blank. "I think you'll find that you will." She spoke a word—a word Imari *felt*, like whispers settling into her bones—and her world went dark once more.

·c⸙⊃·

IMARI WAS JOSTLED awake to muted daylight and thick, looming pines. The Blackwood, she vaguely registered as her body bounced. She'd been slung over a horse like a sack and fastened with rope, and her hands were still cuffed in Liagé binds. There were voices, and the horse stopped.

Boots appeared on the ground before her, and then hands were on her body, loosening the rope but not the binds. Imari started sliding down the horse's back, but more hands caught her before she fell.

She lifted her head and found herself looking into Hersir's cold gaze.

"Stand on your feet," he commanded.

She shifted her balance, steadying her feet, and when he was certain Imari could support her own weight, he let go and moved aside, and Su'Vi took his place.

The mere sight of Su'Vi brought the pressure instantly back. It rolled through Imari's body and pushed against her chest like a scream that could not be released.

"Hold her," Su'Vi said and moved behind Imari while Hersir stood before. He grabbed her arms and held them firmly on either side of her body as Imari glared at him.

Su'Vi spoke a word; metal clicked.

Imari's left hand was free.

A rush of tingling swept through that arm as though a dam

had burst, and a gorge of boiling hot water flooded her body, but then Hersir jerked her arms forward and Su'Vi clamped the binding over her wrist again. It immediately pinched off the Shah, the tingling, and the heat, and replaced it with that sickeningly familiar cold sludge.

It felt even colder this time after the sudden fire.

Hersir, with Karra's help, hoisted Imari back into the saddle, properly this time. Karra climbed on behind her, and they all resumed riding again.

Imari didn't realize she'd fallen unconscious again, but the next thing she knew, her eyes opened to Corinth's southernmost mountain range. It towered before them, and the Blackwood had opened to a stretch of land with a wide river snaking through it.

The Fallows.

The river that provided a natural border between Corinth and Brevera and flowed south to where it eventually dumped into Istraa.

Where they were, apparently, heading.

Su'Vi led their small charge of four, her inhuman form a constant stain upon Imari's view. They did not cross any roads but followed the landscape upon a path of Su'Vi's choosing. Sometimes she stopped to survey the horizon, though Imari sensed she watched for the things unseen. All the while, Imari fought against the sludge in her mind for ideas. How to escape or what she would do if she couldn't. Azir wanted her, but to what end? What could he possibly need from her when he'd destroyed an entire city with his Mo'Ruk and a dozen Liagé?

Thinking on Trier made her think of Kai and Ricón. She wondered if Kai was still alive at the behest of that demon, and where Ricón could be. She hoped he hadn't come home, but she also knew her oldest brother. He would not hide from this.

And neither would she. Azir would pay for every life he had stolen.

Day blurred into night, and they camped just outside the

Fallows but rode on before dawn. Conversation was scattered between Karra and Hersir, and they were careful not to share sensitive information. Still, Imari gathered bits of their conversation as they traveled. She learned that Kyrinne had kept a long and secret relationship with Kormand, and when it'd become clear that Jeric had chosen Imari, Kyrinne had committed to a path that sought to remove the Wolf from his throne. Azir's return had proven to be a nominal complication, as long as the Breveran usurper and his promised queen were willing to hand over the *sulaziér*.

Of course, neither of them had hesitated.

And so when Jeric had returned, Kyrinne had sent word to Kormand, who'd already been enroute to Skyhold due to Jeric's prolonged absence. Kormand had notified Su'Vi, then Hersir and Karra had come along to help with Imari, and also to finalize their bargain with Azir.

Whatever that meant.

Su'Vi never said a word—not one. That pale, glyph-painted skin remained a canvas void of human emotion, those black eyes seeing all things and warming to none. Imari found herself pondering if Su'Vi had been this way in her past life. Had she always been a shell of a human, or had Bahdra resurrected the body but left the soul?

Perhaps that soul had been abandoned long before then.

Whatever the reason, Imari found herself hating the sight of Su'Vi but also unable to stop looking at her. She was a walking and breathing antithesis. A living corruption of something intended for good. Imari wondered what had prompted Su'Vi to reject the Maker's path for this one, when Tolya and Taran had resolutely not.

*You're weak, Prior. The years have not been kind to you,* the legion had said to Taran that night.

Taran, who had been an enchantress. Like Su'Vi. Taran, who had lived during Azir's war one hundred years ago.

Suddenly, Imari understood something she had not before. "You weren't Azir's first choice, were you, Su'Vi?" Imari asked.

Imari expected Karra to strike her for speaking, and especially for not using Su'Vi's title, but Karra did not. Ahead, Su'Vi swayed with the horse and did not turn, though her spine straightened just a little.

So Azir's Mo'Ruk enchantress wasn't entirely devoid of emotion.

"It was Taran of Bassi, wasn't it?" Imari continued. "She was Azir's first choice, but she refused, so he picked you."

Of course, Imari hadn't known for certain, but it made the most sense, and seeing the tension settle in Su'Vi's shoulders, Imari decided she was right.

Still, Su'Vi did not turn, and Karra did not intervene, though Hersir was casting Imari a sidelong glance.

On a hunch Imari could not quite explain, she added, "It happened with Fyri too, didn't it? He chose her first, but she's dead. So now it's finally your turn."

Su'Vi stopped her horse.

Karra stopped theirs. Hersir too.

A hungry wind snapped at Su'Vi's robes, but she sat otherwise inhumanly still and silent.

Imari sensed the shift a split second before it happened. Air punched her square in the chest, like some invisible fist, and the force of it threw both her and Karra from the saddle.

Imari flew through the air, legs flailing, and landed hard on her shoulder. Pain exploded, Imari cried out, and her body rolled. And rolled. Her wrists were bound; she could not stop herself. Finally, her body stopped rolling with her face half-buried in the earth. She spit dirt from her mouth and tried pushing herself up, but the moment she put pressure upon her left hand, she knew she had a problem.

A boot shoved down her left shoulder, and Imari gasped in pain.

"Speak again," Su'Vi said with unnatural calm, "and I will break it." Su'Vi shoved her shoulder once more for emphasis. Imari ground her teeth against the pain, and she hardly heard Su'Vi when she said, "Put her shoulder back in place."

A moment later, Hersir was dragging Imari back to a seated position. His expression was tight as he felt around her shoulder. Imari sucked air through her teeth, clenching so hard she thought her molars might shatter. She'd fixed plenty of dislocated shoulders—Chez's recently—but she'd never dislocated her own. Those stretched muscles were like rope around her chest, making it difficult to breathe, and her ligaments were on fire.

Hersir rolled the joint, and Imari braced herself. Stars, she hoped he knew what he was doing, or he could make it worse. Irreparable.

She felt the moment it slid back into its socket. There was some relief, but the muscles had been stretched too far, and the fire did not leave. She winced as Hersir helped her to her feet.

Karra was still moaning and groaning as she hobbled to their shared mount, with one hand on her lower back.

"I'll ride with her," Hersir said.

Karra gave no response, but—slowly, gingerly—climbed back into the saddle. She cast Su'Vi a dark look that Su'Vi did not see, for she had already ridden ahead. Hersir helped Imari onto his horse, then climbed on after, and Imari did not say another word.

## 36

*I*t took Jeric and the others four days to reach the edge of Stovichshold. In good weather and clear roads, the trek took Jeric half the time. The land between Skyhold and Corinth's northernmost hold was rolling but gentle, with only a few intermittent forests and rivers in between; however, a snow-storm had descended not even an hour after they'd fled the city, and they'd been forced to find cover.

But that storm had probably spared their lives.

Niá had kept them warm and dry with enchantments as they'd huddled beneath trees. Wind and snow railed against them for hours, but the storm eventually subsided, and they went on their way. Stoliks were built to endure the cold and snow, even if their riders were not, so the new drifts did not trouble them.

Jeric was thankful for the drifts, because they had also covered their tracks.

He stopped his stolik on a rise, gazing down upon Stovichshold and the prosperous town huddled at its center: Kleider, where Jarl Stovich had lived and managed Corinth's largest hold and skal mine. Behind rose the southern edge of the Serra mountains—a magnificent range that stretched due north to where it eventually touched The Rim and ended at The Crossing bridge, providing a natural border between The Fingers and Davros, intersecting where Kleider staked its claim.

Which was why Stovich had always kept his army well stocked and fed.

Jeric had skirted these mountains with Braddok and Gerald when he'd ridden to The Wilds, but winter had not yet taken residence. Now, those mountains were buried in snow, as was Kleider and everything else in sight.

A short wall of stone and skal hugged the town, and tall chimneys exhaled wisps of smoke. Towers stood watch over both sides of the main gate, which hung open, awaiting a master who would never return.

Jeric hated delivering this news. He might have had a complicated relationship with Stovich, but the people of Stovichshold respected their old jarl, and Stovich had a brother who would never recover from this.

Braddok stopped his stolik beside Jeric. Snow dusted Braddok's brows and beard, and his cheeks were chapped with cold.

"Do you still have the spyglass, Chez?" Jeric asked.

A second later, Chez produced the spyglass, and Jeric put it to his eye.

"Well?" Braddok asked.

"I don't see any Breverans." Jeric gave the spyglass back to Chez, then clucked his tongue and nudged his horse into a gallop.

They tore across the open land, kicking clumps of snow behind them. The wintry air burned Jeric's eyes and nose and numbed his fingers, but the sight of Kleider was like fire to his soul, and he pressed harder. Figures took shape at the towers, gathering as they spotted the new arrivals, but the gate did not close. Jeric slowed his stolik to a trot, rode right through those broad and open doors, and stopped just inside the walls.

Where about two dozen guards were waiting for them, swords and lances drawn.

Jeric raised placating hands as the rest of his party stopped behind him.

"Your Grace...?" a man suddenly called out from the horde.

Jeric followed the voice and almost sighed with relief. It was Fyrok, a young man in his late teens who'd been hunter Grag Beryn's newest and most promising recruit. Gods above, he hoped this meant Tallyn was here.

"That's your king. Put your swords away," Fyrok barked as he shoved through the remaining guards.

Swords and lances lowered, and Jeric jumped down from his stolik, ignoring the burst of pain that shot through his wounded leg. Niá's enchantment was wearing off. "Is Tallyn with you?" Jeric asked tightly.

"Aye, Your Grace," Fyrok replied, taking in their group at a glance. "He's with Grag, eating in the barracks. We got back an hour ago." Fyrok noted Jeric's leg, and then his attention settled on Jeric's stolik, specifically on its bare and unsaddled back. Worry etched the corners of his mouth, and he turned to Kleider's befuddled guards and said, irritably, "Help them with their mounts."

Sharp, that one, and he had mettle. Perhaps if Fyrok tired of hunting with Grag, he'd consider working for Jeric directly. Jeric could teach a man to fight, but he couldn't teach a man to stand by his convictions, and the latter was so much more difficult to find.

And infinitely more valuable.

Jeric handed his stolik to an older man dressed in worn Corinthian arms while Braddok and the others handed off theirs.

"What happened, Your Grace?" Fyrok whispered to Jeric.

Jeric glanced furtively around. "Not here."

Fyrok's brow furrowed, he nodded once, then asked, "You hungry?"

"Rutting *starved*," Chez answered.

Fyrok acknowledged Chez with a glance, then looked back to Jeric and motioned at them to follow. "I'll take you to Tallyn."

They kept a brisk pace through town, and people glanced over, curious and wary. They crossed paths with a group of children kicking a small bucket back and forth across the street. The children spotted them approaching, grabbed their bucket, and scurried out of the way, though their eyes trailed Jeric and his entourage. Whispers followed.

"Was your shade hunt productive?" Jeric asked Fyrok as they walked.

"Aye," Fyrok replied. "We tracked a pack of them into the Serras. Just east of Vongrüt."

That was Stykken's territory. Jeric remembered the letter he'd sent.

"Is Stykken aware?" Jeric asked.

"We intercepted him on the road back."

Jeric looked sideways at Fyrok, and Fyrok nodded once.

"He'd been tracking the same pack, but he's heading back to Vongrüt to bolster their defenses."

They rounded a corner. This section of city opened up, giving space for a wide pit in the ground: Corinth's largest skal mine. A path corkscrewed around the rim from top to bottom, where Sol Velorian slaves ripped precious skal ore from the earth's dark belly against a symphony of chisels and rolling carts and groaning pulleys. It was the sound of labor, of sweat and blood and pain.

Kleider's guards walked patrol, and Jeric spied some standing upon the various tiers of the three watchtowers, guarding this gaping maw of Corinth's most coveted profits—profits of which the Sol Velorians saw none.

Jeric had released the slaves at Skyhold, but Stovich had refused.

344 | BARBARA KLOSS

"Find me men who will work these mines for free, and we'll talk," Stovich had said.

Jeric watched an adolescent boy, all limbs and elbows and not wearing nearly enough clothing to withstand this cold, pushing a wheelbarrow out of the mine's mouth and up the ramp. The barrel rocked and groaned from all the stone piled into it while the boy fought to keep it from toppling over the ramp's edge. Jeric spotted dark blood stains across the boy's back.

"Your Grace."

It was Fyrok, and he was standing a half dozen paces ahead of Jeric, with Jenya, Niá, and the rest of Jeric's pack.

Jeric hadn't realized he'd stopped, and Niá was staring at him intently.

"Where's Hax?" Jeric asked. Hax was Stovich's brother and second-in-command. He would have overseen Kleider and all of Stovichshold in Stovich's absence.

"With Grag and Tallyn when I left," Fyrok replied.

Jeric peeled his attention from the boy and the mines and followed the others to where Fyrok eventually led them to a wide, low building and opened the door, gesturing for them to step inside. Jeric strode through first, ducking under the low lintel and into a room boasting three tables, a counter where a woman stacked dishes, and an enormous hearth with strong fire that chased away the cold. The air smelled of cedar and smoked meat, and Jeric's stomach growled.

Heads glanced up from the table: Grag Beryn, Tallyn—thank the gods—and a stocky, middle-aged man Jeric recognized as Hax.

Gods, he looked so much like Stovich that Jeric could not look upon Hax without seeing the severed head Kormand had dumped upon the floor of his cell.

Seeing Jeric, the three men ceased conversation.

Hax stood. "Your Grace. I wasn't expecting you."

Grag stood too, but Tallyn remained seated, his one pale eye fixed on Jeric while Fyrok closed the door.

"Marta, tell the cooks their king is here, and he needs to eat," Fyrok said.

The woman at the counter—Marta—dropped the wooden mug she'd been oiling, then gasped and hurried to pick it up off the floor. Her gaze landed on Jeric, cheeks flushed as she bowed her head, and she dashed through a door in back.

"Where's my brother?" Hax asked.

Jeric could not bring himself to say the words, and in that empty space of conversation, the blood began to drain from Hax's face. "He's dead," Jeric said at last, and Hax fell perfectly still. "He was killed by Breverans on his way here. Kormand's taken Skyhold."

Jeric's words were met with a long and heavy silence.

"How in the gods did they break through the wall?" Grag asked with disbelief.

Jeric looked at his faithful hunter. "They didn't need to. Hersir opened it for them."

Grag dragged a hand over his face.

"And the Lady Kyrinne?" Hax asked, sounding as though he feared the answer.

"She's perfectly fine," Jeric laughed darkly, leaning back against the counter to take the pressure off his leg. "She's there now, in fact. Probably arranging her and that Breveran pig's new bedchamber."

At this, all three showed varying degrees of surprise.

Jeric absently picked up the mug Marta had been oiling. "It seems her father wasn't the only one making deals." He set the mug down and looked straight at Hax. To see if Hax had known about Stovich's dealings, because Jeric needed to know how deeply Kyrinne's treachery had rooted.

And Hax paled.

"Did you know about Kyrinne?" Jeric said lowly.

"No, I swear." Hax shook his head, looking dazed as he sat down. He dragged both hands down his face and rubbed at his temples. "I knew Stovich was exchanging supplies with Brevera, but gods—"

"You knew, and you said nothing."

Hax looked at him. "He is my brother. And our people were hungry."

Jeric slammed a fist upon the counter, dishware rattled, and Hax flinched. He wasn't the only one who did. "You sold Corinth to Brevera, you godsdamned fool. I've had men stoned for less. The *only* reason you're still breathing right now is because I can't afford to spare any more men."

Hax's lips thinned, and he looked sharply away.

The quiet stretched; an ember popped upon the hearth.

It was Tallyn who broke the silence. "Tell us everything."

And Jeric did, as much as he could, while the others filled in the gaps. At some point, Marta returned, carrying trays of hard breads and stew, which they all ate as Jeric continued his account. Hax seemed particularly disturbed by news of Azir. He'd heard what'd happened with Astrid at Skyhold, and what'd transpired at Trier, but he hadn't realized Azir's return until this moment, and his physiognomy sagged with defeat, and grief.

"Which is why," Jeric said to Hax, "I need every resource Stovichshold has available to help me take Skyhold from that Breveran usurper so that Corinth will stand against Azir."

And then hopefully he would actually have a chance at saving Imari.

Hax sighed and resumed rubbing his temples. "This is a gods-damned nightmare." He stopped rubbing his temples and looked at Jeric. "It's the middle of rutting winter. A war will not be to our advantage."

"Perhaps you should've considered that *before* you started stealing from me."

Hax's cheeks blotched wine. "My brother's death will hit the people hard, and now you're asking them to fight Azir Mubarék and his Mo'Ruk?" Hax shook his head.

"Well, you're a godsdamned ray of sunshine, aren't ya...?" Braddok said, taking a sip of akavit, which he choked on when Jenya smacked his chalice.

Jeric smiled, all teeth. "Perhaps the wiles that persuaded Kormand to trust you will also aid you in persuading your own people."

Hax bristled. "And what if Kormand's got Liagé working with him? If he's allied with Azir, as you say, it's highly probable he's employed them, and we don't have the means of fighting their kind anymore." Hax gave Jeric a pointed look.

"We do have the means," Jeric said, gesturing at Tallyn and Niá.

"Two Liagé aren't going to turn the tide, no matter how powerful they are."

"*One* managed to sneak us out of Skyhold."

"Luck and sloppy oversight," Hax countered. "We're better served fortifying our defenses here. Wait out the winter—"

"No."

Hax sat forward; wood creaked. "I know you're eager to get Skyhold back, but the resources and manpower are *here*—"

"Kleider is not built for siege, and you know it."

"Then at least wait until the snow melts!"

Jeric pushed himself off the counter and stood tall. Hax slunk into himself, the table fell quiet, and when Jeric next spoke, his voice was dangerously low and even. "There are still Corinthian women and children trapped in Skyhold, all subject to the whims of a man who burned an entire city to the ground just to prove that he could. They will not survive the winter, and Azir will not wait for the godsdamned snow to thaw. Our *only* chance is through Skyhold's defenses, or the Provinces are already lost."

Jeric couldn't help but think how right Imari had been that he contact Brom Stykken. He only wished he'd written sooner, because they needed all the help they could get.

"The Wolf is right," Tallyn interjected, breaking the silence. "We need Skyhold's position, her walls, and all of the enchantments forged in her bones. Kleider will not stand against Azir, and he will come—it's just a matter of when."

At last, Hax sat back in his chair. He stretched an arm across the table and tapped his finger. "As Skyhold is so wonderfully fortified, how, exactly, do you recommend we take her back without reaping hard losses, *Your Grace*?"

Jeric flashed his canines. "In much the same way it was taken from me."

Hax eyed him, his fingers stopped tapping. "You think Lady Kyrinne will come back around?"

Jeric laughed, but there was no humor in it. "No, but I'll worry about the details. You make sure we've got enough arms."

"My godsdamned Scabs can't work any faster," Hax said.

Niá tensed.

Jeric noticed. He looked back at Hax, Kleider's second-in-command, and abruptly started for the door.

"Where are you going?" Hax called after him.

*To do something I should've done a long time ago,* Jeric thought but said only, "For a walk," as he threw open the door and stepped out into the bitter cold.

## 37

*F*or Imari, the next week passed in a monotonous haze of night and day, long rides and quick camps. Su'Vi led them south, along the Fallows' eastern bank. Eventually, snow turned to brown grass then sand, the air lost its bite, and Imari knew they'd reached Istraa.

Su'Vi led them into the sweeping Majutén—the same desert she'd crossed with Ricón a few months ago. How different that journey had been, so full of promise and hopeful uncertainty. Of light.

Now, Imari felt only darkness.

It crowded her every waking moment and ruled every dream, for there was no light in her soul. The bindings had severed it from her, and Imari had never felt more alone.

As they crossed the vast ocean of sand, Imari's attention was drawn west, where a plume of dark smoke rose high over Solán— a city managed by Roiess Avinyar. There, black smoke billowed and climbed as it ate up the sky. Though she could not see the city from here, she knew there had been battle, and Roiess Avinyar had lost. Through the scattered conversation between Hersir and Karra, Imari had learned that Azir's forces were spreading across Istraa, taking all they might add to their number and burning the rest. That pillar of smoke was the Roiess's final beacon of despair, her warning to the world, her ashen flag of surrender: This is your future, it said. There will be no mercy. Run and hide while you can.

Imari glanced away and caught Su'Vi's gaze.

She did not like Su'Vi's eyes. They were like the darkness that always crowded her periphery. Too much time looking, and it might swallow her whole.

Imari looked decidedly ahead, but the plume over Solán was not the last.

She spotted at least two more before they finally reached the opposite end of the Majutén, where it sloped into Trier's valley. Where Imari had stopped with Ricón and laid eyes upon Vondar for the first time in ten years.

Not much was left of it now.

The smoke was gone, but Kazak's fire had destroyed her home. It was a scar upon scorched earth, its once-pristine white towers jutting out of the ground like fractured ribs. Vondar itself remained intact, though battle had savagely charred and muti-lated her face, and all the surrounding structures had fallen at her feet. She was like a lone headstone marking the grave of a once-great empire.

And before it all stood a cluster of crucifixes, exactly like the ones that had existed at the feet of Skyhold's great wall before Jeric had taken them down. The macabre garden of death, where Sol Velorian slaves had been nailed and left for crows.

But these were not Sol Velorians; they were Istraan citizens. Men, women.

A child.

Again, Imari felt a surge of emotion, a burst of pressure, but the Liagé bindings pinched it off, making it momentarily difficult for her to breathe.

Su'Vi continued down the path, though Hersir and Karra had

stopped, gazing upon what had once been Istraa's glory. There was a moment of silence, a sort of horrible reverence for the kind of power that had completely deconstructed a monument of the ages.

Karra cast a quick glance at Hersir, a mark of uncertainty in her eyes, and then she clucked her tongue and urged her horse after Su'Vi. Hersir followed a beat later.

Still, Imari did not say a word.

They crossed the open valley, passing the bleeding crucifixes and vultures feasting upon flesh, into what had been fields, but they'd been reduced to patches of scorched earth. Some of them *still* smoked. They reached the edge of the city proper, where five Sol Velorians guarded entry to a broken arch. They knelt before Su'Vi as she trotted past but gazed curiously at the three who followed—Imari, specifically, and the bindings glowing faintly upon her wrists.

More and more gathered as word of Su'Vi's return quickly spread. All were Sol Velorian, Imari noted, part of the army Azir had brought, and growing fast, due to the additional cities he had destroyed. They'd taken residence in the rubble, building shoddy structures directly along the streets that had been cleared to navigate. Imari didn't doubt the Liagé had helped with that.

So had Trier's Istraan citizens.

Trier's Istraan survivors had been shackled and chained, and Imari spotted many picking through rubble or rebuilding some of the fallen structures under the surveillance of Sol Velorian guards.

Imari wondered if those nailed to the crucifixes were the lucky ones.

They finally reached the broken palace gate, which hinged open like a fractured jaw. Azir had not removed the pikes with severed heads from above the gate, but all that remained now was bone.

Even without the shell, she knew her papa.

Imari swallowed hard, and her next breath pushed against tight lungs.

Su'Vi dismounted at the gate, and an armed Sol Velorian woman bowed and took Su'Vi's horse while Su'Vi gestured at Hersir and Karra to follow.

Hersir did not look comfortable. He was a lone Corinthian in this city, his fair complexion marking him as an outsider, and the Sol Velorians cast dark looks his way, but they did not intervene. Like Imari, he belonged to Su'Vi, and whatever they might hate in the Corinthian, they more feared a Mo'Ruk's rebuke.

Su'Vi eventually led them up the steps and into Vondar. Blood still stained the tiles in places, and all the potted palms were gone, making the halls feel wide and empty and colorless, like the catacombs. More armed Sol Velorians stopped and bowed at Su'Vi but stared after Imari and her escort. Su'Vi led them through an archway and to the main hall, which was guarded by more armed Sol Velorians. Seeing Su'Vi, they stood at attention, bowing to a chorus of "*a'prior,* Su'Vi."

Su'Vi did not speak; she did not break stride nor touch the doors as they swung inward to let her through. Left with no other choice, Imari followed, with Hersir and Karra close behind, and the guards watched as the doors closed behind them.

The last time Imari had set foot in this room had been to face her papa's council when no one could decide how to introduce her back into society. There was no sun to give this space color now, no desert wind to bring it warmth. Two candelabras burned pitifully on either side of what had been her papa's throne, but they could not dispel the shadows that had settled here.

A creature slunk out of those shadows near the dais and into the dim sphere of candlelight.

Astrid.

No, the *legion*, wearing Astrid's skin and smiling with Astrid's cracked and bloodied lips. Imari felt a swell of emotion push against her chest again as she remembered Astrid *before*. That long and silken strawberry hair, those high cheekbones and Jeric's blue eyes. They were pools of shifting black now, and all of her hair was gone, her scalp scarred and scabbed as though she'd ripped it out. Her skin hung like a thin sheet over jagged bones— in fact, the skin had rubbed off completely over her knees, showing white kneecaps beneath—and her right foot had twisted perpendicular to the ankle joint. The only thing giving Astrid's body any fullness was the legion snaking beneath her skin, giving volume where it had none and warping her natural features in the process.

But Kai was not chained to her as he'd been when she'd last seen him. Imari did not see Kai anywhere.

"Su'Vi," said a rasping voice, and a figure stepped inside from the veranda. "I have been expecting you."

It was Lestra. The one who had examined all of Imari's memories with one touch. Azir's Mo'Ruk seer.

Imari flinched with old fear, but her Liagé bindings pushed more cold sludge into her body, burying the fear in ice.

But Lestra wasn't alone. Two robed figures stood with her, a man and woman, both Sol Velorian. They were unarmed, but the glyphs painted upon their faces and every inch of exposed skin marked them as Liagé.

Imari wondered how many Liagé Azir had in his employ now.

"Has my lord returned?" Su'Vi asked.

Lestra stopped before them, the other two Liagé at her sides. "He has not." Her inhuman, milky white eyes landed on Imari. "He will soon." Lestra said this last part distractedly, as if she were witnessing the future event in real time.

Lestra then turned her head to the male Liagé, a man with a wiry frame and unfriendly expression. "Find room for the Provincials to wait until my lord returns."

The man bowed his head and said, "This way."

But Hersir and Karra did not follow. They did not realize they'd been addressed.

"They don't speak Sol Velorian," Imari said in Sol Velorian.

Lestra eyed Imari with that unsettling, milky-white stare.

"Follow Vyzra to your chambers, where you will await my lord's return," Su'Vi said in Common.

Karra's expression opened with understanding. Hersir stiffened. Clearly, he hadn't expected to stay in Trier.

Fool. One didn't bargain with the devil and expect the devil to play by any rules but his own.

Vyzra gestured for Karra and Hersir to go ahead, and they did —Hersir, reluctantly—leaving Imari with two Mo'Ruk and the woman Liagé.

"Remove her binds," Lestra instructed Su'Vi.

A word, a breath. The bindings clicked open, and Su'Vi caught them before they fell, but she didn't catch Imari, who dropped to her knees.

Shah flooded her body as that dam burst open and hot water raged, reclaiming its old pathways. Imari clutched her chest and heaved, gasping for breath as her lungs filled.

And filled.

Every sense opened, every detail defined. She could hear every breath, every heartbeat—even those of the guards beyond the doors—pounding inside of her ears. The world, which had been rendered silent these past two weeks, suddenly screamed at her, all octaves, all at once. A symphony of notes and drums and stars, and Imari pressed her hands to her ears, trying to mute the sound.

Finally, the tide settled, the water calmed, and the screaming reduced to gentle song. Imari drew in a full breath then lowered her hands. She could still hear every heartbeat, every breath, but it was all background now.

Imari looked at Su'Vi, and without those bindings, her rage flared anew. She opened her mouth and started to sing.

No sooner had those desperate notes left her lips than an invisible force barreled into her chest, throwing her back. She skidded across the tiles, slamming right into a column, knocking the wind from her lungs. Pain lanced her spine as she climbed upon all fours, gasping for the air she'd lost, but the Liagé woman stood poised, one hand raised and ready to throw another spell.

A guardian, then. Lestra's insurance.

And then Lestra was there. She grabbed Imari's chin, squeezing it tight, and Imari's present world disappeared.

Like before, Imari was thrown through a blur of time, wrung out like a damp cloth while her precious memories dripped onto the tiles.

Again, she saw the moment Azir had left her at the tree, the moment Jeric had died. She saw herself reviving him, then she saw herself collapse, and Lestra sifted through every moment after. The hidden cave at Av'Assi, and all Imari's moments with Jeric in the privacy of their shared bedchamber. Lestra squeezed and squeezed, focusing on every face in that council room the night Imari had asked for the people's help, and Lestra's attention lingered on Mazz and the bells he had given her.

In the present world, Lestra gripped her chin harder.

Time sped through their journey to Liri, where Lestra paused to observe the monsters that had attacked them, then on to *The Lady* and Kazak's guardian fire. There, Lestra slowed, laboring over every second as Imari closed that wide gap between Kazak and herself through the Shah.

Lestra went back and watched it again.

Time accelerated once more, to Gilder then Skyhold, and more moments Imari did not want to share with anyone but Jeric.

To the tunnel Imari had found and that strange pulse of light.

Lestra paused there as well, stilling the image like a portrait for observation, analyzing it from all sides, and then time flashed forward again, into that tunneling whirl of color. It twisted in a vortex of faces and sound, finally ending with Kyrinne's betrayal.

And then Lestra let go.

Imari collapsed onto the cold tiles, wheezing and dizzy, and then she retched. When she finally finished, someone jerked her hands before her and slapped the Liagé binds around her wrists once more. Cold shocked her blood, severing her from the Shah, and her world became colorless and silent. More hands grabbed her arms and hoisted her to her feet—two Sol Velorian men— and they dragged her after Su'Vi, who strode for the door.

Imari was hardly aware of her surroundings as she stumbled through the palace, held aloft only by those two Sol Velorian men. Her consciousness was still trapped between past and present, her current world distorted by invasive flickers of before.

Su'Vi turned a corner, and Imari realized where the Mo'Ruk was taking her.

They escorted her down the dark and winding stair that led to Vondar's dungeons, and Imari—bound and caught between two strong Liagé men—had no choice but to comply. She staggered down the stairs to the short corridor that Su'Vi had illuminated with a sphere of white-blue light. Su'Vi waved another hand, and a heavy door reinforced with iron bars swung outward.

"Throw the *sulaziér* inside," Su'Vi said.

Imari opened her mouth to speak, but no words came before she was shoved inside, and the door slammed shut to darkness.

Imari sagged against the door, listening to the sound of their retreat until there was no sound at all but that of her own staggered breathing. And then Imari heard another breath, falling out of rhythm with her own.

She was not alone.

## 38

*A*fternoon matured into evening, a youth began lighting the village lanterns, and a cold wind stung Jeric's nose as he navigated the sprawl of Kleider's streets. New snow flurried and danced, dusting the hundreds of footprints that pockmarked the snow-covered paths.

"You walk like a man with destination in mind," Hax said as he caught up to him.

Jeric made no comment as their boots crunched through old snow and new. It wasn't until Jeric's last turn that Hax understood where Jeric was headed.

"You don't trust me to do my part?" Hax asked as they approached the skal mine's foremost watchtower. "I swear to the gods, they've been working overtime since my brother received word that Skyhold's armory was depleted. I can't tell you exact numbers, but Meneike should be able to give you that."

Jeric stopped at the base of the tower, where two guards intercepted them. They nodded at Hax, but their attention rested on the tall and imposing figure beside him.

Apparently, they had not been present when Fyrok had made introductions at the gate.

"Pay your respect to His Majesty, King Jeric Angevin," Hax commanded.

The guards' wariness morphed into shock as they bowed and hastily muttered, "Your Grace."

"Who's in charge here?" Jeric said.

"Uh, Meneike," one replied, head still bowed. "He's at the forge, but I can—"

"I meant who's in charge of your laborers?"

Hax frowned.

"That'd be Roryn, Your Grace."

Roryn. Jeric knew the man. Not well, but well enough to know that he didn't want to know him any better. Unfortunately for Jeric, those were usually the men he had to deal with.

"Where is he?"

"Right here, Your Grace," said a voice from above that belonged to a stout man with graying brown hair, a crooked nose, and a battered Corinthian cloak. The man began descending the tower's ladder while the guards upon the platform peered over the rail, watching the exchange.

Roryn jumped the last two rungs, wiped the winter from his hands onto his breast, and came to a stop before Jeric. He looked softer than Jeric remembered.

"How may I be of service, Your Grace?" Roryn asked.

"Gather your laborers." Jeric gestured at the skal pit. "I would speak to them."

Roryn looked perplexed by the order, but Hax nodded, and within the half hour, every man, woman, and child who'd been working the mine had crowded along the mine's mouth and squeezed onto its winding ramp. More huddled just within the mine, because there wasn't enough room for all of them outside. Jeric counted nearly two hundred in total, and somewhere, a baby cried. They gazed upon Jeric with weary eyes, not caring even as the wind tore through their thin clothes, biting at their exposed skin. Jeric was just another captor, and so they stared blankly at him, awaiting yet another order.

However, some knew exactly who he was. He could see it in their eyes, the deep and burning hatred for the Wolf King who had placed his own worth so high above their own.

So Jeric started down the ramp.

"Your Grace...?" Hax called behind him, but Jeric kept walking. Sol Velorians stepped aside in confusion as he continued down the path, moving through their midst, all the way to where that pit leveled out at the mine's mouth.

Where he was equal with the lowest of them.

They watched him, wary. Hax looked at him with confusion.

And then Jeric dropped to his knees and bowed his head.

No one spoke, though a savage wind howled and twisted around him, kicking flecks of ice and snow in his face. This was the worst thing he could do right now for Corinth, but it was the thing that needed to be done.

It should have been done a very long time ago.

And that is exactly where he began. "I deserve death for what I have done to your people."

Those nearest looked furtively to each other. Some whispered. Some knew his identity, but he could see by the ensuing confusion that many still did not.

He would correct that first and take ownership of the wrongs he had committed.

"I am Jeric Oberyn Sal Angevin," he continued. "The Wolf—and now king—of Corinth."

A blanket of silence fell over the crowd at this confession, and Jeric locked eyes with one man, who stared back at him with fire. In his periphery, he caught Braddok and the others watching from the edge of the shallow pit, but Hax and Roryn had followed him down, looking utterly bewildered, though they would not interrupt their king.

Not yet.

"I know I can't make it right," Jeric added, feeling the cold seep through the knee of his breeches. "No apology will ever be enough to wash away the sins I have committed against you."

Jeric paused to breathe, suddenly overcome by all of those sins, each and every vicious memory.

The baby cried again, and its mother tried to shush the sound.

"If I could go back and change the trajectory of my life, I would," Jeric confessed, unsure as to whom, exactly, he was speaking just then. "But I cannot. I can only walk forward and hope the rest of my life does not reflect the first part, or if it does, it serves only to contrast how truly wrong I was." Jeric looked from face to face, and he did not shy away. He acknowledged their condemnation, their hatred toward him—all of which he deserved. "Upon whatever honor is left within me, you are free to go and live your life. I release you."

His words were met with quiet. Even the wind dimmed in that moment, that pause in time—this unexpected message with a conclusion no one could fathom.

Hax looked aghast, and he leaned in close. "Your Grace, you can't just—"

"*You are free.*" Jeric repeated, louder this time so that those deep in the mine might hear him. "You may stay in Corinth for as long as you need. Indefinitely, if you choose this to be your home, but you are free to choose and free to *live*."

An uncertain murmuring rippled through the crowd.

"But we need them if we're going to win this war!" Hax hissed in his ear.

Jeric stood so abruptly Hax had to jump back.

"Release the workers," Jeric said.

Roryn did not move, his eyes fixed on Jeric as if he hadn't heard correctly. As if he *wouldn't* hear correctly.

"You heard me," Jeric continued lowly. "Instruct your men to unchain them."

Still, Roryn hesitated.

Hax's expression was one of desperation. "Your Grace, they outnumber us nearly two to one, and if they—"

"*Do it now, Hax.* I will not ask you again."

A muscle worked in Hax's jaw. In that second, Jeric wondered how this would play out. If Hax would concede, and if he did not, where Jeric would strike first. In his periphery, he quickly marked every tower, every archer. The position of his men.

But—thankfully—Hax's gaze flickered to Roryn, and he nodded once.

Roryn turned furiously around and barked commands. It took his guards a moment to act; the mere shock of the order made them slow. They were like gears slowly grinding awake, rusted from years without use. They moved through the crowd and begun unlocking shackles, but the people stood dumbfounded.

"What is this, Wolf King?" snarled a Sol Velorian man standing before him. He looked to be about Jeric's age, but his body was hollow with malnourishment, his clothes hung too loose, and frostbite had taken two of his fingers. "You set us free in the middle of winter with nothing but rags."

The woman beside the man elbowed him in the ribs, urging him to be quiet.

"Where are we supposed to go?" asked another, and a few others voiced agreement.

"As I said, you are welcome to stay here until the weather permits your travel," Jeric said to them, then added, surprising even himself, "Or come with me to Skyhold and help me fight Azir."

The couple stopped, and the man glared at Jeric. "You think we would go to war for a *Corazzi dog*?"

The crowd charged with new energy, and a chorus of angry objections crescendoed such that the guards began looking nervous.

"That *Corazzi dog* is trying to save us all from Zussa."

To Jeric's surprise, it was Niá who had spoken. Her voice cut through the din, snapping like a whip over the crowd. People quieted, curious to see which one of their own had spoken, and looked stunned when Niá strode furiously down the ramp to where she stopped beside Jeric.

Her sudden and unexpected appearance caused more whispers, and people inside the mine's mouth craned to see.

"How can you stand beside that monster?" a woman called out, pointing a spear-straight finger at Jeric.

"This *monster* is setting you free."

"He's throwing us into war," shouted another.

"We're already at war," Niá cut back. "He's trying to make sure we survive it."

"No, he's trying to make sure he survives. He doesn't give a dashá about us."

"And you think Azir does?" Niá snapped.

"He's one of our own," the first woman argued. "He's fighting *for* us—"

"He *murdered* my little brother!" Niá cut her off with such raw emotion that those nearest flinched back and the crowd fell silent.

"I know you're angry," Niá continued as tears streamed down her face. "I know that our lives were stolen from us, that our home was stolen. That we've all lost so many we've loved. *I know this!*" Her voice trembled, her tears fell, and the crowd remained silent. "I felt just like you. I joined Bahdra, hoping that revenge against *Corazzi* would make it right, and now I am the reason Trier fell and so many died. I am the reason my little Saza is gone. I am the reason the last thing he saw was Bahdra's *leje* seeping into his body and sucking the life out of it. The same *leje* that murdered my oza. I wanted my freedom and my revenge so badly that I was willing to follow anyone who would grant it to me— even a Mo'Ruk." Niá paused, caught her breath. A few whispered.

"This is not the way," she continued. "Azir is not fighting for you. He fights for himself, and himself alone, and anyone that will help him gain the world, and once you've outlived your purpose, you will be tossed aside as I have been. But this man"—Niá pointed at Jeric—"he gains *nothing* by setting you free."

"Giving back what is already ours by birthright does not make him a hero," a Sol Velorian argued.

"You're right. He's a hero because by freeing you now, with Azir threatening our world, he is putting your lives above his own."

"Those are pretty words, *a'deim*," one of them said, "but there is nothing in this world that could ever convince me to fight for a *Corazzi* dog." He looked straight at Jeric then spat on the ground and strode on through the crowd.

A guard made a move to go after him, but Jeric raised a hand. "No. Let him go."

Thus emboldened, more and more followed after the first, and Niá sagged with disappointment.

"It's all right, Niá," Jeric said quietly, still humbled by her defense.

A muscle worked in her jaw, her gaze hard as she watched them walk away, until only about two dozen remained.

A man approached. He looked about as old as Hiatt and had a kind face and deep-set eyes that had seen many years and many masters yet still burned with that Sol Velorian fire.

He stopped a few paces before Niá.

Jeric tensed out of habit, though he didn't think this man meant Niá harm. In the corner of his eye, he noticed Chez start down the ramp.

"I know you," the man said.

Niá frowned.

"I know your face," the man continued, studying her, while Chez drew nearer and nearer.

"Taran of Bassi," the man said as it clicked. "Did you know her?"

Niá swallowed her emotion, and Jeric suddenly wondered why Niá had left out this detail when speaking to the Sol Velorian people. "She was my oza."

Gasps sounded from a few of the remaining Sol Velorians.

"Taran had no children," someone said.

"She had Fyri," said the old man, eyeing Niá.

Jeric had never heard this, and he suspected it wasn't common knowledge amongst the Sol Velorians based on their startled expressions.

But the old man stood resolute and confident in his assertion, and Niá made no move to deny it. She also would not meet Jeric's gaze.

Taran, the old enchantress from E'Centro, had been Fyri's mother. By the gods...

Which meant Tolya—the one who had raised Imari in the Wilds and was the twin sister of Taran—had been Fyri's aunt. Jeric knew Imari had to be connected to this somehow, but how, exactly, he couldn't figure.

"What is your name, *a'deim*?" the old man asked.

A beat. "Niá."

"Your full name," he pressed, as if he already knew the answer, and he wanted everyone else to know it too.

Jeric thought Niá wasn't going to answer, but at last, like a confession, she said, "Niá Astyrra"—she hesitated a breath—"Mubarék."

Jeric's eyes narrowed on her.

Chez stopped, frozen and confused.

"That's impossible," said a man. "Azir was dead when you were born—"

"Not Azir," she said at a whisper, but it carried through the silence. "Saád."

Saád Mubarék, Azir and Fyri's great-great-grandson, who'd

led the rebellion of Jeric's youth. The rebellion that'd killed his mother. And Saád was Niá's father.

By the gods, suddenly so many things made sense.

Bahdra had to have known. That was how he'd found Niá in the first place and how he'd easily recruited her help: because their common enemy had made a temple prostitute out of Azir's many-great-granddaughter.

And yet Taran—Fyri's own mother—had condemned Azir, because she'd known Fyri *before* Azir. She'd seen how Azir was made and how it'd changed her daughter, Fyri. She had known the world *before* Azir had proclaimed himself a god.

That meant Taran—and, consequently, Tolya—had to have been around two hundred years old. But again, where did Imari fit into all of this?

"Taran of Bassi hid you away when Saád was killed," the old man said.

Niá stared back at him and nodded once. "Saza was just a baby. I've been in Trier ever since."

Where Imari was from, because it was where her father had lived.

Sar Branón. A man who'd fought against Saád nearly twenty years ago, and yet the fallout of that war had left Istraa severely out of favor with the other Provinces. Jeric's father had always accused Branón of growing too soft on the Sol Velorians.

As Jeric had grown soft.

Because he'd fallen for one.

Suddenly, the pieces clicked.

"Saád Mubarék had a sister," Jeric said to Niá.

Niá's brow puckered a little at the unexpected question, and she thought back. "Yes. Jesriel."

Which was eerily close to Imari's middle name: Jeziél.

Rumor was that Saád's sister had betrayed him, which had inevitably led to his demise. Jeric had always wondered what had lured Saád's sister away from his cause, but that was precisely where Jeric had been wrong. It'd never been a what.

It'd been a *who*.

Sar Branón.

And the *sulaziér* gifting only seemed to pass through the women, which is why it had gone from Fyri and eventually to Jesriel, Saád's sister, but not Saád.

Jeric breathed fast, bewildered by the picture that suddenly made so much sense. Imari had faced Fyri in that storm—her own many-great-grandmother.

And now she had Fyri's bells.

No wonder they'd resonated with her. They'd recognized her blood, because they'd seen it before.

Jeric took a step back, and Niá looked confused. She hadn't put the pieces together yet, that she and Imari were cousins, or maybe Jeric had made a mistake.

He looked over at Tallyn, who was watching him closely.

"Jesriel Mubarék was Imari's mother," Jeric whispered.

"Yes, Your Grace," Tallyn said at last. "Yes, she was."

# 39

*I*mari slowly turned, but she could not see. There was no light in this chamber buried deeply beneath Vondar, and her bindings were unusually dark. Still, she could *hear*, and there was definitely another living creature in this prison with her.

More icy sludge pumped into her body, her chest constricted, and Imari tried to calm herself. It was always a battle, this fight between her body's natural reactions and the binding's design to suppress them. To suppress *her*.

But in that moment, as the bindings rushed to capture her physiological response, the wards flared a little, giving light to this dark space, and she saw the figure huddled in the corner.

Her heart nearly stopped.

"*Kai...*" Imari pitched forward and dropped to her knees, straining against the vice now squeezing her chest. She fell on all fours beside him, wheezing, her teeth clenched against the frost in her blood and the acid in her mouth.

Kai lay in a discarded heap, unmoving, eyes closed with sleep, though one was bruised and swollen shut. He was naked and too thin, his bones jutting out at the joints. His hair had been crudely hacked off, and there were more cuts and scratches all over his body. A dark substance stained his backside and legs, and by the smell, Imari knew it was not dirt.

His ribcage shuddered as he inhaled, and, very gently, Imari rolled him onto his back.

Oh, Maker have mercy...

Imari's eyes burned, and she looked away to gather herself. To breathe against the wards that confined her.

They had *emasculated* him.

"Kai..." Her voice broke as she touched his face. His skin was on fire. "Oh, Kai, I am so sorry..."

Kai didn't respond. He was barely alive, and she had nothing to help him or heal him—nothing except her own warmth. And so she curled up behind him as best she could, threaded her legs with his, not caring about his filth, and pressed her forehead to his back. "I am here, *mi a'dor*," she whispered, not sure if he could hear her, but wanting him to hear her voice all the same. "You are not alone."

On instinct, she started to sing, like a mother comforting a child, but her song would not come without Shah, and the bindings glowed anew, flooding her with ice. Imari gasped, her song strangled and died, and she closed her eyes, waiting for her internal winter to calm.

She didn't realize she'd fallen asleep until someone set a bowl beside her. Imari blinked in the torchlight, her sleepy mind struggling to make sense of what her eyes insisted. A Sol Velorian woman stood over them, gazing down at her and Kai. It wasn't the woman from the hall, but Imari had the strangest sensation she'd seen her before.

The woman's eyes met Imari's, faltered, and she strode for the door.

"He needs help," Imari managed, shoving herself to sit upright, though her head spun violently.

The woman walked on through the threshold.

"Please," Imari begged, trying not to vomit. "Let me help"—
the woman slammed the door shut, plunging Imari back into
darkness—"him."

A line of light now shone beneath the door where, presum-
ably, her Sol Velorian guard stood watch.

Very carefully, Imari picked up the bowl and sniffed the
contents: broth of some sort, though the scent was thin. Regardless, it'd been a long time since she'd eaten, and she still needed
to rinse the acid from her mouth.

She set the bowl down, out of the way, and pushed it at Kai
instead. "Kai. *Mi a'dor.* You need to eat."

Kai did not move.

Imari scooted over to him and managed to prop his head into
her lap, then grabbed the bowl, careful not to spill it.

"My hands are bound," she whispered. "I can lift the bowl to
your mouth, but I cannot open your lips. I need your help, Kai."

Nothing.

Still, by that dim line of light, Imari brought the bowl to his
lips, then tilted it just a little to splash broth upon them. To let
him feel it, taste it, awaken his senses.

Still, nothing.

And then—suddenly, thankfully—his head shifted just a
little. Kai's lips cracked open, and his tongue slipped out, tasting.

"There's more," Imari said, her spirits soaring just before the
binds clamped down on them again. She brought the bowl back
to his lips, and this time he drank. He'd finished half the broth
when he groaned and turned his head away, knocking the bowl
from Imari's hands.

Imari cursed as the bowl clattered across the floor, spilling the
rest onto the dirt for the earth to drink, and Kai had already
slipped back into unconsciousness. Imari sighed, rested her
bound hands upon his chest, and tipped her head back against
the wall.

She didn't know how much time had passed, but the door

opened and the Sol Velorian woman returned. The woman looked from Kai to Imari, but this time, Imari did not look up. She lacked the energy.

The woman retrieved the bowl, which lay upside down.

"You didn't eat," the woman said in Sol Velorian.

Imari was too tired to speak.

The woman continued standing there. She looked to the door, back at Imari, then reached into her coat pocket and withdrew a hunk of bread, which she set beside Imari.

"This is for Hizrut," the woman said quietly, and then she left, closing the door behind her.

Hizrut.

Hizrut...

Imari's mind was slow, but then it struck her: Hizrut was the name of a Sol Velorian man she had healed in E'Centro on those nights she'd gone to visit Taran. He'd taken ill, and his wife...yes, that's why she'd recognized this woman. This woman was Hizrut's wife. She'd come to Taran's and solicited Imari's help, though Imari couldn't remember her name.

And now she was working for Azir.

Imari glanced down at the hunk of bread, and her stomach twisted like rope. Stars, she was so hungry. She picked up the bread—it was still warm—and devoured it in two bites. And then, with Kai's head still in her lap, she leaned back against the wall and fell asleep.

A creaking sound woke her, and Imari opened her eyes to see the door swing open. She held her breath, expecting Lestra, but it was the woman again, and she was carrying another bowl.

Stars, how long had Imari been asleep?

The woman stopped just inside the door, torch in hand, and her gaze found Imari.

"I remember you now," Imari whispered.

The woman's expression tightened, as if her resolve were wrestling shame.

"But I don't remember your name," Imari said.

The woman looked away, stepped forward, and carefully set another bowl upon the floor.

"Would you tell me?"

The woman stood. Her gaze darkened on Kai before cutting to Imari. "I thought you were one of us."

Imari regarded the woman. "I am."

"Then why do you care for him?"

"He is my brother, and he is dying."

"I would let my brother rot if he had done what yours has done."

Imari looked down at her brother while silence stretched its bitter limbs.

"How can you serve a Wolf?" the woman snapped.

"I don't serve a Wolf." Imari looked back at the woman, though it was difficult. Her eyes felt heavy, her mind weary. "We were working together to free my people."

"That's a lie."

"It's easier for you to believe that, I know."

The woman's lips pressed firmly together.

"Remember: He is not the one who gave me these." Imari lifted her bindings, which glowed so faintly.

The woman looked at the bindings, and the glow reflected in her dark eyes. "Perhaps you should have listened."

"Ricón said the same when he caught me sneaking into E'Centro every night." Imari closed her eyes, too exhausted to hold them open any longer. "If you prefer a world with ultimatums, then you have chosen the right master."

A beat.

The air shifted, the door latched closed, and the woman was gone.

Imari did not know how much time passed. Her moments were marked by bowls of broth and sleep and comforting Kai through fits of screaming. The first and second time Kai screamed, the woman burst through the door to check on her charge.

"Nightmare," Imari said, drawing her brother close, shushing and rocking him while the woman stood in the doorway. Watching them—watching *Kai*—while Kai sobbed and clung to Imari in pure terror.

"His...wound is deeply infected." Imari gestured at Kai's emasculation, and the woman met her gaze. "There are—*were*—soprese buds in my uki's chambers. *Please*," she begged.

Kai kept sobbing, and Imari kept rocking, and the woman finally ducked out and shut the door. She did not return, and Imari's heavy spirit was once again clamped down by the wards flooding her body with ice.

*You could ask Bahdra,* said a small voice in her mind. Bahdra's talent lay in necromancy, but it was still a subset of restoration magic. Bahdra could help...for a price.

Imari held tight to Kai as he trembled in her arms.

*No,* she decided. *I will not ask that monster for anything. He has done enough to you. I'll do it the old way, if I can. It was good enough for Gamla; it's good enough for me.*

"Can you eat, *mi a'dor*?" she whispered, touching his face. He was still too hot. She didn't know if he would survive the night.

Kai moaned softly, and his head turned to the side. He had not yet opened his eyes, and sweat glistened upon his brow.

*Please*, she begged to the heavens, to the one who had interceded before on her behalf. To the one she had not felt since Su'Vi had snapped these bindings upon her. *Do not take him from me. Not yet. Not like this.*

Imari held Kai, rocking him until the cries turned to whimpers and then fell silent.

"Kai...?"

No answer.

Imari's breath hitched, and more ice flooded her body. "Kai, answer me."

Still, no answer, but his skin was hot and very much alive.

Stars, she was losing him, but it was more than that—she knew. Kai lacked the will to fight.

"Please, *mi a'dor*..." Imari said, holding him tight. "Don't give in. I am here, and I am trying, and..." Her lungs clamped down again, making it difficult to breathe—to speak—though a tear leaked out.

And then the door opened.

The woman stood there holding a candle, deliberating and unsure, and then she set a little bundle beside Imari.

Imari looked at the bundle, at the sprigs sticking out of it, and her gaze met the woman's.

Still, the woman looked uncertain of what she had just done. She awkwardly set down the candle, walked through the door, and closed it quick, as if she could not bear to gaze upon the evidence of this paradoxical decision she had just made.

Imari carefully moved away from Kai and tore open the bundle.

Soprese: its stalks and dried buds.

Technically, she should make a tea from this, but the buds would have to be enough. Imari did not want to press her luck, or the woman's momentary bout of good will, so she got to work plucking the dried flower petals from the stalk. Once she had a little pile, she shoved as many as she could into her mouth and chewed. They tasted like bark, like earth and wood grain. She grabbed the bowl of broth the woman had left—which was mostly water—and poured it gently over Kai's brutal laceration to rinse it a little. She set the bowl down, spit the wet pulp of chewed soprese into her palms, and rubbed it into Kai's wound.

"Hold on, Kai...please hold on," she pleaded.

When she'd finished, she grabbed the bowl. A little broth still sloshed inside, and she chewed the remaining petals, spit those into the bowl, and stirred once with her finger.

"I need you to drink this for me," Imari said.

Kai's head turned slightly to the side, and his eyelids fluttered but did not open.

Very carefully, Imari held the bowl to his lips. Broth spilled down his chin, but his lips parted just a little, and some slipped in his mouth, and once the bowl was emptied, she set it down and lay on her side beside him, brushing the hair back from his forehead. Until Kai's breathing relaxed and his features smoothed. Until she eventually drifted off to sleep.

## 40

*N*iá stood over a washbasin, scrubbing her hands. She still couldn't believe that she and Imari were cousins. Cousins! Niá had *family*—shared an actual blood-bond with a woman Niá had already grown to love like a sister. Stars above, Niá hoped they survived this, that she would get the opportunity to see Imari again, for how cruel would this discovery be if either of them perished before they could rejoice over this revelation *together*.

These thoughts circled in Niá's mind as she spent the evening enchanting whatever skal arms Kleider's citizens and soldiers had brought. Some did not come to her at all, not trusting the work of a "sorceress," though Jeric had done his best to convince them otherwise. Those who *did* come still eyed her with suspicion, but desperation had made them overlook those suspicions—for now.

Tallyn had joined her too, after he'd properly healed Jeric's and Jenya's respective injuries, but the hours passed, her energy waned and her markings weakened, and she knew it was time to stop for the day. How she and Tallyn were to enchant the weapons of an entire army, she had no idea, but they had to try.

They were the only Liagé Jeric had left, and the Wolf King's Corinthian warriors were dwindling.

Many of Kleider's citizens were furious that their king had just released their labor, then furthermore "borrowed" Kleider's stockpile of wools and leathers to send them comfortably on their way. And many more did not trust Niá's heritage, which had circulated fast throughout the evening.

Niá plunged her hands into the ice-cold water and scrubbed it over her face, as if she could scrub away her birthright. It was a stain that had followed her always, a secret she'd hidden so deep. She hadn't meant to admit it today either—stars, she hadn't meant to say anything at all—but seeing Jeric at the bottom of that pit, on his knees before those people...

It had pulled the ugly weed of her own past up by its root, drawing forth all the worms and maggots that'd feasted on the fruit of her poor decisions—decisions that haunted her every second of every day and night.

Niá plunged her hands into the water again, and someone knocked on the door. She stood there, deliberating and uncertain, not knowing who it could be.

But also—strangely—hoping for one. That part scared her more than any other.

She hadn't seen Chez since the crowd, since she'd confessed the truth of who she was and what she'd done, because he'd gone with Braddok and Jenya to send word to Stovichshold's smaller steads, asking for fighting men. He hadn't said a word to her—they really hadn't had an opportunity to talk, period, since they'd found Stovich dead in the snow—and Niá chastised herself for caring.

It didn't matter. *He* didn't matter.

Except she knew that was a lie.

It mattered a lot, and she almost despised him for it. It felt like control, and Niá was done being controlled, but in her more rational moments, she knew she wasn't being fair. Chez was not those other men; he was not guilty simply for being born a man.

Niá very carefully and quietly dried her hands and face on the towel, and the person knocked again.

"Niá, it's me...are you there?" Chez's voice was muffled through the door.

Niá froze; her nerves hummed. She did not owe him an answer, and if she stayed silent, he'd think her asleep and move on.

Niá opened the door.

Chez stopped, clearly not expecting her to be inside, or to be awake, but she was wide awake now. His brown hair was damp from snow and curled softly about his temples, and his cheeks were flushed with winter. He still wore the heavy, fur-lined coat from this morning, though a thick layer of mud caked his boots now. Niá suspected he'd come straight here after finishing his errands.

"Hey," he said.

"Hi."

He dragged a hand along the back of his neck, and an awkward sort of smile pulled at his mouth. "Just wanted to check on you. I...saw that mountain of arms you enchanted." He pulled a carafe of akavit from beneath his coat and held it out between them like a truce.

Niá looked at the carafe, unsure.

He pushed it toward her. "Thought you could use it."

A beat. She took the carafe, and her fingers brushed his. "Thank you," she said quietly, trying to ignore the shock of energy she'd felt from that small touch.

A second passed, and they stood in that awkward space with only the akavit between them.

Chez cleared his throat. "Well. Goodnight then," he said, and started to go.

"Would you share it with me?"

Niá could not say what prompted her to blurt that out, but there it was, and she didn't want to take it back, even though it sent her pulse racing.

Chez paused and looked at her, his expression uncertain. Hesitant and searching.

"I understand if you're tired. It's just that there's a lot here, and I certainly can't finish it by myself"—*Niá, quit babbling!*—"and also, I'd like to hear if you had any luck today," she finished, silently scolding herself for sounding like one of those simpering women she so loathed.

But Chez grinned, his sky-blue eyes brightened, and suddenly she did not care how she'd sounded.

"You're sure?" he asked, but Niá opened her door wider and stepped aside to give him room.

And Chez ducked inside.

Niá caught whiff of woodsmoke and winter upon his clothes as he strode past, then took a slow, calming breath as she closed the door behind him.

Chez stopped with his back to her, appraising the small space Niá had been given to stay, and Niá's heart began to pound. Chez was in her bedchamber, alone. She had never willingly invited any man into—

"Is this all the wood they gave you?" Chez asked, picking through the small sling of wood beside the woodstove, completely unaware of her personal struggle.

Niá sat in a chair and placed the carafe upon the small table. "Yes."

"This won't get you through the night. I'll get more."

"Hax said there wasn't more."

Chez crouched before the stove and opened the glowing grate. "Oh, there's more," he said in a way that made Niá think Chez didn't particularly care for Stovich's brother and that Stovich's brother didn't particularly care much for *her*.

Chez pulled a log from the sling and tossed it onto the stove's greedy flames. Sparks danced, embers popped, and the fire surged anew.

"Were you able to reach everyone?" she asked, setting two chalices upon the table and pouring akavit into both.

"Mostly." Chez closed the grate, dusted his hands, and stood, then made his way to the chair opposite. "There are a few near the river we didn't have time for today, but we were able to get word to the larger houses."

Niá picked up both chalices and handed one to Chez, which he took. "Will they come?"

Chez shrugged. "I don't know. They might've fought for Stovich, but many of 'em aren't too happy with our Wolf right now."

He didn't need to elaborate.

"Cheers." He raised his chalice before his comment could settle and fracture their present levity. "To the gods, may their favor shine upon us."

"To the Maker," Niá corrected, raising her own chalice. "May he spare us from man's boundless depravity."

Chez raised a brow at that and nodded, clanking his chalice against hers. Niá took a sip, but in that moment, she'd forgotten her chalice wasn't full of sweet Istraan nazzat, and the burning akavit took her off guard. She coughed and coughed and set her chalice down while Chez grinned at her over his own chalice.

"I hear it's an acquired taste," he said.

"It's not one I think I care to acquire." She coughed again, and he chuckled.

Quiet settled in once more, and Niá felt suddenly restless. Cornered.

Trapped.

Which was ridiculous, because this was Chez. He hadn't come here to take; he had come to *give*. He was different. This was different.

But for some reason, Niá felt every inch of space between

them. Chez's gaze flickered to her, but then he looked back to his chalice and took another slow sip.

Niá shifted in her seat and tucked her legs beneath her. "Any word from Brom Stykken?" Niá had learned that Jeric had written The Fingers from Imari, just before Imari's capture.

Chez shook his head distractedly as he thumbed the chalice. He looked at her; his lips parted and then closed, and his gaze dropped to the chalice again.

"What is it?" Niá asked.

A crease formed between his brows, and then, "Did you know about Lady Kyrinne?"

Niá inhaled slowly and sat back in her chair. So this was what had been nagging at him. He knew her past; she was the one who'd confessed it. It was no secret she had gathered information for Bahdra and wielded it for Provincial demise, so of course Chez would question how that affected Corinth's welfare.

But the question still pained her.

She looked directly at him. "Do you really think I would've left Skyhold with you that day if I'd known your Wolf was in danger?"

Chez studied her a long moment before saying, lowly. "No. No, I don't think that at all."

"Then why would you ask that?"

Chez held her gaze, seeming to deliberate before answering. "Because...I don't know that my judgment is clear when it comes to you."

Niá's pulse drummed in her ears, and she suddenly found it difficult to breathe. "And why is that?" she whispered.

He looked at her as if she should already know the answer—and she did. She just wanted to hear him say it almost as much as she didn't want him to say anything at all.

"Do you feel nothing, Ni?" he asked, searching her.

Niá went rigid. "Don't call me that." The words snapped out harsh, an instinctive defense, and Chez flinched.

A muscle ticked in his jaw; his hand clenched the chalice.

"This was a mistake..." Niá said suddenly, quietly. "I think you should go." *No, you idiot. That isn't what you want!*

She told herself it was better this way, and she almost believed it.

Until Chez looked at her.

Pain and frustration filled his eyes before he walled them off, and then he smiled at her, all lip. "Well, then, goodnight. *Niá.*" He set the chalice upon the table and stood. "I'll have more wood sent to you."

He started to go.

"Chez, wait. Please."

He stopped, shoulders stiff, but he did not turn, and all her words suddenly tangled up inside.

"I didn't mean...I..."

He waited.

"I don't know how to do this," she said at last.

A beat. "Do what?" Still, he did not turn.

"You...this—whatever *this* is. It terrifies me." The words trembled out of her. In confession, almost against her will. "*You* terrify me."

He glanced back at her then, but Niá could not read the expression there. "You terrify me too," he said. He looked as though he might say more, but instead left through the door and closed it softly after.

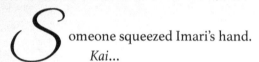omeone squeezed Imari's hand.

*Kai...*

Imari's eyelids flew open, and she looked straight into Kai's eyes. His lids were only half open, but he was awake and sitting back against the wall, looking at her.

*Alive.*

Oh, thank the Maker!

"Kai..." The word wrenched out of her, and her Liagé bindings rattled as she crawled forward, grabbed his face between her hands, and kissed his forehead and each of his cheeks. She pulled back and looked at him as the words mounted between them. As the horror of what others had done to him mounted between them. And then Kai closed his eyes, his expression so full of pain. The kind that had irrevocably injured the soul.

Imari placed a palm to his cheek. Still, he did not open his eyes. "Look at me, Kai. Please."

Struggle tightened his features, and then he said, so softly, "It's hard to look."

Tears stung Imari's eyes, and the ice made her next breath difficult. "I know."

His throat bobbed as he swallowed.

Imari waited, letting him process while she kept her hand on his face. Letting him know that she was there. Letting him draw whatever strength he needed from that gentle *human* touch.

"We're still in Vondar," he said quietly, eyes still closed.

"We are."

Then, "I don't want to be here."

He wasn't talking about her, this prison, or even Vondar.

Imari gently pushed the hair from his brow. "Do you remember that night you found me in the stables?"

Kai did not answer, but she knew he remembered. It was the night Sorai had died, the night Imari had killed her with her music, and Imari had run. She'd run right out of Vondar and into the city. She'd run and run and run, as if she could run away from what she had done, and then she'd heard guards and grown terrified. She'd deserved to die for what she'd done—she'd known—but she'd been too afraid to die, and so she'd run into the closest, safest place she could think: the stables. She'd been there just that morning, in fact. Out for a morning ride with her oldest brother.

She'd slipped inside, completely unseen by the groom, scrambled up the wood and cracks and into the attic, tucked herself into the bales of hay, and tried not to cry.

The groom had heard her, of course, and Kai had been the one to arrive first on scene.

She could still see him standing on the landing below as she stole glimpses through those bales of hay while Kai spoke in low voices to the groom.

"Do you remember what you said to me?" Imari whispered.

Kai's expression broke just a little, and a tear leaked out of the corner of his eye.

"I told you I couldn't come home. That I was afraid to die," Imari continued softly, fighting against the pressure squeezing her lungs. "And you...you told me that you would not let me die.

That the world needed my light, even if I did not need the world." Imari's entire body trembled as she spoke.

More tears spilled from Kai's closed eyes. "I don't have your light, Imari."

"No," she said, grabbing his hand between both of hers and squeezing it hard. "You have your own, and it is here." She pressed their entwined hands to his chest. "And it is brilliant, Kai. Do not give up on it just yet."

Kai's next breath shuddered, and his features strained. Imari moved to sit beside him and drew his head against her chest, and Kai sobbed. Deep and wrenching sobs that groaned from his soul. He gripped her arms as if holding on to her for dear life, and Imari sat quiet, letting him grieve.

His cries eventually ceased as he drifted off to sleep, and the woman opened the door, carrying another bowl. One glance at her and Imari knew she had heard all of it.

The woman's gaze flickered to Kai before she set the bowl down. She started for the door, stopped, and said, "Eat fast. They'll be here soon." And without looking back, she closed the door.

Imari wondered who *they* was, but she did not feel like eating. Kai shifted in her lap and moaned softly.

*For Kai. I need to be strong for Kai,* she thought.

She picked up the bowl, careful not to splash it upon him, and took a sip.

The broth was cold. The woman had been waiting outside the door for a very long time.

Imari had managed only a few sips when the door opened again. This time it was not the woman.

It was Su'Vi.

Su'Vi looked upon her with that black and inhuman gaze, her eyes like portals to a malevolent world, then her gaze fell to the man sleeping in Imari's lap. She stepped aside, and the two armed Sol Velorian men who'd dragged Imari here strode into her cell and unceremoniously jerked her to her feet.

Kai started to wake with a groan.

"I will be back for you, Kai, I swear," Imari cried over her shoulder as they dragged her out of her prison. She caught the gaze of the woman outside her door, who promptly stared straight ahead, her emotion void.

Imari's captors dragged her after Su'Vi, who led them out of the dungeons and into the palace. Though night darkened the windows, Vondar was like a hive swarming with bees. Sol Velorians strode through the palace, stopping to bow to Su'Vi as they passed, and excitement hummed in the air.

The source, Imari could only guess. Regardless, she was about to find out.

They eventually reached the great hall's doors, which were guarded by five Sol Velorians armed in skal and inked enchantments.

Where Hersir and Karra also waited.

Imari wondered where they'd been staying these past... however many days had gone by, but Hersir looked unwell. Heavy bags pillowed his eyes, and a sallow hue colored his skin. His clothes were not pressed; his lines were not smooth. Law had kept Jeric's Lead Stryker in pristine order, but treachery had made chaos out of him.

He met her gaze and promptly looked away, and the guards ceased their chatter.

"*A'prior* Su'Vi." One stepped forward with a bow. Unlike the others, he was armed only in painted glyphs, and he wore a long, black robe. "My lord is expecting you."

He pushed open the doors and stepped aside to let them pass, his gaze lingering on Imari as she walked by him.

And into the great hall.

Her pulse quickened on instinct, though her bindings kept

emotion dull and dim. As before, all the archways were dark, though candles and braziers had been lit, but this time many figures stood near the dais, all of them robed, with visible skin covered in inked glyphs. Imari recognized one as Lestra, though all voices stopped when Su'Vi entered. Faces turned; eyes gleamed.

Su'Vi strode forward. Her black robes rippled in her wake, and her boots were silent upon the tiles. She was in this world but not of it, passing through both dimensions at the same time. Even the shadows seemed to bend toward her, dimming the light in this vast cavern, and at the front of the room, the figures moved aside, revealing the man seated upon Sar Branón's throne.

Azir Mubarék.

There was something undeniably different from the man Imari had last seen outside of the Divine Tree and in her strange visions of him. This Azir was the one from Tallyn's memories— the one who had commanded armies, who had waited at the edge of the battlefield like a god observing his creation. And yet he was also...more. *Worse.* His eyes were pure black—no whites— and shapes writhed beneath his skin, slightly distorting the glyphs upon his forehead and cheeks.

Ice flooded Imari's veins anew, and she stumbled. She would have fallen had her escort not been holding on to her arms.

"My lord." Su'Vi knelt upon the tiles at the foot of the dais, her black robes pooling at her feet. "I have brought the *sulaziér*, as you have requested."

Su'Vi's words echoed in the quiet. Those gathered before the dais stood silent as their lord and master studied Imari as if he would see into to her soul. To every star inside her body, every desire and hidden fear.

"So you have," Azir replied distractedly. His voice was different too, layered with another sound that had not been there before. A diminished tone to his minor.

Zussa.

Karra cleared her throat.

Azir's head turned a fraction, and that otherworldly black gaze settled upon Karra.

"My lord..." Karra said. The words sounded clumsy in her mouth, and so small. "Kormand sent me to...collect the sum you agreed upon."

Su'Vi was still kneeling with her head bowed, but at Karra's words, her head lifted just slightly. Lestra and the other Liagé did not move or speak.

"Sum," Azir repeated, regarding Karra as one might watch a worm wriggling in the earth.

Karra shifted, uncomfortable. "I did not get clarification...my lord. He said you—" Karra's words gurgled silent, and her lips turned black, as though ink bled through them from the inside. Her eyes widened, and she clawed at her neck, stumbling back as that black splintered across her cheeks, moved down her throat, and filled her eyes.

Imari remembered Saza.

Karra screamed, but the sound cut short, and she dropped to her knees. Her body convulsed as that blackness filled her completely, and then she went completely still. A black vapor rose from her body like smoke and ascended into the high rafters that Imari could not presently see in the hall's thick shadows.

On her other side, Hersir had fallen still.

Azir's black gaze settled on Hersir next, where it narrowed slightly. "You are the Corinthian traitor."

Hersir shifted upon his feet. "Yes," he replied, though his voice carried none of its former strength.

Azir flung out a hand—so fast Imari hadn't realized he'd thrown something until a streak of silver flew out Hersir's back and clattered upon the tiles far behind him.

Hersir gasped, eyes wide in shock as he collapsed to his knees. Dark red blood seeped into his tunic, around his heart, where there was now a hole wide enough for Imari to put her hand through.

And then Hersir collapsed, dead.

Imari stared at his lifeless form now bleeding out onto the tiles. She thought she should feel something for the man who had betrayed Jeric, but those Liagé bindings kept that cold sludge stubbornly around her heart and her mind.

And then Azir's attention rested upon her.

If Imari had found Su'Vi's gaze unsettling, Azir's made her feel small and powerless—a mere mortal standing before the unquenchable wrath of a god.

Azir stood, and his horrible magnificence unfurled as his black robes brushed the dais. All power, all terrible glory, this great deceiver. He strode down the short stair, those starless black eyes never leaving Imari's face. He was a night without stars, a form without soul. He strode past Lestra and the others to where he stopped before Imari.

"Look at me, *Sulaziér*." His voice echoed from all directions, as if it had come from the shadows themselves.

But Imari could not bring herself to look into those inhuman eyes again.

"I said *look at me*." Azir grabbed her chin and squeezed it hard, forcing her face up. Forcing her to look at him. His touch was ice—colder, even, than the binds pumping winter into her body—and something slid beneath his cheek, like a snake writhing under his skin, as those starless black eyes bore into her.

"What do you...want from me?" Imari said, though the bindings stole her bite.

Azir glared at her a moment more, then released her chin and said, "Su'Vi. Take off the binds."

Su'Vi waved a hand and spoke a word. Imari's bindings clicked open and clattered to the floor, right into Hersir's dark pool of old life.

Imari's lungs opened up, and she gasped as though she'd been underwater for too long. The Shah crashed into her like the tide, flooding her body as before, and Imari dropped to her knees beneath the weight of it—or *would have*, but Azir grabbed hold of her tunic and held her aloft, her legs sagging beneath her.

And then he jerked her forward and pressed his mouth to hers.

Imari froze, caught between shock and revulsion, her head spinning from the tide of Shah power pouring into her body, and then her world went dark. Not her consciousness—no. The room, and everything in it. She was floating in some endless ocean of black, a world utterly devoid of light, though it screamed in pain. Shrieks of horror and endless torment rattled the dark, trembling through a body she could not see.

Darkness was everywhere. Pain was everywhere, and Imari could not breathe—could not think—trapped in this collapsing cocoon of dark and cold and suffering, and something tingled within...

Her power.

Imari remembered her bindings were gone.

Without wasting another second, Imari sang. Right against Azir's mouth. Her soul ignited at once, and she was suddenly a lone and brilliant sun in this endless universe of night. Emboldened, she sang louder, her star flared brighter. There was a blast of heat, of light, and her vision returned, only for her to find that she and Azir were both sprawled upon the tiles, a dozen paces away from one another, and pain throbbed at the back of Imari's skull.

Imari tried to get up, but an invisible force pushed her back down and held her there.

Kazak.

His arm was extended, his fingers flexed, holding her firmly against the tiles while Azir climbed back to his feet, strode over to Imari, and glared down at her, his eyes molten with hate.

"I won't...help you." Imari struggled to speak, to breathe against Kazak's force and the pain in her skull. "Whatever it is. I won't...do it."

390 | BARBARA KLOSS

Azir crouched beside her and grabbed her hair, and Imari cried out as he jerked her head up. *"You are mine*, little *sulaziér,"* he said in that voice that always haunted her. Zussa's, not Azir's. "Willingly or unwillingly. Just as every *sulaziér* before, since the very first. You—belong—to—me."

"Go to hell," Imari snarled despite the pain pulling through her scalp.

Azir's lips curled in a cruel smile. "Lestra."

A second later, Lestra appeared.

"As we discussed," Azir said.

Imari felt a moment's dread before Lestra placed an ice-cold palm to her forehead. There was that familiar squeezing sensation, and her world blurred into a dizzying whirl of color and sound. When it stopped, she was standing in Jeric's bedchamber.

A fire blazed in the hearth, illuminating the bare skin of the woman in his bed.

Lady Kyrinne.

No...

Not this.

Kyrinne's body arched, and she threw her head back as she moved her hips. Large hands roamed all over Kyrinne's body— hands Imari knew well.

Stars, she was going to be sick.

Jeric hadn't lied to her about this part of his past, but Imari didn't need to *see* it. She did not want this picture in her mind, but Lestra forced it upon her, capturing every gasp, every touch, every hungry kiss in vivid detail. Drawing the focal point closer until Imari was forced to see Jeric's face. To see him lost in this moment, giving himself completely to another woman.

*If you really knew all the things that I've done...* Jeric had said.

Imari reminded herself that he hadn't known her then. That he'd been a completely different person. This was his past, not his present, but still her heart ached, and she felt hot tears slide down her cheeks in the real world.

And then the scene changed, though she was still in Jeric's bedchamber, and Jeric sat in a chair beside the hearth, and his hair was short.

This was recent. Very recent.

Kyrinne rounded the chair and startled him. He said something to her, and she said something back, though their words were garbled in Lestra's version. And then Kyrinne's expression turned coy, and she sauntered toward him and let her robe slide to the floor.

She was naked beneath it.

Imari saw the struggle in Jeric's face, but Kyrinne closed the distance between them and kissed him hard. To Imari's pain, he didn't push her away; he started kissing her back. And then their hands were all over each other. He helped Kyrinne remove his tunic, and she started unfastening his belt...

The scene changed, but Imari hardly noticed. She knelt upon soft earth, surrounded by trees, as she sobbed.

But Lestra did not stop.

The forest suddenly came alive with yips and shouts, and there was a Wolf, cutting down Sol Velorian men and women. A Wolf, unmerciful and cruel, breaking arms and necks, leaving their young to the elements. A Wolf, who dragged men beneath horses, who hung them on crucifixes, who handed them to his inquisitors for torture.

This was the Jeric she did not know—the man *before*. The one he'd warned her about, and the one she'd met only briefly, having witnessed a small fraction of his mercilessness in The Wilds before fate had irrevocably knotted their life strings together and tuned them to sing parts of the same chord. This man was not *him*. This man was a stranger to her, this Jeric with the unquenchable hate in his eyes.

*If you really knew all the things that I've done...*

Those eyes landed on her then, piercing sharper than any blade, colder than any winter. She knew he could not actually see her; this had already happened. Still, she felt that glare to her core—felt his revulsion as it twisted his features. So stunned she was by the hatred twisting his face that she did not realize he had run her through until he was pulling his sword, Lorath, free, and a Sol Velorian woman collapsed beneath her, blood already staining her dress. Jeric spat through Imari onto the dying woman's face.

A little gasp of air escaped Imari's lips, and she stepped back, away from him—away from *this*—as the Wolf whirled on another helpless victim whose only crime was his birthright.

Still, Lestra did not stop.

Scene after scene assaulted her. A dozen murders became a hundred, until Imari lost count and collapsed beneath the weight of all the death Jeric had wrought. Her breath would not come, her lungs panicked, and her heart raced, and she curled her fingers upon the ground, unable to look away, unable to bear the pain in her chest. It bubbled up from her soul and spilled out of her with a violent retch, and then Lestra's visions stopped.

Imari was in the hall again, vomiting horror and agony upon the floor to mix with Hersir's dark blood.

Voices spoke, but she could not hear them. Hands grabbed at her arms, but she hardly felt them. All she could see were flashes of Jeric's past. Blood and screaming, abbreviated by Kyrinne's moans at the height of pleasure.

*If you really knew all the things that I've done...*

"That will be all, Lestra," Azir said.

His voice registered in Imari's mind, her head whipped up, and she met his black gaze.

She had never hated anyone more than she hated Azir in that moment.

Fire seared through her veins, and Imari screamed in fury, threw off her guard, and launched herself at Azir.

His eyes widened seconds before a tendril of inky black smoke lashed out and caught her midair. It whipped her upside down so that she hung suspended by her right ankle, her body dangling. Imari thrashed and kicked and swung, trying to reach for the light inside of her, for the Shah to burn it up as she'd managed before, but another tendril lashed out—from Bahdra—and grabbed her left ankle. Two more whipped out and grabbed her arms as Imari jerked and bucked against them, unable to get her power to move.

Unable to shake Jeric's horrible past from her mind.

"I hate you," she said to Azir while tears streamed down her face and splattered onto the floor. *"BURN IN HELL, YOU RUTTING MONSTER!"*

Azir took two steps and stopped before her. Bahdra held her suspended high enough that their faces were level, and she found herself staring right into those fathomless black holes he had for eyes.

"You will love me, little *sulaziér*," Azir said, stroking her cheek with affection. "And you will unmake what has been made and stand beside me as it is rewritten, for I am your god, and you will serve me in whatever manner I desire. You will worship me, and only me, with every breath that passes through these lips until your last." And then, as before, Azir grabbed her chin and kissed her hard.

Again, Imari was plunged into that dark abyss, that infinite cold sea, but this time she felt no pain, no terror. Her emotions were strangely numb, her body detached. A little voice inside warned her to fight, to sing and draw out the light before the darkness consumed her. And Imari tried—she did. Her lips opened, but her notes fell weak because her heart was not there, too rattled by the memories of Jeric's past. They dampened her song and cast it out for the darkness to swallow.

*You are mine,* Sulaziér. The sound came from everywhere, inside of her, groaning as though the earth itself were opening up.

Imari opened her lips to try again, but more dark and cold

poured into her body like some ravenous beast. It froze her lips on contact and iced over her tongue, burning as it crystallized her lungs, her belly, and then it shoved at the little sun within—her spirit—moving it aside, and she felt her light grow smaller.

And smaller.

To make room for something else.

Imari let out a gasp, a desperate cry, but no one who cared could hear or intervene. A bass suddenly opened within her, a deep and bellowing roar, as something very cold and terrible unfurled.

And Imari's little sun went out.

"Out of despair may grow any manner of horrible things."

~ *Excerpt from the teachings*
*according to Moltoné,*
*Liagé Second High Sceptor.*

## 42

*J*eric turned the skal blade over in his hands. Sleek, well-made, and well-balanced.

"So? What do you think?" Hax asked.

It wasn't Lorath, but it was as close as he was going to get. "Tanyr made this?" Jeric asked. Tanyr was Stovich's skalsmith.

"Aye," Hax replied. "He could fashion one to your specifications, should you prefer something else."

"This will do just fine." He sheathed the blade, then strapped it to his waist.

Footsteps echoed, and a guard appeared in the doorway. "Hax. Your Grace." The guard bowed to Jeric. "Roryn's returned."

To save time, Roryn, Jeric, and Hax had split up to reach whatever steads they could to gather whatever men would fight. Jeric's luck had been marginal. Half the villages had agreed to join, but the other half refused, and Jeric had learned one very important thing: Stovich's power had not been as unilateral as Jeric had come to believe. The people of Stovichshold were divided, and Jeric could only make so many promises from a throne he didn't exactly possess.

It didn't help that many had learned Jeric had just freed Kleider's laborers.

Needless to say, Jeric didn't hold high hopes for Roryn's report, and Hax had seemed even less optimistic. "Send him in," Jeric said to the guard.

The guard bowed and left, returning with Roryn a few minutes later.

Roryn still hadn't forgiven Jeric for freeing their labor, and it was obvious every time he looked—or rather did not look—at his king. Still, Roryn was a tactical man, and he realized the pros of working alongside Jeric far outweighed the cons and thus set his personal opinions aside.

"Your Grace." Roryn bowed his head.

"Leave us," Jeric said to the guard, and the guard departed.

"Well?" Jeric said, moving slowly along the weapons rack. He picked up a small sword, scanned the design, then set it back. "Any luck?"

Roryn shifted.

Jeric picked up a crossbow, aimed it at a wall, and looked down the sight. "Out with it."

"Aldver agreed to send men."

Aldver was a small stead not far from Kleider.

Jeric grabbed a bolt and locked it into place. "That's it?"

"Aye. Hard to convince a man to fight in the middle of winter."

"Not if he's desperate." Jeric raised the crossbow again and aimed it at a dummy.

"They know what's at stake, sire, but they do not want to fight."

"And why do you suppose that is?"

When Roryn didn't respond, Jeric turned his head and looked straight at him. "Come, Roryn. I know you know the answer."

Roryn wilted just a little, and his expression faltered. "The Angevin name does not...inspire loyalty as it once did."

Jeric smiled, all teeth. "There, see? That wasn't so difficult, was it?" Jeric pulled the trigger. The bolt zinged, ripped right through the dummy's forehead, and clattered against the stone wall behind it.

Roryn swallowed. Hax stood silent.

"This has incredible action," Jeric observed, gazing down at the crossbow. "Mind if I give this to Chez?"

A beat. Then Hax said, a bit awkwardly, "As you will, Your Grace."

"Excellent." Jeric set the crossbow upon a bench near the armory door, then moved over to shelves full of braces, plates, and a few shields, scanning the inventory Niá had already enchanted.

"Is there anything more you would ask of me, Your Grace?" Roryn asked.

Jeric chuckled darkly, picked up a set of vambraces, and admired the craftsmanship. "Just be sure we've got enough arms for those arriving."

Which, by Jeric's quick estimation, totaled around four hundred.

"I'm sorry it's not more," Roryn said.

"I'm thankful it's not less."

There was a sound at the door, and Jeric turned to see Braddok walk through.

Jeric glanced back at Roryn and Hax. "Leave us."

Both men bowed and left, greeting Braddok on their way out.

"Fyrok said you returned," Braddok said.

"An hour ago." Jeric perused another rack of weapons. "I wanted to see how things were coming on here." He picked up a spear and tossed it in the air, testing its balance.

"Is there enough?" Braddok gazed about the display.

"Arms or people?"

"Both."

"Yes to the first, but only because it's a hard no for the second."

Braddok let out a sound that was half grunt, half chuckle. "That bad, eh?"

Jeric set the spear back on the rack. "We've caused far more damage with less." Jeric looked at Braddok and winked.

Braddok shook his head with a smirk, and then he plopped down onto the bench beside the crossbow. Curious, he picked it up. "Huh. This is well made."

"It's going to Chez."

"Well, where's mine? There's gotta be some perks to being the favorite."

"There are, but you used them up a long time ago with all your gambling debts."

"Hey, I win fair and square." Braddok pointed a thumb to his chest. "Not my fault Björn's a lying piece of scat."

Jeric grinned, and he tossed a *very* well-crafted dagger at Braddok. Or, more accurately, he threw it at the dummy, which was right beside Braddok, and Braddok flinched with a curse as the blade sank into the dummy's cotton heart. "The hells was that for!?"

"Not having to clear your debts for the past three months."

"You're such an ass."

"Yes, but a generous one."

Braddok snorted and jerked the dagger from the dummy. He appraised the craftsmanship, the engravings, looking impressed as he proceeded to gaze about the room. "She get to *all* of this?"

"She did," Jeric replied. "With Tallyn's help."

A breath of air whistled through Braddok's big teeth as he assessed the arms vault with new appreciation. Then, "We'll get her back, Wolf."

There was a rare and quiet sincerity to Braddok's voice that made Jeric stop and look over. Braddok wasn't just talking about Skyhold.

"Even if it kills us," Braddok continued. "Also, it'll probably kill us."

Jeric's lips cracked into a small smile as he walked over to the bench, sat down beside Braddok, and leaned back against the table.

"Your leg seems better," Braddok noted.

"It is."

"Awfully convenient having a restorer around. Maybe we won't die." Braddok was trying to lighten Jeric's mood.

"I wouldn't fault you if you ran for the mountains," Jeric said instead. "Get the hells out of here. Take Jenya. Start a family. Get on with your rutting life."

"Oh, I plan to start a family with Jen, all right. Problem is, she hates the snow, so I don't think the mountains are gonna work out so well."

"I'd go if I were you."

"No, you wouldn't, you rutting liar."

Jeric glanced sideways at him. "I'm still your king, Brad."

"Only if you've got a throne."

Jeric sighed and dragged a hand over his face. "Gods, what the hells am I doing..."

"Trying to save the woman you love?"

"By leading all of you to the slaughter?"

"You don't know that—"

"Four hundred, Brad. *Four—rutting—hundred.* Not four thousand. Not even close. That's all the support we could find, and that's assuming they all show."

Braddok sat quiet.

Jeric closed his eyes and inhaled deep. He was so over his rutting head with all of this. He thought of the Kjürda, when he'd nearly drowned, right before Imari had saved his pathetic ass.

Perhaps she should've let him drown.

Cold metal pressed against Jeric's hand, and he opened his eyes.

A flask.

Braddok pushed it at him and said, "Drink. You need it."

Jeric looked at the flask, then took it, popped the cap, and took a long drink. Akavit burned down his throat, setting his chest on fire. Jeric held the flask out, but Braddok shook his head. "Keep it. I've got another one back in my room."

Jeric eyed him. "Always drinking on the job."

"Always getting jobs that make me."

Jeric chuckled, then took another long drink. Gods, the fire felt good.

"You gonna be okay?" Braddok asked.

"This helps." Jeric raised the flask.

"Only took you twenty years to agree with me."

"I didn't say it was good. Just that it helps."

·ᑕ᠅ᗡ·

THEY EVENTUALLY LEFT Kleider's small armory to a dark sky and bitter wind. Thankfully, the akavit kept Jeric warm, but it did little to warm his spirits.

*Four hundred* to help them reclaim Skyhold, and then however many left to face Azir. Jeric had faced impossibility before, but this...this felt like suicide. Perhaps if he could convince the other houses, like those in Rodinshold, or convince Stykken to join the fold...

The problem was that required *time*, and time was something Jeric simply did not have. In fact, he should have been on his way to Trier with an army *yesterday*. Instead, Jeric was so rutting far north he was near The Fingers, trying to piece together a band of fighting men. It was easy to cast blame on his father and brother for severing what loyalty had once existed, but blame only went so far. At some point, a person had to step off the path their predecessors had paved and chart their own course.

Which meant he had no idea what in the hells he was doing.

And Imari...

He and Braddok reached the road that led back to the rooms Hax had given them, and Jeric stopped.

"You coming?" Braddok asked.

Jeric glanced at the night as the wind pushed hair into his eyes. His hair was just long enough to tie back now. "I'll meet you in a bit."

Braddok frowned.

"Go on." Jeric waved him on. "I just want to have a quick word with Hax."

Braddok eyed him a second longer, then smacked Jeric on the shoulder and walked on.

Jeric watched him go, then started down a different path. One that did not lead toward Hax but to the gate. People and guards glanced over as he passed them by, though the streets were mostly quiet. A few torches burned, struggling in the savage wind, and snow swirled erratically in the air.

The main gate lay just ahead—closed—and figures stood upon the wall, their silhouettes illuminated by torchlight.

But Jeric did not approach the main gate.

He made a quick right, ducked through an alley, and ascended the stair that switched back and forth against the inside of the wall. A few steps creaked beneath Jeric's weight, but the howling wind sufficiently drowned out his tracks.

He reached the landing, tugged his cloak around his neck, and continued along the narrow walk and parapets, away from the watchtower. Here, at the top of the wall, the wind was greedy, its hungry claws snapping at his clothes and hair. Jeric soon found the small platform that jutted out from the walk. There were rings for torches, and a few metal stands, but this vantage sat otherwise empty.

Jeric stopped at one of the parapet's cutouts and looked across the wide lawn of snow they'd crossed just a few days ago, but the night was too thick to see much else. He gazed down the high wall to where it sank into the snow. It was a good wall, made of stone instead of skal, but it was strong, and it reached just over two stories.

He remembered Trier.

This wall might stand against men, but it would not stand against guardian fire. Only Skyhold had those defenses. It was how Tommad the First, his many-great-grandfather, had finally succeeded in capturing Azir so that the Liagé who'd sided with the Provinces could bind him to that tree deep in the Blackwood. Azir had been unable to bring Skyhold down because Liagé enchantments were not just in the sewers, but all throughout Skyhold's foundation, embedded into the very mortar of that fortress.

Into that magnificent skal wall.

Which Kormand now possess ed.

Jeric curled his hands into fists and dragged his teeth over his bottom lip. Gods*damn*it, he was such a fool.

"You asked me to serve her," Jeric snarled at the sky as ice flecked his cheeks. "But how in the *rutting hells* am I supposed to do that from here?" He paused, feeling that akavit burn deep in his belly. "I need that fortress, and I need an army—neither of which I have—so tell me, oh *magnanimous* Maker, god of the Sol Velorians, who delivers his faithful from their enemies: *Where the hells are you now?*"

The wind howled, but there was no answer. Nothing at all. And the only thing that kept Jeric from picking up a metal rack and throwing it against the wall just then was that it would have made noise and alerted the guards to his presence, and he didn't want to see a godsdamned soul right then.

Jeric ground his teeth and shut his eyes.

*Get your rutting head right!* his own voice chided in his mind.

But all he could see was Imari's beautiful face, and the weight of it all fell upon his shoulders, crushing him. Making it difficult to breathe.

Jeric dropped to his knees, and his hands gripped the cutout,

404 | BARBARA KLOSS

not caring that his fingers ached with cold. "I can't do this," he whispered. "I can't lead these people to their deaths, and I can't let her go, but I don't know how to bring her back. I don't know why you saved her if only to give her to a monster that I don't have the power to fight."

That was what it was, what had been chipping away at Jeric every step of this journey. His entire life had been built upon fighting. On righting wrongs—even perceived ones. In that, he could take control.

But Jeric was coming to find that control was an illusion.

The powers at play were so much larger than him, and for the first...no, second time in his life since his mother's passing, Jeric felt truly helpless.

And he hated it.

He hated that he wasn't enough. He hadn't been enough for his mother; he wasn't enough for Imari. He could give it everything he had, and he would *never* be enough. Not for this. But that was how he'd survived: knowing when to walk away from a fight. This was one such time.

But he could not walk away from Imari.

Jeric knelt there in the snow, numbed by the cold as the wind howled. He could go after her alone. Maybe then he could find a way to sneak in, get past Lestra—something.

*Anything.*

He didn't care about that godsdamned chair, but he would never stop fighting for Imari. That didn't mean he needed to sacrifice four hundred men.

Jeric made up his mind. He looked up, dragged his hands over his face, and froze.

Deep in the darkness, just beyond the snowy lawn, a small light flickered.

Wary, Jeric climbed to his feet. The guards at the tower hadn't noticed, but it was difficult to see. A few large gusts twisted snow in the air, and the light disappeared.

Jeric's gaze fixed on the place it had been, and he wondered if he'd imagined it...

*There.*

And it was drawing nearer.

One light became two. Then three. Then half a dozen as shadows took shape around and behind them.

It was too soon for any of Stovichshold's houses to arrive, and this did not have the form of a Corinthian army. Then...who could it possibly be?

The guards at the watchtower noticed. One pointed, and another ran down the steps, probably to notify Hax. The rest rallied over the gate, and Jeric made his way toward the gate too, eyes fixed on the approaching figures. It was difficult to see in the darkness and snow, but Jeric counted at least a few dozen, and they did not appear to be armed.

But that mean little.

"—ready the slings," said Gavyn, one of the guards at the gate.

Two started to run off.

"Wait."

Jeric's sharp command took them by surprise, and they glanced over, equally surprised to see Jeric standing there.

"Your Grace..." Gavyn said. "There's an army approaching our—"

"That's no army."

The guards stopped, confused.

"Open the gate," Jeric said.

Uneasy glances were exchanged.

"Do it now."

"But, sire, we are not prepared to..." Gavyn's voice trailed as he glanced back at the approaching group. He stared, as if trying to make sense of what he was seeing. The other guards at the gate had fallen silent as all stared into the darkness at the group of Sol Velorians approaching.

## 43

"Open the godsdamned gate, Gavyn," Jeric demanded, then took the steps two at a time, jumping down the last few. He ran to the small stable nestled against the wall, grabbed his stolik, and gave her a soft kick. Her hooves thundered down the path, Kleider's gate groaned open, and Jeric galloped right through.

He tore across the snowy land, wondering what in the world had persuaded the laborers to come back, and he threw a quick prayer of humble gratitude to the one he'd just been cursing from the parapets.

Seeing Jeric, the group stopped, and he realized those lights weren't torches but little Liagé lights glowing in the night. Jeric slowed the stolik to a trot and finally stopped a dozen paces away.

Up close, Jeric also realized these were not the laborers he had set free.

"Who is your leader?" Jeric asked in Sol Velorian.

Some looked surprised he spoke their language.

"I am," said a woman's voice at the front, in Sol Velorian. He did not recognize her from the crowd he'd freed, and yet memory nagged at the back of his mind.

She looked to be in her fifties, though one could never quite know with Liagé, which she appeared to be. Her black hair fell over one shoulder, braided into a rope laced with silver, and painted glyphs covered her face and neck. She wore a plain coat of fur-lined wool, snow dusted her breeches halfway to her knees, and her boots were caked with snow.

"You are the Wolf," the woman said, again in Sol Velorian.

"I am," Jeric said, accepting judgment. "And you are?"

Her dark gaze raked over Jeric, then flickered to the stolik and the city he had left behind. A few behind her bent heads and whispered.

"Maeva," the woman answered.

Jeric studied her. Suddenly, he understood. "You have come from the Serras."

"*Sei.*" A beat. "And *your* family has faithfully kept our population growing."

It was not a compliment; she was referring to all the Sol Velorians who'd sought refuge in the mountains during his father's reign. "But we've never added so many to our number as we did a few days ago."

She meant the laborers he'd freed, who'd gone straight for the hidden Sol Velorian sanctuary in the Serras. Which meant that sanctuary wasn't nearly as deep in the mountains as Jeric had formerly suspected. Still, it did not explain why they were here now. Those Sol Velorians had wanted nothing to do with a Wolf.

"Why have you come?" Jeric asked.

Maeva gazed at him a long moment, as if deciding how best to answer, and finally settled on, "I know Survak."

Jeric drew back, but then he remembered: Survak had been a smuggler. It was why he—the former captain of Corinth's Sunguard—had been cast out in the first place. "He smuggled you out of Corinth."

"When your mother was still alive, *sei.*"

Mention of his mother made his chest constrict unexpectedly.

"Survak said you needed our help," Maeva continued. "I refused him, but then two hundred Sol Velorians appeared at our door, and Corrya asked me to reconsider."

*Survak.*

Jeric never would have guessed that Survak had sailed straight into the inlet at Stovichshold right after leaving them at Felheim.

But then Maeva turned and ushered forth a young woman with long dark hair and a face Jeric recognized, because it was the girl who had stumbled across his fire in the Grays. The one Jorvysk—the Stryker—had tried to take for himself, but Jeric had beat him to death for it and set her free.

Corrya looked at Jeric, her features steel but her eyes full of gratitude, and she nodded once.

"I don't like you, Wolf King," Maeva said sharply. "But Asorai does not care what I think. He sees what man cannot, and it has been made abundantly clear that he has chosen *you,* the least likely of all, to play a part in all of this, and so I am here—*we* are here—to help."

Jeric was suddenly overcome with emotion, and his gaze flickered to the heavens before settling back on Maeva. "Thank you. For coming."

"Don't thank me; thank the Maker, for we would not be here otherwise." Maeva said, and the young woman beside her looked a little embarrassed. "So, Wolf King, do you have room for us?"

MAEVA'S GROUP chose to camp outside Kleider's walls. They pitched tents on the leeward side, right up against the stone, and the Liagé in their midst constructed fires the wind could not steal. Jeric, Braddok, Tallyn, and a few of Kleider's guards brought food and whatever additional supplies Maeva's group needed.

Unfortunately, most of Kleider was not keen to help the Sol Velorians and looked quite unhappy and uncomfortable about the turn of events. Jeric sensed this was exactly why Maeva's group had chosen to sleep *outside* the city walls.

Once their camp was properly situated, Jeric asked Maeva, "A word?"

"Of course." She said a quick word to a few of hers, then gestured at a large, middle-aged man she'd called Akim, who had a brooding disposition and a girth that contested Braddok's own. Akim stalked over to them as Maeva led Jeric, Braddok, and Tallyn to her large tent. Akim raised the flap, Maeva ducked inside, and the others followed.

The space was tight but not uncomfortable, if a little cold, and three spheres of golden light hovered above, giving light to the otherwise dark space. Maeva had already spread out a small pallet, and Jeric noted the stack of old Liagé books beside them. He recognized one as the verses and his heart ached for Imari.

"You know it?" Maeva asked.

Jeric glanced over to find her watching him intently. She'd seen where his attention had landed. "I wish I knew it better," he confessed.

Akim look surprised by this, and then immediately wary. Maeva, however, looked intrigued. Then, "You favor her. Your mother."

The words caught Jeric off guard. "You knew her?"

A small smile touched her lips. "I wish I'd known her better," she said, then, "I worked in Skyhold a very long time ago, but when your father tightened his fist, I began searching for a way out. It was your mother who connected me with Survak."

"What are we talking about?" Braddok interrupted, looking between them.

"He doesn't speak your language," Jeric explained.

"Ah. I am sorry," Maeva said in heavily accented Common.

"But I am...how do we say"—she batted a hand—"getting off topic. There is something you wished to speak to me about, no?"

Jeric would rather have discussed his mother right then, but that was not why he had called this meeting.

"Yes," he said. "I think it would be constructive to give an account for what we've endured and see if—based on your experience—you had any insight on the best way forward."

Maeva looked pleased by his question. Akim still brooded wariness. He was a Liagé guardian. Jeric did not know how he knew that so concretely, but he would have staked his life on it.

"We do have a seer in our midst," Maeva continued a little cautiously, and Akim looked even less thrilled that she'd divulged this information. "She has shared...pieces of your story, which Survak confirmed. But yes. I agree that it would be helpful to hear it from you, in its"—she searched the sky for the Common word—"entirety."

Jeric started at the beginning. From his trek into The Wilds and every moment after. Tallyn and Braddok interjected here and there, and Maeva asked a few questions. Akim even voiced a question when Jeric reached the attack on Trier, namely asking Jeric to better describe the style of attack.

"It's important to know how many Liagé are in Azir's employ," Akim said, not bothering to speak in Common as Maeva had done.

"I agree," Jeric replied in Common, while Tallyn translated Akim's words for Braddok. "Imari counted thirteen at the time, not including Azir's Mo'Ruk."

"He'll have more now," Maeva said, thinking. "We've Seen the flames over Istraan cities."

It was just as Jeric had heard. "How many more?"

"It's hard to say. So many of us have been in hiding for too long. I don't know how many have been hiding in Istraa." She paused. "But *we* have twenty-six."

Twenty-six. It was more than Jeric could have hoped, but would it be enough?

He continued with his story. Maeva was quiet when he reached the part about the tree and Av'Assi, and she and Akim exchanged a long glance.

"You know Hiatt?" Tallyn asked.

"No," Maeva answered, then, "We always believed in this place you mention, but none of us have seen it. Please continue."

So Jeric did, and once he finished, Maeva was quiet for a very long time. She looked at Akim, and the two of them spoke too low and fast for Jeric to follow, though he caught words: *sulaziér*, Fyri, Zussa.

"Maeva, you know Azir," Jeric said. "Do we have a chance?"

Maeva looked at him. Her expression was not hopeful. "Yes, but this fight will only be won by the *sulaziér*, and we must all pray that she does not fall like every other *sulaziér* before her."

"Imari will not," Jeric said. "She is the strongest woman I've ever known."

Maeva gave him a kind of sad smile. "Would that our flesh had the strength of our spirit, young Wolf; then the Great Deceiver would not exist today."

## 44

Rasmin sagged in the dark, drifting in and out of consciousness. He had no concept of time, of day or night, and every breath was a struggle, a fight for existence. They had broken his arms so that he could not fly. So that he could not change or leave this prison, so that he could not aid those who would stand against Azir.

Not a second time.

And so Rasmin remained naked and chained while his guard occasionally brought him water from a dirtied rag. To what end he was being kept alive, Rasmin could only guess, but Azir had always liked to keep prizes. To collect the spoils of his victories and showcase every obstacle he had overcome.

The door winked open, and bright light spilled in. Rasmin winced, blinking as his eyes adjusted. Azir filled the doorway. Or Zussa. They were one and the same now, some sick symbiosis of power.

It was on this point that Rasmin wished he could fly away and warn the *sulaziér*, because they would be too much for her. The only way to stop this was for her to—

"Still you live, Rasyamin," Azir said, though his voice warped with Zussa's otherworldly bass.

Rasmin lacked the strength to answer.

Azir regarded him with those pure black eyes, which settled briefly on the ear he had bitten off, and then he said, "I have brought you a gift."

Intrigue stirred Rasmin's consciousness just a little as Azir moved aside, and a woman stepped into view.

Imari.

Rasmin jolted fully awake, eyes wide with confusion, for Imari was not bound or guarded. She stood full and healthy, dressed in a robe as white as clouds. Independent and free...

Rasmin looked into her face, and he knew. This was not Imari.

There was no mercy in her expression, no love in her gaze. Nothing but cold, unadulterated hate, and a heavy pit settled inside of Rasmin.

"What have you done?" Rasmin said to Azir.

But it was Imari who took a step forward, claiming Rasmin's prison. In that moment, her resemblance to Fyri was uncanny.

"And what have *you* done, Head Inquisitor?" Her tone taunted.

"This is not you, Imari," Rasmin rasped.

Imari took another step, her cold gaze locked on Rasmin. There was nothing tender in it. "Is it identities you wish to discuss, then? Because I would so love to hear your justification for torturing our own in order to *save us*."

Rasmin would not follow her down this path, so he tried another angle. "Jeric needs you."

Imari laughed, though the sound lacked mirth. "The Wolf? You think I mean to help a man who slaughtered thousands of our own?"

And in that one bitter profession, Rasmin understood: Lestra had shown her Jeric's past. Every bloody and grim detail, and it had broken Imari—broken her enough for Zussa to slip in and plant her wicked seed.

Rasmin had watched it happen before.

And how that bitter seed grew fast and furiously, insidiously creeping into every part of Imari's broken heart and soul before choking out all the rest—all the good.

All the light.

What he did not know was if that light was diminished for good or if it had merely been pushed to the furthest recesses of her being.

"He has changed, Imari," Rasmin said desperately, reminding her so that he might bring her back if she was still there. "*Because of you.* You must remember that. Azir wants you to forget everything you and Jeric have fought through together, because otherwise you'll never help Azir finish what he aims to accomplish, but the Wolf is irrevocably on *your* side, Imari. Because *you* showed him another way, and you love him as fiercely as he loves you."

Fire flickered in Imari's eyes, and fury made her features sharp. "Do not speak to me of love," she snarled with a darkness that did not belong to her. She grabbed his chains and jerked him forward so that they were face-to-face. "He will always be a *Corazzi* dog, and you...you are a bird with broken wings."

She looked at him, her eyes burning with hate, and hummed a single note. Just one. It resonated across that small space between them, full of power as it gripped Rasmin's heart and squeezed it silent.

IMARI WATCHED the head inquisitor sag against the chains. His light was gone, strangled once and for all by her song. She spat on his face, watching her spittle slide down the bridge of his beak-like nose. Of course, he did not feel it; he was dead.

Imari felt a slight weight upon her shoulder and turned to face her lord and master.

He touched her cheek. "Well done, my dear *sulaziér*."

Imari closed her eyes and inhaled deep, swelling with his praise. She would do anything for it; it was all she desired.

"I have a gift for you." He removed his hand from her face, and Imari opened her eyes.

A leather strap dangled from his long fingertips and sharp, black nails: Fyri's bells.

*Her* bells.

At the sight of them, Imari felt a sudden and raging hunger. Su'Vi must have brought them back with her, and Imari wanted them *now*.

Her lord smiled as if he felt her urgency. "Take it. It is yours."

Imari took them.

"Shall I help you put it on?" he whispered in her ear.

Imari's eyelids slid lower; her breath trembled. She could not speak, overwhelmed by his proximity. His power. It was everywhere, in the air, in the stones and on her tongue—all of it pressing against her.

He took her hand in his, and his touch sent a tremor through her body as he wrapped the leather around her wrist with practiced ease and fastened the clasp.

But he did not pull away.

Instead, he clasped her hand between both of his, and Imari gazed into his eyes, into that endless well of power—the power of a god—and she wanted to drink from it. She wanted to drink and drink until she was drowning in it.

"Come; there is something I would have you do," he said.

"Whatever you would have me do, my lord, I would do it."

Her lord smiled at her, then let go of her hands and strode for the door, where Su'Vi waited in the hall. She looked from her lord to Imari, and Imari saw a spark of jealousy before Su'Vi fell into step behind them.

*Let her be jealous,* thought Imari. *She is weak and must learn her place.*

They strode through Vondar, and dim light spilled through the open windows. A thick layer of gray clouds hid the sun, and a cold breeze slipped into the open halls, but Imari did not feel cold. Not even through the thin silk and sleeveless gown Azir had given to her, because the Shah was a constant fire in her blood. Like a brazier always burning, always hungry.

Sol Velorian guards stopped and bowed as they strode past, their eyes on Imari. Drinking her in, following her shape—her song—utterly enraptured. One was very handsome, Imari noted. Well-built with strong features and a thick rope of hair draped over his shoulder. His eyes burned upon her, and she smiled coyly at him. He blushed and smiled back. She could take him later, she mused, but decided against it. He would prove only a distraction, and Imari must remain focused on the mission ahead.

On her lord and master.

She caught Azir watching her out of the corner of his eye, and after they passed through Vondar's main doors, he stopped at the top of the stairs, took her hand, and brought it to his lips. Behind them, Su'Vi stopped, watching silently.

"You may take any you wish, once this is finished, but your heart is mine," he said. His long thumbnail trailed over the backs of Imari's fingertips, his gaze locked on hers, and Imari shuddered. "*You* are mine."

"Always, my lord," Imari said, her voice a breath.

He planted his lips upon the back of her hand then released her. Imari wanted him to touch her again. Imari wanted him to never stop touching her.

Instead, he strode down the palace steps, and Imari followed, with Su'Vi trailing closely and silently behind.

They walked past Sol Velorian guards, through the gate, and into what remained of Trier. Much of it lay in shambles, but Liagé had repaired enough to make it habitable while they gathered and waited. Istraan survivors worked to clear rubble from the streets while Sol Velorian guards watched over them with whips and swords.

This was just the beginning of the Istraans' recompense.

Her lord led her to the center of a courtyard, where some Istraans had been gathered at the behest of the Sol Velorians and Liagé guarding them. Imari saw their surprise, their confusion. She recognized a few of them as Istraa's wealthiest and others from previous healing ventures. They looked between her— freshly bathed and dressed as a queen—to her lord, and Imari saw despair set in.

And they should despair.

Her lord led her to a small platform that had once supported a statue of Ashova, goddess of pleasure, and there he stopped.

The crowd waited. Some Istraans called out to Imari for help before struck over the head by a nearby guard, and something inside Imari twisted hard—so hard, Imari gasped. Her lord took her hand, and the strange pressure ceased at once.

"You are gathered here because I would make you an offer, for I am a merciful god," her lord addressed the crowd. "Bow before me now, profess that I am your lord, and I shall welcome you into my new world."

His words trembled through the courtyard, and even when he finished, their memory echoed with power.

A few Istraans dropped to their knees, which persuaded others to follow suit, while murmurs of *my lord* trickled through the crowd. More and more fell, until the courtyard lay prostrate at her lord's feet. However, nine remained standing in defiance, but her lord did not look angry. He simply looked at Imari.

For this was her task, her role in his new world, and she was honored to fill it.

Imari closed her eyes, seeing each and every star, hearing each and every tone of the nine souls before her. Each defiant pitch rang in her mind, and Imari captured them all, held on tight, and raised her wrist—the bells.

She gave the bells the slightest flick, reflecting each tone, magnifying them as she tuned them all into a chord of her choosing. Power tingled within her belly as she took their song and wove them into her own magnificent creation.

It was so simple; she wondered that she had ever struggled.

Those nine points of defiant light grew brighter, trembling with Imari's power, and she tugged them right out of their bodies, letting their lights drift back into the clouds.

In the material world, their bodies dropped like stones. A few in the crowd gasped, and then the courtyard fell silent.

Satisfied, Imari opened her eyes.

And her lord smiled brilliantly. "Ready the others, Su'Vi. It is time."

## 45

"Is that the last of them?" Jeric asked Hax, studying the group of armed Corinthians currently passing through Kleider's open gate.

"Aye," said Hax.

In this group from a neighboring stead, Jeric counted thirty-three in all, ranging from adolescent to middle-age. Half of them bore crude arms, and all of them looked exhausted.

Thirty-three put them just under three hundred, total. They'd lost nearly a hundred men once word spread that they'd be fighting alongside Sol Velorians.

Rutting idiots.

Jeric exchanged a brief glance with Braddok, then jogged down the watchtower stairs, greeted the newcomers, and sent them on with Hax to get situated within Kleider's cramped walls, for Kleider was now teeming with soldiers. Not due to inflated numbers, but because the roads were narrow and Kleider simply lacked space.

Marta had recruited some from the ranks to help with food, and Grag and his men hunted from dawn till dusk to help feed the additional mouths. Still, Kleider could hardly hold or feed any more, and Jeric wondered if, perhaps, it was a blessing that so much of Stovichshold had refused this fight.

He would rather have a small, well-fed army than a thousand starved men. It was why his pack had always been so effective.

"Come on, Wolf. Let's eat," Braddok said suddenly.

They'd been at the wall most of the day, and even though it was now dusk, Jeric did not feel hungry.

"Get that godsdamned despairing look off your face," Braddok said.

"I am not despairing."

"You're a scat liar."

Jeric flashed his teeth, and Braddok laughed, then smacked Jeric on the shoulder. "I hear Hax found Stovich's secret stash of ale, and if it's gone before I get there, I'll kick your ass."

Jeric chuckled at this, then left with Braddok for the hall, but they'd only made it as far as the armory when Jeric heard shouting from the wall, and a horn blared. He and Braddok exchanged a worried glance, Braddok cursed, and they both sprinted back to the gate.

Jeric took the stairs two at a time as anxious guards buzzed around them.

"—army out there," someone was saying as Jeric reached the walk and peered through the parapets.

At the small army approaching.

It was hard to gauge exact numbers through the falling snow, but Jeric counted well over one hundred. Two banners waved, but from this distance, Jeric could not tell who it was. He spied Roryn standing farther down the walk, holding a spyglass, and he pushed his way toward him.

"Who is it?" Jeric demanded once he reached Roryn.

"I don't know. It's hard to see—"

Jeric took the spyglass, startling Roryn, then put the glass to his eye.

Jeric stopped breathing.

Gods, it *was* him.

"Wolf?" Braddok asked.

Brom Stykken *had* come, at Jeric's request, and he had brought an army.

"It's Stykken." Jeric pulled the glass from his eye and looked at a completely stunned Braddok.

"I can't believe the sonofabitch came..." Braddok murmured.

Roryn, however, paled.

"Raise your banner and open the gates." Jeric handed Roryn the spyglass and started for the stairs.

"But, Your Grace...how do we know he's not here to attack?" Roryn asked.

"I invited him," Jeric called over his shoulder, then noticed Roryn hadn't moved. "Godsdamnit, man, open the rutting gates!"

Roryn spun around and started barking commands, and Jeric sprinted down the stairs.

"Don't tell me you're going out there," Braddok said, following after him.

"Done."

Braddok grunted. "Godsdamnit, Wolf."

The gate groaned open like a mouth, and Jeric stepped beneath the portcullis's sharp teeth. Braddok stopped beside him, both of them gazing out at Stykken and his slowly approaching army. Jeric could hear Roryn barking orders above his head, and more guards gathered in the courtyard behind him. The Sol Velorian encampment had also come alive with light and moving silhouettes as everyone looked to see the source of such commotion.

There had to be well over three hundred of them. Gods, if Stykken *had* come to help, it would double Jeric's numbers.

"What if you're wrong?" Braddok asked.

"I'm not."

Braddok didn't look convinced. "I don't like this, Wolf."

"Go have a drink, then." Jeric started forward.

Braddok grumbled and followed Jeric beneath the grate and onto the wide lawn. Their boots crunched in the old snow, which was quickly being covered with new, and the chatter on the wall ceased as all the world stood in apprehensive silence, watching these two nations collide.

Jeric couldn't remember the last time he'd seen his mother's cousin. He'd certainly never seen the man *after* his mother had been killed, though the name had been like a curse within Skyhold's walls. Forbidden from being spoken—forbidden from being *thought*—and Brom Stykken remained a constant splinter in his father's skin.

But Brom Stykken was just as Jeric remembered, built like a warship, broad and thick and strong, able to endure nature's deadliest storms—which he had. Brom Stykken had been born to a line of Stykkens who had fought during Azir's first war, aiding Corinth's warships and leading them all to victory at the seas.

Alongside Jeric's many-great-grandfather, Tommad the First.

That thought gave Jeric hope now.

Stykken was buried in heavy furs and leather, like the rest of his men, but Stykken stood out. He always had, like some jagged stone breaker pushing back a raging sea. The Fingers' citizens had always rallied to him. He was sure, he was safe, he would not shatter beneath the sea's terrifying waves.

No wonder Jeric's father had not liked him. He wouldn't be controlled. No one owned him, and he had no special interest except for doing right by his people, which was inherently problematic for a tyrant like King Tommad.

At a single gesture from Stykken, the army stopped one hundred yards from Kleider's wall. The Sol Velorians crowded at the edge of their encampment, and Kleider's guards stood ready upon the wall, awaiting Roryn's command.

But none of Stykken's men raised weapons as Braddok and the Wolf King steadily approached.

Wind howled, ice and snow swirled, and Stykken

dismounted. The man to his left dismounted too, and both men approached.

Jeric couldn't help but feel as though the past had come to claim the present, and the future teetered on the edge of a blade.

Brom Stykken and his man stopped a few paces away, but Stykken looked only at Jeric, those shrewd, dark eyes assessing.

Gods, even though he hadn't seen his mother's cousin since he was a boy, the sight of him now drew all of those memories close, and his chest squeezed.

"It's been a long time," Jeric said, not without emotion.

"Aye," Stykken replied after a breath. "Last I saw you, you were just a mangy pup tumbling around Meira's skinny legs."

Jeric was surprised to find he remembered Stykken's voice too, its grit and depth, brined like the sea. It made Jeric miss something he hadn't realized he'd wanted.

"You're all wolf now," Stykken said. There was a note of despondency to his words and eyes as he gazed upon Jeric.

"Not *all*," Jeric said. "As it turns out, there's much more of my mother in me than I thought."

This earned Jeric a small, sad smile.

Wind tugged at them, twisting in that space between them.

"You received my letter," Jeric said.

Stykken regarded him. "I did." Stykken started to reach beneath his coat, which made Braddok flinch for his weapon.

Jeric put a hand on Braddok's arm to stay him. *It's all right*, Jeric communicated with his eyes.

Braddok's expression did not agree, but he stayed.

Stykken retrieved a piece of paper, the wax seal broken. The paper itself was crinkled, as if he'd spent countless hours poring over it, probably wondering how to respond. If he should respond.

"Did you mean it?" Stykken asked Jeric.

"Every word," Jeric said, without a moment's hesitation.

Stykken's gaze flitted over Jeric's face, and then he slipped the paper back into his coat. "You favor her."

"So I've been recently told, and all I can say is thank the gods."

This made Stykken chuckle, albeit sadly, and then he took two steps, breaching that distance between them, covering the past with present grace, and embraced Jeric fully.

Jeric wrapped an arm around his cousin and held him tight. A sudden wave of emotion engulfed him, and when both men pulled apart, it wasn't the cold that made their eyes glassy.

"I picked up one of yours on the way," Stykken added. "He found us at Burnam, half conscious. Asked where we were heading and then asked if he could come."

Stykken pointed behind him to a stolik and rider Jeric could just see through Stykken's men.

Jeric froze.

It was Stanis.

And he did not appear well. His skin looked translucent, his eyes sunken—haunted. He was a man who had suffered long nights wrestling with himself. Jeric knew that fight and knew it well. He didn't doubt Stanis still fought, but he was here.

"So?" Stykken asked. "Do we fight this war as allies?"

Jeric peeled his gaze from Stanis and looked to his cousin, hearing all of his father's failings echoed in that one request. "We do," he answered. "So long as The Fingers will also stand alongside the Sol Velorians."

This had been Jeric's uncertainty. The Fingers did not share Corinth's history of brutality toward the Sol Velorians, nor did they possess a kind one. They simply kept to themselves, and The Fingers' harsh climate naturally turned Sol Velorian refugees away—except for those, apparently, in the Serras.

But Jeric would not bend on this point. Even if it meant losing Stykken's support and his army. He had made a promise, and he intended to keep that promise.

*"You might be standing on the same board,"* Imari had said, *"but if you make different plays, you might just find yourself a different outcome."*

Stykken regarded Jeric a long moment. His gaze flickered to the little encampment where the Sol Velorians looked on, and there it rested as the wind howled and twisted all around them.

"You trust them?" Stykken asked.

"I do."

Stykken inhaled deep then looked back at him. "My men won't like it, Wolf. But I do." He paused. "The Fingers will stand beside them; you have my word."

·⟨⟩·

It was late into the night by the time they'd settled Stykken's army outside of Kleider's gates. Tents littered the lawn—Sol Velorian on one side, The Fingers on the other—and countless fires flickered. One tent had been designated for Niá and Tallyn to enchant the arms of Stykken's army, though that had taken some convincing.

Stykken's men were not eager to part with their arms, especially to two Liagé.

But Stykken explained the situation and why it was necessary, and Niá proceeded to give a public demonstration of what, exactly, she planned to do. The first few approached her gingerly, but after a couple of examples, when they realized she wasn't going to turn them into shades, more and more brought their arms. So much so that there wasn't room for her and Tallyn to work, and a group of men offered their large tent for them to continue.

"Are you certain you're feeling up to it?" Jeric asked after they'd moved the arms to the large tent, where Stykken's men piled even more. He knew what enchanting Kleider's arms had cost them.

"We will do what we can," Tallyn replied, determined. "But do not worry on my account, for I would rather perish from my own enchantments than from standing on the receiving end of Azir's."

Niá grunted her agreement as she picked up a particularly large shield.

Jeric exchanged a look with Chez, who stood near the tent's opening.

"I'll stay with them," Chez said.

Jeric nodded, then ducked out of the tent, where Stykken waited.

"Shall we?" Stykken tipped his head, and the two men walked on through The Fingers' encampment.

Thankfully, Stykken had brought his owns tents. Jeric didn't know what they would have done if they hadn't; Kleider had given their spare to the Sol Velorians. Still, Stykken hadn't brought many tents, and his men crammed into them like smuggled cargo in a ship's belly. Others sat outside in the cold, drinking around a fire. Some glanced over as Jeric and their lord passed by. The stoliks had been broken into three pens, all contained by a tight circle of tents. Jeric watched one of Kleider's own wheelbarrow bales of hay to feed the hungry beasts.

"You plan to leave at dawn?" Stykken asked as they walked.

"If your men have the energy."

Stykken grinned, eyeing a particularly loud group that laughed around a fire. "Oh, they'll have the energy, all right. *Or a headache.*"

Jeric chuckled.

Stykken opened the flap to his own tent, ducked inside with a lantern, and Jeric followed, letting the flap fall. The tent wasn't any larger than the others, but unlike the others, Stykken did not share. There was one bedroll, one pack, one lantern, and one blanket spread, littered with maps and scrolls, a compass, and a few odd arms.

They were both much too tall for this tent and had to bend their heads.

"Have a seat, Your Highness," Stykken said, grandly gesturing at the blanket as he took a seat upon it and folded his legs.

Jeric sat across from him, legs stretched as he gazed at the map Stykken had unfolded: a map of Corinth. All of her nooks and crannies, every road and stream and principality.

Every mine.

Jeric's gaze settled upon the three that had originally belonged to Stykken, which Corinth had assumed in the aftermath of Azir's first war. Mines Brom Stykken had attempted to retrieve through Jeric's mother, which Jeric's father had never honored.

Jeric's father had never honored anything but his own desires.

Stykken pulled a long pipe from his sack and offered it to Jeric.

"I don't smoke."

"I hear you don't drink either," Stykken said as he packed dried leaves into the end of it.

"Not if I can help it."

Stykken smiled around the end of his pipe and used flint to catch a spark. "Yes, you've definitely got more of Meira in you."

This made Jeric grin.

The leaves caught the spark, Stykken pulled on the pipe until that spark held, and then he exhaled a cloud.

"That smells like scat," Jeric said.

"We can't afford the good stuff. We grow this on the islands. It's the only thing that'll survive those rutting storms."

Jeric held out his hand.

Stykken eyed Jeric's hand, then passed him the pipe. Jeric put it to his lips, pulled hard, then coughed salt and acid.

Stykken chuckled as Jeric handed the pipe back.

"We'll have to fix that," Jeric said.

Stykken shoved the pipe back in his mouth. "I don't know. I've grown to like it after all these years."

Jeric let out another cough, trying to purge his lungs, then looked down at the map and made a decision. "Kleider is yours," he said. "Cafto and Hestwhich are yours too, but know that I released Kleider's labor one week ago."

They were three of Corinth's most profitable mines, which was why Jeric's father had never honored his agreement with The Fingers.

Stykken slowly pulled his pipe away, exhaled, and gazed at Jeric through the smoke. "You would hand over all three?"

Jeric bent a knee and wrapped his fingers around it. "They belong to you. I am simply returning them."

Stykken regarded him a long moment, then said, "Keep Cafto and Hestwhich. Kleider is more than enough for us."

"But Kleider has no workers."

"She will. My people are eager for honest work."

Jeric looked at his cousin. "I am sorry for my father."

Stykken tapped his pipe against the lantern. "I am too, little Jos."

The name—the *memory* of what was lost—weighed heavily upon Jeric.

Stykken considered him, then said, "I brought you something."

Before Jeric could ask, Stykken stood, stepped over to his bedroll, then peeled it back. Beneath lay a long scabbard. Stykken picked it up and held it out to Jeric.

Jeric climbed to his feet. The leather was old but worn well, and a tarnished skal hilt crowned one end.

"It was your grandfather's," Stykken said.

Jeric's gaze met his, and Stykken nodded once.

This sword had belonged to his mother's father, whom Jeric had never met. Jeric pulled the blade free. The sword was made of skal, light and well-balanced, though the salted air had not been kind to it. Rust had eaten parts away, but nothing a good whetstone and gifted skalsmith couldn't mend.

"It's yours," Stykken said. "If you want it."

Jeric slid the blade back into its sheath. "I would be honored. Thank you."

Stykken looked pleased. He rolled back the bedroll then said, "Tell me everything."

Jeric stayed late into the night, filling Stykken in on all that had transpired, starting with his hunt into The Wilds for Imari. Stykken had already heard about many of the events Jeric mentioned, but he had a lot of questions about Azir and everything that'd followed.

At some point, Hax stepped into the tent and joined them, along with Maeva—while Akim stood by the tent's opening—and the four of them turned their discussion into different strategies for taking back Skyhold from Kormand, but none of them seemed very concerned about that part of their future, with the numbers and various talents now at their disposal.

Unless Azir had already reached Skyhold.

But so far, according to Tallyn and his attempts at Sight, he did not believe Azir had left Istraa.

"We should continue this discussion tomorrow," Hax said with a yawn. "It's late, and we've got many late nights ahead."

Jeric didn't disagree, though he felt an odd reluctance at leaving his cousin.

Stykken must have felt it too, for he wrapped a thick arm around Jeric and clasped him on the back. Jeric returned the gesture and ducked out of the tent after Hax.

The camp was much quieter now, and many of the fires had reduced to hot embers. Maeva and Akim headed for their camp, while Jeric and Hax wound through The Fingers' tents toward Kleider's gates. The light within Niá and Tallyn's tent still glowed brightly, and Jeric stopped by to check on their progress. Their pile of enchanted weaponry was much larger than Jeric had expected, but there was still a lot more to be done.

"You should rest," Jeric said.

"We will soon," Tallyn replied.

Jeric looked to Chez, who shrugged irritably as if he'd already tried—and failed—to convince them to stop.

"I'm heading back," Jeric said quietly to Chez. A silent offer to join, but Chez shook his head.

Jeric patted his shoulder, started to turn, but stopped. "Have you seen Stanis?"

Chez's lips thinned. "No."

Jeric hadn't seen him either ever since he'd ridden through Kleider's gates.

"He was in the barracks, last I Saw," Tallyn said.

"I'll check there, then." Jeric ducked out and walked on with Hax, noting the handful of silhouettes standing upon the ramparts, but the rest of Kleider lay quiet and sleeping.

And gods, Jeric was tired, but there was still one more thing he needed to do.

Jeric said goodnight to Hax, then proceeded down Kleider's dark and snowy streets toward the barracks. They were located near the gate, so Jeric didn't have to walk far before the squat structure came into view. A few lanterns flickered in the foremost windows, and two men stood guard on either side of the door.

On a sudden hunch, Jeric did not approach those front doors. Instead, he walked around the building to the training yard in back.

Where he found Stanis.

Stanis stood all alone in the cold, bow in hand with an arrow nocked and aimed at a straw dummy already skewered with a half dozen more.

"I think he's dead, Stan," Jeric mused, slowly approaching.

String snapped, air whizzed, and the arrow sank between the dummy's eyes.

Jeric raised a brow. "You've been practicing."

Stanis picked up another arrow, loaded it. Never meeting Jeric's gaze. Never even looking in Jeric's direction. He loosed this arrow too, but it sailed high and bounced off the stone wall behind it.

"I'm glad to see you, Stanis," Jeric said. He meant it.

Stanis walked away and tossed the bow onto a table full of weapons. Wood bounced and clattered. "Yeah, well, I don't know if I'm staying."

"I know."

Stanis stopped. He looked over his shoulder at Jeric and growled, "Oh, and what the hells would you know about it?"

Jeric looked at his man, at this sick and struggling soul so determined to be at odds with Jeric and himself, and then Jeric strode forward and stopped right inside Stanis's personal sphere, their faces a handbreadth apart.

"You are so rutting determined to be angry," Jeric snarled, "so stop pissing off and *do something about it*."

Stanis's expression darkened. "Get away from me, Wolf."

"No." Jeric shoved him right into the table.

Stanis staggered back, surprised and nearly stumbling to the ground before he caught himself.

"Get it out, Stan, because I'm rutting tired of this scat," Jeric said, and this time, he punched Stanis in the gut—not very hard, but hard enough to send his point home.

Stanis bent forward with a cough, his features twisted as he lost control of his fury, as all of his anger and torment focused upon the man in front of him, and then he charged. He barreled his head right into Jeric's stomach, pushed Jeric past the dummy, and rammed him into the wall.

"That's better," Jeric said with a laugh, then a wince as his head struck stone.

Stanis murmured something incomprehensible and stormed off.

"Oh, you're just getting started." Jeric pitched forward and kicked Stanis's legs out from under him.

Stanis dropped on his belly, furious as he shoved himself back to his feet. He hardly caught the lance Jeric tossed at him.

Of course, Jeric grabbed one for himself, and he swung that lance wide, giving Stanis just enough time to parry.

But barely.

Stanis managed to deflect the blow at the last second. "I don't want to fight you."

"Lies," Jeric said, delivering blow after powerful blow. "All you've done is fight me since Imari. And yet you keep coming back." Jeric did not stop coming at Stanis, who struggled to stop his blows, but this was the only way he could reach Stanis. This was the only conversation Stanis would ever hear—the only conversation Stanis would ever have.

"Yeah, well, I hoped you'd come to your rutting senses, but then I saw all those Scabs camped at the gates." Stanis snapped his lance upon Jeric's knuckles, and Jeric hissed, shaking the pain out of his hand and barely gripping the lance as Stanis came at him again.

And the blows continued. Back and forth, strike after vicious strike, this dance of predators.

"Yes, it's hard looking at them, knowing what we've done, isn't it? Much easier to run away like a little bitch." This time, Jeric stepped aside at the last second and smacked Stanis on the back —hard.

Stanis cried out and stumbled forward to regain his footing.

But Jeric wasn't finished. "You're angry because I am not the leader you wanted me to be, but I am the one you need, and you rutting know it."

"No..." Stanis spat on the ground and adjusted his grip on the lance. "I'm angry because you rutting *betrayed* us." Stanis whirled on him in a flurry of blows that Jeric worked very hard to deflect.

But then Stanis feinted with his lance while his fist struck Jeric square in the nose.

Jeric heard a crack, pain exploded, and his eyes burned as he whirled his lance, narrowly blocking Stanis's next blow. Something warm trickled from Jeric's nose and over his lips.

Stanis was pissed. Good.

Jeric licked his lips, tasted blood, and smiled as he stopped Stanis's next attack. Their lances crossed between them, trembling as they were caught between two opposing wills.

Jeric flashed his bloodstained teeth. "If you truly believed me a traitor, you wouldn't keep coming back."

"I'm just passing through."

"That's a godsdamned lie, and you know it."

Jeric stopped pushing against Stanis's lance, letting Stanis's own momentum propel him forward at Jeric, and Jeric slammed his forehead against Stanis's nose.

Stanis howled and staggered back, and Jeric whipped his lance around and cracked it against the backs of Stanis's knees. Stanis dropped with another cry, and Jeric stood over him, heaving. Stanis started to rise, but Jeric pressed the tip of his lance to Stanis's throat, and Stanis went still, nose bleeding and sweat dripping around eyes that were locked furiously on Jeric.

Jeric glared back, breathing hard. "I want you back, Stanis, and I know deep down you want that too, but I need you to pick a side, and I need you to pick it *now*, because I will not lead these men and women into battle with a man who can't pull his rutting head out of his own high and mighty ass."

Stanis's jaw clenched; his gaze was fire.

Braddok rounded a corner. "What in the rutting hells..."

"Stay back, Brad," Jeric commanded, his eyes on Stanis.

"But—"

"I said *stay back!*"

Braddok stopped, staring between the two men with fury etched into his face.

"So what will it be, Stanis *Vestibor*?" Jeric snapped that last name, reminding Stanis of where he came from and who he was. "Because if you desert me again, so help me gods, I had better never see your rutting face again."

Stanis's throat bobbed as he swallowed. His gaze flickered to Braddok, who watched, expression dark and arms folded over his chest as if he were just waiting for Jeric's permission to intervene.

And then Stanis's head dropped, and his shoulders sagged with defeat.

Jeric dropped the lance in the snow. In his periphery, he saw Braddok start forward, but Jeric raised a hand.

Jeric looked fiercely at Stanis. "You think I don't understand, but I do. There is no one without blame in this fight, and I want *better*. For all of us. Your father wanted that too. He risked everything for it, and so will I. I'd prefer to do that *with* you."

Jeric offered a hand to Stanis.

Wind pushed through the little courtyard, and snow fell all around them, baptizing them in white.

The silence stretched. Stanis's shoulders expanded with a long breath, but he did not take Jeric's hand.

*So be it,* Jeric thought, feeling a stab of disappointment.

But just as he began withdrawing his hand, Stanis took it. He clasped it hard, as if he were afraid that the moment Jeric let go, he might change his mind. As if Jeric's grip were the only thing keeping that maelstrom contained.

"I hope you brought the akavit," Jeric said to Braddok, whose dark expression cracked into a smirk.

Braddok pulled a large flask from the inside of his coat and sloshed the contents. "Probably shoulda started with this, actually."

"I don't know..." Jeric looked to Stanis and pulled him to his feet. The two faced one another. Stanis's anger was bleeding out his nose, which he wiped across his sleeve. "I'd say we were fairly productive without it."

Stanis chuckled, Jeric grinned, and the two clasped one another on the back. Braddok strode into the courtyard, flask in hand, and cuffed Stanis on the shoulder. "It's about time you came to your senses." Braddok raised the flask. "Welcome back, Pissin' Stan."

## 46

*K*ai lay in the dark and in the cold, awake but not present. It was the space he had sought refuge these past...however many weeks. Months. He did not know. It was all a blur of pain and horror. Too afraid to sleep, but too weary to stay awake, and so Kai existed in a semi-conscious state.

Until Imari had come.

At first, he'd thought her a dream, only all of his dreams had been terror and she was light, and then he woke fully conscious with her holding him, and he had cried.

Because he was still alive.

And then she had left, promising she would come back, but she did not. No one did. Not even to bring food, and Kai felt himself slipping.

And slipping.

He couldn't understand what was taking so long.

Light suddenly cut through the darkness. Kai wondered if this was it—the moment he would join the *sieta*.

Or hell, for that was what he deserved.

A figure moved before him, but he could not see, could not make it out. Everything was hazy and confusing. Warm hands gripped his face, and it took him a moment more to realize that someone was saying his name.

"Kai...Kai, please. Answer me."

Kai blinked at the light. As the shapes began to make sense, a face came into focus.

"Ricón...?" The word came out in a gasp, and Kai coughed viciously.

Ricón said something in a rush, and more figures surrounded him. More hands fell upon Kai's body, and there was warmth, there was tingling from head to toe, and Kai's world faded once more.

## 47

*I*t took four days for Jeric and the three armies to reach Skyhold. The weather, thankfully, held back her fury, though the sun never quite showed her face. Sometimes Jeric glimpsed her through the clouds, but she never made herself known fully. She was a mirage, a gauzy light that sometimes blessed them with her presence to dull winter's sharp edge.

It made him think of Imari. A brilliant star he could not see, obscured to Tallyn's Sight.

Their group was six hundred and seventy-four, in total, comprised of three armies: Stovichshold, The Fingers, and Sol Velorian refugees from the Serras. Their camps did not mix, though Jeric mingled with all, as did the other respective leaders. He rode near the front, often with Maeva, Hax, and Brom Stykken —this unexpected conglomerate of nations set with one common goal: taking back Skyhold so that the Provinces could stand against Azir.

Despite their goal, the three armies still kept a distance from one another. Jeric was not surprised. He couldn't expect this magnificent bridge to be repaired overnight; he just hoped it did not interfere with their ability to fight together.

Trust was so important in battle, if not *the* most important part, and Jeric had to trust that whatever reservations these armies felt toward one another paled in comparison to the resentment they harbored toward Azir.

Tallyn could See nothing where Azir was concerned, and he attributed this block to Lestra. He could not penetrate whatever Sight veil she had erected, and so Istraa was blind to them— Imari remained blind to them, and that consumed Jeric most of all.

He knew she was alive. He did not know how he knew it, only that his soul felt hers, but something was not right, and that feeling chipped at his bones with each passing day.

As they crossed those sweeping, snow-covered moors, Jeric sent messengers west and south to Jarl Rodin and Jarl Vysr, asking for whatever aid they could send. He hadn't dared send word sooner; he hadn't known if Corinth's roads were safe or the extent of Kormand's reach. So far, it seemed the sonofabitch had simply taken Skyhold and stayed there.

It was on the eve of the third night, as they broached the Blackwood's dense wall of pine, that Jeric finally spotted a scout. The figure stood high on a ridge, overlooking the plains Jeric and the three armies now crossed. Truthfully, Jeric was surprised they hadn't seen one sooner, but the snow was deep, and Breverans did not know the Blackwood.

Or perhaps Kormand really was that arrogant.

"Maeva," Jeric said.

"I see them," she replied curtly, gaze fixed where Jeric's had been.

"Are they Liagé?" Jeric asked. This mattered to him more than anything else, because if this figure was Liagé, that meant Azir had settled at Skyhold, and the only positive to *that* was that it meant Imari might be near.

Maeva sat quiet a moment. "No."

Jeric's breath eased.

"I'll go," Jenya said from behind him, urging her stolik on.

"Not without me, you won't," Braddok barked, pushing his stolik after hers.

"Find out what you can, but careful," Jeric said after him. "It could be a lure."

Braddok scoffed. "This isn't my first day on the job, your Wolfiness." Then he and Jenya took off at a gallop, kicking clumps of snow behind them.

Jeric caught Stanis's gaze, and Stanis set his decidedly on Braddok's retreating back.

Stanis had been quiet since their...chat—which had graced him with two black eyes—but that raging fire was gone. Jeric knew Stanis was still sorting through his demons, and from personal experience, Jeric did not think that would ever cease. But Stanis had stayed, and that was enough for him.

It wasn't until Jeric reached the high ridge where they'd first spotted the scout that Jenya and Braddok returned, and Jeric couldn't help the sigh of relief that escaped his lips.

Jeric scanned them for blood but found none.

"He's dead," Jenya said once she reached him. "He was alone, though he did warn that he's expected back, so we might have company."

Jeric's eyes narrowed on the distance, on the wall of trees ahead. "Did he say anything about Azir?"

"No," Jenya replied.

"He *could* have," Braddok argued, "if Jen, here, hadn't slit his throat first."

Jenya's expression darkened. "If you hadn't kept interrupting me, perhaps I wouldn't have had to."

"Well, you were asking all the wrong questions," Braddok defended.

"You *distracted* me."

Braddok waggled his brows. "Just can't keep your eyes off me, can you, Jen? That's the real issue here. You're so rutting *distracted* by me that you didn't notice your prisoner had drawn a knife—"

"Brad," Jeric interrupted.

Braddok folded his arms but kept a big-toothed and goading smile fixed on Jenya, while Jenya glowered.

"Kormand is there," Jenya continued succinctly, though her cheeks flushed with a rare display of emotion. "There are no Liagé on the premises."

"What about Hersir?" Jeric asked.

Braddok gave Jenya a derisive look, which Jenya ignored as she answered, "He didn't say anything about Hersir."

"Then who is he reporting to?" Jeric asked.

"Kormand, directly," Braddok answered this time.

Odd. Jeric exchanged a look with Tallyn, who gazed ahead as though he might See what their human sight could not.

At last, Tallyn shook his head. "Skyhold is still hazy. I would not be surprised if Lestra left something with Kormand to keep it hidden from us."

Which is precisely what Tallyn had done with the aid of one of Maeva's seers: three wards, one for each leader to carry as constant protection against any outside attempts at Seeing them.

They soon passed under cover of the Blackwood. The trees naturally broke their armies apart, like sand through a sieve, and the light dimmed.

"We'll stop here," Jeric said suddenly, right at the forest's edge, surprising everyone.

"We could still cover more ground. The light is still—" Braddok started.

"We will rest," Jeric said. "And we will continue at midnight." He exchanged a long look with Maeva, who had suggested this.

Jeric would rather Azir *not* realize how many were in their number, and the Blackwood would hide them well. And if Jeric's calculations were right, they wouldn't need an army to take

Skyhold back. Kormand certainly hadn't, so Jeric knew it was possible. Braddok thought he was an idiot.

Regardless, the armies settled in, though no tents were erected this night. They took cover against the trees, beneath their wide and sweeping boughs. There was no laughter and hardly any chatter as everyone felt the weight of the perilous future.

Jeric could hardly sit still as he went over the plan in his head. And over it.

Until it was time to go.

Jeric gathered Jenya, Niá, Tallyn, his men, and Akim. "Wait for our signal," he reminded Stykken and Maeva.

"Gods be with you," his cousin said, clasping his shoulder.

They mounted stoliks, and Jeric led their way forward through the dark Blackwood. He soon found the road he had traveled often, during many hunts with his pack, when he had fled the safety of Skyhold's walls to hunt the enemy outside.

It struck him now that the enemy had always been *within*.

He took the longer path, giving Skyhold a wide berth, always watching for scouts, but they crossed none.

Eventually, their path ascended to a small and familiar clearing that gave vantage of Skyhold, and there Jeric stopped his stolik. Wind cut at him, and snow dusted his face as he gazed upon her glittering lights. They were a beacon amidst an endless black sea, and yet all he could see was Kyrinne, holding that bloodied blade as if she couldn't believe what she had done.

He wondered if she was still there.

He wondered if he would kill her if she was.

"You almost wouldn't know," Braddok said suddenly, stopping beside him. "Bastards." He said this last word with bite.

Jeric pressed them on, under cover of the trees. They reached the Muir within the hour, and Jeric followed the dark thread through the trees. The water whispered—a rush of life in this otherwise silent forest—yet Jeric kept vigilant. He did not know if there were shades in this forest. He wasn't particularly concerned over them—not with three Liagé at his side—however, he *was* concerned with their howls. It would draw attention.

Thankfully, they reached the sewer's gate without issue, though Jeric stopped his stolik a dozen yards away, out of sight. Just in case.

He held up a hand to the others and dismounted, his boots sunk ankle-deep in snow. He did not see anyone guarding the entrance, but one could not be too careful.

Braddok dismounted behind him, and the two crept forward while the others waited. A curious wind stirred, but the forest remained quiet.

The grate came in view.

It was unguarded.

This surprised Jeric. Hersir had kept this attended ever since Astrid's attempted coup.

"I don't like this," Braddok said.

"I don't either."

Jeric stopped before the dark grate and peered inside to more darkness. The grate had been welded back into place, letting only water and sewage pass through.

"This isn't like Hersir," Braddok said.

"I know." Jeric stood and waved the others over.

Akim crouched before the grate and appraised the metal. "Did you want to save the grate?"

"Preferably."

Akim tipped his head, then gripped the grate and shut his eyes. He spoke in a whisper, his breath like the wind. Jeric felt the air shift, a change in pressure, and the circumference of the grate began to glow, brighter and brighter until it looked molten. Akim gave a subtle twist, and the grate pulled free. He set it on the ground beside them and looked at Jeric as he stood.

Jeric nodded his thanks, glanced into the darkness, and ducked inside. The others followed.

444 | BARBARA KLOSS

"Light, Tallyn?" Jeric asked.

A second later, a small, white-blue sphere of light appeared, hovering over them as they walked deeper into the tunnel.

"I've never actually been in here," Chez said quietly, though his voice traveled in this empty space.

"Lucky you," Braddok drawled as his boots squelched.

Jeric reached the split and veered left, toward Skyhold, where the air and stink grew thicker, and they all fell quiet. These sewers were a maze, and while Jeric knew his way, there were many tunnels that branched throughout the city's underbelly— many possible distractions. Over the years, he and Braddok had explored some of the other channels and later learned how they connected, but there were still many left to be examined.

"This has always been here?" Akim asked, eyeing the Liagé writing etched into these walls.

"Aye," Braddok grunted. "You people usually bless your own scat?"

"These are not blessings." Akim's voice had turned quiet. Jeric looked at him, and Akim looked back. "I have never seen these words before."

Jeric's gaze trailed one carved deep into the rock like a scar. "You're certain they are Liagé?"

"Yes," Akim was quick to say. "They bear the same strokes, but...I do not know these words."

Jeric looked to Niá and Tallyn, who both shook their heads. Jeric wished he knew; he felt deep down that it mattered.

Eventually, they reached the hatch that led out near the kitchens. Jeric put a finger to his lips and exchanged a knowing glance with the others. The rope ladder was gone, however, and when Jeric looked pointedly at Braddok, Braddok grumbled.

"So help me, if you get scat on my face..." Braddok started, crouching low.

Jeric climbed onto his friend's shoulders, then Braddok

groaned with strain and stood. Jeric could just reach the hatch. He waited a few breaths, listening, but all was silent.

He put his hand to the hatch and pushed.

It didn't budge.

He pushed again. This time, something beyond toppled and crashed. Jeric flinched and Braddok cursed, then…

Quiet.

Jeric waited, and when he was certain he hadn't woken the dead, he pressed his palms to the hatch and slowly pushed. This time, it gave easily. Jeric opened it completely, braced his hands on the edge, and pulled himself through into a dark storage closet.

He inhaled deep for perhaps the first time since leaving Stykken and the three armies in the Blackwood.

Jeric glanced around. There was just enough light from Tallyn's wardlight below to highlight shapes in the shadows, and Jeric found the abandoned rope ladder shoved into a barrel. He pulled it out, tied it back around the metal hinge in the floor, and threw the other end down the opening.

"Oh, thank gods…" He heard Chez say below.

He waited for the others to climb through, then looked at each of them.

*Ready?* his eyes asked.

There were nods, and Jeric cracked open the door. The halls were dark, though he knew the kitchen would be alive soon with pre-dawn preparations. Jeric opened the door wider and looked at Chez.

"Be careful," Jeric said.

"You too," Chez said, then added with a wink, "See you at the gate." Chez gestured for Jenya and Niá to follow.

"You good?" Jeric asked Stanis.

Stanis nodded. "Don't go easy on him," he said, and he and Tallyn took off, with Stanis leading the charge—both groups heading for opposite ends of Skyhold's main gate, leaving Jeric, Braddok, and Akim to deal with the fortress.

Jeric told himself the others would be fine. It was just a bit of tricky navigation through the fortress proper, but as long as they passed unseen—and both Chez and Stanis could do this in their sleep—they should be able to sneak to the wall completely unnoticed.

Still, it didn't stop the rush of anxiety Jeric felt.

Jeric exchanged a look of solidarity with Braddok, nodded at Akim, then started down the tunnel, turned right, and headed up the stairs. He heard a distant voice, which grew even more distant as Jeric stood listening.

Whoever it was had gone.

He didn't know where, exactly, Kormand was staying, but Jeric had his guesses. He slunk out into the hall just as two Breverans stepped into view.

They had been in the middle of conversation, but seeing Jeric, they stopped, their eyes widened, and one opened his mouth. Jeric's dagger was in his chest the next moment, and he dropped dead.

"Hey!" the other shouted, pulling his sword as Jeric charged. The Breveran swung at Jeric, but Jeric jumped aside, seized the man's arm, and flipped the man over his leg and onto his back. Jeric dropped, grabbed the man's head between his hands, and twisted sharply with a soft crack.

The man went limp, and Jeric stood just as another figure rounded the corner.

This figure was not dressed like a Breveran, but wore Corinthian arms, the blue crest and wolf head insignia marking his breast. He took one look at the Wolf King and stopped in his tracks.

It was Kivo, one of Hersir's Strykers. Kivo had never liked Jeric, had never welcomed him into the fold. He'd never trusted Jeric's account of Jorvysk's death, and he'd certainly never hesitated to show his disfavor after Jeric had given back his Stryker ring.

Jeric smiled broadly, which jerked Kivo back into the present, but Jeric had his grandfather's sword at Kivo's throat before Kivo could withdraw his own blade completely.

Kivo froze, face pale and eyes locked on Jeric. Fire burned within.

"The benefit to war is that one learns very quickly who their enemies are," Jeric said lowly, and Kivo's eyes narrowed. "Where's Kormand?"

A beat.

The next second, Kivo struck Jeric's arm in an attempt to knock Jeric's sword away, and while Kivo had always been one of Hersir's best fighters, Jeric was still better—faster. Kivo hit Jeric's sword arm, but Jeric spun with it, whirling around while simultaneously knocking Kivo's feet out from under him. Kivo landed hard on his rear, and Jeric had him in a choke hold in the next breath, with Braddok and Akim standing over him.

"I'll try again," Jeric snarled as Kivo strained to breathe. *"Where's Kormand?"*

"Sleeping..." Kivo managed.

*"Where?"*

"Your chambers..."

Asshole. "And Hersir?"

"I don't know—" Kivo choked as Jeric squeezed harder. "I swear to the gods, I don't know! He left with the Mo'Ruk and the Istraan, and I haven't seen him since...I swear, I—" Jeric exchanged a glanced with Braddok, who struck Kivo over the head with the hilt of a dagger, and Kivo sagged, unconscious.

They quickly dragged the three fallen guards into a dark corridor, stripped them of coats and weapons, which they themselves donned, then checked the hall and kept walking. They kept to the shadows, silent upon their feet, stopping only when they heard voices, but Skyhold was quiet, and Jeric took heart that the others had not yet been discovered.

They finally reached the turn to Jeric's chambers, where two Breverans stood guard. Jeric ducked back behind the corner and raised two fingers to Braddok and Akim, and Akim raised a hand, then pointed at himself.

*Let me do this,* his expression said.

Jeric studied him a moment, but Akim did not wait. He stepped past Jeric and peered around the corner. His eyes rolled back, and his lips moved with the softest sound.

The air shifted; one second passed.

Two.

The guards collapsed.

Jeric looked at Akim. "Why didn't you do that earlier?"

"You didn't give me a chance," he said simply in Sol Velorian, though he was slightly out of breath. "But truthfully, two is all I can handle. I am not *shiva,* and they are not wearing protective wards."

Jeric tipped his head, scanned the hall, and rushed for his door. There wasn't anywhere to hide the bodies, so they dragged them to the sides in case anyone walked past, and then Jeric tried the door. It turned easily. Jeric exchanged a brief glance with Braddok, pushed the door in a crack, and peered into a dark antechamber. Dim light flickered through the open door that led to his bedchamber.

Jeric flexed his fingers around the hilt of his sword and stepped inside, silent as a ghost. Akim followed and Braddok stood guard outside the door, as they'd discussed.

Jeric motioned for Akim to wait just inside the antechamber, and he slipped into his bedchamber.

Where he spotted Kormand sleeping in Jeric's bed with Lady Kyrinne.

"Hello, Kormand," Jeric said.

Kormand stirred, a breath passed, and then Kormand bolted

upright. His gaze roamed wildly as he blinked sleep away, and finally he found Jeric. Shock seized him before he started reaching for the dagger that lay on Jeric's bedside table.

Jeric raised the crossbow he'd pinched from one of the Breveran guards as he said, "Ah ah."

Kormand froze, and Lady Kyrinne shifted beside him. She'd always slept like the dead, and Jeric hated that he knew that.

"How'd you get in?" Kormand demanded. There was no sleep in his face now. Beside him, Lady Kyrinne murmured something to Kormand. Seeming to sense something was wrong, her eyes opened.

Her eyes widened on Jeric, and she sat up, clutching the sheets over her bare breasts. A mixture of emotions passed over her face.

"Where's Imari?" Jeric asked Kormand, that bolt leveled on his face.

Kormand's jaw flexed as he undoubtedly considered his options. Lady Kyrinne was still clutching the blankets, trembling and eyes wide as a doe.

"I will not ask you again," Jeric said through his teeth.

"In Istraa, I imagine," Kormand said at last, through furiously tight lips. "With the Mo'Ruk."

"For what purpose?" Jeric fought to keep his calm, to keep control, while Kormand's stare burned on him.

"I don't know," Kormand answered.

Jeric adjusted his finger on the trigger.

"Godsdamnit, Wolf, I don't know!" Kormand snapped. "Azir asked for the bastard in exchange for Skyhold, so I handed her over."

"You're a rutting fool."

"I'm not the one who lost my throne in my own bath chamber."

"No, you lost it in a bed." Jeric pulled the trigger.

The bolt snapped, and the bolt sank between Kormand's wide

eyes. His body jerked, Kyrinne screamed, and Kormand slumped to the side with blood streaming down his face.

And Kyrinne was still screaming, loud enough to wake all of Skyhold. She untangled herself from the bloodied sheets as she jumped out of bed.

"*Be quiet,* woman," Jeric spat, and Kyrinne stopped screaming as she stood there trembling and naked, her gaze darting from Kormand's dead eyes to Jeric's storming blues.

Gods, he could kill her. He wanted to.

"Jeric..." she started, tears streaming down her face. "I am so sorry...please...I didn't mean for this...I just wanted—"

Jeric snapped another bolt in place and aimed it at her heart.

Kyrinne stopped talking.

Jeric looked at her, his hand trembling. There was nothing to say. He already knew her reasons, and she knew his.

"I loved you," she whispered, nearly pleading.

Jeric couldn't help it; he laughed.

"Wolf, we've got company," Braddok warned from the antechamber.

Scat.

Jeric looked at Kyrinne. Beyond the door, he heard sounds of fighting.

And he fired the bolt.

She flinched, expecting pain, but the bolt did not hit her. It grazed her thigh and sank into the end table behind her.

Her wide eyes found Jeric.

"That's your warning," Jeric said lowly. "If I ever see your face again, I will not miss."

She swallowed, arms crossed over her chest, legs trembling. "But I have nowhere to go!"

"You probably should have considered that before you betrayed me." Jeric grabbed a coat from the chair and threw it at her. She barely caught it as he growled, "*Get out of my sight.*"

"Wolf!" Braddok yelled from the hall, and Jeric left Kyrinne standing there as he bolted into the hall, where Braddok and Akim were now fighting against four Breverans. Three more figures charged down the hall toward them, two Breverans, one Corinthian.

The Corinthian, however, slowed to a stop, stunned as he finally realized the identities of Skyhold's midnight invaders.

"Hello, Galast," Jeric said, ducking beneath a Breveran blade before grabbing his assailant's arm and breaking it over his leg. The man screamed in agony, and Jeric shoved him back into a tapestry; however, the man's weight ripped the tapestry from its fastenings, and it all came crashing down on top of him.

Galast still stood staring while his two Breveran companions joined the fray. Jeric noticed Lady Kyrinne standing in the doorway before she slipped behind Braddok and ran down the hall in the other direction.

Braddok looked over, poised to go after her.

"Let her go," Jeric ordered as he whirled on another and stabbed him through the side. The man cried out, and Jeric shoved him into a man who was attempting to come at Akim. Both men collided and fell, drawing Akim's attention, and with a quick burst of power, Akim produced a rope of light that coiled around the men's ankles and wrists, holding them together.

Jeric wiped the back of his hand across his brow and squarely faced Galast, who held a crossbow in his hands.

Akim and Braddok hadn't noticed—engaged with their own battles—but Galast wasn't looking at Jeric. He was looking *past* as he fired. The bolt zinged before any of them could react, and Jeric heard a sharp cry behind him. He glanced back just in time to see a Breveran man fall.

Jeric looked at Galast and nodded once, sharply.

"Please tell me you're not alone," Galast said like a prayer.

Jeric flashed his teeth just as a keening whistle pierced the night, followed by an explosion that shook Skyhold's walls.

White-blue light flashed through Jeric's open door from the veranda.

Galast cursed, bracing his feet to regain his balance while the overhead chandelier rocked and creaked. "What was that?"

Jeric exchanged a smile with Akim and Braddok. "That, my good man, is our cue. Skyhold's gate is open."

## 48

*J*eric strode for the gate where Maeva, Hax, and Stykken waited. It had been a grueling night after Maeva's screaming explosion of light and fire had streaked through the sky like a shooting star, announcing their arrival.

Announcing certain victory.

As it turned out, Kormand's forces were not many, further weakened without a master to fuel the flames. Those loyal to Jeric eagerly rallied to and around their rightful king, helping him dispose of the Breveran usurpers and Corinthian traitors in the fortress, while the forces outside the walls made quick work of the rest, and by the time dawn glimmered upon the backs of the Gray's Teeth Mountains, Skyhold was—finally—secure.

"What shall I do with this lot?" Hax asked Jeric, who finally allowed himself to breathe in deep.

They'd captured twenty Breverans and fourteen Corinthian traitors, including a furious Kivo. Jeric walked down the line, looking into each and every face. A Breveran spat at Jeric's feet, and Galast promptly whacked him over the head with his crossbow. The man collapsed into the one beside him.

Jeric stopped before Kivo, who seemed to wither beneath Jeric's intense stare.

"Hang 'em in the square?" Hax suggested.

"No," Jeric answered Hax at last. "There has been enough blood spilled today. For now, lock them in the armory."

The dungeons could not hold so many, but the armory could, and it was almost as secure. There was just one thing that needed to be done.

"Akim, will you accompany Chez to the armory?" Jeric asked. "There is one point of security I would like you to reinforce."

Akim nodded. "*Sei.*" He walked on with Chez, and a handful of Stykken's men escorted their captives after them, but when Kivo started to go, Jeric took a step, blocking his path.

"Not him," Jeric said lowly.

Kivo looked at Jeric then, and Jeric saw the stubborn pride in his wild eyes. And the fear.

"You of all people should know that treachery never ends well. *Stryker.*" Jeric said that title through his teeth. "Do you have anything to say for yourself?"

Kivo spat at Jeric's face. "Burn in hells, you rutting Scablicker."

Without warning, Jeric pulled a dagger from within his coat and lashed the blade across Kivo's neck. Kivo's eyes widened as he clutched the gaping wound now spilling his life down the front of his Corinthian-blue coat and onto the cobblestones. He gurgled and gasped and dropped to his knees, and Jeric turned away. He handed the dagger to Braddok, who took it, albeit distractedly.

"Burn his body in the square," Jeric said, and he walked on.

·⟨⟩·

It took the better part of the morning to situate all three armies inside Skyhold's walls. Skyhold was much larger than Kleider, but the streets were still cramped with the addition of so many. They crammed along her maze of streets, all upon the ramparts and watchtowers. Thankfully, grateful citizens opened their homes to some, but it still wasn't enough to house the additional seven hundred men and women who had come to help Skyhold defend herself.

Jeric appointed some to tend to the armies' various needs and ensure that everyone was getting along, and by sunset, Skyhold was alive with laughter and torchlight. Jeric observed it all from a watchtower as Corinthian and Liagé and sea folk communed around a ward fire that the Liagé had set at the middle of a square.

"Never thought I'd see this day," Braddok said beside him.

"I know," Jeric said. The wind tossed his hair as he gazed over his city, at this clash of nations seeking refuge within Skyhold's fortified walls. He suddenly wondered if this was why Skyhold had been built in the first place. If the Liagé of old, in their wisdom, had Seen the days to come and had convinced the Corinthian leaders of that time to build this wall, to let them help and weave the Maker's power into this city, because it was the only thing that might stand against Zussa's inevitable return.

But it was difficult for Jeric to feel any joy for this small victory—this unity of purpose—when the woman he loved was in the hands of a monster.

"Keep an eye on things for me?" Jeric said, pushing off the wall.

"Where you going?" Braddok asked.

"For a walk."

Braddok regarded him. "Want company?"

Jeric shook his head a fraction, adjusted his collar, and strode on, leaving Braddok gazing after him as he walked the ramparts. He moved past guards and racks upon racks of enchanted arms. The wall was alive, and men and women nodded at him with "Your Graces" as he passed them by. All of them waiting.

It was the waiting Jeric always found hardest, because in the waiting, the mind grew unwieldy, and it liked to dwell on all manner of dark things.

Like all the lives Jeric had stolen and *would* steal.

Jeric had long ago severed that emotive arm, but it remained like some phantom limb, haunting him. Imari had eased that. Through her, he'd seen another path, a brighter path, and yet here he was again, armed and ready for battle—ready to take more life.

Gods, he wished the cost of freedom were not so rutting high —no, not *gods*.

God.

Just one. A Maker who had, against all odds, brought him to his knees through the very ones he had hunted and killed.

*You have done the impossible*, Jeric thought as he gazed upon stars he could not see through the snow and clouds. *Do it again*, he pleaded. *Save these people as you have saved me.*

He ascended the steps of a watchtower, past guards, to where Roryn stood talking with Stykken. One of Maeva's seers stood with them as well. Alba was her name, and Maeva had appointed her to the wall so that she could quickly report in case she Saw something their human eyes could not.

"Your Grace," the men said.

Stykken nodded in greeting.

"Anything unusual?" Jeric asked, stopping at the railing.

"Nothing. Other than a small fox."

Jeric looked at the seer.

Alba shook her head. "Lestra's veil is strong, and I cannot See them." She spoke in Common, but her accent was thick.

Maeva and Tallyn had professed the same. They could not See Azir's position, though they'd tried.

A bitter wind kicked, and Jeric shoved his hands inside his coat.

"Have you tried Seeing into Trier?" Jeric asked.

Alba had already attempted to See into Trier along their journey to Skyhold, because theoretically, if Azir no longer occupied Trier, she should be able to See the city.

"No," she answered.

"Try again."

Alba looked as if she were about to remind Jeric of the futility in this request, but then she closed her mouth instead, and her eyes rolled back to whites. Jeric exchanged a look with his cousin, and three seconds later, Alba's eyes rolled forward and fixed on Jeric.

"I can See Trier."

Jeric tensed. "And?"

"The city is... Empty. In ruin. I see fire. And bodies scattered on the streets. And there are birds. So many birds."

"So he's left," Stykken said, then inhaled deep. "Do we have any idea how long he's been gone?"

A chill swept down Jeric's spine and settled in his gut. "What kind of birds, Alba?"

Stykken frowned, but in answer, Alba looked past him—up, up into the starless sky, where Jeric spotted movement.

A bird.

He'd hardly noticed it, black as night. He could hardly see it now even as he was looking straight at it. It floated overhead, riding invisible currents like a ghost. But it was not a ghost.

It was a large crow.

Jeric went rigid. "She's here."

# 49

"*M*ay I ask why we're concerned with a crow, Your Grace?" asked Roryn.

"Because it isn't a rutting crow," Jeric said. "It's Su'Vi."

"The Mo'Ruk seer?" Roryn asked, but Jeric was already at the rail, searching the night to find what he felt so certain were there. All he could see was dark and shadow and the thick wall of Blackwood beyond.

Sensing the shift in the Wolf King, the surrounding guards had fallen quiet.

"You're certain it's her?" Stykken asked.

Jeric remembered the veil Lestra had erected outside of Trier to hide Bahdra's force of nearly one thousand. The one Rasmin had exposed. "Can you illuminate a Sightveil?" he asked Alba.

"I can try," she replied.

Alba closed her eyes, and the air shimmered with power all around her. She raised her hands, curling fingers as if to cup them around some invisible orb, and then a sphere of brilliant, blue-white light appeared, like a miniature sun, which she thrust into the darkness.

It soared, arcing over the quiet lawn of snow.

Jeric held his breath, and the wall fell silent, for all had caught sight of Alba's light.

Just before the Blackwood, it stopped mid-air, striking some invisible barrier. Light exploded, fissuring out from an apex like lightning spidering across a sheet of glass.

Lestra's Sightveil.

Skyhold's wall fell silent as every eye drew to the diffuse expanse of light that had suddenly illuminated the night and shone upon hundreds...no, *thousands* of painted faces and at least two dozen shades.

Jeric's heart seized. Maker have mercy, there were so many of them.

And in that flash—in that split second of revelation—Jeric saw Azir and his Mo'Ruk. He saw them mounted upon black horses, like gods standing over this sea of painted faces, but this time there were five, not four, and a horrible feeling took root in his gut.

"Sound the alarm," Jeric commanded the guards, then bolted down the tower stair, and jumped down onto the ramparts. "To the wall!" he shouted as he ran down the walk. Chatter on the streets below ceased as men staggered to their feet, bewildered, drink and meal forgotten.

And Skyhold's horn blared.

It bellowed through the night, as if the very earth groaned in pain from this terrible inevitability. It rattled the city, shaking all of her men and women to their feet.

Jeric heard a whip of air, the softest whispers, and caught that great black bird diving and darting, straight at him.

He dropped onto the walk at the last second. Wind snapped across his back, followed by an agonized scream, and a man collapsed before him as the bird exited the back of his skull, then dissipated into a screeching black vapor.

The guards near stopped in their tracks, and for a moment, Jeric was too stunned to move.

"Wolf!" Braddok's voice boomed from somewhere below, bringing Jeric back.

"Up here!" Jeric shoved himself to his feet and pushed his way down the walk. "Archers, in position!" he ordered and then in Sol Velorian yelled, "Guardians at the towers!"

The first cannon of guardian fire came without warning, without sound. It arced through the sky as if slung by a giant, its green light casting an eerie pall over the snow below. Guards cried out in warning and fear.

"Hold!" Jeric followed its trajectory with his eyes and prayed that Maeva's protective enchantments would hold—that the wards deep within this skal wall would hold as Tallyn had sworn it would.

The guardian light curved down, its path clear, and the men in its way yelled and started pushing their way out of it.

"*Hold!*" Jeric yelled again, hoping he was right. That he had put his trust in the right pieces.

And then, suddenly, the guardian light struck some invisible barrier. The air contorted with a deep, sonorous boom as it absorbed the force of the blast, and the guardian fire exploded in a shower of green flame that rained upon the snow-covered lawn, sizzling as it melted.

·⟨∶⟩·

FROM ACROSS THE LAWN, Imari gazed at Kazak's brilliant green flame soaring for the Corinthian wall, while the *leje* beside her squealed and bounced with delight. Her lord had known it would not work. He had suspected what protected that great skal wall against Kazak's fire. He knew everything.

Still, he would try. He would tease. He would weaken them with fear, for fear was a man's most valuable weapon, if only he knew how to wield it.

And her lord was master of fear, and deception.

Imari watched Kazak's light explode against the wall's age-old enchantments, watched it fissure into the night and snow where it died, and she felt her lord gazing upon her.

Imari turned her head to face him.

"You know what to do, my dear *sulaziér*." His voice slipped over her skin and wrapped around her with pleasure.

With promise.

Imari's lips curled, and she looked back to the wall, at the mortals lining its heights, as if they could stop a god. Futility, all of it. Small minds and small purposes.

She had been small once.

It did not take Imari long to find the one she was looking for. That king of men and the mortal world. The only one who would stand in her way.

Lestra had Seen it.

*He* was her task, appointed by her lord, and she would not fail her lord in this.

Something inside of her squirmed and twisted, but she ignored it as she urged her horse forward, away from the Mo'Ruk, the *leje*, as she and her lord wove through the ranks of Sol Velorians and ravenous shades. They all parted for them, and eventually she and her lord stepped out of the army and into the wide stretch of snow-covered lawn—alone.

She could almost feel the Wolf King's gaze burning through her from atop that wall. Feel his surprise, his confusion. His fear.

And horror.

Again, something squirmed within, and she strangled it quiet.

Her lord stopped his horse halfway across the lawn, and Imari halted abreast, both of them in full view of those faces lining the Corinthian wall, but she did not look at them.

Her attention rested only upon the Wolf King.

He was at the focus of her world. The only sharp form as the rest blurred, and something inside her squirmed again, harder this time.

She shoved it down.

But that something writhed and screamed within. Imari ground her teeth and commanded it to be still.

It stilled.

"Wolf King," her lord's voice boomed across the night. "Open your gates, and I might have mercy upon your people."

Wind howled, the wall remained silent, and still the Wolf King looked only at her. Behind them, shades snarled and yipped.

"Release Imari, and perhaps I will consider." The Wolf King's voice echoed across that empty space, and again that something wriggled inside of her—pushing so hard she nearly choked upon her breath.

"I cannot release what is not bound," her lord replied, and then he looked straight at her.

His gaze wrested whatever wildness had taken root, calmed it.

And now, it was her turn.

"You cannot win, Wolf King," Imari shouted across the lawn. "Open your gates as my lord has commanded, or your people will suffer."

The Wolf fell very still, the night silent. Many on the wall shifted. They knew her, but they had not expected this.

"What have you done to her?" the Wolf yelled.

Her lord sat perfectly still but for a sardonic twist of his mouth as all the darkness drew into him. Like some lord of night. "I have done nothing," he replied, "but *you* have an entire history of bloodshed toward our people, of which my dear *sulaziér* is now intimately aware. We cannot escape the sins of our past, can we, Wolf King?"

The Wolf King went stone-still. He was a fixture upon the wall, like those half-finished statues of Corinth's feeble gods framing Skyhold's gate.

"Go on, my dear *sulaziér*," her lord said, only for her.

As they had discussed.

Imari glared at the Wolf King, repulsed at even the shape of him, and she raised her wrist. In an instant, her world became light and dark. A night full of stars—full of *souls*, each ringing in unique timbre.

It was so easy for her now. So simple. She could laugh at her former struggle.

She could laugh at Fyri for failing him.

Imari found the Wolf King's tone even before his stars came in view. His bass stood out from all the rest, this cello she so despised. She would silence it forever so that none should suffer his memory ever again.

Again, something within writhed and squeezed.

Imari ground her teeth as she captured the Wolf King's sound into her bell, then flicked her wrist, and a rush of tingling swept through her body.

And yet...

*Her* light flared with heat.

The sensation struck Imari strangely, because she hadn't expected it, and she pressed on, eager to please her lord, eager to destroy this Corinthian monster once and for all. She pushed her power into her bells, reflecting the sound back, to bend his cello until it broke.

Except the moment she started bending the sound, *her* insides twisted sharply. As if she were bending her *own* song.

She held back. Not ceasing, but not pressing forward. Just holding, and holding, waiting for the sensation to ebb while feeling her lord's complete attention.

But the pressure did not stop.

She saw the Wolf King gripping the wall's edge as others tried to rescue him from an ailment they could not see, for it was in another plane.

*Her* plane, but she could not bend his note without bending her own.

She pushed on, but then fire ripped through her chest, and she collapsed forward onto her horse, heaving. Her temples wrenched, and heat burned from her core, melting down her limbs, while she waited—trembling and sweating—for the sensation to pass.

Somewhere, a call to attack was given, shades howled, and the explosive chord of battle rattled the night. Horses and feet trampled past her, all headed for Skyhold's great wall, while a solid arm wrapped around her waist. Her lord dragged her onto his mount with him, and then they were galloping.

Away from the wall, into the Blackwood.

·⌒·

JERIC GRIPPED THE WALL, struggling to draw breath as pain seared through his body. A single note seemed to ring from everywhere. It felt like fire had bloomed in his gut, and then it was as though someone had latched a tether to it and was trying to pull it out of his body through his chest. And just when the pain grew unbearable, it stopped: the fire, the pain, though the ringing still rattled his skull.

Jeric was distantly aware of hands on him, of voices saying his name, but when he opened his eyes, he saw only Imari, just in time to see her slump forward upon her horse. Azir's battle cry rang across the field. Sol Velorians yelled with a charge as shades galloped alongside them, pulling in front, and all the men at the wall raised their arms.

Still, Jeric couldn't speak, couldn't think, his attention fixed on Imari, who was being dragged into Azir's saddle, and then Azir, two Mo'Ruk, and three others galloped in the opposite direction, to be swallowed by the Blackwood.

The sewers. That's where he was heading, Jeric knew without a doubt.

"Wolf!" Braddok gripped Jeric's collar and jerked him back as Skyhold's archers fired.

Flame-tipped arrows sailed, compliments of Maeva's guardians, but as they arced down, air pulsed, the flames ate up the arrows, and ember and ash rained down instead.

Maeva was yelling orders at her Liagé stationed along the wall, while Stykken gave orders to the others. Roryn and Akim pushed through to aid where needed, as did Jenya and Niá and the rest of Jeric's men—save Braddok, who was beside him and still holding tight to his collar.

All Jeric could see was Imari. That look on her face.

The hate.

He had always deserved her hate, but if Imari had Seen everything he'd done, which was possible through Lestra...

Gods, he felt sick.

But the mercilessness on her face—*that* was not Imari; it was something else. He'd tasted that mercilessness too, when Azir's chakran had momentarily possessed him.

With sudden decision, Jeric shoved past Braddok and pushed his way down the walk, right past a startled Jenya, and to the stairs.

"The hells, Wolf! Where are you going?" Braddok yelled after him.

Jeric took the stairs two at a time, but as soon as he got to the crowded street, Braddok grabbed his collar and jerked him back.

"Where are you going?" Braddok asked.

"The sewers, godsdamnit, let go!"

Behind them, battle raged in cries and explosions of light and howling shades. Guards crowded upon the walls, firing arrows. Maeva's Liagé threw spells, while Corinthian and sea folk held formation behind the gate's heavy skal doors.

Jeric threw Braddok off. "Imari has to be stopped, and I am the only one who can."

A muscle ticked in Braddok's jaw. He glanced at the wall, then back at Jeric, and his expression turned fierce. "But will you be able to?"

Jeric heard the question he didn't ask: Would he be able to end her life, should it come to that?

"I don't know," Jeric admitted, answering both questions.

Braddok looked at him. "Then I'm coming with you."

## 50

*I*mari opened her eyes to a grayscale world. There was no light, only dark and darker still. Shapes shifted and disappeared, then reformed, though Imari could not make sense of them. Somewhere, she heard her voice, though she was not speaking. She was not even thinking the words that were coming out of the mouth she could neither see nor sense. The words fell in her voice, but it was not her saying them.

It was the thing that had stolen her body.

This darkness that had smothered her light.

And yet, this fragment of her mind remained her own. This hazy consciousness that contradicted the words she could hear, spoken in her voice, and that single thought—that acknowledgement of self—seemed to give shape to the shadows. It drew them into focus, brought boundary to her presence and localized what had been so thinly diffused.

As her consciousness coalesced.

She was here, but she was nothing. The tendril of a thought floating aimlessly in a vast sea of darkness and cold.

Suddenly, the air stirred. She did not know how else to describe it, only that there was a current to this space when before there had been none. Or, perhaps, that current had always been there, and she just happened to feel it pass by in that moment, like a breeze.

It happened again, stronger than before, and then Imari felt pressure. A great, overwhelming compression upon her thought. The darkness had found her, and it was trying very hard to be rid of her completely.

But Imari knew darkness, for it had been a very old friend of hers. In it, she had always been able to hide, to exist. It was how she existed now, hiding in the nooks and crannies of her mind—a thief, creeping as silent as a ghost, evading the oppressive darkness that would find her and snuff her out for good.

And then she heard a voice that arrested her completely.

It pulled her single thought of existence tight as an oud string. Tighter still, until that string rattled a harmonic, in echo to the voice reverberating through her body and soul.

Jeric's voice.

*Jeric.*

She could not see him through her eyes, for something else had stolen them, but she knew him like she knew the sun on a summer day in the Majutén. It warmed her from the inside out. Little jolts of energy fissured through her, making her think of nerves and synapsis reconnecting.

There was heat.

There was pain.

There was hate.

So.

Much.

Hate.

But it was not hers; it belonged to the thing that had filled her body and shoved her aside.

This bitter, hate-filled piece of Zussa.

Suddenly, her grayscale world turned pale, like a sky milky

with haze. A single silhouette stood upon the horizon, far away, and yet Imari felt that presence *everywhere*.

YOU ARE MINE.

The voice rattled Imari's thoughts, and her consciousness shuddered. Still, Imari heard that rich cello, felt its call, and she held fast to it—this one brilliant tone in her world of cold and meaningless gray.

*No,* Imari thought with everything she had left.

The silhouette was suddenly before her, faceless and soulless. A thing of nightmares.

MIIIIIIIIIIINE.

The sound shook, though Imari held desperately to Jeric's cello, to his warm and distant light, until her thoughts dispersed once more.

·✂⟫·

IN THE REAL WORLD, Imari opened her eyes. The Blackwoods' thick pines blurred past as her consciousness hovered somewhere between actual and ethereal as something twisted and pulled deep inside of her.

*No.* She caught the whisper as it faded into nothing, and the pulling ceased.

"How much farther, my lord?" a woman's voice asked. Su'Vi.

"Not far," her lord replied. His arm weighed heavily around Imari's waist.

Imari was still trying to understand what had happened. Her power had never responded to her like that. It had never attacked *her,* and that was precisely what it'd felt like. Everything she had done to the Wolf King had been reflected back upon her, as if their lights—their souls—were bound, somehow.

Imari snarled as she shoved herself upright.

"There you are," her lord said at her ear.

He did not sound pleased.

Su'Vi rode to their right, Lestra to their left, and three more Liagé kept pace behind them.

"I am sorry, my lord," Imari said in anguish. Her throat felt raw. "I do not know what happened."

"It does not matter," he said, though Imari sensed it very much *did* matter. "The *Corazzi* was not our primary objective, for our purpose lies just ahead." A beat. "Ah, there it is."

The trees opened to a wide river. The Muir, Imari recalled. Still, she did not know what had brought her lord here, but she would not ask. She could feel his displeasure with her, and she would sit in quiet humility until she could regain his favor once more.

Her lord led their horse along the Muir's soft, steep banks, where four figures stood in shadow, waiting with weapons drawn. Two did not hold traditional weapons but had raised inked hands instead. They were prepared to fight; however, they noticed Imari, and confusion made them hesitate.

"Surina...?" one—a man—asked. "What is this?"

Su'Vi raised a hand, curled her fingers, and twisted, and that Liagé choked, now grasping at his throat. The second Liagé—a woman—hissed a curse and pushed both palms forward. A wall of light rushed forth, but Su'Vi threw her hands up, and the light diffused. In the next instant, Su'Vi turned, whirling her fists around one another, drawing all that diffused light back together before throwing it at the Liagé who'd conjured it.

The Liagé woman thrust forth her palms, but Su'Vi's power was too great. It tore right through the hasty veil the woman had constructed and struck her square in the chest. Burning *into* her chest, melting through flesh and bone. The woman did not have a second to scream before she collapsed dead in front of the first.

Leaving two guards—one Corinthian and one from the sea.

Fear opened their eyes wide, and weapons trembled in their

hands. Su'Vi raised a hand, but her lord stayed her with a look. Then he looked at Imari.

And Imari's lips curled.

Even without closing her eyes and moving into that Shah plane, she heard their song. She could pick it out of the symphony all around her, and she focused on those two tones as she raised her wrist. As she wove those notes into a chord of her choosing and reflected it back.

The chord gonged through that Shah plane to be heard by their minds, not their ears. This was not a song for the body, but for the soul, and the moment Imari's chord struck, their eyes dulled, they raised their swords, and they shoved the points deep into their own bellies.

Imari released the chord, the two cried out in pain and horror from what they had done, and then they collapsed beside the other two.

Her lord smiled at her, reaching out across that space, his fingertips dancing across her cheek. "You are exquisite."

His praise washed over her, and her body shuddered with pleasure, but then he lowered his hand and dismounted.

For a moment, he stood there, breathing it all in, and then he stepped forward, past the dead guards and Liagé. His steps fell silent upon the snow, his black robe still despite the breeze. It took Imari a moment to realize what had drawn him to this place, but then she noticed the grate embedded in the rocky part of the bank, just beyond two giant boulders that stood like two figures kissing.

The Kissing Rocks.

It was the exit she would have taken all those months ago had she not sprinted back into the fortress to save the Wolf King from Ventus and then Astrid.

Her lord crouched before the grate, in two inches of standing water, and he curled long, pale fingers around the skal bars.

The grate glowed molten, and metal melted, running over his

hands like water as it fell into the shallow pool below, where it hissed and sizzled. Thus chilled, the skal re-hardened, but the process had happened too quickly, and the brittle skal cracked and fractured like broken glass.

And her lord walked into the tunnel.

Imari dismounted and followed after, with Su'Vi and the others trailing close behind. The tunnel was long and winding and would have been dark; however, her lord had illuminated it with tiny wardlights. Five of them—little stars of white-blue—hovered above his head, as though he were his own constellation, giving light to the endless dark universe.

Her lord had no shadow, Imari noticed. Neither did his Mo'Ruk.

Just then, Imari felt a pull. Not from her lord, but from some-thing else. Something *deeper*, coaxing her faster.

"You feel it," her lord said as she unwittingly matched his stride.

"Yes," she replied.

"Good."

"What is it, my lord?" she asked.

He glanced sideways at her, and that white-blue wardlight danced in his pure black eyes. "Your destiny."

Her lord led them forward, deep into the dark and quiet, and the pull intensified. Imari's steps quickened, and she surpassed her lord without thinking, but he did not move to stop or slow her. When she looked back at him, realizing what she'd done, he only nodded in encouragement.

"Go on," he said, those eyes boring into her with a hunger that made her flush.

And so Imari walked on, her steps falling faster and faster as the tether pulled harder. Whispers sounded on a breeze she could not feel, beckoning her forward, until she spotted a wide crack in the tunnel wall.

Imari ducked through, and the others followed, into a narrower tunnel.

Suddenly, her lord's lights went out. Whispers sounded, and another light pulsed—bright white—as if the tunnel were a vein pumping light instead of blood. It pushed out from where she and the others stood, flowing along the walls like water—from *within* the walls—running to an end she could not see. Then...

Darkness.

Quiet.

Her lord's little lights bloomed once more, but Imari was not looking at them. Her attention fixed on a spot just ahead, along the wall.

Where that pull nearly overwhelmed her.

She started forward, step after step, her gaze fixed on that spot while her lord's wardlights danced, and she stopped before that space.

She had been here before. Stood *right here* and seen it through another's eyes and processed it through another's mind. But those eyes and that mind had not seen the faint inscriptions scratched into the surface: words from *before*. From the beginning, and there were only few who could read them, for they were *his* words.

*Zivi'm verro tai*: Here, I dwell with you.

Her lord stopped beside her, gazing at the words of ages—from a time when *he* had communed with them, here on earth. When he had ruled and set his decrees that all must follow.

Decrees she would grind into dust, and from the dust rebuild.

Her lord stood in silence, filled with both reverence and fury. "The key, Su'Vi."

Su'Vi stepped forward and presented a small object that her lord took and held up to the light: a key, and it was so covered in glowing glyphs that it looked as though it were made of light. Her lord kissed the key with a kind of reverent affection, and then he pressed it flat against the stone, right over the word *dwell*.

All the other words faded but for that one, and it flared bright as lines of light spidered out from the key until the entire section of wall had illuminated in the shape of an archway. The light faded, leaving a dark opening behind.

Her lord's eyes gleamed, and his upper lip curled. "It is time for the unmaking," he said, then slipped the key back into his robes and stepped through, into the shadows.

"For here, in this holy place, Asorai descended from the heavens to commune with his Five Divines. To encourage them in his way, to give strength to their humanity. To dwell among his beautiful creation in a sacred place that could accommodate his richness and glory."

~ Excerpt from Il Tonté,
As recorded in the First Verses by
Juvia, Liagé First High Sceptor.

# 51

*J*eric sprinted for the stables with Braddok. At some point, he caught Jenya running after them, and he'd nearly reached the stables when he intercepted Maeva and Tallyn.

"Azir's taken her to the sewers with two Mo'Ruk," Jeric said.

Tallyn leveled that one-eyed gaze upon him.

"Did you finish sealing them?" Jeric asked Maeva. Last he had heard, Maeva and her enchanters had not finished fortifying the sewers. They'd kept getting pulled away to aid Niá and Tallyn with enchanting Stykken's arms, and the look Maeva gave Jeric was answer enough.

Jeric cursed as the air shuddered with another explosion, and a man screamed.

"I will go," Tallyn said.

"As will I," Maeva added.

"No, I need you at the wall—" Jeric said.

"Akim has the wall. If Azir has taken two Mo'Ruk with him, you'll need far more than your family heirloom." She gestured at the sword Stykken had given him, now strapped to his waist.

She wasn't wrong, and truthfully Jeric was relieved.

"Fine," he said, then looked at Jenya, who'd caught up with them. Her expression dared him to dismiss her.

He did not.

He found Dom in the stables, trying to comfort the horses that'd been startled by that last explosion. Dom looked at Jeric and appraised the group, and understanding passed between the men.

"Last one on the right," Dom said. "She's ready."

Jeric patted Dom's shoulder as he rushed past. Dom untied four other mounts, and soon Jeric and the others were galloping out of the stables, through the frantic crowd, heading for the fortress.

Another explosion rattled the night, louder than before, and Jeric gripped the reins tight. He hated leaving the others to handle that wall, but saving the wall did not matter if Azir made it inside with Imari.

Gods, if only they'd had more time.

Liagé stood there now, but mostly to guard the work Maeva's enchanters had already completed. Jeric had known the sewers left them susceptible; however, the tunnel was narrow, and funneling such masses through a small aperture was never a good tactic for war. No, Jeric had anticipated that Azir would deliver a full-frontal assault, as he'd done in Trier, and so Jeric had prioritized enchanting arms instead.

And Jeric had been partially correct. Azir had *not* led his army through that small and hidden entrance. No, he'd taken himself, five others, and Imari, godsdamnit.

Imari was not something Jeric had factored into all of this. At least, not in this way.

Battle raged near the wall while explosions rocked the air, but they galloped on, over the drawbridge and into the fortress's courtyard, where Jeric dismounted.

The courtyard was empty; everyone had gone to the wall.

Jeric and the others left their horses and took off through the doors, sprinting through a dark hall and down corridors, startling the frightened servants who remained. They made their way to the kitchen—where more servants scrambled to get below to their quarters, to relative safety—then down the quiet corridor that led to the sewer entrance. Jeric's heart beat faster with every step, and when they finally reached the hatch, he was relieved to see it still guarded—by Corinthians, who were quick to greet their king.

They moved aside at a command from Jeric, who then crouched before the hatch, bent his ear, and threw it open.

Beyond, only darkness waited.

He exchanged a look with Braddok, then asked Tallyn, "Can you See anything?"

Tallyn's one eye unfocused for a breath then settled on Jeric. "I can't See anything at all."

Jeric peered back into the darkness and dropped down into it. His boots squelched in mud and sewage, and a light appeared a second later, thanks to Maeva. The little glowing orb hovered above his head as the others dropped down.

"Should we come with you, Your Grace?" one of the guards asked quietly from above.

"No, wait there," Jeric called back, as loud as he dared. "Make sure no one else comes down." He started to turn, but then looked up at the guard again. "If we're not back in an hour, shut this grate and don't let anything back through it. Do you understand?"

The guard's lips thinned, but he nodded once.

Jeric motioned at the others, and they walked on. Water dripped from somewhere, but these tunnels were silent as a tomb.

Jeric didn't trust it.

"You sure these wards will hold?" Braddok asked Tallyn as they walked, gesturing to the wardstone about his neck.

"Against Liagé? Yes," Tallyn replied. "Against Azir and two Mo'Ruk? No."

"Fantastic."

Jeric rounded a bend and stopped. A dozen paces ahead, he spotted a crack in the wall he had not noticed before. At least not that he could remember. It was conveniently masked by the rough texture of the tunnel wall. Jeric had previously dismissed it as a shadow, but right then, light shone faintly from *within*. Jeric held up a hand to quiet the others, then slowly started forward toward that soft light.

Where another tunnel lay beyond.

"The hells...?" Braddok whispered.

They exchanged a look. Jeric drew his grandfather's sword and slipped through the crack, into the narrow tunnel.

This tunnel looked older than the main artery they had just left. The texture was grainy and pockmarked, the ground dry, but there were definitely fresh footprints, and a tiny pinprick of light hovered near the low ceiling, casting a silvery hue over everything.

It was this light Jeric had noticed from the main tunnel.

But it wasn't light that had stolen Jeric's attention; it was the smooth, arched opening just ahead, where there was no light.

Maeva had gone perfectly still, her gaze fixed on that opening.

"You know what it is," Jeric said.

Her lips parted; her gaze flickered to Tallyn's, then she said, "It is said that when Asorai first created this world, he built a temple where he would commune with his Divines. It is what Azir sought the first time."

"What's inside?" Jeric asked.

A beat. "I don't know."

"Well, it's time we find out." Jeric ducked into the opening, Maeva's light followed, and the others joined soon after. Gods, it was so dark, even with the little light, Jeric couldn't see more than a few paces ahead of them.

"Can you push your light ahead?" Jeric asked, and Maeva's light floated farther down to where this new tunnel veered right and out of sight.

Back toward the city.

Jeric pressed on, into the shadows of the past. Here, the tunnel floor remained soft but not wet. There was no sewage, just the natural dampness of deep earth.

And fresh footprints.

Jeric crouched, and Maeva's light hovered over his head. He counted seven prints in total, all heading deeper into the tunnel. Jeric kept walking, following the path as it dipped down and down, as the air turned bitter cold and smelled like sulfur.

"We have to be under the city now," Braddok said quietly.

Their tunnel made a sharp right and opened at a wide cavern. The path ended abruptly at a platform, with stairs descending on either side, where they joined at a courtyard below. And on the other side of that courtyard stood the enormous face of a very old building.

A temple.

It was from another age, built of smooth bricks and white marble, with words carved all over its surface. Long, narrow windows stood dark, and the enormous wooden doors hung slightly ajar.

"It is the first temple," Tallyn whispered, his voice slightly awed. "The holiest of holies. The place the verses have spoken of, exactly as they have described."

Jeric looked at that face, dark and abandoned and buried, and he suddenly realized he knew where they were: beneath Aryn's temple.

The temple to the Corinthian gods, where Rasmin and his inquisitors had interrogated and tortured Sol Velorians. However, Ventus had collapsed Aryn's temple the night Astrid had attempted to take Skyhold. Rasmin had not known why, and Jeric now wondered if this was the reason. If Ventus had been trying to get to this, but why?

"What is in here?" Jeric asked.

Maeva gazed steadily upon the temple face and said, "I do not know, but we had better hurry."

· ⟨⟩ ·

IMARI STARED AT THE TEMPLE. Though her human eyes had never seen its face, her heart knew exactly what it was.

*His* temple.

Asorai's.

Where his five had gathered, and where only one had truly understood the tyranny of it all. That one had fought to break the chains of Asorai's will. That one had fought and failed, but she would not fail this time.

No, there was no one who could stop Zussa now.

She would undo what Asorai had done, and Imari would help her do it. Imari looked at her lord and master as he gazed greedily upon the face of what had once been the holiest of holies. There was such fire in his eyes, that flame of indignation, and when he turned that gaze upon Imari, Imari could not move. Could not breathe. His fire was her fire, his passion her own.

He took a step closer, clasping her face in his hands. "I have waited a thousand lifetimes for this moment, and together, we will put an end to it once and for all."

"I am honored, my lord," Imari replied.

Beside them, Su'Vi watched in silence.

Her lord released Imari and walked on, his gaze burning upon the temple as if it were Asorai himself.

Imari and the others followed to where her lord had stopped before the great double doors that were too tall for any mortal. Upon those doors, engraved in exquisite detail, were scenes from the past. Scenes Imari had seen through Tallyn's memories, reflections of the great tapestry he had shown her— the one that'd been displayed beneath the Mazarat. The image of the Five Divines seated in a circle with a great light at their center.

Her lord raised both of his palms, but he did not touch the wood. Air shuddered, the doors groaned as they rotated slowly inward, straining with the ages, and Azir stepped through into darkness.

Imari followed after him.

A great gust of wind ripped through that space, a hundred candles suddenly sprang to life from the sconces clinging to the walls and columns, from chandeliers hanging from the ceiling, illuminating this magnificent and forgotten nave dedicated to Asorai.

Imari craned her neck to see into the impossible heights, her gaze trailing the gilded archways and intricate stonework. The walls and columns were composed of polished white marble, all of it trimmed in gold and...nightglass. Like sun and stars amidst the infinite black, as though a slice of the heavens had been fused here, in this place. In this perfect joining of mortal and immortal, this bridge between heaven and earth.

Her lord stepped forward, albeit distractedly, as if he could hardly believe where he stood. His gaze trailed the perimeter and candles and high arches.

Remembering.

Five nightglass chairs were arranged at the nave's center, all too tall for mortal form, with seats too wide, as if to remind man how small he was. How insignificant. The enormous chairs had been arranged in a circle, all facing inward to the platform at their center. A platform made of nightglass and covered in etchings of ancient Liagé script, which now glowed faintly, like moonlight.

Her lord trailed long fingertips upon the back of one chair.

There was something familiar about the gesture, the look upon his face.

"This is the Sabbat," Imari said.

The place Asorai had communed with the Divines. Where he had descended from the heavens to counsel his five chosen when they had ruled here, on earth, in the beginning.

"Yes," he said. "It was our appointment. Our duty and our cause...all within the boundaries of Asorai's decrees. All to keep us from reaching our true potential. From becoming our own gods." His voice warped with Zussa's otherworldly bass, and then he glared at the archways above, as if he could see the heavens. A strange light burned in his pure black eyes.

"*I* define truth. I define what is right," her lord growled, the voice more Zussa's than Azir's. "And I have decided that your ways are wrong. That *you* are wrong, and we are all better off without you."

He placed his hand to the back of the chair, and his eyes shuttered close.

Wards ignited upon the chair, as though the chair had been built of words—like the key—and the room glowed with silvery light. The wards burned brighter and brighter until the air smelled like burning, and then suddenly, the chair ignited in white-blue flame. Her lord withdrew his hand, and the chair burned up and turned to ash.

Her lord staggered forward and clutched his chest. Imari could feel the strain on his power—strain because of the binds woven into him simply by being a part of Asorai's creation—and she rushed for him, shoving Su'Vi aside, but Su'Vi was not so easily moved. Su'Vi pushed Imari back.

Imari did not have to think. The note was there before she even raised her wrist, and she used her power to squeeze upon the darkness inside of Su'Vi. To compress its being, to fold it in half. Su'Vi cried out and collapsed, but Imari did not snuff her out completely.

That was her warning.

Imari hurried on to her lord, wrapping her arms around him to give him support where his mortal body was weak.

"Thank you." His voice was all breath as he clung to her.

"Let me do the rest, my lord," Imari said. "You will strangle yourself in his binds. Allow me to unravel them for us all."

Her lord's gaze rested on her, but someone else looked out of those eyes. *Zussa*, though Imari could never tell where she ended and he began. They were a circle of power, both and one, two forms of the same being. Human and god.

Her lord kissed her then, and she kissed him back, breathing in his power, his promise. Wanting everything.

He pulled back, his breath uneven as he said, "Let it be done."

Imari made sure he was stable, then let go and slipped off her shoes. She stepped between the chairs to the platform and gazed down upon the nightglass canvas that displayed Asorai's words.

Asorai's foundation.

Imari closed her eyes and listened. To every breath, to every stirring, to every beating heart. But it was not the material world she needed to reach—it was the world beyond. The world in which Asorai's truths had been written. Truths she needed to unravel in order for her lord and master to write them anew.

The breaths and the heartbeats faded, and Imari heard a new song—a new symphony.

A symphony of stars.

It was the light woven into all of creation, the words Asorai had used to build this word—these constructs to suit his law so that everyone would fall subject to it.

Imari would tear it all apart.

She listened to the notes, all of them together. Let them fill her and stir her soul until she found exactly what she was looking for: the foundational chord—the first tone and tonic. The cornerstone upon which all rested. Destroy that, rip it apart, and all would collapse.

She started with the chairs first, for each sang their own timbre, reflective of the one who had once occupied it. She stepped off the platform and stood first before the *ziat's*—the seer's. From it, she caught a somber dirge, burdened by the time-lines and tragedies of Seeing mankind repeating the same atrocities, over and over again. Forever returning to the depravity of mind.

Imari ripped the notes apart and scattered them to the rafters. The chair exploded into ash and rained upon the pristine floor, coating it in a layer of fine dust.

And Lestra screamed.

She screamed as though her heart were being ripped out of her body and collapsed to her knees in agony. Imari could just hear the erratic pitter-patter of Lestra's heart in the mortal world. Imari did not know if Lestra would survive this, but even if she did not, she should be honored to sacrifice for the greater good.

And her lord laughed. "Good," he exclaimed, his voice still weary from the power he had exuded. "*Good*, my dear *sulaziér*. Do not stop."

Imari moved behind the next chair. The divine *shiva*—restorer. Imari ripped its song apart like the first. However, this chair cracked and splintered like broken bones. All the little flecks of silver within the nightglass turned blood-red and oozed through the fissures, where it spilled onto the floor. The chair finally broke apart, its fragments unable to stand together, and fell into the pool of blood.

Imari heard Bahdra's distant scream—a sound that moved through the Shah plane—while she moved on to the third chair.

This particular song punched through her soul like the blare of a dozen trumpets. *Saredii*. Guardian. Imari reflected the song back at the chair with her bells, and it exploded into a million shards—all of which caught flame mid-air.

Imari felt the slightest shudder to the air and knew that some-where, Kazak was in great pain.

Imari moved to the fourth chair: the *voloré*. Enchanter. Imari looked at Su'Vi and smiled. She held the notes of the enchantress's chair, though she did not split them apart immediately.

And Su'Vi screamed.

Imari wanted Su'Vi to feel her power, to know her place, to know what Imari could do at the mere flick of a wrist. Su'Vi writhed upon the floor in agony, her features twisted in pain as her heart slowed and slowed.

"Imari." Her lord's voice was a light breeze over her skin.

Finally, Imari split the notes apart. Su'Vi whimpered as the chair's enchantments ignited and burned bright, until the chair incinerated into glowing words that rose in a vapor—gone.

Imari breathed in deep, opened her eyes, and met her lord's gaze. He stood just beyond that pile of ash, staring at her with awe, with reverence, and with something else that set her skin aflame.

There was still one more piece left, and then the world would be theirs for creating.

She stepped back upon the platform.

Asorai's place.

And then she heard someone yell her name.

## 52

*N*iá watched the flaming arrows drop like falling stars. They rooted in chests, in faces, and in arms. In horses. But Niá did not stop enchanting them as they flew. She whispered another word, a word of linkage. Of bridging and joining and reaching, until all those little flames reached toward one another, forming a continuous thread of fire across the quickly approaching horde.

The light was a scythe, cauterizing everyone and everything that ran through it. Men cried out, a horse screamed, and this time, the entire front few lines of warriors fell, many of them cut right in half. Chez and all the other archers shot another volley of arrows.

And then a great wind stirred.

Niá heard Kazak's voice upon it, his whisper and his word, and suddenly the arrows were knocked aside and her rope of fire rose into the air like a whip, raised by some invisible hand, and snapped down upon Skyhold's wall.

Right over the gate.

Guards cried out in warning, dashing to either side of the whip's trajectory as it came bearing down upon them. Niá said a quick enchantment to stop it, but Kazak's power was too great. The whip sliced right through her hasty barrier of light, but another barrier materialized—from Akim, who stood at the other end of the wall.

However, it could not stop Kazak's power, and the whip snapped across all the men standing over the gate. Sudden death cut screams short, and bodies toppled over the wall, where shades leapt upon them in a frenzy.

"The gate!" someone yelled, because the portcullis had not closed completely. Guards were running to the gears to finish what their fallen comrades had started when Niá spotted a blaze of greenish light in her periphery.

Guardian fire.

This was much larger than the first, and it was sailing for the gate. Men cried out, and some of Maeva's guardians and enchanters erected a veil to stop it, but it sailed right through.

To where it stopped a few yards before those enormous skal doors as if caught in an invisible net. Niá looked for Akim, thinking he had been the one to stop it, but no—he was caught up blasting a group of shades that had been scrambling up the wall.

No, this...this protective enchantment was buried deep in the wall. From the Liagé of old, when they had once worked in harmony with all the Provinces. Kazak's canon of flame hovered there, casting a sick green light upon the black skal and everyone around, and then Niá felt those enchantments strain.

Kazak's power was too much—unnatural, because of how Bahdra had brought him back. Brought them all back. They were not restrained as they should have been, and Kazak was able to draw upon more Shah. More *darkness*.

The air crackled; the flaming canon sizzled. Without thinking, Niá pushed her palms forth and spoke a word to help, to bolster the wall's defenses, but she was not a guardian, and her power drained fast.

Another one of Maeva's noticed and stepped in to assist. Akim caught on too and thrust his palms forth. For a second, that strain eased, and Niá thought, perhaps, they would be able to throw Kazak's flaming sphere back into Azir's ranks. But then a wave of heat engulfed her, Niá cried out, and the ball of fire pushed through.

It slammed into the doors with such force it rocked the wall, and Niá stumbled into Chez, both of them clutching the ramparts for support. Men and women screamed, trying to flee Kazak's fire. There was a great splintering crack, followed by a deep groaning as the doors turned molten and melted in a heap of blazing green flame. Thus unsupported, the walk overhead collapsed, taking down towers and scaffolding and people with it.

Leaving a gaping hole in Skyhold's magnificent skal wall.

Azir's forces cheered in triumph, and the tide raged forward, bounding and crashing over the doors' remains without a care for the last tendrils of green flame.

And the sea rushed in.

It frothed and spewed its fury while arrows flew and lights flashed, and all resolved to chaos. To blood and light, to screams and shouts as bodies churned like the raging sea. There was no sense to it—none—not even as commanders shouted their orders, trying to protect their small perimeters, and Niá was suddenly struck dumb by the futility of it all.

By the wave of death.

She watched one man knocked down by a shade and dragged under the stampede as he cried out. The archers didn't dare shoot within the courtyard, lest they risk injuring their own. Many of those upon the wall tried to fight their way down to stop the tide from rushing in, but all was a frenzy.

Chez started dragging her farther along the wall, away from the fighting, but Niá planted her feet.

"No," she said. "I am done running."

He held her gaze, then let go of her arm and locked a bolt into his crossbow. "Then we stay here, where both our vantages are best."

And Niá nodded. "Deal."

· ⟨⟩ ·

STANIS DID NOT SEE the doors fall, because he had been running in the opposite direction. He had been standing nearly over the gate when Kazak had turned Niá's rope of fire into a whip that'd lashed across the parapets and taken a dozen good men and women with it. It had nearly taken him too.

And now he was running across the quaking ramparts, trying to keep his footing as the gate collapsed. No, as an entire *section* of wall collapsed. Men and women screamed as they fell, as a watchtower toppled and the wall gave way. Stanis would have fallen too had it not been for Stykken's solid grip on his arm yanking him ahead.

Stanis ran with Stykken down the steps, pushing through guards and Maeva's Liagé for the courtyard, leaving the wall to the archers.

Stanis's sword would be needed for the runoff. And, *gods*, how fast this sea ran.

Azir's Sol Velorians poured through the wall's gaping wound in a clash of steel and light. Azir's Liagé cleared a path with blasts of air, giving room for his non-Liagé warriors to rush in, flanked by shades. Men fell—Corinthian, Sol Velorian, and sea folk—and others rushed in to take their places. To fill the gaps and form a shield wall to hold the enemy back.

But it could not do much against Liagé blasts, and holes were made faster than they could possibly be filled.

Stanis leapt the last few steps and jumped into the fray, hoping Niá's warded necklace would hold. He felt it warm even as he parried a blow, felt it pulse through his skin, and it did not fade. As if the very air were now overwhelmed with Shah power, keeping Niá's ward active.

Gods, he hoped it didn't burn up prematurely.

He pushed his way into the horde, working with Stykken to cut down those who had slipped through their hasty shield wall, while Akim worked fast, wielding earth and stone to fill the gate's hole. In the corner of his eye, Stanis spotted Chez upon the ramparts, shooting bolts one after another, carefully taking aim —which was no small task in this chaos—while Niá stood beside him, giving flame to the arrows as they flew.

Someone barreled into Stanis, and Stanis tripped over a body. He fell into the crowd and tried to regain his footing, to push himself up, but someone else fell on top of him, and he couldn't move. The sea rushed over him, and he was gagging, pinned beneath the weight of it, that undulating surge of bodies.

A hand grabbed his and yanked hard, pulling him right out of the swirling and powerful current.

Stykken's.

Stanis was on his feet again, fighting his way toward the gate, covered in sweat and other men's blood.

He whirled on two, slicing his blade through a gut, a chest, and the ward at his chest burned fire-hot. A great pressure seized his heart and squeezed hard. Stanis cried out as he dropped. He noticed Stykken drop beside him, and at least a dozen more as a robed figure walked through the opening where the doors had once stood.

Bahdra.

·⸻·

NIÁ SAW STANIS DROP. At first she thought Chez had misfired, but that couldn't be right, and Stanis wasn't the only one who fell. Nearly two dozen others had fallen, all Corinthian or sea folk, all clutching their chests, while Azir's forces started ripping their shield wall apart.

But who could have simultaneously overwhelmed so many of her wards at once...?

She spotted the figure passing through the gaping hole in the skal wall, completely unaffected, though battle raged all around him. He was like a great ship untouched by the sea. Always in this world, but not of it.

Bahdra.

The very sight of him filled her with white-hot fury, and she was running before she could think.

Someone in the courtyard below rushed Bahdra, but he extended a hand and an inky tendril of smoke lashed out like a whip, wrapped around the man's neck, and lifted him—screaming—into the air. His neck snapped, his life gone, and Bahdra tossed him aside like a rag doll. The body crashed into the shields and spears, knocking many men down.

But Bahdra was not finished.

He wielded his darkness, raising men and breaking bodies, dropping them by the dozens, while the sea kept rushing in, slowly drowning them.

"Niá!" Chez called after her, but her eyes were only on Bahdra.

A man flew past her, thrown from one of Bahdra's tendrils to crash into a wall and bounce to the ground. Niá ducked and shoved on through the chaos, using the dagger Chez had given her to cut into her palm as she ran. She was small, and her size aided her now. Like a minnow slipping past hungry sharks.

Until she had a clear path to Bahdra.

Bahdra's cowl turned, and those inky tendrils floated in the air around him as if he were underwater. His fathomless black eyes locked on her, and then he smiled cruelly.

"Niá." Bahdra's rasping voice moved through both planes, reaching her even through the chaos.

Niá thrust bloodied palms forward, and a blast of light shot from her palms, but not fast enough. Bahdra snapped his whips, they struck Niá's light, and the light evaporated with a hiss.

Bahdra bared his teeth, his eyes aglow, and someone came at Niá with a scim raised. Niá moved to deflect and was about to throw an enchantment when Bahdra yelled, "*No!* She is mine."

Her attacker left her alone, but in that distraction, Niá didn't see Bahdra's tendril until it was coming right at her.

She didn't have time to throw an enchantment, so she dove. Bahdra's whip struck earth instead, and the ground shuddered and cracked beneath her. Another whip bore down, and she rolled, narrowly missing this one too, but when he struck again, Niá was ready. She shoved both palms up, yelled a word, and white light blasted from her palms. The air sizzled and hissed, and Bahdra's inky serpents retracted and coiled as if to protect themselves.

Bahdra crouched and snarled at her as the darkness gathered around his feet. Niá threw another spell, but Bahdra's whips cut right through it, wrapping around her entirely, and folding her into its depths like a cocoon. They lifted her off of her feet, and then Niá was airborne.

Somewhere, she heard someone scream her name. Her heart jumped in her throat as though she were falling, and then those tendrils abruptly dumped her onto the ground.

Far on the other side of Skyhold's wall, at the fringe of Azir's ranks.

Niá winced and shoved herself upon all fours, heaving as the air convulsed with sounds of war. She was now *behind* Azir's forces, and they began to take notice of her. Suddenly, a vortex of shadow landed before her in the shape of a man, and Bahdra reappeared, standing a few paces before her, his horrible eyes alight with triumph.

Behind him, Niá caught sight of another creature slinking from Azir's ranks.

The *leje*.

Niá did not know how it was still alive, and she marveled that this thing had ever been the Wolf King's sister. Its body was more skeleton than flesh, and where eyes should have been were empty sockets but for a small light that shone from within. It licked bloodied lips as it staggered behind its master's feet.

The last time she had seen the *leje* had been in Vondar, and it had taken Sur Kai as a pet. She did not see Kai now.

She felt a strange prick of concern for him that she did not want to feel.

"You see, Zerxes, I have found you a new pet," Bahdra was saying to the *leje*, his voice eerily calm, and his eyes glittered like polished skal. "What do you say? Is her body acceptable to you?"

"YESSSSSSS..." the *leje* said, more hiss than sound because it no longer had a throat with which to speak. Even now, darkness seeped out of its joints and holes, as if it struggled to hold form.

"Yes, I think you will be pleased with this body, for it is quite familiar with being used—" Bahdra cried out, his words cut short as he staggered forward a step, clutching his heart. His features twisted in pain, and all throughout the battlefield, similar cries echoed.

Niá wondered what in all the stars had just happened, but she did not let herself wonder long. Bahdra was distracted.

Seizing the opportunity, Niá pitched forward, struggling upon legs still dizzied from her unexpected flight. She had only taken three steps, however, when inky tendrils lashed out and wrapped around her torso, lifting her feet above the ground so that she was eye level with Bahdra.

He approached, his black boots striking unsteadily upon the frozen ground. His gaze fastened furiously upon Niá, though his features twisted as he fought to overcome this strange and sudden affliction, and he stopped one pace away.

Niá spit in his face.

Another tendril lashed out, wrapped around her neck, and

squeezed. Niá gasped and squirmed for breath. Even impaired, Bahdra was still too powerful for her to overcome.

"You betrayed me, Niá," Bahdra said through clenched teeth. His pale, inked forehead glistened with strain.

"You...betrayed...our people," Niá managed.

That tendril squeezed tighter. "You are...too governed by your heart."

"What would you know of hearts? You have none."

"I did, but I cut it out." His features twitched, and a small, pained gasp escaped him. "Hearts make us weak."

"Hearts make us human..." Niá struggled to breathe. Struggled to keep her consciousness as her feet dangled.

"I do not wish to be human," Bahdra growled, and Niá suspected his words were not just for her, but for someone else. Someone far greater than either of them.

In that moment, Niá saw her death in Bahdra's eyes—his decision to end her life. To make an example out of her. She had seconds, she knew. She tried to summon an enchantment to stop him, but she lacked the strength. She had exhausted too much already, and slowing Bahdra—even a weakened Bahdra—had diminished what little remained.

Strangely, her only thought right then was Chez and what she should have done the night he'd come to tell her how he felt.

"You are a disappointment, daughter of Taran, though I should have expected nothing more," Bahdra rasped. The tendril squeezed tight, and Niá's consciousness faded.

## 53

*K*ai heard the battle before he saw the war.

But that wasn't really true, Kai mused, because they'd seen the signs before they'd heard the sounds. The crows squawking, that foreboding cloud of wings rising high and flying away. Some circling, waiting.

For blood.

They had been following Azir's tracks for two weeks. They'd initially feared they would be too late, considering Kai's poor state of health and the fact that Azir had at least three days on them.

But it was winter, and Azir numbered many while they were few, and Ricón had vastly underestimated Urri's talents as a healer.

That first night, Urri had not left Kai's side. She had made tonics for him every time they stopped, using her power to keep infection at bay. Kai did not improve at first, and the others in Hiatt's group took turns carrying him upon a stretcher. He'd begged for Ricón to leave him behind, but Ricón would not hear of it.

"What ails him is not infection," Kai had overheard Urri saying to Ricón one night. "He has no will to live."

Ricón had looked over at Kai, and Kai had looked away, but Ricón had walked over and crouched at his side. He'd studied Kai, but Kai did not—could not—return his gaze.

"I told you to leave me," Kai had said, a little defensively.

"I told you I would not."

Kai had looked sharply at his brother. "Let me be, Ricón. You don't need me. I'm a burden, and I deserve what has happened to me. *Let me go in peace.*"

"No," Ricón had said, after some time. "Your work is not finished yet." He'd promptly stood, dropped a lump of bread into Kai's lap, and walked away.

But Kai did not leave. He could not say what propelled him to stay, but he felt a new spark to live. If only for a time, to make things right. Each day grew a little easier and less painful, until he no longer needed the stretcher and was able to walk for long periods at a time.

The others still looked curiously at him. Especially one called Zas, whom Kai didn't really care for, and he suspected Ricón didn't either, but Zas had come, and he was talented with the Shah, and they needed all the help they could get.

Kai knew firsthand the power shared by Azir and his Mo'Ruk.

"It's good to have you back, brother." Ricón had smiled one night and cuffed him on the shoulder, to which Kai only offered a small smile.

And now they were here, hidden within the Blackwood.

Hiatt had enchanted them to hide their presence from Azir and his Mo'Ruk seer, Lestra, and the Blackwood's thick shadows did the rest.

"The war has begun," Zas said after a great trumpet blared. "We need to get moving."

"No, we need to be patient," Ricón said.

Zas took a firm step forward, his expression written in arguments. It was always written thus. "*Patient*? There's not going to be anyone left if we wait much longer. You don't understand Liagé power, and Azir has—"

"We wait," Hiatt said evenly, exchanging a weighted glance with Mazz. Zas ceased speaking, clearly furious but unwilling to disrespect his matriarch.

"And what, exactly, are we waiting for?" Zas asked.

"Distance," Mazz answered. "We cannot afford to be spotted before the battle is fully engaged. You might recall that the Wolf King has *a wall*."

Meaning, they did not.

Zas's lips thinned.

"Can you See anything?" Ricón asked.

"I do not dare call upon my Sight so close to Azir," Hiatt replied.

After what felt like ages, after screams and shouts and explosions echoed through the trees, Mazz announced, "It is time."

They walked on through the thick pines, through snow that would've been too deep to pass through had it not been for the thousands that had already trampled it. Finally, Kai saw the break where the tree line ended and a lawn stretched before a great wall.

Where battle raged.

It was like the sea, undulating and crashing against breakers, frothing like the tide. Shades leapt and lunged, and men crashed against one another as more men streamed through the place where enormous skal doors had once stood. There was no sign of those doors now, nor the watchtowers above them or the scaffolding beside them. It was a great hole in a wall where that sea of battle poured through.

One of Zas's men cursed and made a gesture over his heart.

It was hard to make sense of anyone or anything—it was all chaos, all madness. Corinthians fought along the wall as Sol Velorians and shades tried to climb it, while other Sol Velorians *aided* the Corinthians. Some warriors fighting alongside Corinth were not from either nationality.

"Who is fighting with them?" Ricón asked before Kai could voice his own thoughts.

Hiatt gazed ahead, eyes narrowed with focus. "Brom Stykken."

Ricón looked surprised.

"From The Fingers?" a man called Gezze, a guardian, asked.

Hiatt nodded once, and Gezze frowned. Not with displeasure, but with surprise.

"But where is Azir Mubarék?" Mazz asked, scanning the crowd, the chaos.

"We're missing two Mo'Ruk as well," Hiatt added.

Yes, as Kai studied the battle, he caught no sign whatsoever of Azir, and he spied only one Mo'Ruk. Kazak, Azir's guardian, who fought against what could only be another guardian—a large and fearsome Sol Velorian who stood atop the wall, trying to rebuild the hole that had been made.

But then Kai noticed a vortex of swirling black, and a figure appeared at the edge of Azir's ranks.

Bahdra.

And behind Bahdra, Kai spotted Zerxes.

Kai fell deathly still, and then his body started trembling.

Ricón noticed, and understanding sharpened his features. "Kai, you'll wait here until I give the signal."

Ricón said something else to Hiatt, but Kai's attention was on the figure on the ground before the necromancer. He couldn't make it out from here, but then those inky tendrils lashed out, wrapped around the person, and lifted.

Kai's heart stopped.

"Niá..." Her name fell from his lips like a confession, full of pain. And then he started running.

"Kai!" Ricón yelled after him.

But Kai did not stop. He ran faster than he had ever run

before, not caring for the pain pulling in his mutilated groin. His arms pumped as he sprinted across trampled snow and earth, his sight only on her.

A Sol Velorian man spotted him and turned, sword drawn as he rushed Kai, but Kai ducked aside and whirled, then punched the man in the face. The man cried out and stumbled back while Kai ripped the blade from the man's hands and kept running.

"*KAI!*" Ricón screamed.

More of Azir's warriors noticed them and started for Ricón and the others emerging from the Blackwood.

But Kai kept going, shoving his way into the fringe. He heard a snap of air behind him as someone loosed an arrow at his back, but the arrow caught fire and incinerated instead.

One of Hiatt's had stopped it, and Kai was thankful, because Ricón had been right: His work was not yet finished.

Bahdra didn't see him; all of Bahdra's focus rest on the captive he held suspended in his inky tentacles. Niá clasped at her neck, fighting to break free, to breathe. At the mercy of this monster.

Always at the mercy of another.

Kai growled; his footsteps fell faster.

Zerxes spotted him then. Those white lights glowed in empty eye sockets as it licked cracked lips with wicked delight, and Bahdra's cowl turned. Just as Kai threw the blade.

It zipped across the lawn and sank into Bahdra's back.

Bahdra wailed, a horrible keening sound. The tendrils evaporated, and Niá collapsed into a heap.

Unmoving.

Zerxes hunkered on all fours, snarling as darkness leaked out of its holes. It leapt for Kai, but before Kai could even respond, a blast of white-blue light hit the demon squarely. It screamed as its body ignited, incinerating it completely, though an inky black vapor rose from the falling ash of its host. But that white-blue light did not vanish. Instead, it caught hold of the rising inky black, eating it up, every swell and desperate tendril, until there was nothing left of the demon but the fading memory of its tortured scream.

Bahdra whirled, furious, as he reached behind his back and jerked the dagger free. He looked at the skal, then at Kai, those black eyes glowing with malice.

"You cannot kill *me*," Bahdra spat, though there was great strain in his voice. He threw the knife straight at Kai, and though Bahdra lacked the form and skill with a blade, the inky darkness trailed the blade, adjusting its course and giving it speed. Kai jumped, though not far or fast enough, and it sank right into his gut.

Kai cried out and staggered as fire bloomed inside of him.

"KAI!" Ricón screamed from somewhere, now trapped in battle.

And Bahdra approached.

Tendrils seeped from his palms and snaked around Kai's waist, and Bahdra lifted him up as he'd lifted Niá.

But Kai did not fight. He struggled only to keep breathing. To stay alive.

"I know you, *pet*," Bahdra hissed through his teeth while Kai fought for breath. To stay alive. Just a little longer.

Bahdra studied him. There was nothing human in those eyes. "Do you see, Niá? Love is weakness. He risked *everything* to save you when he must have known he would surely die."

Kai looked at Niá, who had begun to stir. Her eyes opened and settled on him, and then she blinked with confusion.

Then pain.

It was the pain he hated most.

That he had caused it.

"I'm so sorry, Niá," Kai said to her. Tears leaked out of his eyes. "I am sorry I did not do this sooner." And then, in a final burst of strength, Kai pressed the release on his wrist strap and slammed the small, enchanted dagger given to him by Mazz into Bahdra's skull, right between his eyes.

Bahdra wailed, a horrible shrieking and inhuman sound. His body convulsed, the tendrils retracted, and Kai dropped, watching as those tendrils wrapped around Bahdra. Tangled him up in darkness while he thrashed and screamed.

But this time, his power did not heal him—it could not, for it was leaking out of his body.

Bahdra roared in fury as his edges began to dissolve and melt away. Kai looked at Niá, catching her wide-eyed gaze just as the last of Bahdra's tendrils lashed out and punched Kai through the heart.

·⟨⟩·

NIÁ SCREAMED. Kai's eyes opened wide, his lips parted, and he collapsed as Bahdra's darkness melted into the air and dispersed like a vapor.

But Niá did not stop screaming.

She crawled over the frozen ground, through snow—toward Kai—but then a band of Azir's Sol Velorian warriors stepped in and blocked her path.

One raised a scim. "What have you done?" the man demanded in Sol Velorian, looking in horror at the place Bahdra had stood. He looked back at Niá and brought down his blade. Niá was too stunned to move, too sick and grieved to catch her mind up to the present, and it was Sur Ricón's blade who stopped the one that would have cut her down.

Others rallied to him, Istraan and Sol Velorian. Hiatt and the members of her council who had refused Imari's request all those months ago. Niá hardly registered them now or what their presence meant. She was stumbling toward Kai, despite the fighting all around, because she...

She...

She dropped to her knees beside him, though he did not see her. He could not.

He was gone.

His last view of the world had been her, as if he'd known he was going to die, and she had been the very last thing he had wanted to see.

Niá's heart wrenched. "*Why*?" she cried, and her body trembled. Blood soaked his tunic, turning it crimson, and it leaked into the snow. "I meant *nothing* to you!"

She tried to believe it. She wanted to, but her tears fell harder, and suddenly she couldn't breathe.

Someone pulled at her arms, urging her away.

"Why did you die for *me*?" Niá wailed through her tears.

Of course he could not answer, but she knew the reason all the same.

"Niá, we have to go," a man said, tugging firmly on her arm.

It was Chez.

The sight of him gave her a start. He was covered in blood, and there was a nasty gash over his right eye. She had no idea how he'd crossed that distance from the wall to where they now stood, but he looked as though he'd fought through hell to get to her.

And they were completely surrounded.

## 54

*J*eric stared at Imari across the cavernous chamber, frozen in complete shock. She was so close and yet so far away. There, but nowhere to be found, for the woman standing before him was not Imari at all, this figure with hate in her eyes, surrounded by piles of ash and blood.

In that shock, in that moment of profound disbelief, Jeric did not notice Azir raise a hand.

A blast of air struck Jeric square in the chest, and he went flying. He hit the ground hard, and pain ignited in his shoulder as his body rolled and rolled. He finally stopped, only to be lifted by the same invisible force—a force like a giant hand wrapping around his body—and then he was jerked back, like a fish on a line, until he was hovering directly before Azir.

But Azir looked different. He was...more. His edges sharper, his contrasts more defined, and the air around him shuddered with his power.

"Wolf," Azir said in a voice that was his, but also not. It echoed strangely, layered with another sound.

Zussa.

"Demon," Jeric snarled, gasping for breath.

Azir smiled, all cruelty and malice.

"Put him down, Azra," Tallyn's voice boomed from the threshold.

Azir's gaze slid to Tallyn while Jeric struggled in his invisible grip. "I will never understand you, Muzretall. You were created to be free, and yet you keep enslaving yourself to the will of a tyrant."

"There is no such thing as true freedom, for the will of man forever imposes upon another's," Maeva said as she stepped into the room. "It is either Asorai's will or yours, and we will *always* choose Asorai."

Azir regarded her, and his lips curled. "Ah, a remnant. Your ways are as futile as the one you serve." He tossed Jeric aside like chaff and sent a bolt of light at Tallyn even as Jeric hit the ground.

But Tallyn deflected with a wave of his hand, light struck ceiling, and rock crumbled as Jeric got up quick, his attention strictly upon the woman who stared at him with eyes that were not hers. He needed to reach her—somehow.

He would not lose her like he had lost Astrid.

Another blast of light shot past, this time from Tallyn, but Azir pushed his palm out, parrying the light into the wall beside him, and rock exploded. Su'Vi and Lestra hissed, and the other three Sol Velorians drew weapons.

One threw a scim straight for Braddok, but Jenya's saredd reflexes were faster. She charged into Braddok, knocking them both aside, and the scim only nicked his arm as they tumbled to the ground.

But Jenya had thrown a scim on the way down, and it struck one Sol Velorian man between the eyes.

He collapsed, and the other two rushed in while the cavern erupted in light and blasts. Jeric dodged, stumbling as rock exploded, and he headed straight for Imari. That center of calm amidst a storm.

"Come here to die, dog?" Imari taunted in a voice too full of hate.

Jeric ducked as rock rained overhead. The Sol Velorian woman came at him, and he whirled around and tried to deliver a blow, but she was much faster than he'd expected. She feinted and kicked his legs out from under him.

Jeric landed on his stomach, and the impact punched the wind from his lungs. He wheezed and barely shoved himself aside as the woman brought her scim down. Metal struck stone, sparks flew, and Jeric was on his feet with stars swimming in his eyes. The woman came at him again and again as Jeric parried and stepped back. Then, in a move too quick for her to follow, he spun around her and slammed the hilt of his grandfather's sword against the back of her skull. She cried out and collapsed, and Jeric turned back to Imari.

"Imari, I know you're in there. *Fight this.*"

*There.*

The smallest flicker, a fractional twitch. It was gone in an instant, but it was enough for Jeric. She was in there, and he would draw her out, even if it killed him.

"I should have done this a long time ago," Imari said, raising her wrist as before, and like before, Jeric felt the vibration roll through his body, disrupting its natural rhythm. A tone that was everywhere and in everything, and his heart struggled to keep its beat, its rhythm. It panicked against the force trying to stop it.

He gasped and clutched his chest as another bolt of light zinged over his head. But then Imari gasped and stepped back, clutching her own chest, and the pressure ceased. She could not hurt him without hurting herself.

Because the real Imari was still inside, tied to him.

The creature that had taken Imari hissed in frustration, raised her bells, and threw her head back as she sang.

Sound filled the chamber—so loud, the floor shook with it.

Even Su'Vi lost a step, and Tallyn seized the opportunity to blast a sphere of light at her, which threw Su'Vi back into the wall.

Imari's song grew louder, and the wards etched into the platform beneath her feet sprang to life, glowing with that silvery moonlight. Cracks splintered through the platform and spidered across the floor.

She was going to rip this entire chamber apart.

"Imari, stop," Jeric pleaded, making his way toward her as the room trembled, and then he was there before her, holding her face between his hands.

Her power jolted through his body like lightning, and he flinched from the magnitude of it, but he did not let her go.

Her eyes snapped open. There was such fire within, such hate.

He stared right back. "I love you."

"*Don't touch me.*" Imari shoved him back, but he stood firm. As the sound blared, as the world rocked and cracked and bits of plaster fell from the ceiling.

"This is not you, Imari," Jeric persisted. "Fight this."

Imari punched him in the jaw with unnatural strength, and it sent Jeric reeling. He tripped over the platform's edge and sprawled onto the floor, but then Imari was there beside him, and she kicked him in the gut.

Jeric's ribs cracked, and he went sliding again, right through a pile of ash. Imari walked toward him, looming over him as he crawled upon all fours, trying to breathe. She'd broken two of his ribs.

He looked up at her as he winced and strained to breathe. "I love you, Imari."

·⟪⟫·

IMARI FLOATED in that vast abyss, aware that she was...aware. It was like before, when she'd been cognizant of self, but nothing more. Shadows blurred in this grayscale world of dark and darker still, and suddenly she became aware of a distant cello.

It had already been playing, but she had just become aware of the sound. It was probably what had awoken her from...whatever state she had slipped into.

But she wasn't alone.

The darkness crowded all around her, making it difficult to hold on to any thought as it lulled her back to sleep.

Sleep.

Sleeeeeeeeep.

She could let herself drift away, where questions could not bother her, nor pain. Where fear did not exist.

That cello grew louder, insistent, as it said a name.

*Imari.*

It struck her like a bolt of lightning. A flash of blinding white in the dark.

*I love you.*

The darkness showed her another woman, lying in bed with a man she did not recognize, but she felt warmth spring from somewhere, which she found odd, since she lacked form. And then images flashed of this man slaughtering so many others. She couldn't understand why the darkness saw fit to show her these horrible images, or why she should care.

*I love you, Imari.*

A flash.

She saw the man—the man the darkness had shown her— kneeling on the ground before her, gazing at her with eyes storming like the sea.

The Wolf King.

Jeric.

*Jos.*

In a flood, it all came back. Memory after memory until she

was drowning in it, spinning and spinning in a body she could neither feel nor see nor control, but one thing she knew with terrifying certainty: She loved this man with every fiber of her being.

Little points of fire suddenly pricked all over her, poking holes through the haze, and that silhouette appeared against the milky gray horizon as it said: *YOU ARE MINE.*

But those little pricks of fire burned hotter, and Imari yelled: I BELONG TO NO MAN.

The figure distorted, its edges blurred like a mirage as it raged in her mind, and Imari screamed as she threw herself upon it.

## 55

*J*eric watched Imari's features contort, as if they struggled to settle on one expression. One...*mind*. She shook her head as if she might shake the strain away, but still her features twitched and shifted, even as she grabbed Jeric by the collar and pulled him to his knees.

Her eyes bore down on him, full of hate and...something else.

"I saw you," she said suddenly, through her teeth, then she shook her head as if the words had come without her sanction.

But she did not need to explain. "I know," he said. "I'm sorry."

Light flashed. The room shook. More rock rained down, and Braddok called Jeric's name.

"*Sorry*?" Imari moved her hands to his throat. Her features contorted again, but her hands did not squeeze. "You slaughtered *hundreds* of us and left our children for dead!"

"I know," Jeric replied, never breaking her gaze. Not once. He could not, or he would lose her. "Nothing will excuse what I have done. I was lost, but you helped me find my way. You showed me who I want to be."

There was fire in Imari's hazel eyes. Her fingers twitched around his neck. "I saw you with *her*."

Jeric's heart broke, and he struggled to breathe against the pain in his ribs. Struggled to hold on to his consciousness. "I love you."

"Do not speak to me of love," she growled, and he did not try to fight her. He was still beneath her hands, ready to accept whatever punishment he deserved for all he had done.

Imari's fingers contracted, and Jeric flinched, though his gaze never left her face. "I love you."

Her head thrashed; her teeth clenched. "*Stop saying that.*"

"No," Jeric managed. "For as long as I live...I will never stop... loving you."

IN THE GRAYSCALE WORLD, Imari fought. She wrestled and screamed, trying to grasp hold of the one who had trapped her here in her own mind. But it was like grappling sand. It was everywhere, slipping through her fingers as she tried to hold it, and then it would pour on top of her, burying her in dark until she couldn't breathe. Until she couldn't *think*.

*I love you.*

That rich cello resonated through her, making the sand tremble and shaking it from her body so that Imari was able to see again.

The dark figure stood against a milky sky, walking away from her.

Again, Imari ran after it. Or pushed her thoughts at it, for she did not have any body with which to run. She simply focused her thoughts upon the retreating thief, told her mind to go after it, and then her awareness was flying, crossing that distance. Speeding over inky darkness toward the thief, and the thing turned.

It pushed energy at her to knock her down, to push her back

into the infinite dark and horror, but at the last minute, Imari forced her thoughts to the side. Away from the blast.

And the thief's power pushed right past her.

The thief snarled, and Imari's mind crashed into it. There was searing heat and bitter cold. A maelstrom of spinning black and gray and flickers of white, and the thief growled a deep bass that shook Imari's hazy world, her thoughts, her being. It tried shaking her apart, like sand.

*For as long as I live...I will never stop...loving you.*

That cello was spark to her purpose, steel to her will, and the little sun of her being began to glow brighter.

The thief wailed.

Imari held fast to those words, to the song of his voice, and her little sun shone even brighter. Imari's light fissured through the dark, through the cold—poking holes through the creature that had stolen her body and mind. And then all exploded in light.

Suddenly, Imari was gasping—through her lips. And she collapsed—upon her knees. She felt someone's touch upon her cheeks. Her eyes snapped open, and Jeric was there before her, his eyes storming as he held her face in his hands.

"Give me your darkness," he said.

Imari growled through clenched teeth, and she shook her head again as if she might shake out the throbbing pain in her skull. Her insides squirmed, and her body suddenly felt as though it were on fire.

But Jeric did not relent. "Let me carry it, Imari. Give me this burden so that you can finish him." And then he pulled her in and kissed her hard.

There was a moment of revulsion as something else inside of her screamed and thrashed, but Jeric did not let go. His lips held fast to hers as he slid his arms around her and pulled her against him.

Suddenly, her world became light and dark, star and shadow.

She could see his soul shining so brightly, its deep bass so strong, reverberating through her, and her light rang back. It was his bass that had called to her before, when she had not been able to see the world through the thief's haze. This time, she heard her own light singing in harmony.

But there was a third tone—a tone she had never heard before, ringing through them both.

*I am here, Imari,* said a voice that started far away but grew nearer and stronger even as she listened. As if it were trying to reach her but could not because of the darkness inside of her. But through Jeric, through his lips and his light, she could hear it.

The dark mass within her coiled and strained, and Imari gasped in pain. Her muscles seized, but Jeric held tight, kept her on her knees, his mouth still pressed to hers as he said, "Let me carry it, Imari. Give it to me, and finish this."

Hot tears streamed down her face, and her chest suddenly felt too tight. "I don't...I can't—" She screamed as her insides twisted sharp.

She felt as though she were ripping in half.

She could hardly breathe, hardly think. Hardly see. Her vision flickered in and out. Material and contrast. Cavern and stars, as if her eyes and soul fought for priority.

Somewhere she heard her lord call her name.

No, not her lord: Zussa, the Great Deceiver.

It was Zussa who called to her now. Zussa, who had stolen Azir's being, had slipped inside Imari and rooted deep. Zussa who fought against her, calling to that piece of herself buried in Imari's body and demanding it hold.

Jeric was right. She could not give up the darkness that had taken residence inside of her. Once extracted, it would slip right back in, and it would always fight her.

Unless it had somewhere else to go—to someone willing. And Jeric had offered to bear her darkness so that she might save the rest.

She could still feel his lips pressed to hers, though her sight was all light and dark. Writhing masses and glittering stars that struggled to stay lit within the nebulous black.

The corruption.

*I am here,* said that other voice, that pure tone that gave life. It was still distant but drawing nearer. A presence just at the edge of her awareness. One that had always been at the edge of her awareness, though she had not sensed him these past few months. She hadn't been able to, because Asorai would not touch the darkness dwelling within her. It was antithetical to who he was, for light and dark could not coexist.

And she had grown dark.

Asorai was waiting for her to let him back in before everything collapsed.

And it was about to collapse.

Imari kissed Jeric back. A great wailing sounded in her mind, and a burning tear seared through her. She gasped and sagged forward, her mouth still locked with his as he drank her in.

And Imari ripped the darkness free.

A wave of heat shocked through her belly, through her throat and out her mouth as she vomited Zussa's darkness from the depths of her soul.

Jeric gasped as he took it in.

In her Shah sight, she could see that writhing mass fill him, dim his light. She heard his song bend and bend—out of tune, warped from the corruption.

Without Zussa's darkness clouding her mind and soul, the entire world opened up to her. She felt Asorai's presence like never before, and his strength filled her now.

*I am here, and I will give you strength*, he said.

Jeric collapsed in pain and yelled through clenched teeth, his body coiled. Fighting the power his body could not withstand, because he was not Liagé. The Shah was too much for him.

And Imari couldn't bear to watch.

Imari was about to take it back—to kiss his mouth and draw that darkness out of his body and pull it back into hers—when a blast struck her in the back.

She stumbled forward, tripping over the fragments of a chair she'd destroyed, and then another force lifted her off her feet even as she fell.

Azir stood with his hands raised, and he drew her back to him as though she were attached on an invisible tether.

Maeva and Tallyn were pinned to a wall before Su'Vi, and Braddok and Jenya stood, seemingly unable to move as they dripped sweat and blood.

"Asorai makes you weak," Azir said, but it was Zussa speaking now. "I tried to set you free, but like a dog, you persist in returning to your vomit."

Azir's gaze flickered to Jeric, who twitched and convulsed upon the ground.

And Imari was finding it very difficult to breathe.

She could not defeat Zussa in the physical. Zussa was too strong.

*I am with you*, repeated the voice.

And suddenly, Imari had an idea.

"Let him live and I will...finish this, the way I promised," she said, struggling to breathe. "You need me for this, but if you harm him, I will die before I do anything you ask of me."

Azir's black eyes narrowed a little, because he knew that she was right. It was why he'd taken her to begin with: He needed her particular power to unravel the song Asorai had woven—the notes tied into all of creation—and no one else could do it but her.

"You know you need me to do this," Imari pleaded, gasping for air. "*And I will.* As long as you let him live."

Azir regarded her blankly, his thoughts hidden. Then, "Betray me, and he dies."

Azir looked at her and set her down—or, rather, she floated

down to her feet and the pressure ceased. Azir opened his palms. Jeric's spine arched as he gagged darkness into the air. It streamed from his lips and rose like a vapor before seeping back into Azir's palms. Azir's body swelled, and he shuddered as Jeric collapsed on the ground, unconscious, his face pale.

But he was alive.

In that distraction, Su'Vi had forgotten Braddok and Jenya, and, thus released from her hold, both started for Jeric, but not fast enough. Azir waved another hand, sending Braddok and Jenya against the wall beside Tallyn and Maeva. Su'Vi alone remained freely standing.

"Remember what I said," Azir warned, now standing beside Jeric. "Unravel the words, and rewrite them in *my* name."

Imari inhaled a deep, shuddering breath and stepped onto the platform. The skal warmed her bare feet, the glyphs lit anew, and electric power surged through her bones.

Imari closed her eyes, and her Shah sight immediately took over. The chamber was all light and dark. A piece of Zussa's corrupt mass still writhed over Jeric where his star shone, albeit dimly. Thousands of tiny stars shone in this place from the materials with which it had been built, but Imari focused on the current of power surging through her, on the song she could just hear at the edge of her awareness.

Asorai's song, from which he had created all things. A song that needed to be undone so that a new song could be written. Azir wanted that song written in his name, so that all laws of this world would be set according to his ruthless and repressive will, but Asorai wanted something else entirely.

Asorai wanted her to unwrite the song and weave a new one so that *all* could share in his power and glory—not just the Liagé, but all of mankind.

*I need you now*, Imari prayed silently to the one who had created it all and brought her to this place for this moment. *Guide my song, and save them.*

She raised her wrist, helping each bell capture its respective tone, until she held the entire scale in her talla.

In her Shah sight, those words upon the podium burned brightly. They looked like constellations, tethered by a fine line of moonlight.

A line she needed to unravel.

*Show me*, she prayed, as she reflected her song and plucked at the strings of existence. She slowly broke them apart into their constituents. Power strained as she worked, and she felt flashes of heat and cold as she slowly plucked that song out of balance.

The ground trembled beneath her feet, and stars swirled all around her, orbiting her in different directions with her at the center. The more she ripped and pulled with her song, the more the ground shook.

And shook.

Imari adjusted her stance so that she did not fall until, finally, she had all the notes in this place—each and every one—broken apart before her. Pieces of what had been, a broken chord, a scattering of stars, growing dimmer all around.

Because they were not meant to be separate. They had always been intended for a greater picture—a greater good.

*"Their hearts no longer sought to follow Asorai's perfect will, and so Asorai gave them over to their depravity."*

But Asorai was good, and though man had chosen depravity, Asorai had given them a way out. A way that she was going to write, through his guidance and strength.

And so Imari took all of those notes and began to craft a new song. Every note rang loud and clear, full of a power greater than anything that could have come from her, because it was woven with Asorai's pure voice.

Imari had feared that she would not be enough, and in that moment, she realized that she was never supposed to be enough. The Maker would always fill in the gaps.

Even now, he guided her song, giving weight to her notes as

she drew in the stars—not just those upon his podium, but every star in this room, large and small, helping her weave them all into a new creation. Her song spanned every octave, blooming with vibrance, with majesty—embracing all that it was and all that it had created.

Jeric's light grew brighter, caught up in this new piece—one that included him, not just the Sol Velorians—and Jeric's soul ignited.

"What are you doing?" Imari heard Azir ask in the material world.

He had noticed something was out of place.

And Jeric screamed.

The sound wrenched painfully through Imari's heart, but before she could react, Tallyn—in a burst of strength and light— broke free of Su'Vi's hold. Su'Vi's power rebounded, throwing her to the floor, and she did not rise again, not even as Tallyn rushed Azir and fired a sphere of light. Azir waved a hand to deflect, but Tallyn rammed right into him, knocking them both to the ground.

But Jeric had been forgotten, his body relaxed, and so Imari kept playing. She pushed notes into her bells, singing a harmony as she reflected the sound, and suddenly it was as though the heavens had descended all around her, and she was flying through them, capturing stars, drawing them to her and weaving them into her tapestry of light and song. Writing new words into creation. Words she had never consciously known, but her heart knew them, made them, guided by the hand of another.

A mass of writhing darkness slammed into her and knocked her down from the pedestal.

Zussa.

Azir battled Tallyn in the material world, but Zussa had broken free to stop Imari in her world of stars. And the heavens groaned with Zussa's presence, with the strain her darkness inherently pressed upon the stars. That same darkness enveloped

Imari like a cocoon, shielding her from Asorai's presence and strength, and for a moment, Imari was surrounded by cold. A bitter cold that filled her insides, and despair settled deep, alongside hopelessness, futility, and dread.

*Fear.*

These were Zussa's dearest weapons: fear, most of all. But Imari had much experience with fear, and she would not fold beneath this. Through the darkness, through that slowly strangling black cocoon, Imari yelled a note—just one. Sound exploded from her chest in a blast of bass and light. The darkness wailed as it dispersed, only to regroup again in the vague silhouette of a person backlit by stars.

FOOL, boomed the darkness. YOU WOULD ENSLAVE YOURSELF TO HIS WILL WHEN I HAVE OFFERED YOU THE POWER OF A GOD.

"I already have the power of a god," Imari replied in that space. "It is there for me to use, whenever I have need."

The darkness laughed. Its silhouette shuddered with the sound as it writhed and pulsed, then it said, I TOO WAS LIKE YOU, AND THEN I WATCHED MANKIND DESTROY ITSELF WHILE ASORAI DID NOTHING TO STOP IT. HE DOES NOT CARE ABOUT US.

"Then you are the most deceived of them all," Imari said. "Asorai cares more than we can possibly understand, for he has given us freedom to choose, and though we choose destruction, he still sent me to save them all."

A majestic chord settled into Imari's soul, and she pushed the sound into her bells, reflecting it into the heavens. Every star ignited, answering her command. Each star so bright, Zussa's darkness could not stand.

The darkness roared. The sound shook the heavens with defiance, pushing against every star in a desperate attempt to snuff them out.

Imari nearly choked on the backlash, that push of raw fury

and power. It would have buried her had another power not stepped in just then—a greater power, one that was everywhere and in everything, giving her strength where she failed.

"Now!" Tallyn yelled, still locked in battle with Azir, both of them caught in a tumble of light and dark and falling rock.

She strung notes together with bells and with voice. She gave it everything she was, from the depths of her soul, until her voice strained and her lungs ached. Somewhere, she heard Tallyn scream, and she felt the moment his light flickered out. Azir had been too much. Of course he had known that, but still he had tried, to give her the opportunity to stop Azir, and so she did not cease playing. She pulled all the stars together and wrote them into new words around the darkness, which now bucked and thrashed and convulsed, trying to get to her.

Imari wrapped her song of promise around it, her song of salvation, and she heard Azir howl in furious defeat as she strung her final words together and closed the piece, fixing it in place.

*It is finished.*

There was light.

There was heat.

The air shuddered from a blast that ripped through time and space, carrying the promise across all the world, stamping it into the soil, into every living thing—making it new.

The darkness wailed and caught flame—burned up like chaff —and its screams echoed even after it was gone.

*Well done.*

Light faded, the ground trembled, Imari's sight returned to normal, and the temple collapsed on top of her.

## 56

*S*tanis Vestibor was fighting in the courtyard when the ground began to shake. But it did not stop shaking. He had looked to see the source, but he could find none.

He stumbled, nearly tripping right into a Sol Velorian's scim. Thankfully, he caught his footing and dodged to the side. Something shrieked and whimpered, and Stanis glanced back to see a shade tumble past him with a nightglass bolt sticking out of its skull.

Which was when Stanis noticed the cracks. Great, splintering fissures fracturing Skyhold's magnificent skal wall.

Stanis cursed. "Get off the wall!" he yelled, but no one heard, and Stanis shoved two more Sol Velorian fighters.

The cracks began to glow, as if the moon had taken residence inside of them.

"GET OFF THE WALL!" Stanis yelled again. This time, Stykken caught his gaze, then looked to the wall as he pulled nightglass from the belly of a shade.

"*The wall!*" Stykken shouted, and others took notice.

That light shone brighter, as if the moon inside were expanding and pushing against the wall's boundaries. The men atop the wall began to shove their way down, abandoning posts. Leaving a hole for shades to climb through, and they did, scrambling over the ramparts. A woman screamed as a shade picked her off and ripped her apart.

One jumped behind Hax, who was busy ushering everyone down. He snatched a crossbow off a fallen guard and fired. The bolt struck the creature in the skull, the creature yelped, and Hax looked back as the creature toppled over the wall.

But then the wall flashed blindingly, the earth groaned with a splintering crack, and the wall came tumbling down.

· ᒣᔕ᙭ ·

NIÁ MUBARÉK FELT the song first. This strange pressure upon her ears, a distant melody she couldn't quite make out, and yet her soul shook with its reverberations.

But she was not the only one who felt it.

Hiatt and Zas and all the Liagé elders who were fighting alongside Ricón suddenly stopped, confounded as they looked at their palms, over their persons. And it wasn't just them. The Liagé they'd been fighting had stopped as well, confused as enchantments didn't fall.

Someone was disrupting the Shah. Whoever it was pulled upon that well with a force beyond anything Niá had ever felt— so strongly, it sucked the power out of every Liagé standing around her.

*Imari.*

And then that force pulled so hard, it was like someone had jerked a rope tied to her belly, and Niá pitched forward, gasping as she fell to her knees. Hiatt and the other friendly Liagé dropped around her, as well as the Liagé they'd been fighting, and all throughout Azir's ranks, Niá noticed men and women falling, their spells void, while the non-Liagé among them looked on, bewildered.

"Niá...?" Chez asked beside her, his voice heavy with concern.

And then the earth shook violently.

Chez staggered—everyone did, and all the fighting ceased as everyone looked for the source.

The earth groaned like the pains of humanity, as though it were splitting apart from the darkness that had corrupted its perfect soil. As if it would vomit it out.

Suddenly, light exploded from Skyhold's heart—from a central point Niá could not see—and a percussive boom shook the air. That great sphere of light expanded in a blast, incinerating every shade on impact. Their keening shrieks cut short as they turned to ash and rained upon the battlefield.

Even Kazak, who had been wielding his fire against Akim, turned into an amorphous blob of inky darkness as the light pierced him through, melted his human flesh, and disintegrated him completely.

And then...

Quiet.

Light faded, dust settled, and a vibrant sun burned upon the backs of the Gray's Teeth Mountains. Its rays reached across the land like open arms, illuminating the field where bodies lay everywhere, soaking the earth in blood.

The shades were gone, and Niá could not feel the Shah. Not even a little. She couldn't see Kazak either, and there was no sign left of his master. Corinth's great wall was no more than a hemisphere of broken skal upon the soil. An outline of what had once been. But Azir's forces did not press upon the wall. They stood in that haze of confusion and uncertainty, and it wasn't until Stykken and Hax surrounded those who had penetrated the city —which was easily done without Liagé interference—that Azir's ranks began to raise their arms in surrender.

But from where Niá crouched, she could not see the city

beyond. She could not see that where the temple ruins had stood now lay a deep crater in the ground, as though a star had fallen from the heavens and collided there.

And she could not see the woman at its center, hair like moonlight, sobbing over the body of the man in her arms.

"We shall be saved from ourselves, for we—in our depravity—cannot help but seek the things that would destroy us. But one will come and bring Asorai's light so that all may share in his glory."

~ *Excerpt from the teachings*
*according to Moltoné,*
*Liagé Second High Sceptor.*

## 57

*I*mari held Jeric tight. His eyes were closed, his face peaceful, as though he were sleeping, but she knew he was not asleep.

His heart did not beat.

There was no song, no cello that sang over hers—nothing. He was a body without a soul, without light, for that had been taken from his body when Imari had ripped the darkness out of it with her song.

He had been too tied up in it to free himself.

In desperation, she sang, trying to find her light like before, to push her life into his and bring him back.

But there was only silence. No stars, no song, no Shah.

Nothing but a deep and overwhelming anguish.

Imari cradled his head in her lap, pushing the hair away from his handsome face as she cried. Huddled there at the base of the ruin, distantly aware that she was now exposed to the elements, to the dawn brightening the sky above her.

But she did not feel its warmth.

And she grieved its light. That it should start a new day

without him. That it should move on, when her heart would always be here, in this moment. When she could still hold him.

Through her tears, she didn't see the dozens of little lights floating around her like fireflies. She did not see them coalesce above her; she did not realize they were there at all until they slipped between his lips like an inhale.

Imari froze, her breath caught.

The light moved down his throat, visible even through his ashen skin, to where it stopped over his heart, and there it coalesced and shone bright. Jeric gasped suddenly, his back arched with one wheezing inhale.

*Thank you*, Imari cried in gratitude to the one who had given him back to her. *Thank you*.

Jeric's eyes snapped open and landed on her, sharp as a blade, searching. He seemed to realize that she was herself again, and then he threw his arms around her as she clasped him, the two of them holding tight to each other, not noticing the crowd quickly gathering around the crater's edge, watching the two unlikely survivors at its center.

"Jeric, I'm so sorry—" she started.

"*Don't*," he said, squeezing her tighter.

Imari didn't how long they sat like that, clinging to each other, but eventually they pulled apart, and Jeric looked at her. He was covered in dirt, and blood stained his coat and tunic, but his blue eyes shone bright as they held hers. As if he could see every tortured thought, every conflicted emotion. And then he grabbed her face in his hands and kissed her hard. Imari sank into his kiss, pressed her hands over his, but then he pulled back much too soon, holding a clump of her hair between his fingertips.

*Pale, silvery* hair.

"What in all the stars...?" Imari gasped, dumbfounded, as she frantically reached back and pulled more of her hair forward only to find that *all* of it had turned silvery white.

"I like it," Jeric said, brushing it from her shoulder. "It's like starlight."

Imari subconsciously looked over herself, checking for other unexpected alterations, but then Jeric stood, pulling her up with him, and Imari finally noticed the world around them.

The very wide and very deep crater they stood within, where the temple had been.

It was utterly destroyed, as though a meteor had fallen from the earth in this place. All signs of Asorai's sacred place were gone, and yet Imari felt power...*everywhere*, in everything. Not just in her belly, but also in the man beside her and all of those gathered around. Her gaze slid over the flattened bones of the old chamber, over this ruin of time, to where it finally leveled at Skyhold's streets.

Where hundreds of people gathered. Sol Velorians—Maeva's and Azir's—and Corinthian and Stykken's. There was no sign of Azir or his Mo'Ruk or any shades.

To her right, a few paces away, stone tumbled and rolled. As if something were beneath it, trying to get out.

Imari exchanged a quick glance with Jeric, who started forward just as a large hand reached out of the rock.

It was a wide hand, and Imari was surprised to find she knew it: Braddok's.

Jeric was already running to the pile with Imari right behind him, the two of them digging and pulling at rock.

"We need help!" Jeric yelled, but Chez and Stanis and a few others were already scrambling down the crater, and within ten minutes, they'd pulled a battered and bloodied Braddok, Jenya, and Maeva from the rubble. Jenya's arm was broken, and Braddok had to be carried out by no less than five men, who released him once he could balance himself upon his own two feet, while Maeva crawled out dazed but unharmed.

Jenya's gaze whirled, then settled on Braddok, and for the first time since Imari had known the saredd, Jenya's expression visibly opened with relief. Jenya ran forward, clutching her broken arm as she stumbled straight for Braddok, who looked at her with some alarm.

Especially when Jenya reached forward, grabbed one fistful of his dirtied tunic, jerked him forward, and kissed him.

Someone whistled, Braddok blinked, then smiled lazily—still dazed from the temple's collapse—and shrugged off Chez and Stanis to kiss her back. But he lacked the strength to stand on his own two feet, and he would have taken them all down had Chez and Stanis not managed to grab hold of his arms again.

"Took you long enough," Braddok drawled like a drunkard, even as Chez and Stanis strained to hold him upright. "I should've tried to die a long time ago."

"Try it again, and I'll kill you," Jenya said.

Braddok beamed, swaying between Chez and Stanis.

"Where's Tallyn?" Jeric asked, scouring the ruins.

Imari remembered those final moments before she'd ended her song—moments she would not have had if Tallyn had not stepped in to help. "He's gone," she said quietly.

Jeric met her gaze.

"He gave his life so that I could finish." Imari was about to say more, but then someone began to clap. It was Stykken, who stood at the crater's edge, covered in blood and dust as he gazed upon them with pride. The sound rippled through the rest, until Imari's ears filled with their applause.

Imari had a difficult time feeling triumphant. Victory did not come without sacrifice, and this sacrifice had been too much.

"*Surina Imari!*"

The voice cut through the crowd, and Imari looked to see who had spoken—

Hiatt.

A chill swept over her.

Hiatt wore her white prior robe, though it was stained with dirt, and she looked very, very tired. But she had come, which meant...

Imari scanned the crowd. Sure enough, she spotted Mazz, and Urri, and even Zas, and...

"*Ricón.*" The word fell out of her at a whimper, her heart lurched, and she started running. Right for her brother as he climbed into the crater, half running, half skidding down its side. And then he was there, wrapping his arms around her and picking her up as she squeezed him so tight. Her tears fell as she clung to him.

"I was so worried..." She cried quietly.

Ricón touched her silvery hair, and then he buried his face into it while his breath shuddered. "I'm here, *mi a'fiamé.*"

"Where have you been?"

"I went into Ziyan looking for you."

She pulled back and looked at him as more tears streamed down her face. He'd gone into Ziyan...for her.

"You idiot!" she said as she cried. "You could have died!"

Ricón chuckled, and a tear leaked down his cheek as he set her back down. "I would have, but they saved our life." He glanced pointedly at Hiatt.

Seeing Ricón made Imari think of the one who was not with them. "Have you seen Kai?"

Ricón's jaw flexed, and she noticed the deep sadness in his eyes. Imari clenched grief between her teeth as another tear spilled down her face.

"I found him in Vondar, barely alive. Urri did everything she could, and he was doing better, but..."

Imari already knew.

"He...stayed alive long enough to save *her.*" Ricón glanced at Niá, who stood amidst the crowd at the crater's edge, looking as battered as the rest of them. Her eyes were swollen and red.

But then Ricón grabbed her face between his hands. "We're going to be all right, *mi a'fiamé.*"

He said it for her, he said it for himself, and Imari placed her hands over his. "Yes, *tazaviem,*" she said, though her voice trembled. "Yes, we are."

## 58

*I*t took the better part of the week to drag all the dead off the field and from beneath Skyhold's broken wall to where they piled them upon the lawn to be burned. Many of Azir's army had fled when the wall had collapsed and their Mo'Ruk leaders had disintegrated. Hax wanted to hunt them down, but Jeric would not allow it.

Immediately after the dust had settled, Jeric had instructed Hax and Fyrok to throw the nearly two hundred enemy survivors into the empty armory under heavy and constant surveillance. Jeric had known it was a risk, and he couldn't know which of them were Liagé. He'd asked Hiatt if she might use her gift to seek them out, but she hadn't been able to.

The Shah was cut off from her, and all Liagé. They could sense it like balsam in the air, but they could not touch it, taste it, or feel it. Use it.

Strangely, Jeric could sense it too. Everyone could.

What had once only been accessible to the Liagé was now felt by *everyone*, no matter their birth. It was a tingling on the breeze, a stirring in the soul. A warmth and comfort. So far, none of the former Liagé—Imari included—had found a way to channel that power, though they wondered if it would come with time.

But for now, they were all forced to use conventional means to clean up this city: blood, sweat, and tears.

Still, Jeric did not know what to do with Azir's survivors. His former self would have executed every single one, but the idea did not sit with the present Jeric, to Hax and Stykken's dismay. No, it wasn't until Jeric watched Grag pluck a Sol Velorian boy— all covered in old blood, and far too thin—from a hiding place in the Blackwood that Jeric made up his mind.

Grag was escorting the boy, with Hax, to the armory when Jeric stopped them.

The boy still had fire in his eyes, but there was something else there too. Fear. Anger. An expectation that the Wolf would be the monster he had always believed.

Jeric stared down at the boy. "How old are you?" he asked in Sol Velorian.

The boy looked startled that Jeric could speak his language.

"Fourteen," the boy said at last.

Gods, *fourteen*. So young. "Where are your parents? Did they come with you, or are they waiting in the Baragas?"

The boy's expression darkened, though his eyes filled with unprocessed and overwhelming grief.

It was in that moment Jeric looked at Hax, who stood behind him, and said, "Release the prisoners."

Hax looked at Jeric as though he hadn't quite heard correctly. The boy's eyes widened. They widened further when Grag released his hold on him.

"Go," Jeric said to the boy. "Return to your people. Live your life, but remember this day."

The boy stood there a second more, as if not trusting his fortune, and then he bolted off into the woods where he would, undoubtedly, wait to see if the other prisoners would truly be freed.

Grag looked at his king, silently asking if he was sure. If Jeric had changed his mind. But Jeric raised a hand and shook his head, then turned to Hax. "You heard me."

Hax's lips opened. Words came a second later. "But, sire, if we let them all go—"

"There is no *if*, Hax. I said release them."

Hax's jaw flapped closed. He bowed his head and ran off toward the city. For a moment, Jeric and Grag stood gazing upon Skyhold's jagged rooftops and the place where the wall had once stood.

"You know, I never much liked that wall," Grag said suddenly. "Blocked my view of the forest."

Jeric laughed, then sighed. "Gods, Grag. I don't know what the hells I'm doing anymore."

In rare form, Grag grinned. "Well, whatever you're doing, I like this version better."

He rested a heavy hand upon Jeric's shoulder. It was a fatherly gesture, and Jeric was instantly transported to his youth, when Grag had taken him on hunts to teach him how to track in those early years. "Good to have you back, Wolf. Even if it's not for long."

Jeric raised a brow. "Are you expecting me to go somewhere?"

"You're a wolf. You're not meant for life spent in a cage, no matter how pretty it is." Grag glanced at the fortress nestled upon the side of the mountain. He smiled at Jeric, then pulled his hand away and walked on, leaving Jeric marginally perplexed by his words.

Jeric stood there a moment longer, breathing in the cold, and his attention turned back to the field. Four enormous pyres were all that remained of the dead, and tonight they would burn. His gaze settled at the opposite end of the field, where Braddok had worked with Stykken and Akim to erect a few dozen tents for the sick and injured because there was not enough room in the city.

Their makeshift infirmary clustered near the wall's remains, littered by small fires, and Imari and her uki attended all who had need.

Jeric started for the tents, spotting Niá duck out of one and head for the city, undoubtedly to replenish supplies for Skyhold's newest healers. Imari and her uki had worked tirelessly, hardly sleeping, and Jeric really needed to talk to her.

"Wolf," Gamla said, stepping out of a tent. He looked so much like Sar Branon, but without the mass.

Jeric inclined his head. "Is she—"

"That one." Gamla pointed to a smaller tent ahead.

Jeric nodded. "Thank you."

Gamla bowed his head. "A pleasure."

Jeric pulled the tent flap aside and found Imari just inside, as Gamla had said.

She wore a fur-lined coat over fitted brown breeches, heavy black books, and she'd tied back her exquisite silvery hair with suture string. She didn't see him; she was bent over an unconscious man injured by a deep laceration in his shoulder.

Jeric stood in the threshold, watching her. The gracefulness in her motions, the way she pursed her lips when she worked, the clump of hair that hung forward, and the little crease that always formed between her brows when she was deeply focused.

She finished sewing the laceration, rubbed paste over the wound, then wrapped it in bandages, and she was just fastening the end of it when she said, "It's not polite to stare, darling."

"It's a good thing I've never been overly concerned with manners."

She did not turn to him, but by her profile he could see that she smiled. She finished securing the bandage, set down her supplies, and stood, then turned those brilliant hazel eyes upon him.

Sometimes, when she looked at him, he lost himself.

Like now.

She grinned then strode to the other side of the room, where a bowl of water sat atop a stool beside a brazier with fire. They'd moved the brazier in two days ago, when the water kept freezing over. Imari dipped her hands in the bowl and scrubbed the blood and salve from her skin. "And you still prefer lurking in the shadows, I see."

"Only yours," Jeric said as he ducked into the tent, taking quick inventory.

"Niá informed me that one of Grag's hunters found the Lady Kyrinne," she said quietly, though she scrubbed at her hands with added vigor.

"Yes," Jeric answered. Fyrok had found Kyrinne just yesterday, wearing only a stolen cloak and frozen solid upon the Muir's snowy banks.

"I'm sorry." Imari did not turn to look at him, but those two words searched his heart.

"I'm sorry too," Jeric replied, and Imari's shoulders pulled so slightly. "But only because I gave *any* piece of myself to that woman."

Imari's hands stopped in the bowl, and she glanced at him over her shoulder.

He held her gaze, letting the truth in his words settle. Finally, her shoulders relaxed, and he turned his attention to the sleeping man behind her. "He's one of Azir's."

A beat. "Yes."

"Good. Thank you."

He saw the question in Imari's eyes, and up until ten minutes ago, he'd had no definitive answer for her, though she'd asked.

"Hax is releasing them as we speak," he said.

Imari stared at him. She looked back at the bowl. A second later, she resumed scrubbing her hands. "Where will they go?"

"The Baragas, I imagine," he said as Imari dried her hands upon her coat. Then added, "Or Sol Velor."

Imari froze. He could see the tension in her shoulders. The

strain and uncertainty in her face as her gaze moved back to him. "Hiatt told you."

"She did."

Hiatt had intercepted him this morning while he'd been in a short and very heated discussion with Hax over the mines. Hiatt had reminded Jeric who Imari was. About her birthright as Azir's many-great-granddaughter and Hiatt's resolve to resettle Sol Velor as a *sixth* province. She wanted Imari to rule them. The entire council did.

It appeared Hiatt had told Imari too, but the news did not make her easy. How could it? She'd just learned she was a Mubarék.

"I've known for a while," Jeric added.

Imari's eyes strained on him. "How long?"

Jeric rested his boot upon the lower rungs of a stool and leaned forward, forearms crossed upon his knee. "Since Niá told every miner at Kleider that she was a Mubarék."

Imari inhaled deep.

Jeric dropped his boot and crossed the space between them, then grabbed her shoulders gently, holding her before him. "It changes nothing about how I feel, Imari. We are not our ancestors. I am not my father, and you are not *him*."

"Yes, but I..." Her words trailed as she was undoubtedly suffused by the terrible stain of memories gifted her under the possession of a monster.

Her own many-great-grandfather.

"That wasn't you."

"But it *was*," she persisted. "Everyone saw my face, Jeric. That I..." She closed her eyes and took a breath, but Jeric pressed his fingers to her lips before she could finish saying the thought aloud. Before she could confess any other thing she had done while under that demon's control.

"I killed Rasmin," she whispered against his fingers.

Jeric had suspected this, and the sonofabitch had deserved it, but he also knew Imari. She did not have a heart for death—for *killing*—and this would crush her if she gave it reign.

Her breath shuddered; her lip trembled. "And he wasn't the only—"

"*It wasn't you.*"

Imari's eyes snapped open. They were as watery as the Muir, reflecting all the colors of the forest. "It happened with *my hands*, and your people...they saw me standing right beside Azir and his Mo'Ruk, and if I stay here...if we..." Imari swallowed and closed her eyes as tears leaked over her cheeks.

She worried for their future and how her presence here would complicate matters for him, and suddenly Grag's words came back to him.

He understood them now.

"Imari," he whispered. "Imari, look at me."

Imari forced her eyes open.

"I love you so much more than that godsdamned chair."

Imari's brows knit together with beautiful confusion, and he reached up and brushed the clump of hair behind her ear.

"I will go with you," he said.

That little crease between her brows deepened. "But you can't just leave Corinth—"

"I can do whatever the hells I want." Her lips parted to argue, but Jeric continued before she could speak. "My family has ruled too long. There's not a single Corinthian who would disagree— Braddok, especially."

This made Imari laugh, albeit sadly, which then made Jeric really want to kiss her, and he would have, but he needed to settle this first.

He grabbed her face between his hands, and she stared up at him, their breaths mixed between them. "I won't pretend I have a godsdamned clue what comes next. No one can know, but I know that I love you. That is my only certainty. If you want to stay, I will stay. If you want to go, I will go. Wherever you are is where I want to be, so long as you will still have me."

At those last words, a sob escaped her, and more tears spilled over.

But Jeric was not finished. There was still another very important part—one he had wanted to address since he had seen her on that field beside that demon.

"I hate that I've hurt you," Jeric continued lowly, a tremor to his voice as he held her exquisite face so tenderly between his hands. "I hate that you've seen every horrible part of my past. I hate it more than any other thing." Jeric pressed his lips together and swallowed as his eyes burned. "And if you find it impossible to look past all of my many failings, I will understand, but I swear, Imari: I am not that man. Not anymore, I—"

Imari placed her hands over his, her eyes never leaving his as she said, "I know, Jeric." She stopped, gathered herself. "I know. It's...hard for me sometimes. To shake the images Lestra showed me from the man I know. From the man I *love*. But then I remember all the things I have done, and I'm reminded that none of us are perfect. That...we love through imperfection, and that maybe between the two of us, we can make a whole, good person."

Jeric smiled at her, and his eyes burned anew. "No, you are a whole, good person and I am simply here lurking in your shadow."

This made her laugh, and he touched her chin, then trailed a thumb over her full bottom lip. "I love you, Imari Jeziél Masai, and I want to spend every moment of the rest of my days proving it to you."

Imari's breath shuddered as another tear ran down her cheek, and then he bent his head and kissed her. Through her tears, through their shared sorrow and pain, and he kept on kissing her even as the tears stopped.

## 59

By evening, the people of Skyhold and all their new Provincial allies had gathered at the wide lawn to watch the pyres burn.

Imari knew exactly which pyre they'd placed her brother Kai upon, though she could not see him specifically. Still, she watched the flames stretch higher and reach for the sky as if to hand back all the souls that had perished.

She remembered Kai's youth, contrasted by those tortured, final moments, and a tear slid over her cheek. Beside her, Ricón's eyes welled with tears, and she reached for his hand. His fingers locked with hers and held tight, and together they watched the fire take what remained of someone they had loved so dearly.

She gazed down the line, at Niá, who stared at that same pyre, her expression steeled though grief spilled down her cheeks. Chez stood beside her, very close. Eventually, the flames dimmed, snow began to fall, and people returned to the city. However, Imari stayed with Jeric and Ricón.

"You coming?" Braddok asked.

Stanis stood with him.

Jeric glanced at Imari in question.

"You go on," she whispered. "I'll catch up later."

His gaze flickered to Ricón before he bent forward and kissed her cheek, and then he followed after his men.

Leaving Imari and Ricón alone to watch the flames.

"I feel like you're going to tell me something I do not wish to hear," Ricón said suddenly.

This was going to be the hardest part. Telling her brother —*leaving* her brother when they had just been reunited.

Imari produced a circlet from within her heavy coat. "Hiatt gave me this."

Ricón's brows pinched together as he looked down at the little object in her hands. A circle of gold with fives stones of polished nightglass set over the brow.

"It belonged to Fyri."

Still, Ricón did not understand.

Imari held his gaze. "Jesriel Mubarék was my mama, Ricón. My *real* mama."

He pulled back in surprise. She could see his doubt; she could see the moment he began connecting the dots, unable to deny the truth in her words.

And it had been a difficult truth for her, when her uki and Hiatt had come to her in the tent that first night and explained everything. Where she'd come from, what infamous blood ran through her veins. The revulsion she'd felt as she'd suddenly understood that her own many-great-grandfather *had kissed her*, and she—while possessed—had kissed him back.

Stars, even now the thought made her ill, but there was another piece to all of this—a glorious light in the darkness: Niá was her cousin.

Imari had always felt a kinship to Niá, but knowing they were actually related had brought Imari such joy, she'd sprinted right out of that tent, found Niá, and thrown her arms around her tight.

And together they had cried.

Saza had been family too, and Oza Taran.

Tolya.

The knowledge both satisfied and grieved Imari. That she had not known at the time, that Tolya had never told her. Imari understood why Tolya hadn't, but Imari couldn't help but wonder how knowing might have eased the loneliness she'd always felt living in The Wilds. Imari couldn't help but wish that Tolya had told her anyway. Perhaps she'd meant to, but the Maker had taken her before she'd had the chance.

Because *Sable* had not been ready to sift through all its implications.

"It was why Papa would never speak of my mama," Imari continued to Ricón. Because her mama had been a *Mubarék*, a name cursed above all others. It had been Imari's name all along, but her papa had kept her ignorant, attempting to raise her out from the shadow of the nefarious Mubarék legacy. And for the first time in her life, Imari felt pride for the woman who had given birth to her. Because Jesriel had rejected that legacy too. Jesriel had died for it.

"It was why he sent me away," Imari added. "Because if anyone discovered my connection to Saád..." Imari stopped, gathered herself. Saying his name reminded her of Azir, and she still could not think on Azir without feeling shame.

Ricón did not speak. He stood completely still, his gaze now locked on those flames, because he knew what she said was true.

He knew what it would mean.

"You're angry," Imari said.

Ricón looked at her, and his expression softened. "Not at you, *mi a'fiamé*," he said just as soft. "Not at you at all, I just..." He stopped, his expression tightened, and he dragged a hand over his face. "I guess I'd hoped the rumors were not true about papa. I'd...wanted to believe he'd simply taken you in."

Ah.

"I'm going to Sol Velor, Ricón."

Her words arrested him.

"Hiatt asked me to..." Be queen.

She could hardly say it. Could hardly believe it even now, especially that she'd accepted. That she might have the privilege of guiding these people to build a new life and a better world—the one the Maker had intended.

"Your Wolf knows?" Ricón asked, his eyes on her.

A beat. "He does."

Ricón waited. He knew there was more.

"He is...coming with me."

"*He is leaving this?*"

"Yes."

Ricón looked bewildered. "Can he do that?"

"He never asks those questions."

Ricón looked at her and laughed. The laugh tapered, and he combed a hand through his hair with a sigh.

Imari grabbed that hand on its way back down. "I do not want this to be goodbye, Ricón. I want this to be a beginning."

Emotion pulled at Ricón's features, and he clasped their entwined hands before them. "Well," he said at last. "I suppose it's Sol Velor or Corinth, but are you sure I can't convince you to stay in Istraa? It's not in any worse shape than Ziyan—"

Imari chuckled and shoved at her brother.

Ricón laughed then wrapped his arms around her and pulled her close. "I love you," he said, "and no matter what title your people give you, you will always be *mi a'fiamé*."

"And you will always be my *tazaviem*."

They looked to the pyre where Kai's body burned, and they fell quiet. A tear rolled over Imari's cheek, and Ricón squeezed her tighter, knowing this was the last time the three of them would ever be together.

·❁·

NIÁ FOLLOWED the crowd into the city, though it thinned as people stepped off the main artery to head for their respective residences. Many of the guards and warriors from the other two armies returned to the place the wall had been, where they'd made hasty beds this past week. The snow added a slight complication, and they were all cramming beneath awnings or fashioning new ones out of blankets and broken carts, but it was cold, and they were many, and there was no Shah power to aid them now.

Little fires burned everywhere, and men and women huddled around them, but gone was the restlessness, that hum of unease. Though they were cold and definitely uncomfortable, though the quiet of loss settled over them, life echoed through Skyhold's streets.

Relief.

Hope.

For they knew they would be returning home very soon, and the threat to their loved ones was gone.

Niá stopped at the end of her path, absently watching a handful of Stykken's folk sit around a fire, sharing a few flasks of spirits.

Where would she go?

Imari had told her she was leaving. Heading for Sol Velor. Niá couldn't say she was surprised, but what had surprised her was that the Wolf King was going too. Imari had invited Niá to come, and truthfully, it made the most sense. Niá hadn't been eager to leave Sol Velor in the first place, so of course she should be excited about the opportunity to return.

Except she wasn't.

With sudden decision, Niá turned around and strode for the

wall, where she eventually found Chez with some of Stykken's men, stacking wood into a cart to distribute amongst the people.

Snow dusted his hair and shoulders, and he was saying something to one of the men. He caught sight of her standing there, his movements hitched, and then he turned his attention back to the wood he was stacking. "Need some wood, Niá?"

Niá almost walked away. "Can we talk?"

A few of the men glanced over at her.

Chez did not. "I'm a little busy right now."

This time Niá did walk away.

Two seconds later, Chez was running after her. "Niá, wait."

She kept walking.

"*Please.*" He stepped in front of her and blocked her way forward. "Just...that's not what I meant."

"Then why did you say it?"

Chez sighed, closing his eyes as the snow fell all around. "Because...it's hard for me to be around you right now."

Niá felt a crushing weight upon her heart. "Because of what I've done?"

"No...gods." He dragged a hand over his face, opened his eyes, and looked straight at her. "Because I'm trying not to rutting care about you, but I do, and being around you only makes it harder."

Suddenly, it was just the two of them in that street, with snow falling down, and that weight lifted off her heart.

"I don't want you to stay away," she whispered.

He froze, searching her as if not trusting her confession.

"I thought I was going to die out there on that field," she continued. "And the only thing I could think about was you and how I...wished I hadn't asked you to leave that night."

She could not read the expression on Chez's face, but his gaze never left hers.

"I don't know how to do this, Chez," she said, her heart suddenly pounding hard and fast. "But I want to...try. With you.

That's the only thing I *do* know, and I just...that's what I needed to tell you."

Chez didn't move, didn't seem to breathe. His gaze bore into hers.

"Please, say something," she whispered after a moment.

In answer, Chez took a small step closer. He raised his hand slowly and deliberately, as if to give her time to track every motion. To change her mind and back away.

She didn't.

His fingertips touched her brow, and when Niá still did not turn him away, he trailed his fingertips along her brow—so softly, so tenderly—down her temples, her cheekbones, as if memorizing the very shape of her face. Niá's heart hammered in her chest, her eyes locked on his as his fingertips traced her chin.

Still, she did not move. She couldn't. She was frozen in place, struck by the intimacy of this moment and feeling more vulnerable standing before him fully clothed than she'd ever felt naked.

That was the problem with hearts. The small things mattered.

His thumb trailed her bottom lip, so light it tickled her skin, and a fire blushed within her. His gaze slid from her eyes to her mouth then back to her eyes again, hesitant.

"May I kiss you?" he asked.

No.

Yes.

Niá was caught between instinct and...new.

Chez noticed. He started to draw away.

Niá placed her hand over his, holding his palm to her cheek. "Yes."

Their breaths mixed in a cloud between them. "Are you sure?"

"I'm sure." Niá was certain he could hear her heart pounding.

Chez dipped his head slowly, closer and closer, giving Niá every chance to refuse. To change her mind and step away. He hesitated just before his lips touched hers, and Niá's entire body trembled.

And then she stood on her toes and kissed him.

It was the first time *she* had kissed anyone of her own choosing, guided by a heart she'd long thought dead. A heart that suddenly sang as if it'd been shocked alive. Her entire world condensed to that point of contact, to the feel of his lips. They were softer than she'd expected, and he smelled of woodsmoke and winter, and then, to Niá's sharp disappointment, Chez pulled back and rested his forehead upon hers, clasping their hands between them.

She liked how her hands fit inside of his.

"Gods, it's about time," Chez murmured, and Niá chuckled, and then he kissed her for a while longer.

## 60

"*I*s that everyone?" Imari asked as Hiatt took a seat.

All the chairs had been arranged in a circle at the center of the fortress's great hall. The wolf throne stood at the end, upon a platform that had cracked in half, and the wall behind it had collapsed into the ravine below, opening this magnificent hall to a gray and winter sky.

But Jeric had wanted to meet here, before Corinth's throne, because it was the throne they were discussing today.

He'd called for his cousin, Stykken, and Ricón and Maeva, and a few from his guard. Imari had invited Hiatt's party as well, and of course her uki Gamla. Jenya, Niá, and Jeric's men also attended, as well as a few of Stykken's and Maeva's representatives.

Maeva was saying something to Akim in Sol Velorian but then switched to Common as she addressed the group. "I think so." She looked at Jeric. "Will we be discussing the relocation of the Sol Velorians still captive in your holds?"

All eyes turned to Jeric, who leaned in his chair, legs stretched before him and entirely unaffected by the subtle bite in Maeva's tone, "Amongst other things, yes." He paused. His fingers dangled over the end of his chair, idly dancing. "However, first I wanted to inform you that I am abdicating my throne."

The room fell silent. Glances were exchanged. Imari could almost read their thoughts, namely: *Can he even do that?*

She caught Ricón's gaze, and a smile curled his lips. Jeric's men were not surprised. He'd warned them this morning. Braddok had been particularly thrilled and promptly accused Jeric of being a bore as ruler. Jeric had told him not to get his hopes up, because he would be equally boring being married to one.

However, the rest of this hall looked utterly confounded.

"Might I ask *why* you would do this?" Brom Stykken asked at last, watching Jeric closely. Imari had come to appreciate Jeric's cousin this past week. He worked hard, he said what he meant and meant what he said, and she never detected anything duplicitous about him.

Jeric looked at Stykken. "Because I don't want it."

"But, sire..." Hax sat forward. "Our people need you now more than ever—"

"They need someone—yes. They do not need me."

"But to shift power right now...it will make Corinth appear unstable."

"Unstable. Interesting choice of words." Jeric looked pointedly at the gaping hole in the wall behind the wolf throne.

Braddok chuckled.

"You can't just hand your throne to whomever you like," Zas interjected in Common.

Jeric flashed his teeth. "Watch me."

There were a few snickers.

"Hear me," Jeric said suddenly, seriously, bending his legs as he sat forward. "I did not call you all here to discuss whether or not I should occupy that chair. I've already decided. What I need from you is help filling it so that Corinth is relatively stable"—he nodded at Hax—"when I leave. I need to know that whoever steers Corinth has your support and will also honor our new alliances."

"Where are you going?" Hax asked.

Imari caught Jeric's gaze, and she sat forward. "He is coming with me to Sol Velor."

There was quiet, followed by a clash of concerns: "There's nothing in Sol Velor" and "It's too dangerous" and also still "Can he really do that?"

Zas, in particular, did not look thrilled by this prospect. Braddok noticed and beamed, then cuffed Zas on the shoulder as he said, "You lucky bastard."

Beside him, Jenya rolled her eyes to the ceiling, but Imari detected a grin.

"And what of the tyrcorat?" Brom Stykken asked.

"They're gone," Imari answered.

"Then what attacked you at Liri?"

"That was something else. A...vestige of something else. Corrupted Shah power, if you will."

"And how can you possibly hope to settle a land still teeming with demons?" Hax asked.

"If I may," Hiatt interjected in Common and looked to Imari, who nodded at her to continue. "We believe that when Surina Imari defeated Zussa's darkness, she also stripped this world of all things tied to Zussa's power—including her poison that has corrupted Sol Velor all this time. Of course, I can't See into Sol Velor. My Sight is gone from me, as you well know. Should I be wrong in this, our people will search for alternatives, but I believe very strongly that Zussa's corruption is gone, and if it truly is, I know that I speak for many of us when I say that I want to rebuild. I—*we*—want to go home."

Hiatt's words were met with quiet, then people murmured as a few privately discussed. Imari caught Hiatt's gaze across the circle.

Akim tipped his head to Maeva, whispered, then Maeva

nodded and asked aloud, "And would a new Sol Velor have room for us, *a'prior*?"

Everyone looked to Hiatt, who then looked to Imari for an answer.

"Of course." Imari did not hesitate. "If that is what you wish. Prior Hiatt and I have discussed Sol Velor's future at length, and we welcome all who wish to come. We also welcome those who are *not* Sol Velorian but find they prefer the desert, though I might advise they wait a few years to give us time to make her more presentable."

There were a few chuckles at this.

Imari continued, "And with your blessing, we would like to instate Sol Velor as a sixth Province and open peaceful relations between our nations. We would eventually like to rebuild a port at Liri so that it can assume its former position as a pivotal point of trade for all the Provinces, and also stand as a barrier between us and the nations south. We want to rebuild—yes—but we want to rebuild her with your blessing so that we might all enjoy the shared fruits of peace."

A kind of quiet optimism followed, and more glances were exchanged—somewhat circumspect, but also hopeful.

It was Stykken who eventually broke the quiet. "That all sounds well and good; however, I have some concerns. Specifically how it pertains to the working relationship between Corinth and The Fingers." Stykken looked to Jeric. "You're going to be hard-pressed to find a man who will honor your promise."

He was referring to the mines and the fact that Jeric had given Corinth's most profitable mines back to their rightful owner.

"I agree, and that is what brings us back to the reason I called you here," Jeric said. "If we're to move forward as Surina Imari has just professed, appointing the right individual to fill that chair is of utmost importance."

There was quiet, then murmurs.

"Rodin might be up for it," Chez offered. "He was second only to Stovich and will definitely be easier to work with than Stovich, no disrespect." Chez looked to Hax, who chuckled softly.

There was some discussion amongst the council, other names thrown, but Hiatt's gaze locked on Jeric as she said, "You already have someone in mind."

"I do," Jeric replied, and his gaze locked on Stanis. "Stanis Vestibor."

Stanis looked as if he had misheard, because Jeric couldn't possibly be serious, and now he appeared very uncomfortable from all the attention he was receiving.

Because everyone in that room had also recognized Stanis's surname, though they had not previously known he belonged to it.

"As in *Captain* Vestibor?" Maeva asked.

"The very one."

"Wolf—" Stanis started.

"I've worked with Stanis for years," Jeric said. "I trust him with my life, and I certainly trust him with Corinth's future. He's maintained an effective working relationship with the various holds and has oftentimes been the only voice my jarls will entertain. Stanis holds fast to his convictions, no matter the external pressures, and he will honor our arrangement."

Stykken leaned back in his chair, considering Stanis as he tapped his finger. Everyone was considering Stanis as if they were suddenly looking at him in a new, unexpected, and yet promising light.

However, Stanis's features tightened with a thousand objections. "Absolutely not. I don't want it—"

"Which is precisely why you'd be a perfect fit. Men who *want* power are generally terrible with it."

"Pains me to say it, Stan, but Wolf's right. You'd do well," Braddok said.

"I second that," Chez said with a nod. "You've always been the one to knock them back in line when Wolf's been gone."

"Knowing how to threaten a man is different from knowing how to run a kingdom!" Stanis argued.

"Eh..." Braddok disagreed with a shrug.

"That is also why you have a council," Ricón said, in Common. "Pick good men. Considering Corinth's last ruler, you can only improve from there." Braddok snorted from the corner, and Ricón added with a grin, "I was referring to your father."

A few chuckled.

Including Jeric, who went on to say, "And perhaps your ties to *Captain* Vestibor will provide a stronger fleet at both Gilder and Hüdsval, and the seas may lie wide open from Hiddensee all the way to Liri, as they once did."

Stykken sat back and inhaled a slow, deep breath. Imari knew that look. It was hope.

It was relief.

But not Stanis. "No, Wolf, ask one of your jarls—"

"I don't want a jarl," Jeric said. "Corinth needs a leader who will listen first to the needs of her people. *That is you*, Stanis. No one owns you. You are not for purchase, like every rutting one of Corinth's bloodsucking jarls. Their pockets matter far more than the people they're sworn to serve. No, Corinth needs *you*. A man of the people, for the people, but none of this matters if you truly do not want this role. I can't force it upon you, and I will not try, but I want you to know that I believe you are the best suited for Corinth. Appoint a new commander, like Fyrok"—Jeric gestured at the man standing off to the side, whose eyes had suddenly opened wide—"and I do believe the Provinces will know a peace of the likes we have never seen. Though I must warn you: the jarls don't love peace, because it does not make them money."

Stykken laughed and raised an invisible chalice in toast.

"All I'm asking is that you consider," Jeric said. "Please."

Stanis looked around the room, his gaze flickering to the throne and then settling back on Jeric. "Can I think about it?"

And Jeric smiled.

## 61

*One month later...*

"There." Niá grabbed Imari's shoulders, turning her around to face the looking glass, and Imari's breath caught.

For the briefest moment, Imari saw Fyri staring back at her. Even with Imari's pale and silvery hair, the resemblance was so strong that had she not been aware of their familial connection, she would have known then.

Hiatt stood from her chair before the fire. "You look just like her, especially in that gown."

Imari's gown was of the Sol Velorian style, both wrapping and flowing from her body in delicate panels of indigo silk. Indigo had been the color of Sol Velor: the color of monsoons, of desert sunrises and sunsets. Of power. Obtaining such illustrious fabric had proven a bit of a challenge; however, Jeric had been insistent, and they'd eventually found a merchant in Southbridge who could accommodate them. Three from Maeva's party had gotten to work and fashioned this masterpiece that looked more like a waterfall than a gown.

There had been a bit of discussion over style—namely, traditional Sol Velorian gowns revealed a lot more skin than Imari's gown did presently. However, unlike in Sol Velor, they had a Corinthian winter to contend with. The designers had settled on sleeves at half-length that split open at the elbows and fell halfway to the floor, and Imari made up for the rest with a storming-gray fur shawl, tailored from a pelt Jeric had saved since his youth, from a gray he had killed.

She would wear both nations today: Sol Velor and Corinth.

She'd left her hair down, and it nearly touched the base of her shoulder blades now. Niá had painted Imari's eyes in the Sol Velorian way, using heavy lines upon the lids and drawing out a bit from the crease, then used berry to heighten the color at her lips, and Hiatt had set Fyri's circlet upon Imari's crown.

And though the circlet weighed very little, Imari suddenly felt the weight of all the world, resting there upon her brow. What it meant, the responsibility it appointed. Stars, she hoped she would do right by these people, that the Maker would show her how best to move forward.

That she would never lose sight of humanity.

"Sar Branón would be proud," Jenya said.

Imari looked at Jenya over her shoulder. "Thank you," she said, feeling that familiar prick at the loss of her papa. Wishing she could see him now—talk to him—about all of the things she had learned.

Wishing she could see him simply because she missed him.

And then she noticed Jenya had taken more time with her appearance. Her hair fell loose and long, she'd painted her eyes and blushed her lips, and Imari was about to comment when there was a knock on the door.

Imari and Niá exchanged a glance, but then Jenya was

marching for the door as if ready to spear whoever stood on the other side.

It was Ricón.

Jenya moved aside as Ricón stepped into the room, and all Imari could think was that he looked so much like their papa, standing there trimmed in blacks with his hair tied back and a sheathed scim at his waist. He did not wear the traditional sash; they hadn't had the time, but he looked Istraan all the same.

The others dismissed themselves.

"*Sieta*, Imari, you look beautiful," her brother said, crossing the room to her. He grabbed her hands and looked her over. "You've come a long way from a little chimp scrambling on Vondar's rooftops."

Imari chuckled softly, and they both very acutely felt the presence of the man who should have been standing here with her.

"Thank you, Ricón," she said.

He touched her face. "It is my honor." He smiled, albeit sadly. "I always knew this day would come, but now that we're here, I wish it would have stayed away a little longer." He pulled his hand back, then added, "I had words with your Wolf."

Imari drew back, wary, but Ricón only smiled, all taunting and mischief.

"Ricón, what did you say?"

Ricón winked. "That's between us. Suffice it to say that I wouldn't be handing you over to him if I did not believe he loves you as much as I do."

Imari's entire being warmed at that, and Ricón drew her in close, hugged her tight. They stood like that for a moment, the last moment they would have together for a very long time. Ricón stroked her hair. "And whoever else you are, you will always be *mi a'fiamé*." He pulled back and looked at her. "Please don't cry. Niá will kill me."

Imari laughed with a sniffle, and Ricón produced a cloth for her to dab her eyes, and then he looped his arm through hers, and together, they stepped into the hall where Niá and the others waited.

Hiatt nodded, then took the lead through the fortress's sprawling corridors. They were empty, and when they reached the hall's great doors, many guards and citizens of Corinth, The Fingers, and Sol Velor were gathered. All ceased their chatter when they noticed the surina and her entourage, then greeted her as they stepped aside to create a clear path to the doors.

"We'll see you inside," Jenya said, and she slipped through the doors with Hiatt and Maeva. Niá gently touched Imari's hand as she followed after. Imari heard a burst of chatter that set her nerves and heart thrumming, but the doors closed again, muting it all.

Ricón squeezed her arm.

Ten minutes later, Fyrok opened the doors wide, and all heads within Skyhold's great hall turned to look at them.

Imari took a deep breath and walked forward with Ricón. Through the doors and into Corinth's great hall.

Imari had never seen so many people from a variety of nations crowded into one place. Jeric had contacted all of Corinth's jarls, and though she did not know their faces, she picked them out by their stately dress of bold Corinthian blue and the intense curiosity with which they studied her. There were so many faces she did not know, but so many that she did, and they smiled, easing her nerves.

Like Brom Stykken, who stood out in the crowd, this mountain of fur in a sea of people. He looked kindly upon her, and she found herself smiling back. She spotted Hiatt's group off to one side, including Zas, who looked intrigued against his will, and beside them stood Ricón's saredd and guard and many of Maeva's party. Chez and Braddok stood on either side of Stanis, who wore Corinth's polished skal crown upon his head. The three men watched from the front of the room, where Jenya had gone to take her place beside Braddok, and suddenly Braddok's big, beaming teeth were all Imari could see.

And at the front of the hall, right before the podium, stood her uki.

And Jeric.

Imari's heart skipped a beat.

Even without his title, Jeric looked like a king. He'd combed back his bronze hair, and his deep-blue, Corinthian uniform drew out the deep blue in his eyes. A fur-lined cape fell from one shoulder, fastened in place over his breast with a wolf signet, and when his gaze found hers, Imari nearly forgot to breathe.

She was suddenly very thankful for Ricón's hold on her arm.

Jeric's eyes never left hers as she crossed that distance between them, through the crowd, her feet steadied by her brother's stable grip, and when she reached the place where Jeric waited, Ricón took her hand, kissed it, and placed it between both of Jeric's. The men exchanged a long glance. Ricón clasped Jeric on the back then took his place at the front of the standing crowd, beside Jenya and Braddok.

"You are so beautiful," Jeric said softly, his gaze filled with awe and wonder.

She always wanted to remember this moment, the way he was looking at her then, for all the world to see.

But then Gamla cleared his throat, and they turned their gazes from each other to her uki.

Gamla Khan stared down his nose at the Wolf King for what felt like an eternity, and then he looked at Imari.

Those eyes—so like her papa's—made her heart squeeze, especially when they crinkled at the corners as he smiled. Imari knew they were both thinking about her papa. That he should be the one standing there, giving her away.

"I am going to miss you, my little chimp," he whispered only for her, then addressed the crowd and said in Common, "We are gathered here to witness the joining of two nations." A pause. Niá translated for the Sol Velorians, and Gamla looked at Imari. "There are so many words I am expected to say, but I seem to have forgotten all of them."

There were a few chuckles from those nearest. Ricón looked like he might step forward to intervene.

Imari cast Ricón a sharp look as she grinned at her uki. "It's all right, Uki."

"It's not because I don't have words," Gamla continued. "But what they want me to say has no character, and you are too special to waste on platitudes."

Jeric squeezed her hand.

"I look at you," Gamla said, though loud enough for many to hear. "Both of you, and I see promise. I see a Maker who can do the impossible, who orchestrates all for his perfect will, and it restores my hope."

In the corner of her eye, she saw Ricón usher forth a primly dressed young Corinthian boy, who handed Gamla a golden cord.

"Ah, right, then," Gamla said.

Imari caught Ricón's gaze, and he grinned.

Imari produced her right hand, Jeric his left, before Gamla could ask. Gamla smiled, and then wrapped the cord around their wrists, over and under like an eight, then placed his palm over theirs. "Jeric Oberyn Sal Angevin, do you vow to love this woman through sickness and in health, to honor her above your own flesh, until the end of your days, as the Maker has commanded?"

Jeric's gaze never left hers as he said, "I do." His rich cello made her heart sing.

Gamla turned to her, but her eyes were only on Jeric's as Gamla repeated the vow, but with her name in his place.

"I do," Imari replied.

Jeric looped his pinky around hers, and his shoulders expanded with a breath.

"Maker as my witness, you are bound heart and soul, and

what the Maker created separate, he has now made whole." A beat. "Oh, and you might want to kiss her."

Jeric smiled viciously, pulled her in, and kissed her deeply before all the world, just as he had promised.

*fine*

# ALSO BY BARBARA KLOSS

THE GODS OF MEN SERIES

The Gods of Men

Temple of Sand


THE PANDORAN NOVELS

Gaia's Secret

The Keeper's Flame

Breath of Dragons

Heir of Pendel

# ACKNOWLEDGMENTS

After seven years, I am finally drawing this series to a close. I was recently asked if finishing this series and saying goodbye to characters I have been with for so long makes me emotional. I had to think about my answer...because I am *not* particularly emotional, and I wondered if I should be.

But the fact of the matter is that I am at peace drawing this saga to a close. This series has challenged me in ways I could never have expected, and often pushed me to my limits. It has forced me to grow, as both a person and a writer, and if anything I find myself thankful. Thankful for all the help and support and advice along the way, thankful to readers who have believed in this story and these characters. Thankful to close the final chapter on a series that I am proud of, because I know that I have given it my all. It feels...satisfying. And I sincerely hope you are satisfied too.

I've had a wonderful team of people who have been with me from the very start, who have read those earliest versions of each installment, and to them I owe all the gratitude in the world. Carly, Daniella, Jenny, Janice, and Sarah...an author is lucky to have one person in their life who will be completely and utterly candid with them, and I'm lucky to have all of you. Thank you for your honesty, for caring enough to convince me to cut seven THOUSAND words from the beginning (AHEM). For showing me where my supports are weak, and pointing out which ones are rotten, and giving advice on how to fix it. You are all bright stars in my life, and you keep me on track in more ways than one.

To Laura, my editor, who patiently dealt with all of those cuts and changes (after the fact), and who never misses anything. (Seriously I'll never know how you catch even the smallest of inconsistencies.)

Thanks to my Beezies for always cheering me on and building me up, and making everyone read my books. :P Also for indulging me graciously as I talk endlessly about writing. Love you!

Thanks to the love of my life, for always encouraging me, and helping me sneak in those extra hours to work. For being so patient while I approach deadlines and leave the house in ruin. And for showing me what real love looks like.

And thank you to *my* Maker, my reason and my light.

# ABOUT THE AUTHOR

Barbara studied biochemistry at Cal Poly, San Luis Obispo, CA, and worked for years as a clinical laboratory scientist. She was lured there by mental images of colorful bubbling liquids in glass beakers. She was deceived. Always an avid reader, especially of fantasy, she began drafting her own stories, writing worlds and characters that were never beyond saving.

She currently lives in northern California with her gorgeous husband, three kids, and pup. When she's not writing, she's usually reading, trekking through the wilderness, playing the piano, or gaming—though she doesn't consider herself a gamer. She just happens to like video games. RPGs, specifically. Though now that her kids are getting older, she's finding she has to share her gaming consoles more than she would like.

www.barbarakloss.com
contact@barbarakloss.com

Be sure to sign up for Barbara's email newsletter:
https://www.subscribepage.com/barbarakloss

facebook.com/GaiasSecret
instagram.com/barbaraklossbooks
goodreads.com/barbarakloss
amazon.com/~/e/B005V06AoI

CPSIA information can be obtained
at www.ICGtesting.com
Printed in the USA
BVHW032044110222
628406BV00007B/13/J

9 781734 457384